Praise for the Authors of
On the Hunt

New York Times Bestselling Author Gena Showalter

"Bold and witty, sexy and provocative."
—*New York Times* bestselling author Carly Phillips

Shannon K. Butcher

"Unique, magnetic, and unbelievably fantastic—I love Shannon K. Butcher!"
—*New York Times* bestselling author Sherrilyn Kenyon

"Explosive passion and a touch of tenderness combine with fast-paced action." —*Library Journal*

Jessica Andersen

"Raw passion, dark romance, and seat-of-your-pants suspense."
—*New York Times* bestselling author J. R. Ward

"Andersen's got game when it comes to style and voice."
—*New York Times* bestselling author
Suzanne Brockmann

Deidre Knight

"Knight expertly blends scorching passion, gritty danger, and a wildly creative plot." —*Chicago Tribune*

ON THE *H*UNT

GENA SHOWALTER

SHANNON K. BUTCHER

JESSICA ANDERSEN

DEIDRE KNIGHT

A SIGNET BOOK

SIGNET
Published by New American Library, a division of
Penguin Group (USA) Inc., 375 Hudson Street,
New York, New York 10014, USA
Penguin Group (Canada), 90 Eglinton Avenue East, Suite 700, Toronto,
Ontario M4P 2Y3, Canada (a division of Pearson Penguin Canada Inc.)
Penguin Books Ltd., 80 Strand, London WC2R 0RL, England
Penguin Ireland, 25 St. Stephen's Green, Dublin 2,
Ireland (a division of Penguin Books Ltd.)
Penguin Group (Australia), 250 Camberwell Road, Camberwell, Victoria 3124,
Australia (a division of Pearson Australia Group Pty. Ltd.)
Penguin Books India Pvt. Ltd., 11 Community Centre, Panchsheel Park,
New Delhi - 110 017, India
Penguin Group (NZ), 67 Apollo Drive, Rosedale, North Shore 0632,
New Zealand (a division of Pearson New Zealand Ltd.)
Penguin Books (South Africa) (Pty.) Ltd., 24 Sturdee Avenue,
Rosebank, Johannesburg 2196, South Africa

Penguin Books Ltd., Registered Offices:
80 Strand, London WC2R 0RL, England

First published by Signet, an imprint of New American Library,
a division of Penguin Group (USA) Inc.

First Printing, February 2011
10 9 8 7 6 5 4 3 2 1

Contents

EVERNIGHT

GENA SHOWALTER

Chapter One

Meal-on-wheels, eighteen-year-old Rose Pascal thought hysterically. *That's me.*

The bars of her cage rattled as the creatures who'd captured her only an hour before steered her toward a large tent hidden among a thicket of gnarled trees. What awaited her in there . . . Would it be worse than what surrounded her?

Bile burned her throat. These men—*things*—were tall and muscled, with razor-sharp horns spiking down the center of their skulls, black scales that somehow looked as smooth as glass, and too-white fangs peeking from between bloodstained lips. The worst, though, was their glowing red eyes. *Hungry* eyes. Watching her, eager.

Frigid rain pounded from an onyx sky, splashing between the four-by-four iron that imprisoned her. She huddled in a corner, arms around her middle, shivering and freaked. Today was her birthday. She'd stayed up late, hoping to greet midnight—and thereby the shedding of her adolescence—with a laugh and call to her best friend, Claire. But the moment her clock changed from 11:59 to 12:00, her world had utterly shifted.

The indigo walls of her bedroom had faded, as had her bed, her desk, and her computer, only to be replaced by this dark, hammering rain. She'd spun, searching for something, *anything* familiar. No panic, though. Not yet. Perhaps she'd fallen asleep, she'd mused, and nightmares now plagued her.

But the silly hope had lasted only a moment. The monsters had already scented her, racing to reach her before she could figure out what had happened and where she was. Panic? Oh, yes. A tidal wave of it. The creatures had pawed at her, uncaring as she fought and screamed, and tossed her into this cage.

What she'd known then—she'd never been here before. What she knew now—she never wanted to return. How had she gotten to this place? She still had no clue. The . . . things had tried to talk with her before jolting into motion, but they spoke in a language she'd never heard and they clearly didn't understand hers.

The cart stopped abruptly, and she gulped. They'd reached the tent. Her heart pounded against her ribs as one of the creatures unlatched the door, the heavy *thunk* jolting her into action.

"No!" When he stretched an arm inside, she kicked, batting his claws—so sharp and deadly—away. "Leave me alone!"

A grunt, a snarl, and then those claws banded around her ankle, jerking. Rose slid forward and onto her back, skull slamming into wood. Icy air sawed between her lips as her vision swam with winking stars. Another jerk, and she was out of the cage entirely, staring up at the dark, endless sky, raindrops like little needles against her skin. Then multiple sets of those red eyes were peering down at her.

I'm on my own. Helpless. Tremors rocked her, *destroyed* her, because she could no longer move. Death watched her, but she couldn't freaking move. Her blood was like sludge in her veins, weighing her down, pinning her in place.

Tears caught in her lashes before flooding down her cheeks, and even those were cold. "Let me go. Please." A mere shimmer of voice this time.

Angry muttering assaulted her ears. Demands? Threats?

"I don't know what you're saying!"

Firm hands hauled her to her feet and shoved her forward. Rose stumbled, but managed to remain upright despite the rigidity of her body. When she reached the tent flap, one of the monsters held the material up and out of the way, and motioned for her to go inside. Shaking her head, she tried to press her heels into the ground and slow her momentum. Finally, movement, just not the right kind. Her efforts earned her another shove, and this time she fell straight into the tent, smashing her belly, lungs, and face on the ground. More of those stupid stars flashed through her vision.

The flap closed behind her with an ominous *swish*.

Silence.

Her tremors intensified. *Oh, God, oh, God, oh, God.*

No sudden moves, but you have to find out what you're up against. Slowly she raised her head and cast her gaze wildly about. To her left was a bed of furs. *Avoid!* In the center blazed a crackling fire, licking her with welcome warmth. Every cell she possessed craved more. Just beyond those flames was a wooden tub, a shelf of books. To the right, a table piled high with platters of food. Food. How long since she'd eaten? But her empty stomach didn't have time to twist hungrily. Beside that table stood a man. A man who was studying her, casually sipping a glass of amber liquid.

Gasping, Rose jumped up. At six feet, she usually towered over the people around her, yet this man towered over *her*. He was as muscled as her escort, but unlike those monsters, this man had sun-kissed skin, tousled black hair, and violet eyes framed by thick, spiky black lashes.

His face was . . . *beautiful*. Haunting, like that of a favored angel. Seriously, airbrushed models weren't this perfect. He wore a black shirt and black pants, and if he'd unfolded white, feathered wings from his back, she wouldn't have been surprised.

Was she, dared she hope, safe now?

"*Deutsch? Français?* English? *Español?*" he asked.

And he purred. The *oh, God*s in her head instantly changed in tone and volume. From frightened and screeching to awed and whispering. None of the boys at her school spoke like that. "I'm A-American," she said, smoothing the dripping hair from her face. Her black nightshirt and leggings absorbed every drop, and she was suddenly painfully aware of how terrible she must look. *Silly girl.*

"English, then. How many times have you been here, darling? Not many is my guess."

Darling. The endearment soothed like balm. "Th-this is the f-first time." Stupid chattering teeth. The cold and waning shock had caught up with her.

He smiled over the rim of his glass. "Happy eighteenth birthday, then." Gaze never leaving her, he drank what remained, ice cubes clinking, and set the cup on the tabletop.

That smile nearly stole her thoughts as well as her breath. "How did you know today is my birthday?" For that matter: "Where am I? Wh-what are you going to do with me?" Chattering teeth couldn't be blamed for that last stutter. She wanted to blame renewed fear, but . . .

"One question at a time, yes? *After* we're comfortable. Be a good girl and sit down for me."

"N-no, thank you. I prefer to st-stand." She was less vulnerable that way.

His eyes darkened, narrowed. "I don't recall asking what you preferred, darling." The purr was gone, and in its place was a cold demand for absolute compliance. Instinct told her that refusing meant suffering.

Yes, renewed fear. Though she wanted to run screaming, Rose sat, her knees buckling under sudden pressure. She tried to scramble backward, but again, her body acted the traitor and remained in place.

There was something odd about this immobility. Immobility that was far worse than what she'd experienced outside, because there was absolutely no hope of overcoming it. She was stuck.

Why can't I move? Because of him? Quaking, she fought a fresh round of terrified tears. She wasn't safer with this man, this *fallen* angel, she realized with certainty. Not even close.

"Good girl. Now." He dragged a chair in front of her and eased down, resting his elbows on his thighs and leaning toward her. He smelled of peat smoke and wildflowers, of all things, and the fragrance made her . . . ache. From more of that fear, surely. "What's your name?"

Too close. He was too close. And that ache, it was too unsettling, born of fear or not.

"Name." Another demand.

"R-Rose."

"Pretty. My name is Vasili, and I'm going to ask you some questions, Rose, and you're going to answer. If you lie to me, I'll know, believe me, and I will not be happy." He waited until she nodded in acknowledgment before continuing. "Do you know what happens to people who fail to make me happy?"

She gulped, shook her head.

"They die. Slowly, painfully."

Said so easily, he left no room for doubts. One lie and he *would* kill her. *Dear God. Breathe.*

"Why are you here, Rose?"

"I—I don't know. I swear to God, I don't know," she rushed out, expecting him to punish her for her ignorance.

He merely arched a black brow. "You weren't told to spy on me? To hurt me?"

"No! I don't even know who you are."

"What a terrible blow to my ego," he said, clutching his heart.

Life and death rested in his hands, and he . . . teased? Sparks of anger bloomed inside her, numbing some of the fear and kicking her common sense in the teeth. "I'm sure you'll survive," she replied before she could stop herself. "Unfortunately."

"What's this? Spirit from my little mouse?"

Now he mocked her. Several more sparks joined the fray.

Don't forget a predator lurks under that easy charm.

Thank you, Common Sense, for finally coming out of your coma. Wisely, she offered no reply to him.

"Do you know what you are, Rose?"

What kind of question was that? "I'm human. Educated. Civilized. Unlike—" *Uh-oh.* She'd forgotten. *Rein in the temper*—a temper that had always been her downfall.

"Unlike me?"

Her lips pressed together in a mulish line. Again, he'd get no reply from her. Her, a "little mouse." Oh, how that still burned. She liked to hunch her shoulders, sure, to make herself appear smaller, and she'd always preferred to blend into the background of a room, rather than stand out. And yes, she avoided confrontation whenever possible. But sometimes she snapped and lashed out, consequences be damned, and those "sometimes" were not pretty.

"In this, you clearly have no education," he said, tapping the tip of her nose with a strong finger. As if she were a naughty child. "But allow me to instruct you. You are what's called a Dimension Walker. You crossed from your dimension and into this one, the dark side of your golden world."

"No." What was he talking about? Dimension Walker? "No, that isn't possible. That only happens in books and movies."

"Then you tell me. How are you here?" He spread his arms. "What is this place?"

"I don't know. All I know is that what you described is—"

"Ridiculous?"

She nodded firmly. "Yes."

He ran his tongue over his perfectly white teeth, considering her for a moment. Firelight glimmered over his fallen-angel features, stroking him with loving fingers. "Your father and mother . . . tell me about them."

The subject change threw her, a pang of homesickness suddenly bombarding her. She was about to graduate high school, and for the past few months had most looked forward to moving out of her parents' house and into a tiny apartment she'd already picked out with Claire. But oh, just then, she wondered why she'd ever wanted to leave. Just then, she wanted to cuddle into her mother's arms and never let go.

"Rose. I issued a command." Steel seeped into Vasili's voice. "Do I really have to remind you what happens when you fail to please me?"

She swallowed the lump growing in her throat. "My father is a science teacher, junior high, and my mother is a receptionist at a law office." Perfectly middle-class, which was why they'd placed such strong hopes on her medical degree. Only, she didn't want to be a doctor. She didn't know what she wanted to be. Or do. Nothing . . . fit. Yet. She'd figure it out, though. She always did. Problems were simply opportunities for finding solutions.

"Well, that doesn't help my case as I'd hoped, does it? So, let's pretend for just a moment that I'm right. That I've met others like you." Bitterness joined the steel. "Let's pretend for just a moment that of the two of us, I'm the more educated. I would know that you were born to your world, but are bound to this one. Now, does anyone in your family disappear every year on their birthday? Maybe they say they like to be alone for the big event."

She didn't have to think about it. "No."

"Are you sure? No one has told you they were moving away, yet never wrote or called?"

"No." Truth.

"No one has told you scary stories about a land that has no sun? Where monsters roam and a cruel king slaughters?"

"No." Those kinds of stories a girl would remember.

"Pity." His gaze raked over her, hot, lingering. "If you'd had just one Dimension Walker in your tree, I would have had a use for you."

So. His questions hadn't been asked for her benefit, to convince her. He'd merely sought to learn about her family. Cruel of him. Still. That sultry gaze made her think of one thing and one thing only: sex. And she liked the shiver that followed—which made her feel stupid. And guilty.

She had a boyfriend. Hoyt was an inch taller than she was, which was why *she* had asked *him* out. (See. She wasn't a mouse!) They'd dated for seven months, he'd been her first, her only, and she loved being with him. Loved how gentle he was with her.

"Y-you shouldn't look at me like that," she said.

"Well, you shouldn't enjoy when I do. But concentrate on my threats, darling, nothing else." So amused. "I can't be interested in bedding you. You're a little too ... young for my taste."

The hesitation implied he'd wanted to say something else. Like ... too silly? Too timid? "Good," she found herself snapping. *Temper, temper.* "Because you're far too *old* for me." And too dangerous. And too mentally unstable.

A muscle ticked in his jaw. "I'm not too old for anyone."

Clearly, she'd made a direct hit, and the idea of besting him, even in so small a way, filled her with a sense of power. "Whatever you say," she replied, offering him a sugar-sweet smile.

"That's right. As I was *saying*, darling"—a growl now—"you're of no use to me."

Which meant ... what? Nothing good, that was for sure. *Get yourself under control before you push him too far!* "I just remembered! I know someone who, uh, disappears. Like you said."

His own smile was slow and wicked, the best of a charmer and the worst of a bastard. "Now you're lying, and I believe I warned you of the dangers of that. I murdered the last Walker who did."

The rest of her anger drained, and more intense tremors rocked her. He'd committed murder—*do not think about that; don't you dare think about that*—and once again she tried to pop to her feet and run. Still her body refused to obey. "I . . . You . . . *Please*. Let me go. I'm not a walker or whatever you think I am. I'm just a girl."

"Ah, there's my little mouse. I missed her."

This time his mockery failed to chase away a single thread of terror.

"I wonder . . . Do you have *any* fighting instinct?" Before she could form a reply, his fist whipped out.

She didn't have time to flinch. Could only squeeze her eyelids closed . . . waiting . . . dreading . . . but impact never came, and her lashes cracked open.

He had stopped just before contact. Now he sighed and lowered his arm. "None, then. Too bad." He unfolded from the chair, his form as dark as the sky outside and as menacing as a blade. "That would have made our next dealing more entertaining."

Oh, God. "What are you going to do during our next dealing?"

One step, two, he strode away from her. At the table, he poured crimson wine into a waiting glass. Rather than drink it, he stood there for a moment, his back to her, fingers drumming against the surface. Thinking of the best way to dispose of her?

There was no better time to run. But yet again her brain issued the command, and yet again her muscles ignored it. Truly, what held her down? She wasn't bound. *That you can see* . . . She shuddered. If he really was responsible, that would mean he was powerful in a way she couldn't comprehend. And maybe . . . maybe he had been telling the truth.

Finally, he nodded, as if he'd just reached a decision,

and returned to her, arm outstretched, eyes glittering.
"Drink this."

Hell, no! If he thought to poison her ... "I'm not
twenty-one." The only excuse her frantic brain could
come up with.

"Well, I won't tell if you won't."

"No, I—"

"Drink."

Another steely command. With trembling fingers, she
claimed the glass. She drained the contents before she
could talk herself into defying him. And possibly getting
herself killed "slowly and painfully." The thick liquid
burned her mouth, leaving a metallic taste, then scalded
her throat before cooling in her stomach.

After taking the cup from her and tossing it aside,
he knelt in front of her, clasped her wrist—his skin, so
warm, so calloused—and lifted. She was ashamed of
herself for not trying to pull away. But how could she?
Where he touched, the ache inside her finally subsided,
offering her the slightest glimmer of relief.

Gaze intense, he stared down at her open palm. And
there in the center, her skin split. He hadn't moved,
hadn't even raked a nail over her, yet blood welled. Her
jaw dropped in shock. She'd felt no pain, then or now.

Oh, yes. Powerful in a way she couldn't comprehend.
"What—"

Without a word, he raised the wound to his mouth
and licked.

Her stomach quivered and she told herself it was in
disgust. "That's gross." *Oops*. She'd sounded breathless
rather than creeped out. "Why did you do that?" Still
embarrassingly breathless.

Another sweep of his tongue, and the skin wove
back together. Rather than answer, he said, "Wherever

I walk, so, too, shall you. Now you," he prompted. He maintained a firm grip on her.

"What?"

"Say those words. Only I want you to say them for yourself, not me."

Her brow furrowed in confusion. "'Wherever you walk, so, too, shall I'? Like that?" What did that mean?

"Yes. Now, this next part might hurt a bit. Say my name."

"Vasili." A wave of heat suddenly slammed through her, burning her up, blistering her inside and out, and flaming her to ash. But before she could scream, cry, beg for mercy, those ashes began to rebuild, locking together, re-forming her into a new person. A person who hungered for the man in front of her. Desperately. The ache he'd assuaged? Once again caught fire and spread, leaving no part of her untouched. It was harsher now. Harder. More commanding and utterly consuming.

What. The. Hell? She tried to jerk free, but he held firm. "What did you do to me, you—"

"Hush. Vasili's talking. I've decided I can use you after all. Tomorrow, you'll wake up at home. I suggest you do whatever it takes to find out if there are others like you. Find out who they are and when they travel here."

"And if I don't?" Breathless again, damn it. All that ferocity could be hers—all she had to do was lean into him. . . .

"Then you'll be of no use to me when you return, just as I first assumed, and I'll have to kill you."

This threat lacked heat and conviction, something the others had had in spades. She trembled. *Don't lean. Don't you dare lean.* Wait. When she returned, he'd said.

"How am I supposed to find them?" she squeaked out. She'd address his concern first, then hers.

"I'm sure you'll find a way. Also, you should know that you can return here anytime you'd like now. The gate will always be open for you, but you should also know that I will—"

No, no, no. "I don't ever want to return." She shook her head to emphasize her refusal.

"Sorry, darling, but you'll return on your next birthday whether you wish to do so or not." His thumb traced the lines in her palm. "You'll return every birthday for the rest of your life. That's just how the bond to this world works."

She had trouble focusing on his words. That touch . . . the intensified ache . . . She moaned. *More.* Discarding all common sense, she finally allowed herself to lean toward him.

"Another suggestion," he whispered, stopping her. The space between their gazes crackled. "Use the next year to prepare. Learn how to fight, and fight dirty. With guns, blades, even your hands." He placed a soft kiss on the hammering pulse in her wrist before at last releasing her and straightening. "Or don't. Survival will be up to you."

Chapter Two

One year later . . .

Exactly five minutes until midnight.

Perched at the edge of her bed, Rose stared at the clock sitting on her desk. Dread coursed through her, as did anticipation. And fury—so much fury.

Would she or wouldn't she?

Would *he* be there or not?

In the twelve months since meeting Vasili, she'd had time to build him up and tear him down. Romanticize and vilify him. She'd had time to accept what had happened and rationalize what couldn't possibly have happened.

After his parting words, she must have slipped into a deep sleep, because the next thing she'd known, she'd woken up in the hospital, groggy and incoherent, her parents frantic. She hadn't responded to their morning knock or subsequent shaking, so they'd called 911.

The doctors claimed she'd suffered from a drug overdose, though they hadn't been able to identify the drug. Clearly, Vasili had slipped something into the wine he'd forced her to drink. *Bastard*.

Four minutes.

Something had happened to her that night. Something besides the drugging. In the weeks that followed, she'd tried to move on with her life. Tried to forget. Only, everything had changed. She'd been irritable, hungry, aching unbearably, unable to focus or sleep. Her parents had tried to talk to her, and at first, she resisted. But finally she'd broken down and hinted at what she'd seen. They told her she'd hallucinated. She insisted. They asked her if she was still using. She *really* insisted, giving them every single detail.

They had her committed.

Upon her release, she'd begun searching online for others like her, desperate to prove herself sane. What she found shocked her. There *were* others like her, and their experiences matched her own. Their description of the world—Nightmare, they called it—matched, too.

Sometimes people "stepped over" and never returned, she'd been told, and the other Dimension Walkers suspected the monsters had butchered them. Which was why they were looking for ways to sever the "birthday bond." So far, no luck.

She'd spent so much time researching, she'd failed to enroll in college. She hadn't gotten an apartment with Claire, either. And Hoyt . . . The first time he'd kissed her upon her return, she'd begun to sicken. And the more his tongue had twined with hers, the sicker she'd felt—until she'd finally had to pull away altogether. Miraculously, she'd felt better an instant later.

Still. She'd assumed she had caught a virus. Until he tried to kiss her a few days later. That time, there'd been no warning. She'd jerked away, her body wanting no part of him, and vomited. A few days later, *she'd* tried to kiss *him*, hopeful, perhaps desperate to make things work. But once more, she'd vomited.

There'd been no fooling herself after that.

And there'd been no keeping him. He'd moved on, leaving her brokenhearted. For a few months, at least. Eventually, she'd gotten over him and tried to move on herself. That ache . . .

Then a new guy had finally caught her eye. Nick. Handsome, sweet, with blond hair and brown eyes—she now avoided guys with dark hair and light eyes because they made the ache so much worse—and, best of all, six foot one and a Dimension Walker.

Three minutes.

Everyone used fake names online, but after trading war stories with Nick, she'd given him her phone number. Their first date had been amazing. They'd understood each other, talked, laughed, *connected*. He'd walked her to her door, and she'd hugged him, once again hopeful for the future.

Until their second date. He'd walked her to her door, and that time, she'd tried to kiss him. Immediately, her stomach had threatened to rebel. She'd jerked away and barricaded herself inside. She'd avoided his calls ever since.

The only time she left the house anymore was to train. Guns, knives, hand-to-hand combat, just as Vasili had instructed. She would never be so helpless again.

Two minutes.

A cold sweat beaded over her skin. Each minute seemed to tick by faster than the last.

Would she even see Vasili this go-round? According to her sources, she would land in a different place every time she traveled.

One minute.

Rose stopped breathing, stood. *Steady*. She had a semiautomatic stashed in the waist of her pants, extra clips in her pockets, blades sheathed inside her boots, killer barrettes in her hair, and an innocent-looking pen strapped to her thigh. That pen was actually a syringe filled with enough sedative to knock out an elephant.

Kill as many of those monsters as you can, so many Walkers advised. She couldn't, she wouldn't, unless they threatened her. Vasili, though . . . she owed him.

Twelve o'clock.

Would she—

In a single heartbeat, the world around her vanished, a new one taking its place. Indigo walls were replaced with the white fabric of a tent, and her bed and desk with furred rugs. This time, there wasn't a table. Not even a single chair. The books and tub were gone, too. There was only open space and that fur. And rather than a crackling fire, torches hung along the walls.

But she'd landed in Vasili's tent. She knew it.

"Well, well, well. The mouse took my advice and armed herself like a lion. I'm impressed."

Rose nearly swallowed her tongue as she spun. And there he was, golden lamplight caressing him. The dark prince of her nightmares. He hadn't changed. Same inky hair, though the strands were now wet and slicked back, and same feral eyes. Same imposing height and muscled width. Same haunting beauty.

Just as before, he clutched a glass of liquid amber and ice, sipping as he studied her. He wore a black shirt that hugged his massive biceps, and black pants that were ripped and stained with . . . blood?

"Forgive my appearance, darling." *Oh, sweet heaven.* There was his seductive purr, all magic and moonlight, shivering over her. "I had to race to get here."

Her gaze snapped up, and his lips lifted in a slow, sensual smile, revealing those perfect teeth. Her heart finally kicked back into motion, fluttering wildly against her ribs. *He's a self-professed murderer. Don't forget.*

But, God, he's gorgeous.

Concentrate!

I'm trying, damn it. But already the ache, that constant, cloying, demanding ache, had sprouted wings.

"What? Nothing to say? Well, no matter. I'm not done talking. Happy birthday, darling. You're a stunning nineteen. Almost a woman."

The mocking tone hadn't changed, either.

"Did you do as I asked?" A casual question. "Did you search for others?"

"Yes. I did. And you were right. There really were others like me."

He stiffened. "Their names. Tell me." No longer casual, but almost . . . desperate.

"I didn't get them," she lied. The only name she had was Nick's, and she wasn't sharing that.

The hand at Vasili's side fisted.

Attack him before he attacks you. She merely shifted from one foot to the other, glaring over at him. Too well did she recall how he'd frozen her in place. And she *would* learn how he did that—and how to combat it. "Plan to kill me now?"

Disappointment and anger battled for supremacy on his face, but all he said was, "I'm feeling generous. I'll punish my bad, naughty girl for not doing as she was instructed rather than kill her. How's that?"

"How about you answer my questions, before *I* punish *you*." He would find she wasn't as easy to intimidate this time. "What did you do to me last time I was here?" No one else had experienced anything like that stupid ache or comalike sleep. Not even a little.

"Better question. What kind of greeting is that?

We've been parted for so long, yet chastisement and an inquisition are the best I get?" He tsked quietly. "Someone in this room needs to work on their manners, and I'll give you a hint. It's not me."

"Oh, I'm sorry. Did I fail to make a proper introduction?" She closed some of the distance between them, that ever-present temper making her braver than was probably wise. She didn't stop until she could smell the peat smoke and the wildflowers that wafted from him. God, she'd missed that scent.

Missed? No, no, no. Wrong word. She'd *dreaded* that scent. Better. "Here, let me fix that," she said. "Rose's knee, meet Vasili's ball—"

With a laugh, he stepped backward, out of reach. "None of that, now."

God. Even his laughter was perfect, taking his sexy voice and mixing it with velvet and melted chocolate. Her nipples pearled, the ache intensifying. *Concentrate.* "If we're done with introductions, then, why don't—"

"Vasili's turn," he interjected, serious again. "Has anyone contacted you? Asked you to hurt me?"

"No." Truth. No one had contacted her specifically. But a lot of Walkers wanted the creatures here destroyed. Some even bragged about the ones they had killed.

"That's good."

"I answered you, so answer me. What the hell did you do to me?"

"I'm afraid I don't know what you mean. Explain."

"Liar! You know!" *Steady.* Slowly she reached back and curled her fingers around the handle of her gun. *Good, that's good.* "You did something. I can't desire a man without—"

"Sickening. Yes. I know," he said dryly. "But, darling.

One thing you should know about me. I never lie. There's no need. Lying is for those who fear consequences. I do not. Now, then. What type of man—men?—did you desire, hmm? Whom do I have to kill? The boyfriend you mentioned last time?"

She didn't know Vasili well enough to know whether or not he was teasing about the men he needed to kill, or whether he could even travel to her world. "Answer me. Please, Vasili. What did you do?" Hopefully her pleading would keep him distracted while she did . . . this—metal whizzed through air as she aimed the barrel of the gun at his chest. She tried not to smile at her success. "Tell me or I'll shoot."

He rolled his eyes. "Put the gun away before you hurt yourself."

Not the reaction she'd expected. Why wasn't he scared? Did he think she lacked the guts to squeeze the trigger? Could he freeze her finger in place before she moved? Or would bullets not hurt him?

Her stomach twisted into hundreds of little knots. She hadn't considered that possibility before, but . . . Was he even human? Or was he more like those monsters than she'd realized?

"Rose. Gun. Now." Gone was the charmer, and in his place was the commander. "Right now, there's only one thing you need to know about me. I will slaughter an army before heeding an enemy's demand. Put the gun down and ask nicely for the answers you want. That's the only way you'll get them."

"So I'm the enemy?" Another distraction meant to keep him talking despite his objections.

One that failed. "Gun," he growled.

Clearly, he'd answer *nothing* until she complied. Biting the inside of her cheek, she sheathed the weapon and waved her empty fingers at him. "Happy?" If he made an aggressive move in her direction, she could withdraw a blade and gut him. Simple, easy. *I've got this.*

Negligent shrug.

All that protest, and *that* was what he did when he won? *Bastard.* He really *hadn't* changed. But at least he wasn't gloating. "What. Did you. Do to me?"

"Now. Isn't that better?" He tossed his glass over his shoulder. "I did what was necessary. I bound you to me."

She watched the ice scatter across the furs. Anything was better than peering at Vasili. As he'd spoken, heat had sparked in his eyes. So much heat. Her skin tingled, pulling tight over her bones, and she had to fight the urge to rub her arms, her thighs. Had to fight the urge to beg *him* to rub her arms and thighs. "What does that mean? Bound me to you?"

"Anytime you enter this world, you will come directly to me."

"Imposs—" *No.* She had long since struck that word from her vernacular. *Nothing* was impossible. "How? How did you do that?"

"Remember the words you spoke? The wine you drank?"

"The poisoned wine," she snapped, at last facing him again. He was closer to her, so close. *More tingling . . . no fear . . .* "Because of you, my parents thought I was doing drugs."

He reached out and smoothed a lock of hair behind her ear. "And that pained you. I'm sorry."

Ignore the contact . . . the fever now spreading . . . the shock of his words. "Thank you," she said, backing as far away from him as she could get. "Now stop threatening and stop stalling. The wine? What was in it?"

Another shrug. "My blood, among other things."

"Blood?" No. No way. She would have known. Wouldn't she?

"Afraid so. Must say, watching you drink it was the *grossest* thing I ever witnessed." He shuddered.

Gross. Exactly what she'd said to him when he'd lapped up *her* blood.

Rose's eyes widened as the consequences of his consumption hit her. "You licked my wound." A wound she'd later convinced herself she'd imagined, since a scab had never formed.

"Yes," he agreed easily. "I did."

"So you can't . . ."

"No. I can't." Anger had infused his voice that time. "And yes, that makes you my child bride. No need to thank me. Twelve months of torturous abstinence is thanks enough."

Hell. No. "Why would you do that? And by the way, we are *not* married."

"A moment of insanity, that's all. And yes, we are. But really, I suffer only as long as you're alive."

She raised her chin. "You don't scare me, Vasili." *Much*.

"Don't I?" He closed some of the distance between them. "Let's see if I can change that."

Steady.

More of the distance was swallowed by his steps. When their toes touched, when she could once again smell the peat smoke, the corners of his lips twitched as if her refusal to run amused him. She didn't mean to, but she breathed deeply, savoring, wanting so badly to arch into him. Why had she let him come? Why hadn't she pulled a knife?

"We're going to spar, you and I, whether you wish to or not, so I can judge your skill. But how about this? Every time you strike me, I'll answer a question."

She gulped. The one thing she couldn't resist: information. "No threats of endless pain to get what you want?" Of course, he could be lying, meaning to attack to kill, as he'd implied, and not merely to judge.

"Not this time."

She didn't trust him, but she said, "All right," and meant it. And her capitulation had nothing to do with a raging desire to put her hands on him and have his hands on her. If necessary, she would *force* the information out of him. "Just to be clear, I can ask any question I want?"

"Absolutely any."

"And you'll answer honestly?"

"I always do."

"Even if I ask how to divorce you? And live?"

He pretended to wipe away a tear. "That hurts, darling. It really does."

"That's only the—"

She never saw him move, but he managed to kick her feet out from under her while shoving her down. On impact, her brain rattled against her skull, and she choked on that delicious breath she'd just taken.

No time to react. He pounced while she was prone, pinning her shoulders with his knees and her stomach with his ass. *I shouldn't like this.* Yet her body sighed in contentment, as if this was what it had craved the past year.

"First order of business. Disarming." Five seconds flat, he had every single one of her weapons thrown to the side. Would have been two seconds, but he studied the syringe before chucking it over his shoulder. "Bring a machine gun next time, darling. They pack more of a punch."

Terror should have filled her, but anger did instead.

Mocking bastard. At least he didn't go for the kill shot. And how did he know so much about her world? Had he been born there? If so, did that mean he was a Walker, too?

"Second order. Distraction." He waited, peering at her expectantly. When she remained silent, he sighed. "Darling, this is the part where you apologize for being so distracted during my brilliant tutorial."

She flashed her teeth in a snarl. "No, this is the part where I—" *Smash your nose into your brain*, she thought as she jabbed the heel of her open palm toward his smirking—kissable—face. Wouldn't do to warn him.

Just before contact, he rolled out of the way. Suddenly she could breathe. She found herself gasping, sucking in mouthful after mouthful of air, shocked that she'd gone so long without it and hadn't suspected.

"Third order. Fighting past the pain. You're just lying there, daring me to attack while you're vulnerable. Were you anyone else, I would. Up."

With stars winking behind her eyes, she pushed to her feet and faced him. "You rotten piece of—"

His laughter was the only warning she had. In the next instant, he was on her, once more shoving her down. This time, he didn't pause and explain his actions. He simply taught her the consequences of daring someone to attack. For hours. She grunted, she groaned, she ached—a far different kind of ache—and she bled. Oh, did she bleed.

A few times, she thought he even broke her bones.

That didn't stop or slow him. He really was determined to kill her, she supposed. That didn't stop or slow her, either. Every time he knocked her down, she got up. Every time he cut her, she wiped the blood on her shirt and smiled. After her second smile, the instructions began. In English at first, and then in his language. She shouldn't have understood him, but as he translated his meaning, she began to learn far more easily than should have been possible. As if the language had always been stored in her brain, and she just hadn't unlocked it yet.

Vasili told her what she was doing wrong and what she needed to do to improve. Again, for hours. An eternity. But not once did she strike him.

"Stay down, damn you," he finally snarled after tossing her to her ass again. "Stay down, and the pain ends. You've had enough."

Never. Rose lumbered to her throbbing feet. Her eyes were swollen, her line of vision shit, but she waved her fingers at him. "Come on," she said haltingly, the harsh words of the new language weird on her tongue. She would *not* give up, and she *would* have her curiosity assuaged.

For a long while, he remained in place, a few feet away, panting, studying her. Then he tangled a hand through his hair, disrupting the dark locks and sending them falling over his forehead. "Stubborn little baggage, aren't you?"

"What? Too sweet to take me?"

His lips twitched again, and her heart raced. No one should be that handsome. Especially a man who had just kicked her ass. Although, in his defense, he'd never struck her in anger. Every move he'd made had been designed to teach her.

"Darling, you just asked me if I was too sweet to take you."

As her cheeks heated, she switched to English. "You know what I meant. Too *tired* to fight me."

He laughed outright, then frowned, as if the laugh angered him. "One question," he said flatly. "You can ask me one question."

Not enough, she wanted to scream. One wasn't enough. She wanted to know about this world—what he called it, what the monsters were, why those monsters deferred to him. She wanted to know what else Vasili knew about her origins, what he planned to do with her, why he'd bonded them. She wanted to know how he'd controlled her body that first time and why he hadn't this time. She wanted to know . . . what he thought of her, if he liked her. Who he was. *What* he was.

"Hurry. Before I change my mind." Disgust layered his tone, as if he couldn't believe he'd even made the offer in the first place. "You don't deserve it, after all, and I have never—"

"How—how do I come here at will?" The words left her mouth before she could snatch them back. She never wanted to come here again. Even on her next birthday. *Damn, damn, damn.* Of all the stupid things to ask! But to her knowledge, no one else could do so. They traveled only on their birthdays.

He spun away from her—but not before she saw the flicker of surprise in those magnificent violet eyes. He strode out of the tent, leaving her standing, stunned, and unsure. Should she follow him? Should she— He stomped back inside, holding two glasses of that amber liquid.

His hair was wetter, his clothes plastered to him. He demolished the distance between them, steps clipped, his expression blank. "Why do you want to know how to return?"

"I don't have to answer that." Besides, she didn't have an answer. "Explaining the reasons for my questions wasn't part of the deal."

A pause. Then, "When you want to return, say my

name, the vows we spoke to each other. Picture me. Your body will find me." He held out a glass. "Drink."

She shook her head and twined her swollen fingers behind her back, and oh, that hurt. "No way. I'd rather fight you again than let you drug me."

"I hurt you; I'll make it better."

"And your liquor can heal me?" she asked dryly. "Rather than make me pass out?"

"Yes." Perfectly serious.

Was that why he'd been drinking it earlier? Had someone hurt him? That blood on his pants . . . Her stomach clenched. In fear? At the thought of this man injured? What was wrong with her?

Angry—with him, with herself—she claimed the glass and drank. Unlike the red wine/blood of last time, this went down smooth and warm, little butterflies taking flight inside her and spreading fairy dust. "If you poisoned me, I'll . . ." Within seconds, cuts wove back together, bones realigned, and the threat died on her lips.

"There's my pretty girl," he said, and if she wasn't mistaken, there was affection in his tone.

Affection? No way. Her imagination, surely. Not once had he copped a feel or tried to kiss her. *The bastard.*

Yes, something was definitely wrong with her.

"Rose, darling. You should know that next time, if you don't have the answers I want, I'm going to push you harder than you've ever been pushed. I'm going to make you bleed and beg for mercy I don't have. So I'd be careful about visiting unannounced, if I were you."

Chapter Three

Vasili remained in his war tent a long while after Rose disappeared. Twelve hours. That was as long as a resisting Walker remained before their world sucked them back—unless they were bonded to someone here and returned on their own. Then *they* could decide how long to stay. Would Rose dare?

He breathed deeply. The scent of her lingered. Roses, like her name. Dewy, uncut. Unexpected.

Beautiful female. *Foolish* female. She had no idea of the danger she was in.

She should have died a spy's death that first night here, for that was what his army had assumed she was. A spy from one of the three kingdoms surrounding his. And as protective as they were of him, spies *suffered*. But Vasili had been in camp and they'd given the honor of killing her to him. One look, though, and he'd known. Not a spy. A Dimension Walker.

Had his men realized the truth, a spy's death would have felt like foreplay to her. But unlike Vasili, they hadn't spent most of their life hunting Walkers. Slaughtering them. Most Walkers were male, and that was what his people expected, but every so often, a female came. Rose had been far too timid to be a spy, and he'd recognized that wild, confused look in her eyes. Many a Walker had died by his sword wearing that same expression.

Foolish *man*. He should have killed Rose himself. Anyone else would have.

Walkers were born in her world, but bonded at least one day a year to this one, just as he'd told her. Why, he didn't know. What he did know: Walkers were the only ones capable of moving between the light—her world—and the dark—his.

Decades ago, his people had welcomed them. Given them food and shelter, protection. They had been taken to the royal palace, questioned by the king himself, for the king had hoped to find a way for his people to travel into the light. But though many Walkers had mated and decided to stay here, they'd never gotten over their fear of the Monstrea, the "monsters," and decided to destroy them.

Thus began the process of the Walkers finding one another, building their army, planning the perfect way to strike and cut down the royal family. *Vasili's* family. As a boy, he'd watched his father, mother, all three of his sisters, and one of his brothers fall to guns and grenades. He and Jasha, his youngest brother, had barely escaped alive.

The Walkers would have gotten away with their crimes, never to be punished, but like Rose, they had to return at least once a year. Though Vasili had been crowned king of the Northern Realm immediately after his father's death, he'd spent most of his time hunting— and slaying—Walkers rather than leading his people.

And even though he'd already punished the ones who'd taken his family from him, others still came. Others he hunted. They'd learned how to hide, and hide well, but he always found them. Or so he'd thought.

Rose might not have hurt his family, but she was one of them. And if she was to be believed, she had found Walkers he had not. What if they did as before? What if they worked together to destroy him?

Yes, he should have killed her. But at that first meeting, he'd thought, *I can use her to learn about the ones I cannot find.* He could learn how many were out there, where they traveled, when they traveled, their strengths, their weaknesses. Yet at this second meeting, she'd given him nothing. And *still* he hadn't hurt her.

And he looked forward to their third meeting, not to learn from her but to see her.

"I'm more than a fool," he muttered.

He'd had his men prepare this tent in the woods surrounding his palace. On his way here, he'd been ambushed. A fight had broken out—damn King Greer and the Eastern Realm—and he almost hadn't reached the tent in time. Rose would have appeared wherever he was, out in the open and in front of his men. There would have been no denying her origins then.

She would have been put to death, and his questions wouldn't have been answered. Questions he'd had no business entertaining. Like, how had time changed her? Like, how would she react to him? Like, what would she say to him?

Like, would those liquid silver eyes of hers sparkle as her temper flared?

Time had indeed changed her, adding more curves to that slender body. She'd lashed out at him, dared him, defied him, and yes, those eyes had sparkled.

His neglected body had reacted. He'd wanted to touch and to taste. *Too young*, he'd had to remind himself. Over and over again. That hadn't stopped his mind from screaming, *Mine*. A hazard of the bonding, he knew, and not of a particular woman's appeal. Though she was. Appealing. God, was she appealing. She'd been soft under his hands, her height making her a perfect fit to the hard line of his body.

Would she have welcomed a kiss?

He was thankful he hadn't found out. Sex with a Walker—he would never live it down.

Should have killed her, he thought again. Instead, he'd tested her strength, her endurance, her combat skills. He'd even *instructed* her on how to be better, wondering how *her* people would react to her origins if they ever found out. Thinking he wouldn't be there to protect her. Thinking if she ever decided to live here, she had to be prepared for *his* people.

What was wrong with him? Live here? She *couldn't* live here. His people hated her kind. And if Jasha ever found out . . . Vasili sighed. There'd be no living that down, either. Worse, his brother's disappointment and hurt would slay him.

As if his thoughts had summoned his brother, the tent flap rose, and Jasha strode inside. His right-hand man, Grigori, trailed behind. Both were dressed in the clothes of a warrior. Leather breastplates, pants, and dusters. Boots with daggers in the toes. Both men were dripping wet.

Jasha was a less . . . hardened version of Vasili. Wavy black hair cut haphazardly, violet eyes, tall, muscled. Though his first instinct wasn't always to kill—as Vasili's was—he was no less skilled with a sword. And no less savage when riled. Vasili had made sure of that. He loved his brother more than anyone or anything, and had wanted the boy well able to care for himself. He'd trained his brother exactly as he'd trained Rose: without mercy.

"There you are," Jasha said with a grin. He spoke in Drakish, their language, and Vasili made a mental note to do the same. No more of Rose's English for him. "Are we interrupting something?"

Clearly, he'd been hoping to do so. "Not at all," Vasili offered casually.

His brother's expression fell. "We heard female grunts and groans. Which means that after a yearlong abstinence, our king has finally shown interest in a woman. Who is she? More important, where is she?"

"Long gone," he answered truthfully. And was that . . . displeasure in his tone? That she *hadn't* stayed?

Well, he hadn't wanted her to stay. After he'd so stupidly told her how to return to him at will—*after* going to such lengths to keep her out of the palace and hidden—all he'd wanted was her absence. No question.

His hands fisted. What would he do if she appeared in front of his brother? What would he do if she appeared during a battle? *Stupid, stupid, stupid*, he thought again. He'd known it then, yet still he'd told her.

And now he wondered if she would visit before her next birthday. If they'd spar and tease and touch . . .

Blood . . . heating . . .

"You should be embarrassed to have finished so quickly." The picture of a confident male, Grigori crossed his arms over his chest. "Had I been here, she would still be shouting my name."

Twelve hours was finishing quickly? What the hell did Grigori do with his women? Like half the beings in this world, Grigori was of the Monstrea. He possessed sharp, poisoned horns along his hairless skull, black-diamond skin, claws, fangs, and glowing red eyes.

The other three kingdoms considered the Monstrea to be nothing more than expendable soldiers. Slaves. Unworthy. Vasili did not and never had. He respected strength and loyalty, and that was what he got with the Monstrea.

"You wear them out, so they never want to come back for more," Vasili told his favorite warrior. "Mine *always* come back." Not that he welcomed them. When he was done, he was *done*.

He should take Rose and finally be done with her.

"I just wish I could make *one* come," Jasha muttered. His cheeks reddened when he realized what he'd admitted.

Vasili slapped his brother on the shoulder. His easier manner should have brought him favor with the ladies of their kingdom. Not so. Well, not anymore. Jasha was shy and bumbling around the fairer sex, and always had been.

At first, when he'd reached maturity, they'd wanted him feverishly and had thrown themselves at him. He'd had difficulty speaking to them, had sweated uncontrollably, and hadn't looked anywhere but at his feet. They'd teased him, which had only made his shyness worse. Now he avoided them.

"You can have any woman you want. You just have to stop running from them. They only bite if you ask them nicely."

Grigori laughed.

"What's her name?" Jasha asked, refusing to be baited. "The one you were with today?"

He saw no harm in answering. "Rose."

"Rose?" His brother choked on a gurgling laugh of his own. *"Rose?"*

"What? It's a fine name," he growled, unsure why

currents of fury blew through him. Rose was the enemy. Anyone could make fun of her. Especially his brother.

"Yes, but *Rose*? Like the tattoo you had inked into your arm last year?"

His jaw clenched so painfully he feared the bone would snap. "No. Not like that," he managed, the words so raw they sounded as if they'd been pushed through a meat grinder. "Not like that at all."

He didn't know why he'd gotten the tattoo. He hadn't wanted to analyze the desire then, and he didn't want to analyze the desire now. He knew only that when he looked at the night rose, he wanted to smile.

"You've known her all this time?" Grigori tsked, just as Vasili liked to do to Rose. Surely *he* wasn't that irritating. "And yet you never breathed a word about her."

"He must have feared one of us would steal her away," Jasha said with a mystery-solved nod.

Before Vasili could form a reply, not that he knew what to say, they turned to each other, cutting him from the conversation.

"No wonder he raced from the warm, dry palace to get here. He missed his woman," Grigori said, then cooed mockingly. "The poor baby."

Jasha stroked his stubbled chin with two fingers. "She must be hideous if he feels he must hide her away like this. Or perhaps she's too precious for our *poor baby* to share."

Vasili felt privileged. No one else ever saw them like this, relaxed and teasing. To the rest of the world, Grigori was a snarling beast, too savage to handle, and Jasha was quiet and withdrawn. They saved their charm for him, as if he were special to them, and he was glad. They were the most important part of his life. Therefore, he didn't mind their teasing. Much.

"So, what are you doing here?" he asked, inserting himself back into their chatter.

They chortled.

"We must find him someone new," Grigori continued to Jasha. "This one obviously didn't work him from his yearlong temper."

More stroking of that chin. "We've tried, placing female after female in front of him. He sends them away in tears."

"I asked you a question," he said on a sigh.

And still they continued.

"Perhaps we should ask around," Jasha said. "Find out what others know about this Rose. Where she lives, why she leaves her man in a bad mood."

Grigori massaged the back of his neck. "And we should instruct her on the proper way to treat a king. I do my best instructing naked."

Oh, no, no, no. He couldn't have them asking others about her. And he couldn't even contemplate Rose and Grigori in bed. Not without foaming at the mouth. "Why. Are. You. Here?"

Finally. They focused on him. To his irritation, both flashed him unrepentant grins.

"We heard of the ambush," his brother said, slapping *him* on the back now. "We came to offer you our aid."

"As if I can't handle a few enemy soldiers on my own." Greer, the king of the neighboring realm, wanted possession of Vasili's, and constantly struck at random times, in random ways, before scattering with the wind. "I sent the men back to their leader. Minus their heads."

"Perhaps that's why he failed to satisfy his Rose," Grigori said to Jasha. "She was too frightened of him to enjoy him."

"Surely not. That would mean she rejected him, and

my brother will be the first to tell you how irresistible he is."

Enough. "Let's return to the palace. I'm in need of dinner and a bath." And a woman, damn his always aching body, but he couldn't have one of those. Unless Rose returned.

Too young, damn it! She'd lived nineteen years. He'd lived thirty-three. Until twelve months ago, she'd been his fearful little mouse. He'd been a lion his entire life.

Part of him wished he could have followed her to her world, though, where he could have her without (much) worry. No one to disturb them, no one to threaten her, no painful past to remember. He hated that part of himself. This was his home. He wouldn't leave for any reason.

"Look at you. So serious all of a sudden," Jasha said. "You're right, Vash. It's time to return to the palace and feed you. I want my impious, pain-in-the-ass brother back."

He snorted, but allowed the men to lead him outside, puddles splashing at his feet. As the rain continued to pour from the darkened sky, he mounted his horse. Many Monstrea and human guards waited nearby, acting as his protection as he'd ordered, ensuring that no one entered—or left—his tent without his permission. Except for Jasha and Grigori. They always did what they wanted.

"Leave the tent," he told them, "and go home." No reason to have them out in the rain. Not that the rain ever stopped this time of year. And the command had nothing to do with maintaining a hideaway for Rose in case she visited without warning. Of course.

Everything taken care of, he spurred his animal into motion. He almost hoped someone else ambushed him tonight. He itched for another fight. Something, anything to release some of the tension coiled inside him.

Yet, deep down he suspected only one thing would release that tension—and he might not see her for another year.

Chapter Four

She didn't visit.

For the next year, Vasili looked for her in every shadow, waiting. Hopeful, damn him, for a glimpse of her. He spent more time in "their" tent than he did in his palace. Or training. Or hunting.

Because of Rose, he was distracted, on edge, and too fucking needy. His people were now leery of him, afraid he'd snap their heads off. And he just might. Damn *her*!

He liked women, and he liked sex, but the two had a place in his life—and that was right after everything important. Doing without shouldn't have bothered him. But he kept thinking about Rose, and his body kept reacting. He wanted her. *Badly*.

In one week and twenty-three hours, she would be twenty years old. No longer too young for him. And despite her origins, he could finally have her. But only after he punished her for reducing him to *this*. A grumpy king, a disgruntled suitor, and a terrible brother.

She owed him, and he would collect. You didn't ask someone how to reach them, and then never try to reach them. It was rude. And Vasili had always believed in the power of civility. Fine. He was a recent convert. But because she'd made him wait—and wait and wait—he was having one of his night-rose tattoos removed.

Yeah, he'd gotten another one. Stupid wine. He hadn't meant to consume so much last week, but his mind had wandered—about Rose, *of course*—and he'd thought a second tattoo would look amazing on his other arm.

Jasha hadn't stopped teasing him since.

He would punish Rose for that, as well.

After he tasted her. By now he'd realized that she was nearly too lovely to resist. Too stubborn, too. Which, despite everything, made him proud of her. Hell, these days he was always proud of her.

She was resisting him with a strength he himself did not possess, and he was proud.

Last time, she'd armed herself, and every time he remembered it, he was proud. She'd fought him with more skill than he would have guessed, and he was proud. She'd asked him how she could return, and he was fucking proud. It was disgusting. Next he'd be claiming his husbandly rights. Not just sex, because that was on the menu no matter what, but *everything*. Her presence, her constant attendance to his needs. Her heart.

Rights that belonged to him. No one else. Any man who touched her would— Nothing. His shoulders slumped against his throne. He couldn't reach them. Which was frustrating and damned irritating. He was a king. He could control people with his mind. Their actions, their words—even rip their skin open with only a thought. Yet he couldn't cross a stupid threshold of shimmering air and check on his property.

Yes. Property. That was what she was, he decided with a smile, already imagining how she would react when he informed her of her new status. Most likely, she'd finish the introduction of her knee to his balls.

"You're scaring the guests." Jasha's deep voice drew him from his dark musings. "Honestly, that smile is evil. You look ready to torture someone."

They were seated side by side on their royal dais, a party in full swing around them. Soft music played, every note perfect. It should be; the orchestra was comprised of the best of the best.

"They don't like the look of me, they can leave." But even as he spoke, he gentled his expression. He needed a distraction, damn it. Otherwise, he'd never survive the next seven days, twenty-two hours, and forty-three minutes until Rose's birthday.

He scanned the room. Gold filigree lined the walls in circling patterns, gleaming in the light cast by the many chandeliers. Windows arched under each golden circle, rain pattering against the glass. There were too many lords, ladies, and Monstrea dancing and laughing to see the gold-veined marble floors he wanted to lay Rose upon, stripping her, touching her, finally tasting her.

His fingers curled around the arms of his throne, and if those arms hadn't been made of onyx, he was certain he would have bent them. As it was, his fingers cracked the stone.

Distraction. What to do, what to do. He continued his study until his gaze caught Grigori's. The Monstrea stood in the far corner of the ballroom, armed for war.

His friend nodded, silently telling him all was well. A surprise. Half of the attendees were from the neighboring kingdom—and his enemies—so he'd expected a fight to break out. But they were here to make nice, to offer him a peace settlement, as well as one of their princesses, so they were on their best behavior.

Relax. He returned the nod.

Grigori's glowing red eyes shifted back to the dance floor, and for a second, only a second, Vasili would have sworn utter longing claimed the man's expression. Interesting. Now, there was another surprise. Vasili followed the line of his friend's gaze, but couldn't pinpoint a specific female. Just a group. What he did notice, however, was that everyone in that group was human—and all four of the visiting princesses were there. Twice as interesting. One, Monstrea usually mated only with other Monstrea, and two, King Greer was especially prejudiced against the warriors.

In fact, the king had threatened to leave if Vasili didn't send them away. After Vasili showed the king to the door, the man had grudgingly withdrawn his ultimatum.

"Is Grigori seeing anyone?" he asked his brother.

Jasha's head tilted to the side as he considered. "Not that I know of. Why?"

"Just curious." If the warrior hadn't talked about his love life with Jasha, Vasili wouldn't do it for him. "How about you? Anyone special?"

"No." Hard tone, no room for discussion.

Hint taken. And discarded. "I've been wondering something. Are you still a virgin?"

His brother sputtered, cheeks red. "I'm not answering that."

So yes, yes, he was. Unbelievable! "Let me pay for—"

"But you . . ." his brother interjected loudly, as if Vasili hadn't spoken; then he lowered his voice. "You're still seeing your Rose." Wouldn't do if one of the princesses overheard. They were currently walking to the dance floor, all four of them, though each continually cast hopeful glances his way.

Peace he would give. Marriage, no.

"Yes. I'm still seeing my Rose." No reason to deny it. Not when she would be here in one week, twenty-two hours, and thirty-seven minutes.

"Two years, and there's been no one else for you."

He wanted to say, *That you've seen*, but the words refused to form. They would disrespect Rose. *Stupid!* When she arrived, he planned to disrespect her plenty. In a bed. In a tub. On the floor, as he'd already imagined.

"I want to meet her."

"No," he rushed out. Jasha wouldn't recognize what she was. Not on sight. But if Rose were to accidentally reveal the secret of her origins . . . Not just no, but hell, no. *Change the subject.* "Think Greer truly wishes peace with us?" Excellent. Bloodshed and mayhem. A much safer topic.

"Hardly. He's wily, always planning, and, as you know, his offer of alliance makes me uneasy."

Vasili sought the man in question. He stood at the back of the ballroom, three lovely ladies surrounding him. They fed him tiny pieces of fruit, caressed him, doted on him, laughed at his coarse teasing. He was older than Vasili by at least twenty years, yet no less muscled and honed.

"But I hate the danger you are continually in," Jasha went on. Then he sighed. "Perhaps you should take him up on his offer and wed one of his daughters. Perhaps that will finally mellow him."

"And be stabbed while sleeping for my efforts? Please." But to be honest, Vasili might have risked such a union had he not already bound himself to Rose. Like Greer, he now wanted peace. His people deserved it, he would be able to hunt other Walkers on a permanent basis, and, well, he didn't want Rose in danger when she visited—and eventually moved here.

Which he wanted her to do. Desperately. But only because he could not bed another female. Not because he couldn't get her out of his mind. Not because she intrigued him and made him laugh. Not because the scent of a night rose now caused his cock to stand at attention.

He shouldn't have married her, he thought darkly. Look what she'd reduced him to. An obsessive, frustrated, pathetic bag of hormones. After he tasted her, he should kill her rather than convince her to move here with him. Finally give her what she deserved. That way, he would stop craving, stop waiting. He was so sick of waiting. He was—

Seeing things. Rose had just appeared in front of him. Not on the dais, but just below, dancers twirling behind her. She shook her head, pale hair waving around her shoulders, and blinked, gaze roving, searching. . . .

Vasili leaped to his feet, blood heating in his veins. He should be worrying that someone had seen her simply appear out of nowhere. But all he could think was, *She's here.* At least she wore clothes similar to what his people usually wore. Black shirt, black pants. Though right now his followers were dressed in gowns and formal attire.

Still. His woman was lovely. The loveliest in the room. *And she was here.*

"Brother?" Jasha said. "Everything all right?"

"Better than all right." *Touch* . . . He had to touch her.

He pounded down the steps, hands clenching and unclenching.

Rose spotted him, raked that silver gaze over him, and her jaw dropped. She'd never seen him in the royal uniform before. White shirt, dark breeches. Knee-high boots.

Did she like?

When he reached her, he grabbed her by the forearm

and ushered her into the nearest hallway, away from the crowd. Such small bones, easily breakable. He gentled his hold. He was thankful she didn't struggle.

That lack of struggle could mean only one thing: She liked.

"I warned you of the dangers of coming unannounced, Rose." *But thank you for ignoring me.*

"I can't believe it worked." She spoke in Drakish, his language, halting and stilted, but understandable. "I can't believe I'm here."

Her voice . . . richer than before. Huskier. His shaft twitched, thickening, hardening. And he'd thought his body desperate before. Now that she was here . . . "So you thought to test my claim?"

"No. I had a question for you. But before you interrupt me, no one has contacted me, and no one has asked me to hurt you. I know you always want that information first."

He believed her because he wanted to, he was stupid, and his cock was thinking for him, but he didn't care. "What's your question?" Any chance it would be, *Will you strip me?*

Silence.

Guess not. He glanced at her, just a quick look. One he hoped would not affect him. *Fail.* His blood heated another degree, and his cock filled the rest of the way. Soft lamplight caressed her, highlighting the delicacy of her skin, the frosted pink of her cheeks.

She was studying the murals on the walls with wide eyes and awe, her lush lips parted, just begging for a kiss.

He hardly noticed those murals anymore, but just then he studied them through new eyes. Armies marched, human and Monstrea, attacking a neighboring kingdom. Blood spilled, and victory awaited.

She should have been disgusted, not awed. That she wasn't ... *Damn it.* He was proud of her. Again. She must appreciate strength as much as he did. He guessed he'd have to take her against the wall, as well. For her. Since she liked them. Would be a favor to her. Of course.

"Beautiful," she said on a wispy catch of breath.

"Yes," he said, his voice breaking.

Her gaze flittered to him. "Where are you taking me?"

"To my chamber. The walls are just as lovely there."

"Why does that matter? No, wait. Stop." Finally she tugged from his clasp, forcing him to come to a halt. There were guards posted at every door in the hallway—all Monstrea—but she paid them no heed. Or perhaps she hadn't noticed them, too focused on the scenery and then Vasili. "My question."

His jaw tightened as he turned to her completely, allowing only a whisper of air between them. He motioned to the closest guard with a tilt of his head. Her gaze followed, and she gasped. She even scrambled backward several steps before realizing what she'd done; she rooted her feet in place and withdrew a semiautomatic.

The guards reacted instantly, jolting into motion, meaning to take down the threat to their king. Vasili froze them in place with only a thought, swiped the gun from Rose, and sheathed it at the back of his waist.

"She means no harm," he told the men. Then he released them from his mental hold and they stumbled over themselves in their efforts to slow their sudden, renewed momentum.

Every member of the royal family possessed an ability like his, though everyone's was different. His father had smoothed the harshest of emotions with a blink of his eyes. His mother had pushed images into other people's minds. Jasha could listen to a conversation from hundreds of miles away—if he so wished. But his brother never intruded upon Vasili's privacy, and Vasili never held his brother immobile. A courtesy to each other.

He wondered, now that Rose was wed to him, if *she* possessed a new ability. Or perhaps her ability to walk from one dimension to the other qualified.

"Leave us," he added.

With only the slightest show of hesitation, they marched away. And now, Vasili was alone with his Rose. As he'd dreamed for nearly a year. Unable to help himself, he crowded her, getting in her face and backing her into the wall. Why wait until they reached his room?

When she could go no farther, she flattened her hands on his chest. Warm, soft. But she didn't push. His heart thundered to meet her touch as he breathed her in, all the floral sweetness of her. Too long. He'd been without her for too long.

She gazed up at him, lashes long and black and gorgeous, and gulped. "Why do they defer to you?"

"Is that your question?" He leaned down and nuzzled her neck, not quite touching but close enough to tease. "A question you risked your life to ask?"

"No."

He answered anyway. "I'm their king."

A gasp. "I think the meaning of what you just said was lost in translation. You're a *king*?"

What was so hard to believe about that? He exuded power, just as a king should.

"Never mind," she said as if she didn't care. "Can I bring someone here?"

Every muscle in his body locked down on bones. He cupped her chin, lifting her head so that he could glare into her eyes. "Who do you want to bring?" If she named a man, he would find a way to reach the bastard. Tear him from limb to limb.

"My parents."

Vasili relaxed. "No. You can't. They'll die. Only Walkers can cross. Why do you want to bring them, anyway?" And why did he suddenly want to meet them? To see the man and woman who had created her?

She traced the collar of his shirt. "I no longer have any kind of relationship with them, and I miss them. I just thought that if I proved myself to them, they would know I'm not crazy or on drugs and . . . I don't know . . . like me again."

His skin tingled where she stroked. "You can't tell anyone what you can do, Rose. It's dangerous for you. For them."

"But I'm . . . lonely."

He didn't like the thought of her alone and sad, and now wanted to meet her parents for an entirely different reason. To *destroy* them for causing her pain. "Is that how Walkers are treated in your world? With disbelief?"

"Yes. We're considered crazy. Locked away."

"You were locked away?" The words lashed from him.

"Only for a little while."

Rage hammered through him. "If that ever happens again, come to me. Immediately." *Calm. She's here; she's fine.* Desire returned, blending with the declining rage. "Now, is this the only reason you came to see me early?" he asked silkily.

"No." Defiance suddenly flashed up at him. "I wanted to tell you how much I hate you."

"You hate me?" Anymore, females ran from him. With good reason. He had a fierce, frightening temper and held life and death in his hands. Still Rose clashed with him, unconcerned. Oh, yes, he felt pride. "Prove it," he said in that same silky tone.

She shivered. "You've threatened me, fought me—I'm better now, by the way, and will kick your ass if we spar—and cursed me. I *should* hate you."

He settled his big hands on her hips, allowing the tips of his fingers to slide under her shirt. More skin, more warmth and softness. "I taught you to fight, to speak properly. And you've been practicing, haven't you, Rose?"

A grumble.

Because deep down she knew she belonged here. "I know you have."

"Did you hear nothing else I said?" she demanded.

He sighed. "Cursed you how?"

"To *suffer*." Accusing.

To ache, she meant. "But I can ease your ... pain." Oh, the ideas pouring through his head ... the many ways to sate her. He'd start with her breasts, tonguing her nipples, and work his way down. But not yet. First, he'd gentle her. He wanted no resistance when the passion claimed them. "Did anyone hurt you during your training?"

A tremor, a slight arch of those hips, closing the distance. "Of course." Breathless.

Another inch and her core would brush his throbbing cock. Was she as eager as he? "Bring them here."

"But that will kill ..." Slowly she grinned. "Why, Vasili. I think you're a romantic at heart, wanting to slay my dragons."

"Romantic, no. Desperate for you, yes."

She licked her lips. "I thought I was too young for you."

"That was when you were a mere nineteen."

"My birthday isn't for another week. I'm not officially twenty."

"Did I fail to mention we celebrate early here? Also, I have a present for you."

"If you say it's this"—she trailed her hand down his stomach and cupped him—"I'll accept."

Yes. She was eager, and there would be no resistance from her.

His restraint broke. "Then let's get you ready to accept." With a groan, he fisted her hair and smashed her lips into his.

Chapter Five

Finally.

A man's tongue in her mouth, thrusting, tasting, taking, giving. Rose's stomach clenched in pleasure rather than pain. A man's hands on her body, squeezing, kneading, rough, calloused. Her blood heated rather than chilled. And that the man was Vasili . . . heaven and hell, salvation and ruin.

His face could reduce a woman to a slave. His *scent* could reduce a woman to a slave. *She* was a slave. One sweep of those dark lashes, one curve of those soft lips, and one thought would prevail above all others. *Yours*. That was what she'd come to realize this past year. He'd enslaved her, changed her entire focus to being with him. Like this.

Shouldn't have allowed the kiss.

But she'd had to know his taste—a dark, spicy drug. Had to know his touch—an electric current. Had to immerse herself in the peat smoke and wildflowers. All dangerous. Had to have more. Had to let him please her. Had to *force* him if necessary. Just once. Then she would know. Then she would stop wondering, stop remembering the way he'd taught her to fight, his hands all over her but not where she needed them most. *Then* she could finally think straight, recall just how mad she should be with him for bonding them, making her feel this way, and finally demand the answers he'd never given her.

Nothing else had helped. In the last year, she'd gotten her own place, started teaching others self-defense, and trained with a vengeance herself. But always she thought of this man, wondered what he was doing, whom he was with.

If he'd turned those violet eyes on another woman, Rose would kill her.

A thought she'd had before, and one that scared her. Because she meant it.

She was too obsessed with him. She knew it, hated it, and had tried to prove to herself that she could live without him. That this man who liked to threaten her, but only ever protected her, wasn't the only reason she lived.

Only one more week; that was all she'd had left to wait. But then she'd thought, *How wonderful to catch him unaware.* To see him outside the tent, if at all possible. To see him interact with other people—and warn away any women who thought to win him. *Mistake.* He'd stridden from that platform, black hair in disarray, eyes bright with welcome and longing, biceps hugged by soft white fabric, cock practically on display in fawn-colored pants.

To hell with *yours.* She'd thought, *Mine.*

"Someone could see," he said roughly. His lips moved to the base of her neck, and he licked and sucked at her pulse. "You've been warned. Now you'll be allowed no quarter."

"You're a king." What, exactly, did that mean here? The same as in her world? Not that she would ever obey him. "Make them go away."

He uttered a rasping chuckle. "What my queen wants . . ."

They'd switched to English, she realized, as he kicked her legs apart. Unprepared for the action, she could only fall. Until he inserted his hips between her thighs and her core rubbed against his erection. A needy gasp escaped her. She closed her eyes and clutched at his shoulders, nails sinking deep.

"Again," she demanded.

He pushed against her. Another gasp. Hers, his, she didn't know anymore.

He plumped her breasts. "I want to see them. Show them to me."

Maybe she would obey him just this once. Too hungry, too achy to be shy or modest, she ripped her shirt over her head and dropped the cotton to the floor. The black lace bra latched in front, so she snagged her finger in the center and tugged.

A low, base curse filled the heated air between them. He stared, just stared while she panted, trembled.

"Mine." His pupils expanded until black overshadowed violet. He bared his teeth, feral just then. Losing control. "These are mine." He squeezed, hard. "Mine."

Thank God. She remembered how much she'd liked Hoyt's gentle caresses. *Silly girl.* So far Vasili had been anything but gentle, and she'd never been gladder. "You like to prove things. Prove it."

As he squeezed, she rolled her hips forward, once again sliding against his thigh. *Yes!* The pressure that had been building since their first meeting expanded, drawing her taut, like a rubber band ready to break.

"Taste."

His head swooped down, his tongue flicking out, back and forth, before his teeth nibbled. There was a sharp sting. She moaned. *More.*

Had to have more. Two years, damn him. Two years

she'd lived without this, hungry, sensitive, dreaming of him at night, fantasizing about him during the day. So many times she'd almost come to him. Once, while pleasuring herself in bed, not that her own hand ever brought her relief, she thought she had. She'd cried his name, his image in her mind, and in the next instant, she'd thought she spied him sleeping next to her, but she'd panicked and rolled away, only to fall onto her floor.

Now she was here. She was with him, and he was still cupping her breasts, his finger toying with her nipples in between bites. *More.*

"Had I known these awaited me, I never would have resisted you this long."

"Sweet words later." She jerked him forward, meshing their mouths, feeding him a kiss, her soul—whatever he wanted he could have.

Their tongues thrust together in a fight for dominance. Their teeth scraped. She swallowed his breath, desperate to have any part of him inside her. All the while she writhed against him, trying to pump herself to orgasm, so when he moved back, preventing her from touching him that way, she bit his bottom lip in a fury.

"More."

"Yes." His fingers ripped at her darkened jeans, popping the button, almost breaking the zipper, revealing black lace panties. He didn't pause to look. Just sank his hand inside. Warm skin on wet flesh, past her small thatch of curls and—

"Yes!" There.

One finger pushed deep while the heel of his hand pressed against her clitoris. She should do something for him, touch him like he was touching her, reach into his pants and fist his cock, but as he inserted a second finger, her thoughts fragmented. *More.* A third finger. *More!*

Stretching, burning. So long, too long. He drove those fingers in and out of her, and she was so wet they glided smoothly. Pressure, still building. Blood, like fire in her veins. She wanted to come, was desperate to come, but just as she neared satisfaction, he stopped.

"Bastard!" She slapped his shoulders.

"This bastard wants you to come in his mouth." He dropped to his knees.

Oh. "Good . . . boy . . ." Rose lost her anchor and fell back against the wall, giving it all of her weight. Vasili didn't bother trying to remove the panties; he just shoved them aside, and his gaze again locked on hers.

Hoyt had never tasted her. She wasn't sure she would have let him had he tried. Those days, she'd been self-conscious. Had preferred to be with her man in the dark. Had been too unsure of herself to say what she needed. Now she had no more experience than she'd had then, but she was a different person. Stronger, more confident. Haunted by desire. She doubted Vasili would have let her hide in the dark, anyway.

He was too sensual a man. More driven than she was. "Do it. Please."

"Pink. Wet." His words were slurred. "Mine." And then he was there, tonguing her clitoris, and she was moaning, fingers tangling in his hair, arching into every stroke, gasping his name, shouting his name.

He sucked and he *devoured.* Anyone could have walked out of the ballroom, just as he'd told her, but she didn't care. Was lost. Was climbing higher and higher, the pressure finally uncoiling, promising satisfaction. Almost . . .

"Harder. More. Don't stop. More. Stop and *die.*" The commands left her in a rush.

His fingers joined the play, three thrusting up inside her without any more preparation or warning, and she shot off like a rocket, screaming, pressure finally breaking completely, stars exploding behind her eyes, inner walls clenching around him, holding him captive.

"Fuck," he growled, and she wasn't sure if the word was a command or a curse. He jolted to his feet, those fingers sliding out of her, and she moaned. She might have come, but she wasn't done with him. Needed more, still had to have more.

His lips smashed against hers, and she tasted herself. She ripped at his pants, finally freeing his cock. Her fingers curled around it—but only briefly before he batted her away, positioning himself for penetration. In those brief seconds, she thrilled at how big he was, how hot and hard and ready.

"Do it," she commanded. *Please.*

"Vasili?"

He turned his face away from her with a snarl. "Leave!"

It took Rose a moment, but she snapped out of her sensual haze and followed Vasili's example, turning and looking. Several men stood at the end of the hallway, peering over at them. Two were grinning—one of them a monster, one of them a younger version of Vasili—and the rest quickly spun, offering their backs.

The monster caught her eye and his smile fell away. Shock registered on his features, then fury, hate.

She shuddered and switched her attention to the Vasili clone. He continued to radiate absolute amusement in a way that Vasili never had. Was that what Vasili would look like if ever he lost his dark edge?

She adored his darkness, but also realized she wanted to make him smile like that.

"Go," Vasili snapped, even as Rose disengaged from him and, like the guards, gave the newcomers her back.

She bent down, blindly reaching for her shirt and bra, and tugged them on as she straightened. *Dear God. Now* she cared about an audience. She would have run, but Vasili clasped onto her arm, holding her immobile.

"Now!" he shouted.

"You can't ... do that here," the younger version of him said. "There are guests, and they can hear you. *Greer* can hear you, and he isn't happy."

Rose's cheeks flamed. She was as embarrassed as she was suddenly curious. Who was Greer? Why did his happiness matter? "I should go," she whispered, careful to use his language. She'd practiced at home, alone, and quite often, but even though the language seemed to be embedded inside her brain, she had yet to master it, because no one could tell her what she said correctly and what she didn't.

"No," Vasili snapped. Then more gently, "No. Not yet. Please." Finally he released her and fixed his clothing. "I'll be right back," he threw over his shoulder, ushering her farther down the hall and away from the men.

She didn't protest. Not until they'd snaked around a corner and were once again alone. Then she pulled from his grip and whirled on him. "I should go," she repeated.

He scrubbed a hand down his face. "No. We're not done. Wait in my room, and I'll return as soon as I can."

Wait for him to fuck her? Hardly. No matter how much she wanted it. "Is that an order, Your Majesty?" she asked dryly.

"Yes."

Her eyes narrowed. "I'm not your—" *Shit!* What was the word? She didn't know, so she ended with, "I'm not yours."

He got in her face, madder than she'd ever seen him. "You are. You're my wife."

Oh, how her body liked hearing that. Every cell she possessed purred. "By force, so it doesn't count," she said, lifting her chin.

"Many women would kill to be in your position, Rose."

"Yeah, well, many men would kill to be in yours."

His nostrils flared. "They try, and they'll die."

There was a commotion around the corner, voices—male and female—then stomping feet. Then the clone, the monster, four females and another, older male were bearing down on them.

Vasili stiffened as he turned. He stepped to the side, in front of her, shielding her.

"Who," the older man snapped while trying to glare at Rose, "is that?"

A moment passed in heavy silence. During that moment, Vasili's entire countenance changed. From glaring, snarling beast to wicked charmer. "Greer," he said. "Princesses. So lovely to see you."

Princesses? Were they his sisters? His daughters?

Rose studied the females. Three were petite, slender. One slightly taller, but plump. Two had silky brown hair, one red, and one honey blond. The brunettes were pretty, the redhead plain, and the honey blonde stunning. Each wore gowns of sparkling velvet, jewels dripping from their ears, necks, and fingers. They radiated wealth and confidence, even the plain one.

"The girl," Greer insisted. He had thick silver hair, scars lining his face, and the body of a warrior.

"My apologies if I gave you the impression you had the right to question me about my people," Vasili replied in that smooth, humming tone, and the older man narrowed his eyes. "Now let's all return to the party, shall we?"

"Father," the redhead said in a gentle voice—to the old man. Not Vasili's sisters or daughters, then. Potential girlfriends? Rose wanted to hate them, but their eyes were kind. "Perhaps the girl would like to change into a gown first?"

"What a kind little thing you are, darling." Vasili patted the top of her head. "But she won't be joining us."

Darling. He'd called the redhead *darling*. A moment ago, he'd called Rose by her name. And with that thought, she realized that he hadn't called *her* darling. Not once during this visit. Not while he'd had his fingers inside her, not while he'd tongued her to orgasm.

Disappointment rocked her. No endearments. Did that mean his affection for her had waned?

Oh, he wanted her; she knew that much. He was still hard, after all. But you could screw a woman, even a wife, and not truly like her. And he'd bonded them, so he couldn't sleep with anyone else. She was the only outlet he had.

"May I escort you back to the ballroom, Your Majesty?" the redhead asked. Without waiting for a reply, she reached out and took Vasili's hand.

Now Rose hated the girls. *Mine*, she wanted to scream. *He's mine*. No one else was to touch him. Ever. Even so innocent a touch. He'd just had that hand on Rose's body, inside Rose's body, and to casually touch someone else . . . Her teeth ground together.

"Actually," she said, raising her chin, "I would love to join the party. As is. So . . . let's do this. *Maj-ass-tee*."

Chapter Six

He'd had her, Vasili thought, but he hadn't *had* her. And now he had to parade Rose around the ballroom with his enemies surrounding her—and there wasn't a damn thing he could do to stop the madness. Not without drawing more attention to her. Worse, he had to do it with the intoxicating taste of her in his mouth, the feel of her burned into his hands. And a hard-on only *she* could relieve.

She remained by his side, at least, as she watched the happenings through wide eyes. Both a blessing and a curse. She was here, but he couldn't claim her. Couldn't stop every single man from staring at her. Men he wanted to kill, his own as well as Greer's. But he couldn't blame them. She was enchanting. That fall of white-blond hair, those cherry red lips swollen from his kisses. Even dressed like a warrior, she was the most elegant woman in the room.

And she was his. He wanted to announce that fact more than he wanted to throw her on his bed and strip her. Well, maybe not quite that much. But damn it! Everyone needed to know whom she belonged to! In time, he promised himself. After he'd assured her safety. Maybe.

He led the group—Rose, Greer, Jasha, Grigori, and the princesses—to a quiet corner, as far from the masses as possible. There, he positioned Rose against the wall, with half of his body shielding her from the others.

Awkward silence seized them. He was glad. He preferred silence to questions. But, of course, a few minutes later Greer had to ruin everything. As always.

"So tell me, King of the North. Which of my daughters do you favor?" Greer asked him. "Which will you choose to be your bride and end the war between us?"

Rose stiffened. "Bride?"

He reached back, grabbed her wrist, and squeezed, all without looking at her. At the moment of contact, he hissed out a breath. So hot, so soft. So *his*. He wanted more. Wanted her under him, over him, shouting his name. "Now is not the time for such a discussion."

"When, then?" the king insisted. "That's the reason I'm here, isn't it?"

Rose dug her nails into Vasili's hand, drawing blood.

"You're here for peace talks, nothing more," he said.

A vein nearly burst from the king's forehead as another bout of silence settled over them. The princesses inched away from their father, as if they feared being struck. They probably did. Vasili had heard about the king's fearsome temper.

"Prince Jasha," the redhead said with a shy—desperate?—smile. Funny. She knew all of their names, yet Vasili couldn't recall hers. "Would you care to dance?"

His brother's violet gaze dropped to his boots. He opened his mouth to reply, but no words emerged. Finally he shut his mouth and gave the redhead his back, glaring out at the circle of ladies closest to them.

Her cheeks flamed with embarrassment as she lowered her arm.

"Men," Rose grumbled with sympathy, speaking in Vasili's language. "Forget him, sweetie. He's obviously an ass."

Vasili pressed his lips together to stop his laugh. At least she'd spoken the correct words.

"What's your name, girl?" Greer snapped at Rose.

"She's mute," Vasili said. "And her name is unimportant."

"What's the matter, *darling*?" Oh, the anger in that tone. She would punish him later, though he wasn't exactly sure of his crime. "Embarrassed of me?"

Embarrassed? When he wanted to beat his chest and warn every other man away? When he would have been happy if she tattooed his name on his chest? A suggestion he would later make. Still. He wasn't sure how she affected him like this when no one else ever had. Surely the bond wasn't fully responsible. He'd reacted to her *before* bonding them, or he wouldn't have fucking bonded them.

"Like I said," he snapped. "*Mute.*"

Greer watched the entire exchange with anger sparking in his eyes. "A slave would never make a good wife, you know."

She isn't a slave! "You know this from experience?" he asked smoothly.

Rose's nails were now embedded in his bone. He could feel warm drops of blood sliding down his arm. He reached back with his other hand and applied pressure to the center of her palm, harder ... harder ... but she held steady. Damn her, when would she give?

He eased the pressure rather than break her bone.

Finally she released him. He wanted to smile. She'd out-lasted him, and he was irrationally proud of her. Again.

"Yes," Greer said. "I do. Though I have not bonded with any of my women, I keep five of them to attend my needs. One is a slave, and she is by far my biggest mistake. Greedy, grasping, desperate. So keep your girl, if that's what you wish, but take one of my daughters. I want peace, but I cannot trust you without the marital bond."

Nails raked down his back, hard, and he nearly hissed in pain. And pleasure. He'd endure Rose's torturing over any other woman's caressing. The little wildcat. "When you yourself refuse to wed any of your women? Besides, Greer, I'm not the one who attacks without provocation."

Those nails began to pet him. Again, he wanted to smile.

Greer ran his tongue over his teeth. "I have other offers, you know. Other kingdoms eager for an alliance."

"Yet you came to me first. I'm moved, really, but that doesn't mean I'll give you what you crave."

A growl. "The Western and Southern kingdoms despise you for your strength, yet they have not risen against you. Yet. But they will. Mark my word, they will. There is already talk."

He reached back a second time—he couldn't *not* touch her—and traced his fingers along the waist of Rose's pants. Felt her belly quiver. Cut off his possessive grunt of approval. "They fear my strength as much as they hate it. They will not attack."

"They will when I agree to help them defeat you. Which I *will* do if you refuse this opportunity."

He stiffened. "I don't like threats."

"And I don't like issuing them. But I want this alliance, more than anything."

The man's desperation relaxed him. He resumed his exploration of Rose's pants, twisting the button, moving the zipper. His finger glided over her panties, and she gasped. Her nails dug into him once more, but not to hurt. To urge him on. "And what's in this for you, hmm?" Had that breathless tone been his?

Greer sighed. "I'm old. I'm tired of all the fighting. I want to ensure my kingdom is properly cared for when I'm gone."

Truth or a lie, Vasili didn't know. But the sentiment he understood. He wanted his kingdom safe, as well—but he wouldn't be backed into a corner. "I could kill you and place a new king on your throne. One who will adore me. What think you of *that* plan?"

"I like it," Rose whispered. She arched against him, a command to attend her. He did. He cupped her between her legs, rubbing. Even with the thin cotton barrier, he could feel her moisture, her need for him, and he reacted. His cock, which had never truly deflated, grew and hardened.

He fought the urge to whip around, press himself against her, drop to his knees, taste her again, to have her, here, now, in front of everyone, or drag her away without a word to his guests. He needed her, wanted her, had to have her, and the wait was impossible. But he didn't allow himself to do any of that. He would be patient, take care of territory business like a good boy—no matter the cost to his sanity—and *then* himself.

"You need a new plan," Greer said. "Before I die, I'll either have joined with you or defeated you. That, I swear."

Vasili stilled, the vow ringing in his ears. If he failed to wed one of the princesses, Greer would ensure their minor skirmishes became full-blown battles. That was what he was truly saying. People would die. Lands would be burned. Was one life—Rose's life—worth that? These people trusted him. Needed him. Relied on him.

"I need time," he gritted out.

Greer nodded, as if that were the answer he'd expected. "Do not take too long. But meanwhile. Girls." He waved them closer. "Tell King Vasili all about yourselves so that he might know you better."

"Wait, what?" Rose suddenly demanded, pulling from his touch entirely. "Did you just say you needed time? To decide among them?"

He wanted to howl.

"Isn't that just a party in a box?" she gritted out. "I'm outta here."

"No! You—"

"I'll do it," Jasha said, cutting him off. "I'll wed one of the princesses."

Vasili stopped breathing, afraid he'd misheard. "Are you sure?" Whether his brother's claim was a token or not, Vasili didn't care. He grasped onto the offer like a lifeline.

His brother nodded. "I'm sure."

To save Vasili from losing Rose, or because Jasha desired one of the princesses for his own and was too shy to say so? Again, Vasili didn't care. Sweet, sweet lifeline.

"Do you find this acceptable, Greer?" he demanded.

The old king thought for a moment, then nodded. "A union with royalty is a union."

"Good. It's agreed. Jasha may choose one of your daughters and wed her, and you will leave my people and my lands alone. Forever."

"Agreed. But the wedding must be soon," the old king insisted. "I was willing to give you, the king, time. The prince will not be afforded the same luxury."

Jasha gave a stiff nod. "I don't care when it happens. A wedding is a wedding."

Vasili could have kissed him. "Enjoy the rest of the party, men, ladies. Now, if you'll excuse me." Vasili grabbed Rose's wrist and dragged her out of the ball-room for the second time that night.

"Dismiss the guard," she ground out when they reached the hallway. "I want to talk to you. And by *talk*, I mean peel the skin from your bones and hear you scream."

"Kinky, but no." He wasn't taking a chance that they would be interrupted again. "This area isn't private enough." He didn't turn back to her, but coiled around several corners, pounded up a flight of stairs and down another hallway. Finally, he reached his wing of the palace.

Servants were tending to the party, so each room was deserted. He bypassed the bathing room, his workout room, his entertainment room, and headed straight into his bedroom.

Large bed. Four posters, velvet sheets. Silver, the color of her eyes. He'd had them made earlier that year. He stopped at the edge and turned to face her.

Her eyes were narrowed, her lips pulled tight in a scowl. She was panting, shoulders lifting and lowering in quick succession, as if she wanted to punch him but was restraining herself. Just barely.

"You needed *time*?" Although they were alone, she still spoke in his language.

She wanted to hash that out now? *Fine*. He would multitask. "Yes," he said, unbuttoning his shirt. "I called you a slave and a mute, too, so feel free to slap me around while you shout."

"You threaten me and call me names, and that's al-ways been foreplay. But the fact that you needed to think

about whether or not to kill me so you could marry one
of your princesses is insulting!"

Insulting? Try ingenious. His shirt fell from his shoulders, leaving his torso bare—except for the blades he
had stashed on his arms, both of his tattoos covered. "I
would never kill you, Rose. Ever."

"Rose." She laughed without humor. "There you go
again, calling me by my name. You bastard!"

A bastard? For *that*? "I'm lost," he admitted, kicking
off his boots before unfastening his pants, pushing them
to the floor, and stepping out of them. There were blades
strapped to his thighs and ankles, too.

"What happened to 'darling'?" she lashed out, careful not to look at the hard cock peeking from the waist
of his underwear.

He blinked. She was angry that he hadn't called her
darling? A meaningless endearment he used for everyone?

"Were you going to pick the redhead?" Her voice
rose. "You called *her* 'darling' fast enough. Never mind.
Don't tell me. Just tell me how you were going to manage a new marriage if you weren't going to off me. I
seem to recall you telling me death was the only way
out of the first one."

"And that's still true, baby, but here are the facts. I
can't think when I'm with you. I'm reduced to two words.
Mine and *more*. And I don't call you *darling* anymore
because—" He pressed his lips together. *Do it. Tell her.*
But he'd never said the words before. Never *thought* them
before. "Because I don't want to call you what I call everyone else. You're special." She meant something to him.

Her features softened, those silver eyes going liquid.
"Really?"

"Yes." He closed the distance between them and

cupped her jaw. So soft, so delicate. "And I never would have abandoned you. I was going to toss the princess in a palace far from here, let her call herself my wife, and shack up with you." War averted, body and mind satisfied. "But now I don't have to. Now we can be together." In secret, he thought with a frown.

He didn't want to hide her, though. But he would. To keep her safe, he would do anything.

Rather than softening her further, his admission left her sputtering. She jerked from his clasp and backed away, his hands already mourning the loss of her. "How sweet of you. And how about this? I'll go find another man, let him live in my apartment, let him tell everyone he's my husband, and then I'll return to you."

Oh, hell, no. He got in her face, breath suddenly like fire in his nose. "Touch another man, call another man *anything*, and I will find a way to enter your dimension and murder him in front of you."

"I'll take that as a 'Do whatever you want, *Rose*.'" She pushed him, hard, and he stumbled backward. "To get here, all I had to do was think about you. To go home, I figure all I have to do is think about my apartment. Right?"

"You're staying right here." He lunged.

She waved her fingers, smiled too sweetly and—

Disappeared.

He flew through air, just missing her. "No. Rose!" Righting himself, he swung left and right, searching for her, any sign of her, his heart pounding against his ribs, that heated breath still sawing in and out. There wasn't a single trace of her.

"You little witch!"

She'd gone home. Well, *this* was her home now, and it was time she learned and accepted.

She'll be back, he told himself. One week, and she would be back. She wouldn't be able to stop herself.

He almost rubbed his hands together as his blood flamed yet another degree. He did laugh. This, he realized, was just foreplay for him. Like the threats and the name-calling were foreplay for her. Every time she left, he only wanted her more.

Oh, how he enjoyed her.

Oh, how he would have her. In every way imaginable.

One week, he thought again. He had some planning to do.

Chapter Seven

Maybe she'd overreacted, Rose thought the next day as she cocooned herself in the cold sheets of her bed. Alone. Aching. As if the fire Vasili ignited had never been doused. Had she stayed with him, she could have woken up in his arms. They could have made love. Down and dirty, nothing taboo. She was more certain than ever that he wouldn't allow insecurities or hesitation on her part. He would demand everything. And she would give it. Willingly. Eagerly.

But he'd thought about making another woman his "wife" and she'd felt as if he had just punched her in the stomach. Her fury and her jealousy had raged out of control. She couldn't stand the thought of him with someone else, even for appearances. Even to save his people and his land.

Selfish hussy.

She wished she had a girlfriend to talk to about him, but over the years she'd cut everyone from her life. Or they had run from her. She worked, she trained, she thought about Vasili, and that was it. Which was his fault, damn it! After that first visit to his world, she'd begun to pull herself out of this one. She knew that now. As if she'd known she no longer belonged here. As if she belonged with him.

I want to be with him. Forever. She should have shied away from the thought, but couldn't. It felt too ... right. Too perfect. To be pleasured every day the way he'd pleasured her yesterday ... yes, yes, a thousand times yes. But ... did he want forever from her? They'd never been together more than a day at a time. Maybe they'd hate each other after a week. Maybe they weren't compatible. Except in bed. There they'd be magical. No question.

But the get-along thing she couldn't work out in her mind. Would they or wouldn't they?

There was only one way to find out....

Return and stay, without letting him drive her away. No matter how much he annoyed her. She nodded, instinctively liking the thought. Yes, she would return and stay for a week.

But first, she wanted to find out some stuff for him. He'd asked her numerous times for names of other Walkers and the dates they visited. She would find out, but she wouldn't give him the info until she knew why he wanted it.

Moaning, she lumbered from the bed, showered quickly, and dressed in jeans and a T-shirt. Then she made a call.

"I was surprised when you contacted me."

Rose peered over at Nick. Her kind-of ex. They were inside a coffee shop, a round iron table between them, people coming in and out, and bright, hot air blustering through the door. Too bright, too hot. She suddenly missed the dark and cold of Vasili's world.

What did he call his land, anyway? "Nightmare" just didn't fit anymore.

"Sorry," she said, fingers tightening around her mocha latte. "About ignoring you." For more than a year. "That was rude, and immature, and I feel terrible."

"I would have appreciated a reason," he said. His hair was a darker shade of blond now, and his face a little lined. From stress? His cheeks were gaunt, as if he weren't eating properly, and his clothing was wrinkled, as if he no longer cared about his appearance. Still, he was a handsome man, and more muscular than most humans.

"I . . . kind of have a boyfriend. We're on again, off again." Truth. Vasili claimed they were married.

And part of her believed him. Because part of her *wanted* them to be married. Even though they saw each other only once a year. *That's about to change. Soon you'll have your week.*

And then . . . more?

Hopefully. He'd put his hands on her, kissed her, tasted her, and oh, she needed more. With every minute that passed away from him, being with him stopped being a want and became a need. Like breathing. She had to have him. More of his touches, all of his kisses.

"I see," Nick said, drawing her from her daydreams.

"I really am sorry," she repeated. "I liked you, I did, but . . ."

"You liked him more." A defeated sigh. "Does he know?"

About Nightmare, Nick meant. "Yes. He knows." *Because he lives there.*

"Is he a . . . *you know*, too?"

She shook her head.

Nick's dark eyes widened with shock. "And he accepts you?"

"Yes."

He frowned, but that frown soon became tinted with sadness. "You're very lucky."

Lady troubles? Had someone rejected him because of what he could do? Probably. Rose could relate. She hadn't lied to Vasili. Her parents barely spoke to her anymore, and each encounter stung worse than the last.

After they'd institutionalized her, she'd never again spoken to them about Vasili or his world, but that hadn't mattered. The damage had already been done. They'd known her before, seen the changes in her, and hadn't liked who she'd become. No longer their sweet little princess, but someone a little dark, a lot stubborn. Beyond harsh.

Finding a way to escort them into Nightmare had been a last-ditch effort to salvage their relationship. To make them believe. But she was almost relieved that she couldn't take them. Vasili was her safe haven, her fantasy in the flesh. She didn't want to share him. With anyone.

"So why'd you call, Rose?"

Nick's question once again dragged her back into the present. God, she was easily distracted today.

"I have questions. About"—she looked around, made sure no one was paying them any attention, and whispered—"Nightmare."

He, too, looked around. A habit every Dimension Walker probably possessed. "Okay. Ask."

"Why us? Why can we do this and no one else? I mean, none of us are related that I'm aware of, so it isn't genetic."

A shrug. "You've read the theories online, I'm sure."

She nodded. "One is that we're supposed to study them, learn from them. Another is that we're ambassadors, meant to pave the way for when the two worlds collide." But no one could prove the two would ever collide. "Another is that we're supposed to kill them. What do *you* think?"

He shrugged again. "I believe that last one. That we're like vampire hunters, special, meant to destroy evil."

Destroy evil. The words echoed through her skull. She sipped at her mocha, though it had chilled and settled in her stomach like lead. After that first visit, she would have agreed with him. Now? Not even a little. Vasili was important to her, and the thought of him being hunted, hurt, caused rage to burn through her. A lot more Walkers probably thought like Nick.

She released her latte before she crumpled the cup. "Have they ever hurt you?"

His chest puffed up with pride, and for a moment, she saw the man she'd dated: strong, healthy, determined. "I haven't given them the chance."

"And yet you still think you're supposed to kill them? What if they're chasing you to talk with you? To learn from you?" She remembered the people at the party last night. How they'd laughed and danced. How harmless they'd seemed. Even the monsters.

Nick gaped at her. "You've seen those red eyes, right?"

"Yes. So?"

"So, you know those creatures don't want to talk to us."

But they hadn't hurt her. That first night, they'd taken her to Vasili. "Can *they* travel here?" She would love for Vasili to show up unannounced and uninvited—at least she would pretend he was uninvited—and sweep her off her feet—only to throw her on her own bed.

Wait. He'd said only Walkers could travel between the worlds. But maybe there were Walkers in his world, too.

"No." Nick shook his head. "Many have tried to bring one over, you know, to prove there's another side, but the bodies disintegrate every time. Dead or alive, no one from here or there can be taken from one world and placed in another unless they're a Walker."

Wow. She felt no pain when she traveled. Just blinked, and boom, she was in another time and place. Yet others burned to death? *Just . . . wow.* "Can any of us go there on our own? You know, without it being our birthday?" She could, but what about the others?

"No, and thank God for that." Again, he frowned. "Why ask? Tell me you don't want to spend *more* time there."

"Of course I don't," she rushed out. A lie, and one she didn't feel guilty for telling. She didn't need him trying to talk her out of returning. Or rallying others of their kind to do so—forcefully. But why could she travel at will and no one else? Because she was "bonded" to Vasili?

"So why all the questions, Rose?" Nick asked.

"My birthday's approaching, and I'm just trying to figure things out, that's all." *Good, that's good. Keep it casual.* "So . . . when do you go back?"

"Next month." Bitterness laced his tone. "August eighth."

She made a mental note.

"I've always dreaded going back, but now . . ." He shuddered, the action making several strands of hair dance over his forehead. "In the last year, several Walkers have failed to return. Did you know that?"

"No. How do you? Hardly anyone shares their name." Too afraid of being labeled a crazy, as she well knew.

"The day before their birthdays was the last time they posted online."

Yes. Telling. Or maybe not. "What if they just decided to stay?" Could they stay, though? Maybe she was the only one who could stay for extended periods of time, just like she was the only one who could travel at will.

Nick snorted. "Who would want to live in constant darkness?"

If you were in bed with a sexy man who had his hands and mouth all over you, there was a definite appeal to all that darkness. "Have you ever met a man named . . ." She hesitated, as if saying his name were a betrayal to him. But she had to know. "Vasili?"

"Met? No." A hard glint darkened Nick's eyes. "But heard of, yes."

"Tell me!" Did she sound too eager? Look too eager? She was leaning forward, hands wringing together.

Clearly. Nick regarded her strangely as he pushed aside his cup and drummed his fingers against the table-top. "He's the king of the Northern Realm. Have *you* met him?"

"Well, uh, I . . ."

He took her stuttering as a yes. "Can you get close to him? Kill him?"

"No!" And anyone else who tried would feel the sting of her wrath. Sadly, that "anyone" might be Nick. At the moment, he glowed with determination.

But if she had to choose between them, she would choose Vasili. Always.

"Too bad. See, from what I've been able to piece together, I know there are four realms. North, South, East, and West. A different king rules each. The North and East are at war, and the South and West are allies who refuse to take part."

Vasili, at war. With Greer. But that war had been averted, since Jasha was marrying one of Greer's daughters. She mentioned none of that, though. She wouldn't aid Nick's cause with information.

"If we could kill Vasili," he continued, "one of those realms would fall and that's one less to worry about."

Now her eyes narrowed, and she knew the hard glint he'd had earlier was suddenly mirrored in hers. "That would make you a murderer, Nick." *And me, as well, since my first reaction will be revenge.* "You don't want to go there. Believe me."

"Well, I'm sick of the birthday curse," he burst out. "Sick of dreading the darkness and the rain, the monsters and their chase. They always scent me out immediately, and I always spend the entire twelve hours I'm forced to stay there running for my life."

"I'm sorry." And she was. But she still would not accept his intentions.

A sandy brow arched. "That hasn't been your experience, has it?"

"No," she admitted. "They aren't so bad."

"They're monsters, Rose."

"Yes, but they've never hurt me." Sure, Vasili had threatened—she shivered, still uncertain why the thought of Vasili's naughtiness thrilled her so much— but he'd helped her instead.

Nick scrubbed a hand down his face. "Look, there are others like me. Tired and craving an end. We want those things *dead*."

"What are you planning?" she whispered, gripping the edge of the table.

He shrugged. "We've been talking about it, *trying* to plan. But that's hard to do when no one trusts anyone else, so nothing's been solidified yet. I've got an idea, though. One that might bring us all together."

Oh ... shit. Another reason to visit Vasili. To warn him.

*   *   *

The next day, Rose shimmied into a lacy ice-blue dress and matching heels. Vasili had never seen her in anything but pants, and at the ball, as all the women had danced around her in those velvet gowns, she'd felt drab. She'd wanted to show Vasili that she, too, could look pretty.

After doing her makeup and hair, she packed a bag. All her toiletries, lots of lingerie, a few more dresses, and some pants and tees. She'd stay all seven days, no more, no less. No matter how much he pissed her off. Then, if things worked out as she hoped, she'd return here, say good-bye to her parents, find out if Nick and the other Walkers had "solidified" anything yet, gather the rest of her things, and finally shack up with Vasili for good.

If he was on board, of course.

He'd better be on board. Rose strapped her blades onto her wrists and thighs. She recalled the weapons Vasili had worn last night, and shivered. *Sexy.* She'd wanted to eat him up. *Now you can.* She grinned as she checked her .45, threw a couple clips in her bag, and tried to anchor the gun to her waist—oops, no room. The blades took up too much space under her dress.

She slung the bag over her shoulder, keeping the gun in hand, safety on. She wouldn't use it on Vasili, of course. Unless he pissed her off. Better to shoot him than to leave before her time ended. And the monsters she'd seen last time had looked so civilized, she doubted she'd have to use it on them. Besides, they hadn't attacked her, and hadn't acted as if they even *wanted* to attack her. For the most part, they'd kept their eyes averted. They'd even danced with the humans, those claws gentle on their partners and not drawing a single bead of blood.

Vasili clearly liked them, and they clearly respected him. So Rose planned to make an effort to befriend them, too. That didn't mean she'd head into that palace defenseless, though. Last time, she'd meant to stay only a few minutes, so she hadn't armed herself quite so fiercely. Plus, if another Walker showed up looking for trouble, she would be able to deliver.

With a deep breath, she closed her eyes, the white walls of her bedroom fading away. For a moment, she remembered Vasili's bedroom. The difference between hers and his. Hers, plain. His, decadent. Hers, small. His, unbelievably spacious. Hers, dowdy. His, a rainbow of colors, textures, and patterns. Murals painted along the walls, murals of the sun and flowers and battles. Marble floors veined with gold. Alabaster columns, windows of sparkling crystal. Dark velvets and— Her mind locked on that thought. She would wrap Vasili in that velvet, then unwrap him, one inch at a time, kissing every piece of skin she bared.

His eyes would be heavy lidded, his lips parted, his expression strained.

Perfect. She repeated her vow to him, and her feet lost their anchor. For a moment, she was weightless, a little dizzy, and then all was well. Except for the sudden blast of noise and the shower of pounding rain. Her eyelids popped open, and she gasped in horror.

The dark of night, just like that first time, and hammering rain. Somehow torches were lit and remained so, illuminating a battle scene of violence and fury, far worse than anything that had been painted on the walls. Swords arced. Blood sprayed. Mud splattered as bodies fell. Monsters, so many monsters. Eyes red, glowing. Teeth bared, chomping. Men flailed, grunted.

A tremor slid down her spine. Where was Vasili?

Had the Walkers already attacked? Had Greer betrayed him?

Her wild gaze scanned, searching . . . searching . . .

so many bodies, so many injured.... There! He held a sword, swinging the long blade, connecting with a human. That human hunched over and Vasili kicked him, sending the man reeling backward. He didn't get up.

She wanted to shout Vasili's name, but knew she would distract him. As every single one of her instructors had told her, distraction could kill you faster than an opponent. She looked around. She was a few yards from the action, and hadn't been noticed yet, hidden by shadows as she was. She would have joined the fray, anything to protect Vasili, but she didn't know who was on his side and who wasn't.

What should she do?

Calm, steady. She couldn't leave. Or rather, she wouldn't. She would not be able to live with herself if something happened to him and she hadn't been here to save him. So she dropped her bag and slinked farther into the shadows, inching closer to him. When she was but a few feet away, she crouched, wiped the frigid water from her face, and looked him over. He was cut, bleeding. Mud was splattered all over him.

Two humans launched themselves at him, and her breath caught in her throat. His swords whizzed through the air, slicing through the one in front and the one behind at the same time. Yet he didn't see the third man running toward him, blade raised high, descending....

Rose aimed and fired, no hesitation. Kill shot. The man grunted and fell. Vasili must have heard the boom because he whipped around, searching the dark. When he spotted her, he snarled.

"Go home!"

"After I rescue my damsel in distress," she called.

Another man raced up behind him. She switched her attention, fired again. He, too, fell to her bullet. She'd never purposely hurt anyone before—not with the intention of utterly destroying—and would have thought she would feel guilt and sadness. All she felt was savage satisfaction that she'd protected her man.

For a moment, she thought she saw sparks of pride in Vasili's violet eyes. Then he spun from her and rejoined the fray. If she'd thought him brutal before, he soon proved her wrong. Now he was ferocious. He gave no quarter. Showed no mercy. Moved with lethal grace, blades slicing and dicing. Men fell all around him, and every so often he looked back at her. To make sure she was watching?

Was he . . . showing off?

She nearly grinned. He was. He really was. And she was impressed. Here was a man who would always be able to protect. He would defend with a strength few possessed. He would—

Someone grabbed her from behind, hard arm winding around her neck, choking, hot breath fanning over her cheek. The other arm batted the gun out of her hand.

"Who are you?" a male voice demanded at her ear.

"Let me go," she snapped.

"*What* are you? A Walker? Yes, I think so. I saw you appear. I saw your weapon. Saw you help that bastard king."

This was not Vasili's man, then. No panic. She'd trained. She knew what to do. Rather than tug at the arm choking her, as instinct demanded, she reached back and jabbed him in the eye. His hold loosened, enabling her to turn. Immediately she slammed her knee between his legs, and he doubled over.

She kneed him in the face, sending him flying to his back. When he hit, he gasped for breath he couldn't quite catch. As she approached him, withdrawing her knife, he regained his bearings and kicked her, hard. Now *she* lost her breath and stumbled backward and he was able to hop to his feet.

"Bitch."

He flew toward her. To his surprise, she met him in the middle. He was able to disarm her as they punched and dodged, punched and dodged. She landed three hits. He landed one, and for a moment, she saw fireflies dancing around her and had to spit out blood. But she didn't slow or stop or cry or panic. And soon she landed her open palm against his nose. *Crack*. Blood sprayed and he fell.

An unholy roar sounded behind her. Then there was a whirl of black, a hard breeze wafting over her, and she could only stand there, amazed, as she realized Vasili was on top of the man and beating his face into pulp.

At first the man struggled; then the struggling ceased. Vasili continued to punch and punch and punch. Rose approached him slowly, gently, and flattened her hand on his shoulder.

"Stop now, darling," she said. "Yes?"

He did, as if her voice had penetrated that fog of rage. Panting, he swung narrowed eyes to her. Blood and mud were caked all over his bruised face, the rain dripping over him and streaking both along the rest of his skin. He was brutal and all the more beautiful for it.

"You're all right?" he demanded.

"Yes. You?"

"Yes."

"But he hurt you," was the ragged reply, as if he couldn't believe that fact.

"I'm fine. I've endured worse during training."

"But he hurt you. I saw him." With that, Vasili turned back to the man and punched him again.

"He's already dead," she told him gently. No way anyone could survive that kind of beating.

"But he needs to die again." Another punch.

Rose tugged him to his feet, forcing him to face her. For a long while, they simply stared at each other, the rain pouring between them, the darkness thick, their breath rough and misting.

"You came back early," he said, and reached for her. Gently, so gently. His fingers traced over her bruised jaw.

There was a tingle, that ever-present ache. "I couldn't stay away. I . . . missed you."

Before he could reply, a hard voice called, "The rest have fallen back, my king."

Vasili's hands didn't leave her, but he did move his gaze to the newcomer. "Gather their dead and send them back home with a message. 'Attack again, and the same will be done to your families.' "

She looked and saw Grigori, the monster from last night. He nodded, his red eyes bright, and swung around to instruct the men.

"You won," she said to Vasili, returning her attention to him.

"Yes."

"Against Greer?" Had the old king tricked Jasha into agreeing to wed one of his daughters, and then attacked while everyone was complacent? "Or Walkers?"

Vasili gave an abrupt shake of his head. "Neither. The other realms heard of my alliance with Greer, and attacked to prevent it. He warned me they would try, but I didn't believe him." He dropped his forehead to hers, his hands spanning her waist, and tugged her close. "I saw you here, amid the battle, and I almost died. We have to work on your timing, sweetheart."

Sweetheart? She melted against him. "You have to admit I saved you."

He snorted. "I'll admit no such thing. *I* saved *you*."

Now *she* snorted.

His heated gaze traveled the length of her, and he licked the raindrops from his lips. "You're wearing a dress." He sounded shocked, awed.

"And heels. Not that you'll get to enjoy them. They're trash now."

"They were for me?"

A nod.

"I love them."

"I'll love them when you peel them off me."

"My little Rose is eager. I'm a lucky man. But I'll never hear the end of bringing a female into battle."

"You didn't bring me. I brought myself."

"You are never to admit that." Harsh, rough again. "Promise me."

He would rather be teased than reveal the truth? Why? He'd once told her that he never lied, that he didn't care about consequences. But he kept doing so. *She's mute. She's a slave.* For her.

A hard shake. "Promise, Rose."

"Promise." She wound her arms around his neck, so happy to be here, enjoying him, touching him. So happy that they were both alive. "Can we go to your bedroom, get cleaned up, and argue about who saved whom there?"

He placed a soft kiss at the base of her neck, where her pulse hammered wildly. "Oh, yes. But you should prepare to admit defeat, love. The things I'm going to do to you . . ."

Chapter Eight

The battle had taken place right outside the palace, so the walk to Vasili's wing wasn't a long one. And yet to Rose, every step was torture, every second an eternity. People tried to stop them along the way, but Vasili kept moving, dragging her behind him, directing the intruders to Jasha and Grigori, the two he'd left in charge.

Finally, they reached his chambers. When she was inside, he released her, faced her, and leaned into her. She tingled, expectant. Only, he didn't touch her. He flicked the door with his wrist, sending the wood slamming closed. Then he straightened—and still he didn't touch her. He pivoted on his heel, gaze locked on her until the last possible second, and freaking walked away.

What the hell?

There was a wet bar in the corner, she noticed. He poured two glasses of that amber liquid and returned to her, one hand extended. She accepted with a small smile. A fire blazed in the hearth beside her, the heat licking over her wet skin, making her crave this man so much more.

"What is this stuff?" she asked just to break the taut silence.

"Medicine." He drained the contents, and she did the

same. Then he claimed both glasses and returned them to the bar.

Warm and sweet, the medicine slid into her stomach and quickly spread through the rest of her. The little stings and abrasions she'd acquired began to heal. "How are you so advanced in this way?" Her world had nothing that healed instantly. "Yet so antiquated in others?"

"We were once so highly advanced we managed to destroy our sun and most of the population." A few steps, and they were facing each other again. "What you see now is centuries of rebuilding."

"Oh. Neat." Shaking with anticipation, she glanced at the four-poster bed. "Do you want to . . ."

"Yes, but we can't. Not yet. We need to talk."

Guttural tone, ominous words. She licked her lips, nervous and achy at the same time. "Okay. What about?"

"Outside, you mentioned other Walkers." His eyes blazed.

A stark reminder of what she needed to tell him. "Yes." Now she gazed down at her feet, cold seeping through the heat. His safety came before her pleasure. "Why do you want to know who they are and when they come?"

"That's not important now. We need to—"

"Why?"

He sighed. "To protect my people."

"How do you protect them from Walkers?"

Silence.

She looked up at him through the shield of her lashes. He plowed a hand through his hair. "How?" she insisted.

"I kill them."

He'd stated the words so simply, without a hint of remorse; she could only blink at him. "Without knowing their intentions?"

A nod. Stiff, suddenly angry.

Clearly, she couldn't tell him when Nick would come. Not yet. "Why?"

"They're dangerous."

"I'm not. Others aren't."

"You're different. They aren't." Firm, flat.

"How do you know?"

"Rose!" Hard fingers twined around her upper arms and shook her. "That doesn't matter. And I've changed my mind. I don't want to talk about the other Walkers. Let's discuss the fact that you showed up unannounced. Again. And in the middle of a battle, no less."

Having him this close, finally touching her, yet not skin on skin, was complete torment. Her breathing quickened, and goose bumps beaded. Her chest constricted, even as her belly quivered. She loved looking at him. Especially now, as water dripped from his hair and caught in his eyelashes. As color deepened his cheeks, and mud and blood streaked his bare arms and torso.

"No. Let's continue talking about the Walkers. I met with one," she said. "And you're right. Some of them are dangerous. This one told me he's been talking to others, and they want to plan a way to destroy this world. He has an idea to join them, to team up with others who share the same birthday week, and each bring their weapon of preference and strike, so it's one tragedy after another here, and there's no time for you guys to protect yourselves. But that's because they're scared. If you showed them a bit of compassion, they would—"

"No." Still stiff, again angry, though far more so now, he dropped his arms away from her, severing all contact. "That's not up for discussion."

"Fine. Then maybe we should take sex off the table, too." If he wanted to play stubborn, so would she. This was important to her. *He* was important. "I need a bath and a change of—" *Shit!* Her bag. "I dropped my bag outside. When I . . . landed."

There was a glimmer of fear in his eyes, there one moment, gone the next. "I'll return shortly." He didn't wait for her reply, but strode to the door, tossing over his shoulder, "Do not leave this room. Bathe, eat, whatever you want, but do not leave."

"I didn't mean you had to—"

Thud. Alone. Frustrated, she glanced around. Through an open set of doors on the left, she spotted a large pool, steam curling in the air. He'd mentioned bathing. She stripped along the way, leaving her wet dress and heels strewn on the floor, part of her grateful for the reprieve. She stepped into the hot water, submerging herself, and sighed with pleasure.

Though she wanted to relax, she hurried through the bath, lathering hair and body with a bar of soap that smelled like wildflowers. No wonder Vasili always smelled so sweet, though she was surprised he'd *chosen* such a feminine scent for himself. Unless a female had chosen it for him.

Did he entertain women here? Let them bathe? Watch them? Pleasure himself while doing so? Probably.

The jealousy and possessiveness that swept through her were hot and undeniable. He was hers now. *She* would be seeing to his needs, just as he would be seeing to hers. If he would just return with a better attitude, the jackass.

After she rinsed, she stepped from the pool and searched for a towel. She found a closet full of his clothes and weapons, but no towel. Not knowing what else to do, she used one of his shirts, dabbing the material against her body to absorb the moisture, then grabbed a soft sheet from the bed, wrapped it around herself, and sat in front of the fireplace to dry her hair. And plan. If she could negotiate a peace treaty between Vasili and the Walkers, they wouldn't try to hurt him, and he would be safe.

An eternity later, hinges creaked, and then Vasili was striding back into the room. No closer to answers, Rose popped to her feet. He was wetter than before, muddier, and had her bag slung over his shoulder. He had a new cut on his cheek, and blood trickled. He threw the bag down as he searched. . . . Their gazes collided. He stilled, jaw clenched.

"What happened?" she asked.

He looked her over, nostrils flaring, pupils expanding. "You're naked under there." A growl.

"Yes, but—"

He was in front of her a moment later, gripping her waist and hefting her up. He turned without setting her down and tossed her. For several seconds, she was airborne and confused. Then she hit the bed, bounced on the mattress, and knew. He was going to have her.

"Vasili, we really should talk about how to combat—"

"I don't want to talk about the other Walkers anymore." He strode to the side of the bed and ripped off the sheet, his hot gaze raking over her. She didn't move, allowed him to look his fill. And look he did. That gaze was as intent as a caress, lingering on her breasts, causing her nipples to pearl for him, then dipping to her thighs. "I don't want to talk about the danger you placed yourself in. Not now."

Something had set him off. Something had shredded his control. She liked it, loved it, wanted it, but all that ferocity . . .

"Spread your legs," he commanded harshly.

She trembled. "What's wrong with—"

"Talk after. Spread."

Seriously. What had come over him? she wondered, even as she obeyed. As she'd already learned, sometimes doing what he wanted paid off.

He sucked in a breath. "You're wet."

For you. "Always."

His lips pulled tight as he reached out and ran a finger through her tiny patch of curls, then through her lips, then against her clitoris. "You're mine."

Her back arched, and she had to grip the sheets to keep from grabbing his wrist and holding his hand in place. "Y-yes." She couldn't deny it.

He severed the contact, and she moaned. But then he brought his fingers to his mouth and licked, his lids dipping to half-mast. "You're not going to leave this time." A brutal command. "Not until we're both sated."

"I'll stay."

As if the admission broke him down into nothing but sensation, he ripped at his pants, kicked off his boots. When he was finally naked—gloriously, wonderfully naked—he pounced, diving on top of her. His weight crushed her, but she didn't care. They were skin to heated skin at last, his long, thick erection rubbing against her core.

His tongue thrust into her mouth, as demanding as his tone had been. Savage, showing no mercy, dominating. She loved it, meeting him thrust for thrust, taking and giving. One of his hands squeezed at her breast, his naughty fingers tweaking her nipple and shooting sharp lances of pleasure through her.

She bent her knees, rubbing them against his hips, offering a deeper cradle for his penis. He didn't take the hint. Rather than push inside her—even the thought made her moan—he inched down her body and sucked a nipple into his mouth. Her fingers tangled in his hair. He played for a little while, teeth nipping, hands lowering, exploring, tracing over her core, but never actually touching. Mostly, he dabbled behind her knees, at her ankles, the curve of her ass after flipping her over.

"Vasili," she moaned. The ache was consuming her, that ever-present ache. She was leaning into his every glide, trying to force him to head in the direction she wanted.

He flipped her again and kissed a path to her stomach, tongue swirling in her navel. Her muscles quivered. He followed that quiver with his tongue, licking straight into her core. Finally, blessedly. A moan tore from her.

The other day, she'd come and he hadn't. She should be going down on him. "M-my turn to do that to you," she rasped. *But don't stop. Please don't stop.*

He didn't pause, just kept lapping at her, sucking on her clit, making her writhe and pant and pull at his hair. Heat poured through her, burned her up, singed, then exploded, careening through her, spinning her mind, flashing white lights.

As she cried his name, he flipped them both over, and she found herself on top of him. His features were tight with tension. Seeing him like that, so aroused for her, had the ache roaring back to life as if she'd never climaxed.

"Stroke me."

She rose up and straddled his thighs. His erection strained proudly between them, and she wrapped her fingers around the thick base, gliding upward, engulfing the head and dampening her palm with the moisture beaded at the tip. "Like this?"

His hips arched into her touch. "That's good, but I want—"

She didn't let him finish. She bent down and sucked him into her mouth, until he hit the back of her throat. He bucked, a hoarse groan leaving him. God, he tasted good. A sweetness that could only be passion. Her jaw stretched and burned to accommodate his width as she rode him up and down.

He fisted her hair for a moment, then released her, as if afraid to hurt her. She heard flesh slap against metal and assumed he was now gripping the headboard. She didn't stop to look, just kept eating that hard length, consuming it.

"Going to . . . if you don't want . . ."

Faster . . . faster . . .

"Rose!" He roared her name as his seed jetted into her mouth.

She swallowed every drop. And when he calmed, she lifted her head with a satisfied smile and a lick of her lips. The ache hadn't left her, had only increased. She wanted more, needed more. He would, too. She knew it.

He was panting, gripping the headboard as she'd supposed, his lips bleeding from chewing them. Her gaze moved to his arms, to the muscles straining there, and she gasped. There, on both of his forearms, were roses. Roses, like her name. Once again her chest constricted. He'd marked himself permanently, inked those symbols on his body for all of his days. For her . . . She knew they were for her.

"Lift up," he suddenly growled.

"Am I too heavy?" She climbed to her knees.

"Hardly." Immediately he inserted two fingers inside her.

Her head fell back, hair tickling her skin, breasts arching toward him. She cupped them, moaning and pumping against his fingers. Fucking them the way she wanted him to fuck her.

"My Rose is still wet."

"I liked the taste of you." Up, down. More, more. She knew there was something they should discuss, something all lovers should discuss . . . oh, yes. "I'm on the pill, can't get pregnant, not diseased." There. "Vasili, please. Unless . . . unless you need time to recover."

"I'm not diseased, either." His fingers pulled from her. He gripped her hips, lifted her, and slammed her down, his cock suddenly filling her, stretching her. She had to brace her hands on his chest to hold herself upright. But finally, he was inside her, all the way, hers.

"Yes!" she screamed.

Air hissed from his teeth. "Move on me."

"Yes, yes." At first, she moved slowly, torturing them both, driving them to insanity. As he began to thrust up, meeting her downward glide, his fingers digging into her waist, bruising, spurring her on, she increased her speed, taking more, giving more, demanding more. Soon they were both writhing, both reaching, hands everywhere.

"Kiss." He cupped the base of her neck and jerked her down, tongue stabbing into her mouth.

She came instantly, inner walls clenching around him. That was when he flipped her to her back, thrusting harder and harder, deeper and deeper, one of her knees caught under his arm, allowing even deeper penetration, his cock like a jackhammer against her clit, and then he was shouting her name, spending himself inside her, and she was shouting his, clamping around him yet again.

When he collapsed on top of her and rolled them to

their sides, she was still twitching from that second—third?—consuming orgasm. He didn't release her, but held her tight. *Thank God.* She couldn't have existed on her own, she didn't think. She was panting, sweating, floating. Lost.

Her eyes were heavy, and she wanted to sleep. Was even drifting off, content for the first time in years, when his voice roused her.

"Did I take you from someone you loved, the night I bonded us?" he asked gruffly.

Was that what had been bothering him? She forced her lids to remain open. "Yes. No. I don't know. I thought I loved him at the time, and I thought he loved me, but he ran pretty quickly when I could no longer put out."

"Poor, stupid bastard. The running, though, is what has saved his life."

She chuckled. "Did I take *you* from anyone?"

"No one special." His fingers stroked her back.

"Good. Because I brought my gun, and I'm not afraid to use it."

"As I have seen." His fingers lowered to her ass and spread, squeezing. "I must admit, I like my woman jealous."

She liked when he called her his woman. She liked *this*. Being snuggled against his side, listening to his heart pound, rubbing her knee up his legs, feeling his shaft harden again.

"Stay," he said, suddenly serious. "With me."

Hearing the words—he wanted her the way she wanted him!—caused relief to bloom. "For one week, I'm all yours."

His grip tightened. "Stay longer."

God, she liked the sound of that purring, commanding voice. The needy ache sprang back to life, joining her relief, and she rubbed against him like a cat. "We don't even know if we're compatible."

He rolled her to her back, his weight nearly crushing her. "We're compatible."

"Here." Would she ever get enough of him? She arched against him, breasts pressing against his chest. "But what about out there?"

His nostrils flared. "In the palace?"

"In . . . life." Her legs wrapped around him, ankles locking on his lower back.

He considered her for a moment, pushing all of his weight between her thighs and holding her steady. "We will take this week, then, and see how we get along. But you aren't leaving. And you can't tell anyone what you are."

"Why can't I tell anyone? And will you please get inside me? Unless you need that recovery time?"

"That's the second time you've asked if I need recovery time. How you wound me. You, I always want." His cock twitched against her, slid inside her, and his pupils expanded. "Just don't tell anyone what you are. Please."

Yes! "Thank you." There was something he wasn't telling her, but she didn't have time to reason it out. He was inside her, but he wasn't moving. "I won't tell. Now thrust!"

"Lusty wench. But let's see if I can finally sate you."

He spent the rest of the night trying.

Chapter Nine

Vasili held a sleeping Rose tight against his body, breathing her in, savoring her warmth, her softness. He hadn't pleasured a female in two years, but he'd *never* slept near one. He'd never trusted his lovers enough to be near him during his vulnerable sleeping hours, and besides that, he hadn't wanted to promote a familiarity he hadn't—and would never—feel.

Attachments weren't something he formed.

Until now.

He'd had Rose in his bedroom, and rather than strip her as he'd planned, he'd found himself scared. For her. She'd met with other Walkers. That was what he'd always wanted. That was why he'd bonded them. For information. But the thought of her with other Walkers, so far away from him, him unable to protect her . . . He'd wanted to roar. And then, when she'd mentioned she had left her bag outside where his army roamed, searching for the dead, true panic had set in. If they found the bag, they would know a Walker was nearby. And they'd seen her, so of course they would know she was that Walker. They wouldn't simply think she'd been living in the woods, seen the fight, and decided to help, as he had planned to encourage them.

He'd found her bag in Grigori's possession. His favored guard had been livid with him, though the Monstrea had admitted he'd known what she was the moment he'd seen her at the ball.

You have to kill her, Grigori had said. *Otherwise your people will revolt.*

Vasili had been terrified of just that, which was why he'd rushed back to Rose, to guard her. One look, though, and he'd had to bind her to him sexually. He'd had to have her, to reaffirm that she was here, she was his, and to prove to her that they belonged together. Forever.

He loved her.

His world might be dark, but she was his light. She amused him, challenged him, fought for him, delighted him. Pleased him. Oh, did she please him. He had never enjoyed a woman the way he enjoyed her. Her taste was addictive, her long, slender body the perfect fit to his bigger, harder one. She wasn't shy or coy, but gave herself fully.

She'd ruined him for anyone else, and it had nothing to do with their blood bond and everything to do with her smile, her stubbornness, her wit, her playfulness, her lustiness. Perfect. Fit.

Now he had one week to convince her to stay with him. Because he couldn't live without her. *Wouldn't* live without her. The risk from the other Walkers, the risk from his own people, he would figure out, deal with. Somehow, some way. But he would have to do so without alerting Rose. If she discovered how much his people hated her kind, she would be hurt and afraid, and would possibly leave.

That, he couldn't allow.

*   *   *

Only two days into her stay, Rose realized she could live with Vasili forever. Sex anytime she craved it—and she craved it often. Vasili ensured she was fed, and the food was divine. He dressed her in lavish gowns, like the ones she'd seen at the party. He made her laugh, touched her often, even when he didn't realize he was doing it. If she neared, he wound his arm around her waist. If she placed her head on his shoulder, he petted her hair and urged her into his lap.

They rarely left his rooms, but when they did, he had rules for her. No speaking in English, and no mentioning the word *Walker*. The only dark spot on her happiness was that Vasili refused to explain why. Yeah, he'd told her the Walkers were dangerous. But *why* were they dangerous—besides what Nick and others might be planning? What had been done in the past?

Anytime she asked, Vasili changed the subject.

But now he'd been called away by his brother. Why, she didn't know. But he'd left her sleeping in bed. Or so he'd thought. Rose hopped up, quickly bathed, and dressed in a violet gown to match his eyes.

She left the chamber and strode along the halls, down the winding stairs, and into the dining room. The few times they'd roused from bed, this was where he'd taken her, and she'd memorized the path. Someone was always in here, she'd noted. Maybe because there was a long wooden table always piled high with food. Like an all-day buffet.

The walls here were the same as those in the ball-room: swirling gold circles surrounding windows that looked into the dark, rainy ever-night. The royal colors must be burgundy and gold, because those colors were everywhere: tapestries, carpets, furniture.

Today, there was only one occupant. One of the Monstrea, as Vasili had told her they were called. Grigori was his name. She wasn't afraid of him. He might look like a demon, but his love for Vasili was proved every time he spoke with his king.

"Has Jasha picked a bride?" she asked as she filled her plate. She was careful to pronounce her words slowly, just right.

"Greer died in battle the other night." His tone was gruff. "The rush for the alliance has ended."

"Poor princesses." To have lost their father to violence. "But Jasha still intends to wed one?"

"Yes."

That was good. "Who?"

"The redhead." Eye twitch.

Interesting. "Want her for yourself, do you?"

Silence.

She'd take that as a yes.

"Enough talk of unimportant issues. What are your intentions toward the king, female?"

"Dishonorable," she said with a grin, and claimed the seat across from him.

His claws scraped at the table. "You mean to kill him?"

Don't provoke the beast, idiot. "Hardly. I lo—like him." She loved the man—she had to, since she was willing to give up everything for him—but Vasili hadn't said the words to her, so she wouldn't say the words to him or anyone else. Another game, she thought with a secret smile. The first one to crack would be teasingly tortured forever.

"I know what you are, you know. I remembered the talk about you from that night, so long ago. I wasn't there, but I heard. You were thought to be a spy."

"So?" She popped a grape into her mouth, the sweet

juice running down her throat. She'd learned that they had greenhouses and other places that were able to grow the fruits from her world.

Those fiery eyes widened. "So?" he whispered darkly. "You are no spy. Twice I have seen you dressed in pants, and your language is rough. You appear out of nowhere, and no one has ever heard of you. You are a Walker, and you're going to get him killed."

Her brow scrunched. "What are you talking about?"

"Your kind is hated here. Slaughtered."

Answers. He offered answers. All she had to do was ask and finally, she'd have them, but just then she wasn't sure she wanted them. Still, the first question rushed from her mouth: "Why is my kind hated?"

"You once destroyed our royal family. *Vasili's* family. His parents, his siblings. He watched, bound, helplessly waiting his turn. They even held a gun to his father's head and made the man choose which of the girls, Vasili's sisters, would die first. And die they did. Every one of them."

"Not me," she said brokenly, tears springing to her eyes. Poor Vasili, losing practically everyone he loved in a single night. But now she understood why he had refused to answer her questions while she'd held a gun on him. He must have been reminded of that night.

God, the fact that he hadn't killed her astonished her.

"Not you, no. You are too young. But those like you. My people couldn't help all those years ago because you went after us first. Explosions everywhere. So many fires. Innocents, children. All gone in a single night."

"I'm sorry." So sorry. She wanted to stop this now, run away, but persisted anyway. "How . . . how did Vasili escape?"

"So many of us were running around, screaming,

confused, but he managed to get free while the Walkers were distracted, find Jasha, and haul him into the forest, where they hid for days before the remaining army found them. That's when it was decided—by all of us— that Walkers would be killed the moment they entered our world."

Poor Vasili, she thought again, the tears running freely now. She wanted to hold him, to chase away his pain.

"He bonded with you, did he not?"

She nodded, unable to speak. There was a lump in her throat she couldn't manage to swallow.

"Foolish man, thinking with his cock. Some of our people did the same with other Walkers all those years ago, but those Walkers were put to death after that night. The wives fought us. Their Walkers were peaceful, they claimed. But still we killed those bound to your world. How would it look if they discovered Vasili, the king, had kept you alive?"

Bad.

"If the people ever find out, they will rebel against him. They haven't forgotten what was done to their loved ones. And if his own people rebel while he battles other kingdoms . . ."

Oh, God. Oh, God, oh, God, oh, God. She swallowed the lump. "I'll . . . I'll leave." She would have to. To save him. *Oh, God.*

"But you'll return." An accusation.

"Because I can't stop myself," she growled, swiping at her cheeks with the back of her hand.

"He knows what you are, but pretends you are one of us. How long do you think that lie will last, since you'll appear right in front of him every time you arrive?"

She closed her eyes, heartsick.

"The bond must be broken."

Her lids popped open. "I'm not going to kill him, and I'm not going to kill myself."

"And because you are his, he will never forgive the one who does kill you."

Does kill, as if it were already a fact. No wonder Vasili had taught her to fight. He'd known what would happen if she were ever discovered. He'd wanted her to have a chance. But *why* had he wanted her to have a chance? He should have hated her. Yet he'd bonded her, saved her.

Would the hate return in time? Would he grow to resent her?

"When is your next birthday?" Grigori asked.

"In . . . three days."

"So you came early. To see him." A statement, not a question.

She answered anyway. "Yes."

"You love him?"

"Yes." No denying it now, as she thought about losing him forever. The game was over.

"Do not tell him what we discussed. There is much I need to think on."

She nodded, even though she suspected he meant to think about ways to kill her without Vasili finding out who had done the deed. She had to find a way to stop traveling here. Not just her, but *all* the Walkers.

She could travel at will, so it stood to reason that she could *prevent* herself from traveling through that same will. Right? But the others couldn't travel at will. So they wouldn't be able to stop themselves.

Damn it!

That would save her—and save Vasili. Except for the bond . . . They couldn't be with other people. But she couldn't deny that she was *glad* he couldn't be with other people. Even if that meant suffering herself. Because she couldn't imagine wanting anyone else. Not after experiencing that tongue, those fingers . . . him, only him.

She needed distance, time to deal. To think. Surely she could find a solution if she tried.

"Tell Vasili I said— No." Any parting words would only deepen the connection between them. She needed anger. His, hers. For with anger would come distance. "Just tell him I left."

Grigori nodded.

"Thank you for the . . . conversation." Translation: *I hate you, but I can't hold it against you because you did it for him.*

Another abrupt nod.

She closed her eyes, pictured her house, and let her body do the rest. Seconds, that was all it took, but she knew it had worked, because for a moment she felt weightless. Dizzy. Then perfectly fine. Physically, at least.

She opened her eyes, and four white walls surrounded her. There was her couch, the fabric torn. There was her coffee table, the wood scratched.

Walkers had killed Vasili's family. Walkers were even now trying to think up ways to hurt Vasili. She had to talk to them. Give them the facts, bare her soul. No matter what they thought of her or tried to do to her. She had to make things right.

Chapter Ten

"Vasili."

He must be imagining things, Vasili thought. There was Rose's sweet voice. But he was drunk, as he had been for the past three days, sitting in his room, alone, all lights extinguished, rain pattering outside. After a panicked, frantic search for Rose, Grigori had admitted what had transpired.

If he heard "for the best" one more time, he was going to stab someone. Namely Grigori. The bastard was lucky to be alive. To have sent Rose away like that . . . He *would* kill him, Vasili decided.

"Vasili, darling."

There was her voice again. He closed his eyes, savoring. She wasn't due to arrive until later tonight, just four hours away. He was going to punish her for leaving him—the chase-and-retreat game no longer amused him. He wanted her always. Then he was going to make love to her, beg her to stay, tell his people to fuck themselves, and if she still refused to stay with him, he would try to cross into her world. To do so, he'd have to hold on to Rose until they both left his world. If he died, so what? He couldn't live without her. Not anymore.

"Are you listening to me? No? Let me help you." An open palm slapped his cheek, leaving a heated sting.

He blinked. A hallucination wouldn't have been able to hit him, would it? "Rose?"

A sigh. "Who else?"

He hopped to his feet, his eyes quickly adjusting to the darkness. There she was, right in front of him. His arms banded around her—solid, warm, real—and he jerked her into his chest, all thoughts of punishment fleeing. "I thought I'd lost you. Don't ever do that to me again."

She hugged him back. "I want to be with you," she said, shocking him. "Forever."

"Thank you. Thank you. You won't regret—"

"But the hate has to stop."

"Anything." He would deny her nothing. Not anymore.

"There can be no more killing Walkers just because of what they are."

"Done." He wouldn't argue. He would outlaw the practice immediately, and his people could protest all they wanted. They could rebel, kick him off the throne. Whatever. As long as he had Rose, nothing else mattered. Hopefully, his people would learn, as he had, that these Walkers were not the vicious race from the past. How could they be, when Rose was among them?

She cupped his cheeks. "I love you."

"And I love you. So much."

Slowly her lips lifted in a beautiful grin. "Call a meeting with your people. As many as you can fit inside the palace. And no weapons. They aren't to bring weapons. And they aren't to attack, no matter what they see or hear."

"What are you—"

"Please, Vasili. No questions. I need you to do this quickly. One hour. Please."

"It will be done."

With that, she disappeared.

Vasili had his army gather his citizens and "gently" usher them inside the palace ballroom. Yes, threats of force abounded, but finally the task was done. Jasha and Grigori were beside him, the princesses seated on the dais but against the wall. They weren't sad that their father was dead and, in fact, seemed lighthearted.

Jasha had decided to wed the redhead, to which Grigori had only this morning said, "Not that one." Which meant the Monstrea wanted her for himself. Jasha had shrugged—almost with relief, as if he hadn't wanted to pick her but, because she was the plainest, thought she would have been the easiest to deal with—and next decided on the blonde, who watched him now with awe in her eyes. Jasha continually cast her stealthy glances.

It would be a good match, Vasili thought, making Jasha king of the East. He'd take care of that just as soon as he finished with this.

The crowd grew restless, their curiosity intensifying, and his army had to form a blockade around them. Vasili had only one order for his soldiers: Kill anyone who threatened Rose.

When would she appear? What did she plan? He would support her, whatever she did. He should have talked to her, told her, but he'd feared losing her.

She suddenly materialized in front of him, pale hair cascading down her back, silver eyes bright. She wore jeans and a T-shirt, every inch the Walker. Their gazes met briefly, his heart slamming against his ribs, before she turned and faced his people. They gasped in astonishment, in disgust. In hatred. Murmurs of, "Murderer," arose.

Vasili leaped to his feet, a brutal scowl contorting his features.

"Yes," Rose said, splaying her arms. "I'm a Walker."

"She's also my wife," he shouted, daring them to comment.

She tossed him a quick smile over her shoulder. "There are others like me. They come here on their birthdays, and you chase them. Hurt them. Kill them. They fear you, which makes them want to hurt you in return. But it doesn't have to be that way."

Silence. Perhaps because he scowled at them murderously.

"Yes, Walkers hurt you in the past." She cast Vasili another glance, this one sad and apologetic. "But to condemn them all for what others did . . . I'm sure you wouldn't welcome being condemned for the sins of your fathers."

More murmurs. Fortunately, these weren't quite so rancorous.

"I went online and told them who I was, where I was, and what I could do. I told them I could stop their visits to Nightmare. That's what they call this place, you know. They fear the people here. But it doesn't have to be that way," she repeated. "Not for you, and not for them. And so, they came to me. I want you to meet them. See them. Welcome them. I promise you, be nice to them and they will be nice to you."

With that, she disappeared.

Now there were gasps.

Meet them? How was she going to—

She reappeared, holding the hand of a young man with pale hair. That man gaped when he saw the crowd of people and tried to back away.

"You didn't say you were bringing me here," he growled.

Vasili hopped from the dais.

"Nick. Just stay here. Nothing bad will happen to you," she said. "Vasili," she then called. "He's not armed. Protect him." She disappeared again.

Vasili went to Nick's side. "Don't hold her hand again," he said, patting the man on the shoulder and nearly drilling him into the floor. He'd never thought to find himself the protector of a Walker—Rose excluded—but he did so now without reservation. Just because his woman had asked him.

Dark eyes swung to him. The man remained in place, though he trembled.

Rose reappeared with someone else, introduced him, then left again. Over and over she repeated the experience, until there were sixteen Walkers. They were scared, but didn't move from their spots. Perhaps because they were surrounded.

"How did you get them here when it isn't their birthdays?" he asked her when she settled beside him.

"I think because I'm bound to you, I can move between the two worlds at will. And I figured I could move other Walkers with me whether it was their birthday or not. I was right."

Smart girl.

"Now let's make nice between your people and mine so we can be together. Unless . . . I understand if you can't," she said, unsure. "If it's too painful. Your family was taken. All I ask is that you let me return these men without harming them. I just thought this would be—"

Vasili planted a kiss on her lips for all to see. "*You* are my family now, and I will do whatever is necessary to protect you. Even this."

Grigori stepped from the army ranks and joined them, placing his hand on Rose's shoulder in a show of support. "You have my protection, as well." His voice was gruff, but he was not a man to make false promises. He always meant what he said. "I have never seen my king so happy—or so upset when he thought he couldn't have you. I will do whatever is necessary to give him the life he deserves."

Tears filled her eyes. "Thank you."

"You have my support, as well." Jasha closed in their little circle and placed his hand on Rose's other shoulder. "Like Grigori, I want my brother happy. Always. No matter what that entails."

God, I love my family. They might not agree with him, but they would support him. Even in this.

"Thank you," Rose said again, chin wobbling. "I won't let you down. I swear."

Vasili's people watched, listened, and issued no more protests. That was a start.

And so, with Jasha and Grigori at his sides, he introduced himself to the Walkers and offered a vow to protect *them*. Most flinched under Grigori's stern gaze, but they seemed to lose a sliver of their fear.

"You don't have to run from us anymore," he said. "Our goal is no longer to harm you. You are my wife's people, which means you are also mine." He reached back. "I protect what's mine."

Rose knew what he wanted, and once again settled in at his side. She twined their fingers and gave a comforting squeeze. "Let's learn from one another," she said, the tears now flowing freely down her cheeks. "Let's embrace peace."

She waited until each Walker nodded before at last taking them home. Vasili rushed to his bedroom, and when she next appeared, he jerked her into his arms. "You've given me so much, I'll never be able to repay you," he told her.

"I can think of a few ways you can *try*."

"It's like *my* birthday today."

She chuckled, the sound of her amusement warming him. "Then happy birthday, love."

He grinned down at her. "Are you my present?"

"Well, my heart is yours. Now, forever."

"Good, because that's exactly what I wanted."

THE COLLECTOR

SHANNON K. BUTCHER

*For Julie Fedynich, the best cheerleader
an author could ever have*

Chapter One

The woman had something Neal Etan wanted and he wasn't leaving until he got it.

He hurried up the cement steps leading to her front door, his booted feet leaving behind tread marks in the dusting of snow that had just begun to accumulate. With any luck at all, he'd convince Viviana Rowan to give him the gadget Gilda said might cure his friend's paralysis, and be back on the road home to Dabyr before dark.

Synestryn demons got more hours of playtime during the long winter nights, and Neal needed to be done with his errand and back out there fighting, ready to stop them before some unsuspecting human became a meal. Not to mention the fact that he really needed the physical outlet to help control his pain—an outlet only a good dose of hack-'n'-slash fighting or hot-'n'-sweaty sex provided.

He wasn't going to get either in the house of some stuffy old antiques collector, so he needed to get in, get the gadget, and get out. Fast.

The pain was grueling today, grinding against his bones until even his hair ached. The two hours of meditation he'd done earlier had barely eased the pressure of the power growing inside him. He told himself it was because he'd just lost another leaf from his lifemark—the living image of a tree that covered his chest—but he knew it was more than that.

His time was running out. The leaves were falling faster now, thanks to a jolt of power a stun-gun hit had given him last summer. He'd absorbed a year's worth of energy in one instant, and he still had the nightmares and cold sweats to prove it.

With only twelve leaves left, he knew the remainder of his life could now be measured in months. Maybe even weeks. And that was assuming that one of the Synestryn demons he fought didn't get a lucky shot in.

Not that he was complaining. He'd been around nearly four hundred years now. It was a good run. He'd slain a lot of evil in his lifetime. He'd served his purpose and done his job. And when it came time to take his own life so he wouldn't become like the evil he was sworn to fight, he'd do that, too. No complaints, no regrets. He was a warrior destined to die for his cause, and no amount of wishing for things he couldn't have was going to change that.

Just because other men like him had found the women who could save them didn't mean Neal had gone all soft in the head, thinking he would, too. He knew better than to let false hope sway him to hang on longer than was safe. This time next year, he'd be dead. No sense in getting all sappy about it.

Neal's knuckles rapped on the frigid door, and a moment later, he could hear aging floorboards creak on the other side of the wood. It slid open two scant inches, revealing one long-lashed, hazel eye.

"Yes?" said the woman, her voice low and soft.

"I'm Neal Etan. I have an appointment with Ms. Rowan."

"Is it four thirty already?" She sounded bewildered.

"It is."

She swung the door open and stepped back for him to enter. "I'm sorry. I was studying a new artifact and must have lost track of time. Please come in."

Neal stared at her in a long moment of surprise.

She was taller than he expected—only a couple of inches shy of six feet—and much, much younger. He'd had an image of some dried-up, bent old woman, someone who fit in with all the ancient items she was reputed to have collected—one of which Neal wasn't leaving without.

Instead, he guessed her to be in her late twenties, though her prim business suit and spinsterish bun gave her a more mature air. She was pretty in an untouchable kind of way—the kind of woman a rough man like Neal avoided when possible. He'd either shock her or hurt her or both if he was around long enough.

He hoped he could conclude their business and be on his way before that became an issue.

Neal stepped over the threshold as she extended her hand in greeting. "I'm Viviana Rowan."

He didn't want to touch her. Her long, elegant fingers seemed too fragile for his sword-calloused hand. But even more than that, he didn't want to offend her—not when they hadn't even begun to negotiate.

With an inward sigh of resignation, Neal took her offered hand, thinking of blown-glass sculptures and hollow eggs so he'd keep his grip light.

He'd intended to make the contact as brief as possible, but the second his skin touched hers, his world fell silent. Decades of pain evaporated like snowflakes over a fire. A buoyant, weightless bubble swelled inside him, driving away the pressure of the massive power he stored but could not use. The hair along his limbs lifted from his body, and a fine shiver eased down his spine, warming him as it passed. Even his shock at the reaction couldn't seem to penetrate the overwhelming sense of peace that settled over him. He was content to stay here in this quiet, warm peacefulness for the rest of his life.

And then he felt her fingers slide from his grip and reality came crashing down on him once again. Pain thrashed inside him, as if angry that he'd had even that brief respite. It lunged against his bones, pummeling his organs as it punished him.

Neal gritted his teeth against the scream that was crawling up his throat and locked his knees so he wouldn't collapse in a heap at the woman's feet. A cold sweat beaded up along his hairline, and his stomach gave a hard, sickening twist.

"...you okay?" Her soft voice lapped against his nerves, quieting their rioting dance. "I'll call for an ambulance."

"No," croaked Neal. "I'm fine." He was anything but fine, but the last thing he needed was to be dragged away from here and have human doctors poking at him. Not only would they be freaked-out by his lifemark, but he'd have a hell of a hard time explaining why there was an invisible sword strapped around his hips. "Can I have some water?" he asked, just to get her to leave him alone for a minute. He needed to collect his wits, and he really didn't want this woman to see him weak like this.

She shut the front door behind him and hurried off, her heels clicking against the hardwood floor.

Neal sagged against the wall and blinked to clear the black spots from his vision. He was shaking like one of those scared little purse dogs, and about as tough as one right now, too. Sunset was in just over an hour, and he had that long to get his shit together and fix it before the nasties came out to play.

One thing was certain: There was not a force on earth that was going to pull him away from Ms. Viviana Rowan's side until he figured out what she'd done to him.

And how he could make her do it again.

Viviana filled a glass with water and guzzled it down before she remembered she was supposed to get *him* the water. Her heart was racing, and her hand was trembling so hard it kept slipping from the faucet handle.

When he touched her, something happened. And she wasn't entirely sure she liked it. She'd felt like someone had sent an electric current through her skin, making it tingle and buzz from the inside out. A swath of heat swept over her, emanating from his wide, rough palm. His touch had been gentle, but that had somehow allowed her to feel each ridge of his calluses, every minute detail down to the whorls in his fingerprints.

That simply wasn't right. It had to have been some kind of hallucination. Maybe his skin had been drugged with a contact poison.

Even as the thought entered her mind, she dismissed it. Deep down she knew what this was. She'd felt it before, albeit never so intensely. That buzzing, resonant humming that filled her wasn't new to her. She'd felt it every time she touched one of the precious artifacts she collected.

The only problem was, Neal Etan was not some centuries-old artifact. He was a living, breathing, incredibly warm man. One who was waiting in her foyer.

What was she going to do with him? He couldn't stay.

He was here to buy one of her artifacts, and although she hadn't before suspected he'd want one from her special collection, she now realized that had to be the case.

She wouldn't let him have one of those. They were hers—the only things that made her feel connected to this world. Without them, she would be doomed to live with that meaningless, disconnected feeling she'd suffered through most of her life. She couldn't let that happen.

Not that she could keep him from taking something he wanted. He was far too big and powerful to stop. She was going to have to outsmart him and get him to leave as soon as possible. She could not let her entire life's work be torn apart. Especially not so soon after losing Mother.

This was going to be her first Christmas alone with only her collection to keep her company.

Viviana covered her mouth with the back of her hand to stifle a whimper, and swore she could smell his masculine scent lingering on her skin. It soothed her nerves, which only frightened her more. She'd never had a reaction like this to a man before, and she hoped it was only temporary.

She scrubbed her hands in the sink to rid them of his scent, and then hurried out with his glass of water. The sooner she got him to leave, the better.

She rounded the corner and nearly ran right into his broad chest. He grabbed her arms to steady her, and she was thankful the layers of fabric between them muted the effect of his touch. Only a trickle of that tingling energy reached her skin, but it was enough to heighten the trembling of her hands, causing water to slosh over the side of the glass onto his boot.

"I'm sorry," she said, as she tried to step back out of his grasp.

He let her go, but his dark blue eyes slid over her face, lingering at her mouth.

He was handsome in a deeply masculine way. His features were big and bold and starkly angular. The wide ridge of his jaw was sharp, shadowed with new beard growth. His neck was thick, as were his thighs and arms beneath the snug leather jacket. There was nothing soft or gentle about this man, making him completely unlike the men she chose to date. Though, why she'd make such a comparison was anyone's guess. He wasn't here to ask her out. He was here to take something precious from her.

She thrust the glass at him, hoping it would distract him and that steady gaze. Instead, his fingers grazed the back of her hand as he took the water.

Instantly, another jolt of power shot through her, ricocheting inside her heart until she was panting for air.

"Who are you?" he asked, his deep voice tinted with suspicion.

She tried to sound unaffected, but her words came out breathy and panicked. "I know I promised you a meeting, but I forgot about an incredibly important appointment. I'm afraid I'm going to have to cancel."

"Like hell."

"Excuse me?"

"You made me a promise, and where I come from, that means something." He started to set the glass down on a seventeenth-century writing desk, and Viviana lunged to stop him before the damp glass could make contact.

Her hands closed over his and that resonant energy

flooded her system, weakening her knees and making her eyes flutter shut. A deep groan of satisfaction rose between them, and she couldn't tell if she'd made the noise, or he had. Not that she cared. Whatever he was doing to her—whatever poison or magic the man possessed—she was starting to like it.

That thought jolted her, forcing her to remove her hands from his. She'd sacrifice the writing desk to a water mark if it meant he'd leave before setting his eyes on any of her treasured artifacts.

As she broke contact, he sucked in a pained breath and doubled over. The glass slipped from his hand, shattering against the floor.

"Sorry," he grated out.

She didn't care about the glass. She only wished she could say the same for the man. But she did care. She hated seeing any living thing in pain, and that included big, strapping men who were here to ruin the calm of her peaceful existence.

"Sit down before you fall down," she ordered as she guided him to a chair in her living room. She was careful not to touch his bare skin, choosing instead to use the sleeve of his jacket to tug him in the right direction. He landed on her settee with a thud, making the delicate wood creak in protest of his weight.

One of his thick arms was wrapped around his middle. His head hung down, propped against his hand as if it weighed too much to support. On that hand he wore a ring that pulsed and swirled in a mesmerizing combination of colors that reminded her of aged parchment and ancient wood.

Viviana stared, wondering where he'd found such an interesting item. It was definitely old. She could feel the vibration of years emanating from it, along with something else—something faint and elusive.

She reached out to touch the tip of her finger to it, but Mr. Etan saw the movement and leaned smoothly away, out of her reach. "How about we both keep our hands to ourselves for a while so we can talk about the gadget, okay? I'm not sure how much more of a beating I can take right now."

She wasn't sure which part of that confused her more—the part about a gadget or the part about him hurting. Fortunately, she had manners to fall back on in such an occasion and gave him a prim nod. "Certainly. I'm not usually so forward. But as I said, I have an appointment, so we'll need to reschedule."

He gave her a disbelieving look. "Listen, lady, I've driven for hours to get here. I made a promise to bring this gadget home and that's exactly what I'm going to do."

"Gadget?"

He reached into his back pocket and pulled out a folded piece of paper, which he smoothed flat against his thigh before he handed it to her.

Viviana took the paper, being careful not to make any further contact with his skin. She sat down across from him, putting some much-needed distance between them.

On the page was a printed image from her Web site of one of the artifacts from her special collection. It was a carved wooden box, and inside, snuggled into perfectly shaped recesses, were two engraved metal disks. The markings on both the box and the disks were elaborate and painstaking in their detail, covered with trees, leaves, and vines. She'd found this item in the attic of a three-hundred-year-old home that she'd bought with the plans to restore it. And while she had no idea as to the artifact's purpose, it belonged in her collection, and she wasn't going to part with it.

"I'm sorry," she said, giving him back the paper. "It's not for sale."

"So you do have it?"

"Yes."

"Show me."

The demand in his tone made her spine straighten in indignation. "Even if it was here, which it isn't, I wouldn't show it to you. Not if you're going to be rude and demanding."

The man rose to his feet, looming over her. At five-ten, she wasn't used to it, so she stood, trying to put them on a more even footing. Even with her in heels, he was still a few inches taller. The hard set of his jaw and the way his nostrils flared made him even more imposing.

"Rude? I'm sorry if I insulted your delicate feelings, but I don't have time to be all nicey-nice right now. A friend of mine is dying and that gadget may be the only thing that can save him."

Viviana scoffed. "Nice try, but I'm not an idiot. Those disks don't hold medicine, and if they did, I'm sure it would be all dried up by now."

He frowned at her. "You have no idea what you've got or how important it is. I'll pay you whatever you want, but I need that device now. Tonight."

"Impossible. It's not here and it's not for sale."

"Fine. I'll rent it, then. I'll pay you whatever you ask to use it, just for a few days."

"Use it? They're paperweights. Beautiful, certainly, but nothing more." Even as she said it, she knew it was a lie. There was something special about the artifacts she collected. She could feel it. Perhaps Mr. Etan knew the answer to that mystery. The question was, did she dare spend enough time with him to find out?

"Just tell me where the gadget is. Please." That last bit sounded like it cost him more than a little effort. Clearly, he wasn't used to asking for things.

Poor baby. He was just going to have to suffer.

"No," she said. "It's time for you to go."

"I'm not leaving here without it."

"Yes, you are." She pulled her cell phone from her pocket and waved it in front of him. "If you prefer to do so with a police escort, I'm happy to provide one."

His mouth tightened and his eye twitched. He crossed his arms over his wide chest, making his jacket creak as his biceps bulged against the leather.

His size contrasted with the gentleness of his touch earlier. She was used to soft, intellectual men with smooth hands and wool suits, not brutes in leather. And although he'd been nothing but careful with her, Mr. Etan was definitely a brute. A man didn't get to be as big and muscular and . . . imposing as he was without also adopting that barbaric kind of demeanor.

He was a man misplaced in time. Centuries ago, he would have been a prize, but now, in modern civilized society, he had no place. There was no purpose for all those muscles other than vanity. And attracting women.

Viviana would just bet he was used to having women hang all over him, cooing and fawning and simpering like idiots. She could hardly stand the mental image.

He stared into her eyes for a long moment—long enough that Viviana began to heat under his gaze. She knew better than to be drawn to a man like him, but apparently her body did not. Apparently, there was some vestigial part of her that had woken up and taken notice of him and his outdated muscles.

She told that part of her it could just go right back to sleep as soon as he left her home.

"We're not done, you and I," he said, making it sound like a promise. "Wherever you go, I'll be there. Call all the cops you like. It won't change a thing. I'm getting that gadget for my friend and that's final. As soon as you get sick of having me breathe down your neck, I'm sure you'll see things my way."

The idea of his breathing on any part of her was more than a bit intriguing, which only served to anger her further. "Good night, Mr. Etan."

"Call me Neal," he said as he turned to leave. "I have the feeling the two of us are going to be spending a lot of time together."

Chapter Two

Viviana stood there, flustered and flushed. Her whole body was shaking by the time she heard her front door swing shut.

She hurried to check and make sure he hadn't faked her out and gone roaming her home. She wouldn't have put it past him to do just that—stomping through her personal, private space as if he owned it.

Through the curtains, she saw the big shadow of his body move smoothly down her steps and out onto the street. She parted the lace panels and watched him go. He had far too much grace for a man his size. It was hard not to stare as he moved, his long limbs loose and strong as he strode away. He almost seemed to glide across the snow. Only his big footprints gave away the fact that he walked like anyone else, one foot in front of the other.

A passing truck obscured her vision, releasing her from whatever spell he'd had on her.

She turned, refusing to look again for fear she'd be sucked back into his gliding stride.

He was bluffing about staying nearby. She was sure of it. It was just a tactic meant to force her to comply with his wishes.

As if she would bend so easily. She might not be some

huge, hulking man, but she was no wilting flower, either. She hadn't yet met the man who could make her back down. That *gadget*, as he'd called it, was hers and she was keeping it, regardless of any lies he might tell her about his dying friend.

Avid collectors would say anything to acquire an item they sought. He was just one more.

Viviana locked her door and fetched a towel, broom, and dustpan to clean up the broken glass. Her hands were still shaking, and as she picked up a large shard of glass it sliced across her finger. A few drops of blood stained the towel as she finished cleaning up the mess.

Irritation tightened her shoulders. It wasn't like her to let a man—or anyone, for that matter—rattle her so deeply. She needed to find her sense of calm and put him out of her mind. She refused to dwell on Mr. Etan for one more moment. She had more important things to worry about, like why a living, breathing man felt the same to her as the artifacts from a long-dead ancient race.

Maybe it was that ring he wore. She'd never seen anything like it before. Maybe it was an artifact that called to her, not the man himself.

That made much more sense and settled her nerves. Her shoulders relaxed as she decided that must be the case. The answer would be somewhere in her books. All she had to do was find it.

Viviana went to her third-floor study, and had just laid out the first ancient book in her collection—the one with a barren tree embossed on the leather cover—when she heard a faint scratching sound.

She peeked out the window, expecting to see animals pawing through the trash cans in the alley below. Instead, when the noise came again, it was behind her, in the hallway. Inside the house.

She whirled around, her heart pounding in her throat.

She told herself it was just a rat. She'd call an exterminator and the problem would be solved.

Instincts that were rusty from disuse screamed otherwise. There was someone in the house. Or something.

Her imagination ran wild with the images of horrible beasts she'd seen in her texts. Claws and teeth and horns mingled together into a massive collage of childish nightmares.

Viviana picked up a hefty brass candlestick. The smooth metal slid around inside the white cotton gloves she'd donned to handle her books. She gripped it tighter and stepped to the right to peer into the hallway.

She'd turned the hallway light off in her determination to be more environmentally conscious. Stupid, stupid move. Now she couldn't see a thing.

A feral hiss rose up from the darkness, positioned too high to have come from a rat on the floor.

She kicked the door open wider with the toe of her shoe, hoping to shed some light into the hall. A faint glow reached halfway across the space. Beyond that light, she saw glowing eyes at about waist height. They were a bright, sickly green. That green glow flared brighter and the hissing noise got louder.

The scratching sound came again, closer, and this time she heard it for what it was: claws on her hardwood flooring.

The thing stepped forward, landing one foot in the rectangle of light. The paw was huge. Furry. Easily as big as her hand, tipped with oily black claws.

Whatever it was, it was definitely no rat.

*   *   *

Walking away from Viviana Rowan had been one of the harder things Neal had done in a long time, but it was necessary. He didn't think she'd be the kind of woman who would fold under a little pressure. Better to ease off and rethink his strategy, figure out what she wanted.

Not that he was thinking too clearly right now. The woman had rattled him.

He'd heard the rumors about Drake and Helen and how they'd met. She'd taken away his pain when they touched. Was it possible he'd found another one of their women? A female Theronai?

A bubble of hope swelled inside him, and despite his best efforts, he couldn't seem to make it stop. He knew that when it burst, he'd suffer, but he couldn't seem to stop that fragile feeling from gaining momentum.

Neal slid behind the wheel of his truck and dialed Drake. If anyone could help Neal figure all this out, it would be his buddy and fellow Theronai.

"Hey, Neal," answered Drake. He was out of breath, but the sun had been down for only a few minutes. It hadn't been dark long enough for the couple to be out fighting yet. Which left one other reason for all the panting.

"I interrupted you and Helen, didn't I?"

There was a smug smile in Drake's tone. "A couple of minutes earlier and you would have. What do you need?"

"I met this woman tonight. When I touched her, the pain . . ." He didn't know how to describe it. "It faded. But then it came back so fast and hard I thought I'd lose my mind."

Drake's tone was sharp and clear, all business. "When you stopped touching her?"

"Yeah. Sound familiar?"

"Absolutely. Who is she?"

"Her name is Viviana Rowan. She collects antiques."

Hope rang pure and clear in Drake's voice. "Tell me about what you felt."

Neal didn't much like talking about his feelings, but for Viviana, he'd make an exception. "It's like I said. I shook her hand and the pain just . . . fell away. When she pulled her hand back, I thought I was going to be crushed under the pressure. It happened twice. I wasn't sure I'd survive a third round."

"Did your luceria react?"

Neal glanced at his ring. There might have been more movement of color in the iridescent band, but it was hard to tell in the dim confines of his truck. "I don't know. I wasn't thinking about it at the time. I was too busy trying not to puke up my guts on her floor."

"Does she bear the mark of a female Theronai?" asked Drake.

The ring-shaped birthmark. Neal had nearly forgotten about that. No women of their kind had been born for so long, their men had all but stopped looking for the signs. "I don't know. She was clothed from her neck down, all prim and proper. I didn't ask about any birthmarks, and if I had, she probably would have kicked me out sooner."

"You're not with her?"

"I'm in front of her home. Outside on the street."

"Where are you? Has the sun set there yet?"

"About five minutes ago."

"Get the hell back in there and don't you dare leave her side," ordered Drake. The note of fear in his voice was contagious.

Neal was already out of his truck when he asked, "Why?"

"Because if she is one of ours and you touched her,

you might have destroyed any natural defenses she had. The Synestryn might be able to find her now, especially if she bleeds."

The broken glass.

Stark, ragged fear sliced through him as he slammed out of his truck. He ran across the street, cursing at the passing cars in his way. "Thanks, Drake. I won't leave her again until I know for sure if she's ours."

"I'll send Logan to you. He might be able to verify her bloodlines."

Neal didn't like the idea of one of those bloodsuckers anywhere near her. Her neck was far too pretty, her blood far too precious. "No. I'll find out myself, even if I have to strip-search her."

"Helen and I can come. Where are you?"

Neal didn't answer. If Drake came, he might bring some of the other men—men who might be compatible with Viviana. Neal didn't want to take that risk. He'd already gotten off on the wrong foot with her. If she was one of their own, the last thing he needed was competition. He'd found her, and as barbaric as it might be, that meant she was his. At least for now.

"I've got it covered," he told Drake. "I'll check in later."

Neal hung up, and out of the corner of his eye he saw a shadow dart down the alley beside Viviana's home. It could have been a large dog looking for scraps in the garbage, but the hair standing up on the back of his neck told him that was wishful thinking.

He didn't bother knocking on the door, doubting she'd answer. Instead he ran through the alley to the back of her house and dialed the number he'd called to set up the appointment. He hoped it was her cell phone and not some office line.

It rang once before he heard her frightened voice. "Mr. Etan? Please tell me that's your dog in my house."

Relief at the sound of her voice was quickly washed away by the implications of what she'd said. "Dog? What did it look like?"

"Big. Furry. Black claws. Glowing green eyes."

That was no dog. It was a sgath. A Synestryn demon.

Neal's limbs iced over. If that thing so much as scratched her, she'd be poisoned, and that was the best-case scenario of what could happen if he didn't get in there and stop it.

"I'm coming. Where are you?" he demanded.

"Upstairs. Third floor. It's in the hall. I closed the door, but I don't know how long that will keep it out."

Not long.

Neal reached the back door of her home. It was hanging wide-open. The doorknob lay on the back step, crumpled and torn from its mooring. Paw prints were easily visible in the snow. More than one set.

One sgath had already found her. He didn't stop to study the tracks to find out how many more were inside. He'd find a way to deal with as many as it took to get her out safe.

He drew his sword. It became visible as it left the sheath mounted to his belt.

He heard a heavy thud from upstairs, followed by a frightened shriek coming through the phone.

Neal sprinted for the stairs. "Hang on, sweetheart. I'm coming."

The heavy wooden door shuddered against another attack by the giant dog.

Viviana yelped and clutched her cell phone in one hand, her candlestick in the other. There were no weapons in here—only a store of books and trinkets so old they'd crumble if she held them too hard.

Mr. Etan had said he was coming, but she had no way of knowing how long that might take. By the way the door was rattling, she guessed it wasn't going to be fast enough.

She wriggled between the side of a low bookshelf and the corner of the room and shoved hard, hoping to use the shelf as a barricade to keep the door shut. The shelf was laden with books and seriously heavy, but it scooted a couple of inches.

The dog slammed into the door again, only this time one of its claws punctured the wood, shooting shards of splinters into the room.

Viviana clamped her lips shut over a scream of fear and pushed harder. She still had five feet to cover before the shelf was going to do anything to impede the dog's progress.

If it was a dog. She was beginning to wonder if it wasn't something . . . else.

Her books were full of images of horrible, writhing beasts and monsters so terrifying there was no way they were real. And whatever was outside her door was definitely real.

She pushed that train of thought from her mind. If she survived this, she'd dedicate as many hours to the question as necessary, but for now, she had to focus on staying alive until help arrived.

The shelf moved another few inches, giving her enough room to use her legs to better advantage.

Another loud, hammering blow to the door sent more wood flying into the room. This time, the opening was big enough for an entire paw to reach through, searching blindly for her.

That was most definitely not a dog. Its claws were way too long, its paw too wide, and its arm was at least as long as her own, thick as a man's leg. Maybe it was a bear or some kind of large, black jungle cat escaped from the zoo.

Whatever it was, it was closer to those terrible images in her books than to anything that belonged on a leash.

The thing let out a vicious snarl, lashing the air with its searching paw. A second later, it yelped in pain and two feet of severed, furry leg dropped through the opening onto her floor. Black blood oozed from the severed end, somehow burning the floor, sending plumes of thick, oily smoke up into the air.

Viviana froze in terror, unable to make sense of what she saw.

The door flew open, batting the furry limb across the floor toward her. She shrieked and jerked away, only to find she was trapped in the corner, unable to move any farther. Her elbow jabbed the wall behind her, sending zings of sensation out to her fingertips.

"Viviana?" came Mr. Etan's deep, worried voice a second before his head appeared around the doorframe.

She didn't answer him. She couldn't. Her mouth was too dry, her throat too constricted for any words to pass.

In one hand he held a sword covered in the same oily black fluid that was burning her floor. The other hand—the one with the ring she'd noticed earlier—was held out to her.

He took a step toward her. "We have to go. There are more sgath in your house."

Viviana looked at his wide hand, then down at the paw of the thing he'd called a sgath. He'd killed it. With a sword. How was any of this even possible?

His voice was confident, steady. He showed no signs

that anything that had happened seemed odd to him. "Sweetheart, I know you're scared. I know all of this is a lot to take in, but now is not the time for hesitation. We need to go."

Go. Before the other sgath in her house found them.

She gave herself a hard mental shake, then reached for his hand. She didn't know this man, but she knew he'd killed to save her. For now, that was going to have to be enough.

Her thin cotton gloves were damp with sweat, but she didn't dare take them off. She remembered how odd she'd felt when they'd touched before, and she really couldn't stand any more bizarre stimuli tonight.

The heat of his skin sank through the glove, and along with it came that odd resonance she'd felt before, only this time it was muted. Even so, it was still enough to make her suck in a startled breath. A shiver wriggled up her back, allowing some of the too-tight muscles there to loosen.

He gave her a tug. "Come on. We need to hurry."

She didn't know where they were going, but for now, she was happy to be leaving behind all this strangeness. Once she was away from here, she'd figure things out and make some sense out of it all. For now, leaving sounded like a fantastic idea.

She stepped over the severed paw, and now that she was able to see through the doorway, she saw the remains of the sgath. It was in four pieces, and each one of them was leaking black blood, sending thin tendrils of smoke up from her floor. The head lay against the banister, its sightless eyes staring up at the ceiling. At least they were no longer glowing.

Mr. Etan helped her step over the biggest part of the

carcass. She clutched his arm tight, feeling the dense, thick muscles beneath his leather jacket. She'd never been more thankful for a brute than she was in this moment. He may have been misplaced in time, but none of the men she'd dated would have stood a chance against the thing he'd just killed. Maybe all those muscles were for more than just vanity's sake.

"Thank you," she whispered, finally finding enough of her voice to speak.

"Sure thing, sweetheart, but we're not out of the woods yet. Stay close."

The way he was holding her arm in a death grip, she didn't think any other option was possible.

From the stairwell somewhere below them came a caustic, angry growl.

Mr. Etan stopped. "It's caught our scent. Is there any other way out?"

"Fire escape down to the alley."

A blur of movement caught her eye, but by the time she'd turned her head to see what it was, Mr. Etan was already in motion. He pushed her behind him, letting out an agonized hiss. It looked like he was fighting the need to double over in pain, but in the end, he stood straight and tall, his blade ready for the sgath that leaped up the stairs, gouging deep grooves into the wood. It didn't even bother to use the treads—just bounded between one railing and the other, hopping up each flight of stairs in two giant leaps.

It lunged at Mr. Etan, but he stepped aside at the last second, pushing her along with him. It bounced against the wall next to her head, ripping the plaster from the wall with its teeth.

Mr. Etan ducked low and spun so fast his blade was

a flashing arc of silver. One of the thing's legs flew away
from its body, streaming oily blood as it went. A drop of
it landed on her suit jacket and began to sizzle.

Mr. Etan shoved her back with one big hand, forcing her to stumble away from the sgath. "Get out," he
ordered.

Viviana regained her balance and jerked the jacket
off her body before that blood could touch her skin. By
the time she had, Mr. Etan had landed another solid
blow to the sgath's side.

It roared in pain and its green eyes flared bright. For
a moment she was frozen in place, struck by the oddity
that the green color reminded her of all those Mr. Yuck
stickers her mother had placed on the chemicals in their
home when Viviana was in elementary school.

"Go!" he shouted. "Now."

She gave herself a hard shake to rid herself of the
need to stare at that eerie light and turned to run. She'd
made it only two steps toward the fire escape when another one of those sgath creatures lifted its head and
peered into the window.

The sgath snorted out a heavy breath, making the
glass fog up. Before that misty spot had completely
cleared, the monster lunged for her, shattering the
window.

Chapter Three

Neal heard the sound of glass shattering. A second later, a blast of cold air hit him.

Viviana let out a yelp of fear and bumped into his back. "There's another one," she yelled.

The sgath he'd fought tonight were bigger and stronger than those he'd been fighting for decades. Maybe the things had found a stockpile of steroids or something.

He shoved forward, blade first, lunging to push the sgath back on its one remaining leg. It stumbled and fell in an awkward heap.

Normally, he would have finished the thing off, but apparently there were more urgent matters that needed his attention, like an uninjured sgath going after a defenseless woman.

Neal spun around, tracking Viviana's position as he moved. Even though he couldn't see her, he could somehow feel her presence, like sunlight glowing against his skin. She gave off a subtle kind of humming he knew he'd be able to track even if he were blind.

He grabbed her arm and hauled her through the bedroom door into the room with the new sgath. He booted the door between them and the injured sgath closed, hoping for a few seconds to deal with the new threat.

Viviana wielded a crystal lamp like it would actually do some good against the demon, and while he admired her courage, she was just going to get herself killed if she tried to fight it.

Before she could, Neal charged, pulling out all the stops. He let loose all the pain he'd carried for too long, his anger at the time that damn stun gun had stolen from him, and his worry for the woman at his side. Fueled by that rage and fear, his body exploded into motion, going through a series of coordinated, powerful movements he'd practiced more times than he could count.

He met the sgath midcharge and used its momentum against it. His sword sliced deep, sending a thick spray of black blood across the cheery yellow wallpaper.

The sgath screamed, but its vocal cords had been severed, and the noise came out as more of a breezy hiss.

The cut was deep, but apparently not deep enough to stop the thing. It opened its jaws and raised its front claws to strike.

Neal was in a bad position, and as the nanoseconds passed in an adrenaline-slowed crawl, he realized he wasn't going to be able to recover his stance in time to dodge the blow. His flank was unprotected, and in another heartbeat he was going to lose a big chunk of flesh between his ribs and his hip. There wasn't time to do anything to stop it.

Out of the corner of his eye, he saw a sparkling object fly past. It slammed into the head of the sgath. Crystal prisms erupted into the room, casting pretty rainbows over the sgath's matted fur.

It reared back in shock, shaking its head as if stunned.

That motion gave Neal enough time to recover and avoid the incoming blow. He took a half step to his right, tightened his grip on the hilt of his sword, and shoved it into the sgath's chin and up into its brain.

It wriggled there for a moment, lashing out blindly before it fell still and silent.

The bedroom door burst open, bouncing off the wall so hard it nearly closed again. Only the hulking form of the injured sgath charging into the room kept it open.

Neal didn't have time to release his sword, so he hauled the heavy body of the dead sgath along the blade, using it to bat at its own kind. His muscles strained under the added weight, but his blade held strong and solid.

The injured sgath flailed and hit the wall hard.

Neal shoved the dead sgath from his sword with his boot, and wasted no time in finishing off the last threat to Viviana.

He wiped the blood from his blade on the dead sgath's fur, and turned to the woman.

She was standing in the corner, taking up as little space as possible. She had some kind of ceramic figurine in her gloved hands, clutching it like it might save her life. Her hazel eyes were wide with shock, and her slim body was shaking so hard he could see her silk blouse shimmering with the tiny tremors.

Neal moved to her as he scanned her skin and clothing for signs of blood splatter. He found none.

Keeping his voice calm, he said, "It's over now, but we need to go."

She didn't seem to hear him, so he eased the little figurine from her fingers and took her hand. He could feel her chilled skin, even through the glove, but he'd get her warm soon enough. He just needed to get her out of the house and into his truck so they could avoid any more unexpected guests.

He tugged her forward and she took one stumbling

step. Clearly she was still in shock, not that he could blame her. A lot had happened tonight.

But if he didn't get her out of here, a hell of a lot more was going to happen.

Rather than trying to talk her down, he wrapped his arm around her slim waist and lifted her over the sgath corpses. By the time he set her on her feet at the broken window, she was batting at his hand. "I can walk."

If her legs were as shaky as her voice, she was going to tumble down the fire escape. "I'm sure you can. But it's icy out there. We're safer if we stick together."

Neal scanned the alley below and saw no signs of more Synestryn. It was going to have to be good enough.

They went down the steps. He kept a firm grip on her arm in case she froze up or slipped. The last few feet were a bit slow, but they made it down into the alley.

He helped her over a mound of trash, and then he picked up the pace, heading for his truck. Snow crunched under their feet as they went, and accumulated in their hair.

Viviana was shaking like crazy, and Neal didn't know if it was more from shock or cold. He slipped his jacket off and draped it over her shoulders. She clutched it closed at her throat.

"Thank you."

"No problem."

He waited for the first safe break in the traffic and hurried them across the street, ignoring the horns and outraged shouts from the cars he forced to slow so they wouldn't hit them.

The lights on his truck flashed as he unlocked the doors. He didn't bother taking her around to the passenger's side, but instead opened the driver's side, lifted her onto the high bench seat, and got in behind her, crowding her so she had to scoot over to make room for him.

The engine started with a deep rumble. He cranked up the heat and leaned over so he could buckle her in. Then he shoved his way into the oncoming traffic, drawing yet more blasts from car horns.

Whatever. He wasn't in the mood to be a courteous driver. He had more important things to worry about.

Like what the hell he was going to do with her now.

The St. Louis skyline was well behind them when Viviana's mind finally stopped sputtering and started running again.

She'd been attacked by monsters. Three monsters. Mr. Etan had killed them all to save her.

She turned her head the slightest bit, trying to look at him without appearing like she was. She'd never seen anyone move like that. He was mesmerizing. Brutal grace. Beautiful death.

He hadn't said a word since they'd gotten in his truck. There was no radio to block the silence, only the humming of the pavement under his tires and her too-fast breathing.

Viviana didn't know what to say. "Thank you" seemed a bit inadequate. In fact, she wasn't even sure if she should thank him at all. For all she knew, he'd sent those things after her so he could save her and impress her enough to let him have the *gadget* he wanted.

"Shouldn't we go back? Call the police? Or animal control?"

"No."

"Where are you taking me?"

"South."

"South where?"

"I don't know. I haven't thought that far ahead yet. I just wanted to keep moving so the truck would warm up. You were shaking."

She still was, though she wasn't nearly as cold now as she had been, thanks to his leather jacket and the delicious heat that was pouring out of the truck's vents. She pulled off her cotton gloves and held her hands close to the dash to warm them.

"Do you want something to eat?" he asked.

She looked at him to see if it was some kind of joke. He wasn't smiling. "Are you serious? We nearly died and you want to eat?"

He lifted one thick shoulder in a shrug. "We're still alive. Gotta keep our strength up."

"I'd rather talk about what happened back there."

Guilt flattened his mouth. "That was my fault."

"You brought those things with you?"

He spared her a quick, appalled glance. "Hell, no. I'd never do that. But I think it's my fault they found you."

"Care to explain that?"

He shook his head. "It's a long story, but the short version is too shocking to blurt out."

"I'm tough, Mr. Etan. I think I can take it."

"Neal," he said. "Call me Neal. And tough or not, I'm not sure you need another shock so soon after being attacked by sgath."

"How about you let me judge whether or not I'm able to handle more. I assure you my constitution is not so delicate as you might think."

He grunted his disagreement as he pulled into a fast-food restaurant and parked. "If it's like the rest of you, it is."

Indignation was swiftly burning away all traces of the fear she'd felt earlier. "I think I should get out here and call a cab. Thank you for saving me. You'll understand if I prefer never to see you again." That last part was a bit of a lie. She'd enjoy seeing him as often as possible. He was the epitome of the term *eye candy*, but that didn't mean she would indulge.

She unfastened her seat belt and reached for the door handle.

Neal moved so fast she didn't even have time to yelp. He grabbed her hips and pulled her back across the leather seat until she was practically in his lap. She felt the hardness of his body behind her, the heat of his big hands sinking through her skirt.

When he spoke, she could feel his breath brush past the top of her ear. "If you leave me, you probably won't live to see sunrise."

Her insides began to quiver, and she wasn't sure if it was his extreme prediction or the feel of his hands on her that caused the odd reaction. That resonant vibration was back, streaming through her, pooling in her belly, and expanding to fill up all the empty spaces.

"Don't be ridiculous," she said, her voice shaking as much as her body.

"I'm not. Those sgath found you once; they can do it again."

"You said that was your fault. If I'm not with you, it won't happen again."

"Wrong."

She wasn't sure, but she thought she felt his mouth make the briefest, fluttering contact with her ear. She shivered, though she wasn't sure if it was his touch that made it happen, or merely the thought of him touching her that did it.

Either way, she wasn't going to sit here and be man-handled. "Let me go."

Slowly, he released her hips, dragging his fingers over her wool skirt so slowly it was almost a caress. "Please don't try to run," he told her, the warning ringing clearly in his tone. "I can't let that happen."

Viviana scooted back across the seat as far as she could go. She faced him, determined to watch those too-fast hands of his. "Why not?"

"I nee—" He cut off whatever he'd been going to say and started again. "We still have the matter of the gadget to settle. I can't go home without it. My friend's life is at stake."

She gave him a steady stare. "So is yours if you grab me again like that."

A small smile played about his bold mouth, giving her the sudden urge to reach out and see if his lips were as soft as they looked or as hard as the rest of him. "Fair enough."

She straightened her skirt and smoothed her hands over her hair to make sure her bun hadn't come undone in all the excitement. "Let's start with this friend of yours. How is it you think my artifact will help?"

"It's some kind of healing device. My friend is suffering from a progressive kind of paralysis. Without this gadget, he'll die. I won't let that happen."

"Stop it with the thinly veiled threats, will you? If I lived through those horrible creatures, I can certainly live through whatever you have to offer."

"Don't forget I was the one who killed them."

Which reminded her . . . "Your sword. Where did it go?"

He patted his side. "It's here. You just can't see it."

Viviana snorted. Her mother would have frowned

in censure at the noise, which brought about a wave of grief and loneliness. She missed Mother so much—even her annoying parts.

Viviana closed her eyes and suffered through the unwanted emotions. Her heart had been through a workout tonight, and she couldn't find the strength to keep everything in check like normal.

"Hey. What's wrong?" asked Neal gently a moment before his hand settled on hers.

An effervescent tingling wove its way through her arm and into her chest. It expanded into a plume of warmth that drove away all thoughts of grief and sadness. For a single, shining moment, Viviana felt safe and happy. Like she belonged.

She'd spent her entire life standing outside, looking in. She'd never been like other children. As an orphan, she'd begun life as an outcast—an infant no one wanted. Her mother had adopted her before any of Viviana's memories had begun to form, but it hadn't seemed to save her from the knowledge that she was different.

Mother said she was special, but Viviana knew that was simply a euphemism for someone who didn't fit in.

"I'm fine," she managed to say.

"You don't look fine. You look like you just found out someone killed your kitten."

Viviana swallowed and collected her wits. "Too much excitement for one night. That's all."

She started to pull her hand away, but Neal's grip tightened slightly, holding her hand in his. "Not yet," he said. "I'm not ready to start hurting again."

She blinked in confusion. "What?"

"Let's get back to the gadget, shall we? You were just about to tell me where it was so we could go get it and save my friend Torr."

"Nice try, but not good enough. You were going to show me your sword."

Viviana was sure she'd seen the intricate vines winding around the hilt. Even as fast as he'd moved, she knew what she saw. And if she was right, his sword was made by the same ancient people as her treasured collection.

Neal lifted a brow. "You want to see my sword?"

"Yes."

"If I show you, will you tell me where the gadget is?"

"Maybe."

His thick chest expanded with a heavy sigh. "Fine."

Slowly, so slowly she could feel his touch over every nerve, he pulled his hand away from hers. The moment their skin broke contact, his whole body went tense. Sweat broke out over his forehead, and his breathing was fast and shallow.

Worry for him hit her, worming its way so deep it was almost as if she'd known him for years. "Are you okay?"

"Just give me a minute."

She did. Seconds ticked by, and slowly his body relaxed.

"Damn, that gets worse every time," he said, panting.

"What gets worse?"

He shook his head and pinned her with his glittering gaze. "That's all part of that long story. Suffice it to say that when I touch you it feels really good. When I stop, not so much."

She felt the same way. She opened her mouth to tell him to just keep touching her before she realized how it might sound. She didn't even know the man. She certainly wasn't going to offer to let him put his hands on her, no matter how lovely the idea was.

He moved and a sword appeared in his hand, as if conjured from thin air. "How did you do that?"

"The sword is invisible when it's strapped to my body. Keeps the locals from freaking out."

"But . . . how?"

"Magic."

Magic. The word trickled into her, shifting puzzle pieces in her mind. What had been a confusing set of facts before now became a clearer picture. If magic was real—and she was looking at proof that it was—then that explained a lot of things. All those stories she'd read. All those artifacts that seemed to have a purpose, but no one could ever determine what it was. It was all beginning to make sense.

Neal laid the flat of the blade against his forearm, pointing the pommel toward her. She leaned over the piece, enthralled by the power of it. It was beautiful, a thriving, pristine work of art. The detail was incredible. Intricate leaves etched with such precision she could see the veins wove around on a vine, forming the guard. Part of the detail in the hilt had been worn away with use, making her wonder just how old this piece was. "Where did you get it?"

"My father had it made for me when I was born."

Part of her excitement deflated. He couldn't be more than thirty-five, making the piece a beautiful replica, but nothing more. "Did the metalsmith pattern it off of an antique? Is that why it looks so worn?"

"It looks worn because it is worn."

"It would take decades of hard use to manage that."

"Yeah. It would."

"What? You're saying that you've done that? You can't have even been using it for more than a decade or two."

"I'm older than I look."

The way he said it gave her pause. She wasn't sure

she should ask, but she really needed to know. "How old?"

"You sure are a curious thing. I think I should stop answering your questions until you start answering mine."

"The only thing you seem to want to know is where the artifact is."

"Now you're catching on."

"If I tell you, what's in it for me?"

"How much do you want?"

"I'm not interested in money. I want your sword."

He let out a hard laugh. "Not on your life. This sword in the wrong hands could be dangerous."

"It's dangerous in the right hands, too."

He gave her a slow wink. "Glad you noticed."

Another shiver coursed along her limbs, and this time it had nothing to do with his touch. All he had to do was give her a wink and she melted.

He sheathed his sword and it faded out of sight. She was dying to get her hands on the sheath to see how he managed it, but she didn't think he'd appreciate her making greedy, grabby hands, especially near his manlier parts.

Not that she was thinking about his manlier parts. She simply knew they were there. She was not going to look, no matter how much she'd piqued her own curiosity with the thought.

Her eyes slid down his torso, admiring the way the mock turtleneck hugged his muscular contours. She'd almost embarrassed herself by staring at his crotch when his voice jerked her attention back to his face, where it belonged.

"See something you like?" he asked.

She cleared her throat, ignoring his question. "So, if

I can't have your sword, do you have any other items I might be interested in?"

"I don't know. What kind of things do you collect?"

"Items from a long-dead group of people called the Sentinels."

Neal went still, his eyes glittering in the dark confines of the truck. "Where did you hear about the Sentinels?"

"Books. You should give them a try sometime."

"I'm sorry to break it to you, but those books of yours had at least one thing wrong. They're not long-dead, sweetheart."

Viviana's body went numb at those words. "What do you know of them?"

"More than you, I'm sure. I happen to be one."

"Liar," she spat out before she could stop herself. It was easy to say he was one of them, but for all she knew, he'd researched her obsession with the Sentinels in order to win her over so he could get what he wanted from her.

There was one way to test him. "Which race are you?"

His brows lifted in a show of admiration. "You really have done your homework."

"That doesn't answer my question."

"Theronai," he said, waving the ring on his finger in front of her face. "Though I would have thought the luceria would have given it away."

Luceria. She rolled the word around in her head, letting the sound of it soak into her memory. "I don't remember any mention of a luceria."

"Guess you don't know everything, then, huh?"

"I know there's one sure way to prove what you say is correct."

"What? You mean that slaying those sgath wasn't proof enough? What about the way you feel when we touch? I bet no human man has ever made you feel like that before."

"I don't feel a thing," she lied. She couldn't remember reading anything about feeling odd at the touch of a Theronai, but that could have been the fault of her translation, too.

"No?" he challenged. "So you wouldn't mind if I touched you again, then?"

Yes, please. She'd like that very much. Not that she'd ever tell him so. This man needed no more weapons against her now that they shared a common interest. Sure, he said he was a Sentinel, but that had to be a fabrication. They were all dead.

Weren't they?

"Show me your lifemark," she demanded.

A slow, hot smile spread out over Neal's face. "If you wanted to get my shirt off, sweetheart, all you had to do was ask."

With that, he pulled the long-sleeved shirt off over his head, baring his chest.

Viviana stared and forgot to breathe.

Not only was he a living sculpture of masculine perfection; he was also telling her the truth. He was a Theronai. The giant tree spanning his chest, stretching from his left shoulder to well below his belt, was proof of that.

The detail was astounding. Even in the dim confines of the truck, she could still make out each individual leaf and twig. The bark was so lifelike, she itched to feel the texture of it under her fingers. As she watched, the tree seemed to sway with some invisible wind.

It had to be an optical illusion caused by the steady expansion of his ribs as he breathed.

Viviana reached out a hand. The compulsion to touch such an amazing work of art was uncontrollable.

Her fingers came to rest lightly on the image, and only then, when she felt the warmth of his skin, did she remember that this was no mere image on a canvas. She was touching a living, breathing man.

Beneath her fingers, she felt the branches shift, swaying toward her touch. An electric current flowed out of him, tingling her fingertips.

Neal sucked in a breath and held it. "I was right. You are one of ours."

"One of your what?"

"People. You're a Theronai. Like me."

Shock jolted Viviana's gaze up to his. He wasn't teasing. His dark blue eyes were steady on hers and there wasn't even the faintest hint of a smile anywhere to be found.

She started to pull her hand away, but he flattened his palm over her hand, holding it in place. His warm skin was stretched tight over hard muscles. She could feel the subtle vibration of his pulse pounding in his chest.

Her breathing was too fast when she finally found the ability to speak. "I don't understand."

"You're not the first woman we've found who didn't know she was one of us. There are others like you— women fathered by men from another world. I know this all must be really confusing to you, but believe me when I tell you that you, Viviana Rowan, may be the only person on the face of this planet who can save my life."

Chapter Four

Neal could hardly believe his eyes. Only the chaotic swirl of colors in his ring proved to him that he wasn't just experiencing a bout of wishful thinking. Viviana really could save him.

If she chose to do so.

She tugged on the hand he had pinned against his chest, but Neal wasn't ready for her to stop touching him yet. He was dealing with enough without adding an avalanche of pain on top of it.

"What do you mean?" she asked. "What's wrong with you? You seem perfectly healthy to me."

"How much do you know about lifemarks?"

"I read they were magical images put on men at birth that marked them as one of the Theronai."

"That's partly true. We're born with the mark, though it's merely a seed at that time. It sprouts and grows as we do."

"How is that possible? A tattoo doesn't grow."

"It's not a tattoo. It's a living mark that's as much a part of us as freckles or a birthmark—like the ring-shaped one you have."

She sucked in a shocked breath. "How did you know about that? I know you haven't seen it."

The fact that she bore the mark of a female of his race was simply more proof he was right.

Neal smiled and leaned closer. "Where is it, sweetheart? Want to show me? I showed you mine."

She turned a lovely shade of pink and her spine straightened. "You were explaining to me exactly how I'm supposed to save you."

"See how bare my lifemark is?"

She looked down and he knew what she saw. He had only a few precious leaves left hanging on.

"The leaves are gone."

"That's right. When the last one falls, my soul starts to die. I'll become evil and twisted. Unless I kill myself first, which I'd planned to do, right up until I met you. You can save me from that fate."

To his relief, she didn't seem appalled at how much he needed her, only curious. "How?"

"There's power inside me, power I can't use. I've been collecting it since I was a boy, saving it for the one woman who could use it. You're that woman, Viviana."

She let out another indelicate snort—the only unladylike sound he'd heard her make all night. Even her screams of fear were prim and proper. "No, I'm not."

He pressed his hand harder over hers, pushing a few sparks of energy from his chest into her skin. "If you weren't, you wouldn't feel that." He lifted her hand to his mouth and kissed her palm. More sparks fled his lips and jumped eagerly into her as if they'd been waiting to make the trip for years.

"This can't be happening."

"Why not? You said you've been studying us. You should know all about this."

"None of my books covered . . . this. It's all too much. I need some time to think."

A pang of disappointment fell over Neal, but he was tough. He could take it. Some things simply couldn't be forced. Getting a woman to commit the rest of her life to him was definitely one of those things.

"Okay. I'll back off, but not about the gadget. I need it. Torr needs it. I won't take no for an answer."

She gave him a shaky nod. "All right. It's obvious to me there are a lot of things I don't know. If you promise to take me with you and answer my questions along the way, then I'll take you to the artifact."

"It's a deal."

Neal pulled up to the home of the retired Professor Reynolds, the man who had possession of the healing device.

"All the lights are out," said Viviana. "I hate to wake him."

Her slender fingers were laced through his, and even though it made driving harder, he wasn't about to let go. He'd been pain-free for nearly an hour now, and it was enough to make him euphoric.

"I'm sure he won't mind, considering this is an emergency."

"I want to tell him about you. He loves these artifacts as much as I do. That's why I loaned the disks to him."

"Maybe some other time. I'm not sure I could handle another barrage of scholarly questions tonight. I might go hoarse."

Truth was, he hadn't minded her nonstop questions at all. The fact that she was interested in him and his people was just going to make her transition into his world that much easier.

He knew how hard it had been on Helen to leave behind her human upbringing. He hoped Viviana's background would make it easier on her.

He really did want things to be easy on her. The thought of her suffering made him want to pound on something with his bare fists. Not good for his carefully held control.

Neal kept her hand in his as he hopped out of the truck. She scooted to the edge and stopped. Her hazel eyes were dark with worry as she stared at him for a long moment. "What am I doing?"

"Helping a man in need?"

She looked at their joined hands. "I can't stop touching you. I feel like a kid with a crush, and I don't even know you. This is not like me at all."

She was getting cold feet, letting all the confusion and questions sink into that clever head of hers. "No? What are you like?"

"Slow. Methodical. I think things through. I don't jump into trucks with strange men in the middle of the night and hold their hands."

"I'm your first, then?" he teased.

She didn't smile. "I'm scared, Neal. This whole thing scares me more than those monsters ever could. You're telling me that my whole life has been a lie. That I'm not even human."

"Nothing about your life is a lie. You just didn't know your own family tree, that's all."

"You think I'm going to save your life."

"I won't pretend it's not what I want. I don't want to die. I want to keep fighting. I honestly never thought I'd find you in time, but now that I have . . ."

"You want to keep me."

"We'll go slow," he promised. "I still have time. I'm not going to force you into anything you don't want."

"My life as I know it is over, isn't it?"

He trailed a finger over her cheek, reveling in the

softness of her skin. She was so pretty. So elegantly un-attainable. He had no business with a woman like her, even if his luceria thought otherwise. "I prefer to think of it as the start of a new life for you—one surrounded by the people you've been reading about for years. This will be your chance to study us in a way no one else ever has: from the inside."

"You're pushing all the right buttons to gain my co-operation, aren't you?"

"Sweetheart, if I'm ever lucky enough to push your buttons, you won't wonder why I'm doing it. You'll know."

That delightful pink flush rose up from the prim collar of her shirt, making Neal wonder just how far down her blush went. He could think of a lot better ways to be passing the night with her than showing up uninvited at some stodgy professor's house.

He'd strip her out of all those proper clothes and get as much skin-on-skin contact as possible. The play of sparks between them—the feel of minute traces of his power soaking into her skin—would be enough to light the sheets on fire. And even though he wasn't supposed to want a woman like Viviana, the luceria thought they'd be good together.

Who was he to argue with centuries of proof that the system worked? If the luceria wanted him to have her, he was going to enjoy convincing her to play along with tradition.

And part of that convincing was getting her thinking in the right direction.

He cupped the back of her neck and pulled her toward him. She went along for the ride, closing the distance between them. She slid forward on the seat, which shoved her skirt up her thighs.

Neal stepped up, wedging himself between her knees so he could get as close as he needed to be.

Her eyes slid to his mouth and he knew in that moment that he had her. Victory surged through him, making him feel stronger, more powerful. Just the thought of this woman wanting to kiss him was enough to send him into overdrive. Bring on the battle. Let a dozen charging Synestryn bear down on him. He'd take them all out. Not one of them would get close to his lady.

A low sound of warning rose up from his chest and there wasn't a thing he could do to stop it. He felt Viviana stiffen slightly under his hand, but it was too late for second thoughts now.

He pressed his lips to hers, forcing himself to keep things light. No open mouths. No tongue. Just the contact of her lips on his.

It wasn't even close to enough.

He wanted more. Desire spread through his body, pooling in his gut, making his limbs vibrate. His luceria was freaking out, hopping around on his skin as if celebrating the contact.

Against his will, his fingers tightened around her neck, stroking slightly over her bare nape. He wanted to taste her there, to kiss and suck and bite while he took her from behind.

His cock was throbbing and swollen, and the need to push her legs wide and rub himself against her was swiftly taking over all rational thought. He slid a hand up her thigh, feeling the silkiness of her stockings, then the even softer texture of her bare skin. Thigh-highs. Naughty girl under all that prim-and-proper.

Just the thought made him lose control.

Neal opened his mouth to deepen their kiss, but she was way ahead of him. Her tongue danced across his lips, flicking against his, making his blood heat. She fisted her hands in his shirt, jerking him closer, and all he could think was that he wished he hadn't put it back on. He'd give anything to feel her palms against his bare chest again—feel his lifemark arcing to connect with her.

She slid to the edge of the seat, widening her thighs to make plenty of room for his body. The bite of her fingernails through his shirt was an exquisite torture, but not nearly as good as the sharp little nips of her teeth on his bottom lip.

A soft, feminine moan filled the space between them. Cold air swirled around them.

He'd have to keep her warm, cover her body with his. Not that he'd mind. He'd be her living blanket any day of the week and count himself a thousand kinds of lucky.

Neal cupped her breast, feeling the slippery silk fabric of her blouse warm between them. Her nipple puckered in his palm, though the damn layers of fabric she wore kept him from feeling it the way he wanted. He wondered if her nipples would tighten like that for his mouth, too.

Only one way to find out.

A sound of cracking ice came from behind him. Instincts as deeply a part of him as his own bones rose up, shouting a warning.

Neal ripped himself away from Viviana, drawing his sword as he moved. A dump truck full of agony unloaded on his head, tearing a pained cry from his throat.

He fought the need to double over, gritting his teeth to stay standing. The tip of his sword trembled, but he kept it up.

"What is it?" asked Viviana, her voice tight with sudden fear.

"Heard something."

Slowly, the pain receded until it was no longer draining him of strength. It still pounded through him, but now it was at the level where it was just pissing him off.

He searched the area, channeling tiny motes of power to his eyes so he could see through the murky darkness.

Nothing. No movement, no glowing eyes, nothing but the white landscape and the muted silence of snowfall.

"I guess it was just a tree branch cracking in the wind," he said. His instincts weren't usually so faulty, but he had been more than a bit distracted a few seconds ago. "We should go inside." Where he could protect her better if the shit did hit the fan.

He turned around just in time to see her pull her skirt back down, giving him only the briefest of glimpses of black silk stockings against pale, smooth skin.

Her mouth was red, and a few strands of hair had escaped her spinsterish bun. He could see her rapid pulse shimmering in the fabric covering her breasts. Her nipples were still hard, making Neal's mouth water.

He promised himself they'd get back here—to where her mouth was on his and he could feel the damp heat between her thighs against his fly. They'd get back to that moment, and when they did, he wasn't going to stop until she lay hot and sated beneath him.

Maybe not even then.

Unfortunately, business came first. Once they got the gadget, he'd take her back to Dabyr, where he could take his time with her. Linger. He definitely wanted to linger over the lovely Viviana Rowan. No question there.

Being careful not to touch her skin, he zipped his jacket up over her to keep her warm. The thing was way too big, falling over her hands, but it would work until they could find something that fit her better. And if any demons came their way, the magically enhanced leather would provide her with at least a little protection.

Once she was bundled and warm, he turned his attention back to the job at hand.

Professor Reynolds lived in an old farmhouse in the country, with only a few neighbors visible in the distance. Round bales of hay dotted the surrounding land, their tops covered in the accumulating snow. Everything was white and pristine, including the sidewalk leading up to the professor's front door.

Neal helped Viviana traverse the slippery sidewalk in her high heels. She rang the bell. Neal looked up at the house, but no lights came on.

"Maybe he's a heavy sleeper."

She rang again. And again.

A bad feeling started to creep up Neal's spine. "Could he be out of town?"

"I talked to him earlier today. He didn't mention anything like that."

Neal reached for the knob. It turned easily. "Unlocked."

"Not much need for locks out here. The professor likes it because it's quiet and he can work without interruption."

The house was dark. Neal stepped inside, drawing his sword. Just in case. "Stay behind me."

The foul smell of sewage filled the air, and beneath that was a musty animal smell. Synestryn. They'd been here.

There were stairs leading up on his left and three doors exiting the entryway.

"His study is to the right," whispered Viviana. He could hear the fear in her voice, the worry. As much as he wanted to comfort her, now was not the time.

Neal peered through the doorway she indicated. Snow had made it bright outside, and some of that light streamed in from a window behind a huge desk. A man was slumped over the desk, lying at an odd angle.

Neal hoped the man was just asleep, but he doubted they'd get that lucky.

He stepped inside the door and positioned Viviana with her back to the wall. As he moved, he inadvertently cleared the path for her to see the professor. She let out a frightened gasp and started to move toward him. Neal grabbed her arm and pushed her back. "Stay here. I'll check him out."

"Something's wrong with him, isn't it?"

Neal didn't reply. He crept forward, keeping his eyes open for signs of movement. Some of the Synestryn were small and he didn't want any of them getting near Viviana.

A cold tendril of wind wrapped around Neal's legs, and as he stepped forward, he could see the window had been broken out, leaving a gaping, bloody hole. He could also see that the bottom half of the professor's body was missing. The top half was lying on the desk and blood dripped down onto the leather office chair.

"Oh God," breathed Viviana. She was right next to him now, staring in horror at her friend's remains. She stepped forward, but Neal caught her before she could get too close.

"There's nothing you can do for him. We need to get the gadget and go." Before the Synestryn found them, too. "Where would he have kept it?"

Her eyes were brimming with tears, and the tendons in her neck were standing out as she struggled not to cry. "We need to call the police. Find the person who did this."

"It wasn't a person. It was a demon, like those that came for you tonight. If we call the police, chances are we'll just get them killed, too. We need to focus."

She was staring at the body, her eyes wide, her chin quivering.

Neal moved to block out the sight of her dead friend. He cupped her face in his hands and tilted it up to look at him. Her skin was so soft and warm under his fingers. He felt delicate sparks of energy jumping from him into her, making his palms tingle. "I'm sorry, sweetheart. I wish we'd gotten here sooner."

"He was a sweet old man. Why would anyone do this?"

Good question. Clearly the man wasn't blooded, or they'd have taken the whole body and not left a pool of blood lying wasted on the floor. Synestryn fed on traces of ancient blood running through certain humans. They used it to fuel their magic, but this man hadn't been killed for that, which left only one reason. "He had something they wanted."

"The artifact he was studying for me?"

Neal figured it would crush her to think she'd been the cause of her friend's death. "We can't know for sure. What I do know is that we need to find it."

She sniffed and nodded. Her eyes closed and he felt the strangest sensation vibrate in the air between them. It was almost as if she were pulling on those sparks he kept giving off—like they were iron filings and she was a magnet.

A moment later, the feeling subsided and she opened her eyes. "There were two disks in the box. One of them is still here. Nearby. The other . . ." She shook her head. "It's too far away for me to feel it."

"Feel it?"

Her gaze drifted to the floor as if she were ashamed. "I don't know how it works, but I can feel certain artifacts when they get close. Those disks were like that for me."

That news left Neal reeling. Every female Theronai seemed to have some kind of specialty, but if hers was finding Sentinel artifacts, she was going to be invaluable to them.

Assuming she agreed to become part of their world.

He couldn't forget that other women like her had balked at the notion of leaving their human world behind. Viviana had already been through a lot tonight. He couldn't push her, no matter how much the need to do so burned in him.

Right now, when he was touching her like this, and the pain was gone, it was easy to be patient. But as soon as he had to let go, and that mountain of pain came crashing down on top of him again, patience was a lot scarcer.

He couldn't force her to accept his luceria. It had to be her choice, and lingering here in the room with the body of her dead friend was not the way to convince her to make the right one.

"I don't want you to watch," he told her. He was going to have to move the body and he didn't want her seeing anything ... upsetting.

She gave a tight nod and turned around, pulling from his grasp.

Neal clenched his muscles, readying himself for the agony he knew was only a heartbeat away. He tried to prepare himself for it, but there was no preparing for the seething weight that bore down on him, crushing the air from his lungs.

A high, strangled sound hissed through his teeth, and he reeled inside the grip of that pain, powerless to stop it from tearing him apart.

Long seconds later, he was sweating and shaking, but at least his vision began to return.

If anything had happened during that moment of incapacitation—if the Synestryn had attacked—there wouldn't have been a thing he could have done to stop it. He would have been unable to protect Viviana.

And that thought was the one that changed his mind about patience. He had to convince her to take his luceria and end his pain. Tonight. It was the only way he could ensure that she stayed safe.

But not here. Not in this house. He couldn't do that to her.

Neal made quick work of searching the professor's desk for the disk. When he didn't find it, he moved to the man's pockets, and there, deep inside the pocket of his sweater, lay the cold, metal, palm-size disk.

He shoved it into his jeans pocket and eased the man's remains to the floor. He grabbed a crocheted throw from the back of a nearby recliner and draped it over his body.

"Time to go," he said, grabbing Viviana's arm with his clean hand as he left the room.

"Did you find anything?"

"Yes." He ducked into a bathroom he found down the hall and washed the blood from his hand, keeping the light off so she didn't have to see the mess. "You said you can sense these objects?"

"If they're close."

He hurried them out the front door, keeping a grip on her arm so she wouldn't slip. "How close?"

"I can usually tell whenever one of them comes into the city."

He had to find that second disk. From what little Gilda had told him, he didn't think the gadget would heal without both halves, and Torr was running out of time. "Do you have any sense of direction as to where the second disk went?"

"I don't know. I have to concentrate," said Viviana.

"Got it."

They got in his truck and he fired up the engine and drove back down the gravel driveway.

"Where are we going?"

"Just warming up the engine so we can get some heat," he lied. Truth was he didn't want any nosy neighbors to see his truck and report it to the police when they eventually found the professor's body. With any luck, the truck's tire tracks would be filled in with snow before anyone else knew of the professor's death.

Neal drove a few miles and pulled into the entrance to some farmland. A snow-covered chain barred his path, but for now, this was as good a place as any to stop. It was nice and open around them, giving him a clear view if any monsters headed their way.

"Okay. Do your thing," he said.

Her body was rigid in the seat, and he could see shiny streaks where her tears of grief had finally fallen.

Neal wanted to pull her into his arms and offer some kind of comfort, but he didn't dare. He still felt battered from the previous time he'd stopped touching her bare skin, and he wasn't sure how much more punishment he could take. If the pain did eventually kill him, she'd be left unprotected.

Viviana closed her eyes, squeezing out more tears. Seeing her cry damn near broke his heart, but there was nothing he could do to bring back her friend. He didn't even have a freakin' tissue to give her. The only things he had to offer were a strong sword arm and his desperation for her to save him. It made him a needy bastard, but there wasn't much he could do about that.

A few seconds later, she let out a disheartened sigh. "I can't feel it. It's too far away. I'm sorry." Her eyes started tearing up again, and Neal couldn't stand it any longer.

He slid across the seat and gathered her in his arms. She tucked her head against his shoulder, melting into him. Her fingers clenched in his shirt and he could feel the tremors of her grief tumbling through her. "It's okay, sweetheart. Don't worry. We'll figure something out."

"I killed him. I gave him that artifact and it brought those things here."

"We don't know that's what happened."

"Don't patronize me. That's exactly what happened. And now I can't even find the artifact they stole."

Neal hesitated only a moment before he made up his mind. Sure, she knew little about his world or who she really was. And no, she didn't know about what he was going to ask her to do or what it might cost her. But what he did know was that the luceria thought they belonged together, and after seeing the happy matches his Theronai brothers had made, he wasn't going to question the gift that was being offered to him. He was going to grab it with both hands and hold on as tight as he could.

Viviana was meant to be his, and he was going to make it happen.

"I can help you with that," he offered. "I've known women like you before who had powers and I know how to amplify them. Make them stronger."

She pulled away enough to look into his eyes. "How?"

And here was the tricky part. He fished the humming band of the luceria out from under his shirt to show it to her. "All you have to do is wear my luceria."

Chapter Five

Viviana was weighed down by the loss of her friend, but even through the foggy haze of grief, she could tell Neal was hiding something from her. "It's magic, isn't it? Like the disks?"

Neal nodded, his dark eyes glittering with hope.

"What does it do?"

"The luceria is two parts of a whole. We each wear one. It will connect us and allow you to tap into the stores of power inside me. You can use that power to fuel your ability, which will amplify it."

"You think that if I wear that necklace, I'll be able to sense where the second disk went?"

"I do."

That artifact had caused enough pain and suffering. She needed to find it and put it where no one could ever get hurt again.

She held out her hand. "Give me the necklace."

"That's not the way it works. You have to take it off me."

Viviana's hand shook as she reached for the luminescent band. The swirling display of earth tones intensified the closer her hand got. Of all the Sentinel artifacts she'd seen over the years, this one was the most intriguing. It felt . . . alive. She could almost feel some kind of intelligence working within it.

She slid one finger under the band, enjoying the supple warmth and the slippery texture. A flowing plume of bronze spiraled out from her finger and it seemed to heat. It was going to feel so nice against her skin and look so pretty around her neck.

The band broke open and slipped down beneath Neal's shirt. He pulled it out and took the loose ends in his blunt fingertips. "Are you sure?" he asked.

Viviana nodded. She wanted to know what it felt like to wear something so beautiful and magical, even if it was only for a little while.

Neal reached around her neck and she heard a subtle click as the ends locked shut.

He leaned back, his eyes fixed on the band. His voice was a reverent whisper. "You have no idea how long I've waited for this moment. I don't want to mess it up or scare you."

"Why would you scare me?"

"I'm going to cut myself a little now and offer you my promise."

Confusion swept over her as she watched him strip off his shirt. "Cut yourself? Why?"

"It's the only way to finish the process of connecting us." He drew his sword, making it appear. He sliced a shallow cut over his heart with the edge of the blade. "My life for yours," he said, then gathered a drop of blood on his fingertip and pressed it against the necklace. "You have to give me a promise of your own now to complete the process."

"I don't understand."

"I know. I'm rushing you. I didn't want to, but I can't seem to stop myself," he said. "Just follow your instincts."

A promise? She had no idea what kind of promise he wanted, but she could sense the magic of what they were doing surrounding her. With the snow falling outside, there was a hushed kind of reverence in his actions, the quality of an ancient ceremony. She really didn't want to ruin that. "I promise to help you find the artifact and put it somewhere safe so that no one else can get hurt."

She saw disappointment flash across Neal's face a second before the band around her neck shrank until it fit close to her skin. Her vision wavered until the confines of the truck disappeared and she was suddenly somewhere else. Overlooking a valley. It was dark—the kind of dark one found only well outside the light pollution of cities. There was an old log home nestled below. It was a tiny, one-room structure with smoke billowing up from its chimney. There were no security lights, no propane tanks, no vehicles. It appeared to be a scene from sometime long ago, though she couldn't imagine how that was possible.

A few yards away, a small barn sat huddled against the roaring wind. The prairie grass was brown, the trees bare. She could smell spring on the wind, but it had yet to take hold of the land.

A man on horseback was on the opposite hillside, outlined against the starry night sky. The sword in his hand reflected moonlight as he sat there, still and silent. The horse beneath him quivered, as if sensing danger. She had no idea what he was doing out here in the cold when there was a safe, comfy cabin not far away.

She opened her mouth to shout at him to get inside, but nothing came out. Wherever she was, she had no body. She was simply a presence hovering in the night sky.

The man turned his head and the moonlight fell over his features.

Neal. The man standing in what looked like a scene from the long-dead past was the same man sitting next to her in the truck.

Viviana struggled to make sense of that, but like a dream, there was no logic to be found.

From the hilltop to her right, she saw several low shapes slink forward. An eerie howl split the air, making the wind seem quiet in comparison. The horse stomped nervously for a moment before Neal spurred it forward.

The shapes rose up, solidifying into the form of those things that had attacked her earlier tonight. Neal charged them. The first sgath leaped into the air, lunging for Neal's throat. Instead, it was his blade that hit, and the monster flew past him in two spinning pieces.

Two more of the sgath attacked, and Neal cut down each one with the same competent efficiency. Never once did he do anything showy. Every movement was smooth and easy, with no wasted effort. The lethality of his grace stunned Viviana even after she'd seen it before.

Neal wiped his blade clean on the dead grass, remounted his horse, and rode away.

Below in the valley, the door to the cabin opened. An old, bent woman stood there for a moment, staring in confusion into the darkness. She never saw Neal or the threat he'd eliminated.

Viviana's vision wavered again, as another battle was shown to her. Then another, and another. In each one, she saw signs of different eras, different times and places—none of which Neal was old enough to have lived in, and yet there he was. He fought off dark, terrifying monsters for people who didn't even realize he existed. He never once asked for thanks or praise for his deeds; he simply left when the job was done.

When the interior of the truck finally came back into

focus, Viviana was exhausted. She felt like she'd been gone for years and was just now coming back home.

Neal was staring at her with the oddest look on his face. It was part sympathy and part pride, and she wondered if he was upset by what she'd seen.

"What was that?" she asked.

"The luceria shows us pieces of each other—things it thinks we need to know to help us grow closer and speed up the bonding process."

"What bonding process? You never said anything about that."

"It's how we connect. It's how you reach my power. The luceria makes that connection possible, but the amount of power that can flow between us is directly related to how much we trust each other."

"And those visions of you fighting monsters were supposed to make me trust you?"

"Did it work?"

In an odd way, it did, but no more so than seeing him fight for her life earlier tonight. It was something else that pulled her in—the part where he seemed to have visited other times. "I thought I saw you a long, long time ago."

"You did."

"How? Does your magic allow you to travel through time?"

"No. I've lived a long time." He smiled, and it made her insides quiver in response. "Just like those artifacts you like to collect."

"How long?"

"I've lost count. Four hundred fifty-something years now, I guess."

"You guess?"

He shrugged, drawing her attention to his bare shoulder. Even that small movement caused delicious muscles to ripple beneath his skin. "It stops mattering after a while, though I may start counting again if things with us go the way I hope."

"What do you mean?"

"I mean you don't have to be alone anymore. You don't have to feel like you don't fit in. You're one of us now."

Viviana's insides iced over with worry. "What did you see?"

"You. Alone. All your life. You've always set yourself apart from other people because you knew you weren't like them."

Humiliation stiffened her spine. "You had no right prying into my past like that."

"Sorry, sweetheart. That's the way it works. You got to do the same with me."

"I don't like it."

He took her hand and flattened it against his bare chest. His skin was hot and tight over hard muscles. Streaming sparks flowed into her, making her dizzy.

"You like that," he said with complete confidence. "And I like not hurting anymore. Thank you."

"Don't get used to it. If this luceria lets you pry into my private life, it's coming off."

"Not until we find the gadget. You promised. Besides, by then I hope to change your mind."

"About what?"

"Taking it off." He leaned forward, a hot smile on his lips. "If I have my way, you'll never take it off again."

Shock rattled through her and she sat silent for a moment, trying to make sense of his words. "I don't understand."

"I know. That's my fault, but I'll spell it out for you.

You saved my life by putting on my luceria. Before I met you, I was dying. The power inside me was killing me slowly. And now I'm fine. I've also seen inside you. I've seen how gentle and caring you are, how driven you can be. You are everything I've ever hoped for in a partner, and if I get half a chance, I'm not going to let you go. Ever."

"You need to stop right there. I don't even know you and you're talking about us being together?"

"In ways you have probably never imagined."

Her face heated, as did the rest of her. "I only said I'd help you find the artifact."

"I know. I'm counting on my powers of persuasion to change your mind."

She opened her mouth to ask him what kind of powers when a wave of something hot and delicious slid into her skin, emanating from the luceria. It floated down her body, making her grow languid and needy as it passed.

Neal speared his fingers through her hair and lowered his mouth to hers. He didn't touch her, but he was close enough that she could feel energy sparking between them.

"I'm playing dirty," he told her, "but I need you too much to let it stop me. We're meant to be together. The luceria knows it. I know it. So will you."

He kissed her then, and she didn't even think to try to stop him. His mouth felt too good on hers. Too right. Her whole body quivered in excitement at his touch, and wherever his bare skin touched hers, heady streams of power raced into her, making her feel more whole and alive than she ever had before.

In this moment, she was swept away, ready and eager to go along with whatever insane plan he had. Let him think they were destined to be together. What did she care? As long as he kept kissing her, he could be as crazy as he liked.

A deep howl cut through the cold December air.

Neal stiffened and pulled back with a caustic curse. "Fuck. My blood. They can smell it."

He moved to his side of the truck, leaving Viviana feeling cold and alone. She didn't like it. She wanted back that feeling he gave her—that sense of belonging, of being needed. It took every ounce of her willpower to stay put rather than slide over the seat so she could cling to him.

She was not a needy woman. She did not cling.

He slammed the truck in gear and pulled back out onto the snowy road. "I'm sorry, sweetheart. You're so damn sexy, you go to my head. I should have known better than to stay put after cutting myself."

Viviana cleared her throat and fastened her seat belt to give her head time to clear. "I'm not sexy. I never have been. I'm tidy. Neat."

He shot her a grin full of heated promise. "You won't be when I get done with you."

"I am not going to have sex with you."

"No?" He didn't sound convinced. Or concerned.

"No. I don't know you."

"You will. Count on it."

Chapter Six

Neal told himself to back down. He was coming on way too strong. The connection the luceria had forged between them had already grown enough for him to sense Viviana's anxiety.

"You're quite full of yourself, aren't you?" she asked.

He bit his tongue to hold back a comment about how he'd rather *she* be the one full of him. That was way too crass for his sweet Viviana.

His.

Neal was already in trouble, already feeling way too possessive. She wasn't ready for that. Hell, for all he knew she never would be. He needed to calm the hell down before he screwed up his one chance to keep breathing.

"I didn't mean to offend you. I'm sorry." He guessed he was going to have to get used to saying those last two words a lot—assuming she stuck with him long enough to let it happen.

"Where are we going?"

"A safe house. I need to clean up." He looked down at his chest. The wound had already healed, but the blood was still there, drawing every Synestryn for miles, no doubt.

"You said they can smell your blood."

"Yep. I need to wash it off ASAP."

There was a nervous lilt to her voice. "What about my blood? Can they smell that, too?"

"Absolutely."

"I cut myself earlier tonight. On the glass. That's why they came, isn't it?"

The thought of her being hurt made his stomach twist in a combination of anger and pain. "Let me see."

She ripped off a small bandage and held up her hand. A short, shallow cut crossed her palm—little more than a paper cut.

"Did it bleed?"

"A little."

"Toss the bandage out the window."

She did, letting in a cold gust of wind. Without his shirt on, he felt every degree in the drop of temperature.

"Will that work?" she asked.

"Not with me in the car, but I don't want you walking around with blood on you."

The next thing he knew, she was kneeling on the seat beside him, using one of those white cotton gloves to wipe away the blood on his chest.

"You're already healed."

"I heal fast. It's necessary for the job."

She made quick work of cleaning him up, her movements efficient and matter-of-fact. "Job?"

"Killing Synestryn. Protecting humans."

She brought the glove to her mouth and wet a spot to scrub away the dried blood. Then, as if she realized what she'd done, she stammered, "I-I'm sorry. I should never have put my saliva on you without permission."

Neal stifled a laugh. She was so prim and proper. "Honey, the way we kissed, I'd say it's a bit late to worry about that. Hell, I've fantasized about things involving your mouth that would make you blush."

And just like that, she did, and quickly changed the subject. "You called those things that attacked tonight sgath."

"Sgath are one type of Synestryn. There are lots. All butt-ugly. All deadly."

She finished the job, went back to her side of the truck, and the cotton glove went out the window. "And you fight them."

"Nearly every night."

"What would I do? I mean, someone who planned to continue her association with you?"

That made Neal grin. "Association? Sounds like our names should be on a business card together. You think that's what we have going here?"

"I don't know what to call it, and you shouldn't make fun. I've been through quite a bit of stress tonight."

"I'm sorry, sweetheart. You sure have. I should be more understanding."

Silence greeted him and he left her alone. She did have a lot to digest. It was barely past midnight. He'd met her eight hours ago and in that time, she'd been attacked, lost a friend, and joined herself to Neal in a way she couldn't possibly understand.

But he did. He knew what her commitment meant to him and what it would mean if she decided to walk away. Still, even the fear of dying couldn't stop him from celebrating what he had now.

He was fulfilling his purpose in life. He was united with a woman who could wield his power—one he was sworn to protect so she could blow away the demons that plagued Earth. Together they would be unstoppable. And not just on the battlefield.

The brief glimpse he'd had of her life still haunted

him. Even though her adoptive mother had loved and cherished Viviana, she'd still felt alone. It was as if she knew she was part of something bigger than herself. She'd tried to fit in as a child, and as an adult, she'd found people who accepted her for her quirks. But it had never been enough.

Neal didn't just accept her; he reveled in her. Everything about her was fascinating—from the prim bun she wore down to those naughty stockings under her skirt. Her love for ancient Sentinel artifacts only added to her appeal.

He wanted to be part of her collection. A permanent part.

As much as he hated feeling needy and demanding, there was nothing he could do to stop himself. Without her, he would die. No matter what it took, he was going to spend what little time they had before they found the gadget convincing her that he was the kind of man worth keeping.

She was quiet as they drove. Every few minutes, he could feel a subtle tug on his power, as if she were testing the waters. Knowing that if he said anything, it would only discourage her, he kept quiet, pretending he didn't know what she was doing.

Slowly, her attempts became bolder. More power flowed between them, easing the crushing pressure inside Neal. He couldn't remember the last time he'd felt so good.

Despite how much he needed her, despite how much he wanted her, the need to protect her tender feelings rose above all else. He promised himself he wouldn't push her for more. At least, not yet. Let her discover her newfound power on her own so she wouldn't balk at accepting it.

Two hours later, Neal was regretting his decision to let her find her own way. He kept getting glimpses of her—little fleeting images of things she felt and wanted.

He was at the top of the list. As proper as his Viviana seemed, she was all hot, passionate woman beneath that prim exterior. She kept having fantasies of her hands on his bare skin, stroking his lifemark. Every few minutes she'd glance his way and get caught up staring.

Apparently, she liked the way he looked, which worked for him. He'd never really paid much attention to the texture of his skin or the play of shadow over his muscles, but she did. And seeing that through her eyes— the way it turned her on—was making it hard for him to keep his hands on the wheel.

All he could think about was how good it felt to slide his hands up her thighs until the smooth skin above those stockings greeted him.

By the time they pulled into the driveway of the Ge-rai house, Neal was shaking with lust. He was careful to keep it from her—block her from sensing his thoughts— though he knew that worked against his need to bind them together. She wasn't ready for his desire yet. She was still dealing with too much. It would be unfair of him to ask her for more when she'd already given him more than he'd ever hoped to have.

Neal pulled his shirt back on before braving the cold. He found a key tucked behind the porch light and let them into the small farmhouse.

The air inside was chilly, but all the makings for a fire were laid and ready to go. Neal made quick work of getting a nice blaze going before raiding the fridge for food.

"Is this your house?" Viviana asked when he returned with some sandwich fixings.

She was curled up on a corner of the couch nearest the fire. She still wore his leather jacket, which made her look small and vulnerable.

Protective instincts rose up in Neal, and he had to

fight the urge to reach for his sword and bare his teeth against an invisible threat.

"No. It's called a Gerai house, named for the group of humans who keep it stocked with food and supplies."

"Gerai?"

"They're blooded humans—humans who have ancient blood running through their veins. Synestryn will attack them for their blood, so we protect them. In exchange, they help out where they can, like giving us a safe place to rest when we need it."

"So the Synestryn can't get to us here?"

"Oh, no. They can get to us, but it's harder to find us here than in other places, since Gilda has woven some magic that helps shield us here."

"Gilda? Who's she?"

"A powerful Theronai. She and her husband, Angus, have been together for centuries. She's the one who told me about the gadget. She has amazing power."

"And she uses it to protect these Gerai houses?"

"Among other things. But yes, I can sense her touch on this place. Unless we do something to attract attention, we should be safe here."

"That sounds nice."

Neal heard fear wavering in her voice. "I don't want you to be afraid, sweetheart. You're safe with me. I'd give my life to make sure of it."

"I'd rather you didn't. I don't want anyone else to die because of me."

He set the food on the coffee table and sat next to her, taking her hand in his. Her skin was smooth and flawless, unlike his own scarred hands. Her bones were delicate, her limbs breakable. He had no idea how he was going to keep her safe long enough for her to learn to wield his power, but he knew he'd do whatever it took to make that happen.

Neal made sure she was looking in his eyes. He couldn't stand knowing she was being eaten up by guilt. "The professor didn't die because of you. You have to believe that."

"Would those things have come for him if I hadn't given him the artifact?"

"How many people have you allowed to study your collection?"

"Several."

"Were they attacked?"

"No."

"Then there was no way for you to know what would happen. You can't blame yourself for the evil of another. All you can do is use the power you now have to stop them from doing it again."

"Is that what you do?"

He shook his head. "I can't do a lot with magic. I can use a little bit, but nothing compared to you. The best I can do is cut them down."

"You're good at that."

"Nice of you to notice."

She was silent for a long moment. "What's it like living in your world?"

"Normal. It's all I've ever known."

"Killing monsters and fighting demons is normal? I don't think I could ever get used to that."

"There's more to being a Theronai than killing. We have a home where we take care of humans—orphaned children, mostly. We're helping rebuild a stronghold in Africa that was destroyed. And we stand guard over the Gate."

"Gate?"

"To Athanasia, the place where our magic originated. Chances are good your father was from there."

"Where is it?"

Neal shrugged. "Another planet, I guess. I never really worried much about the details. I fought when I needed to, protected when I needed to, and in the meantime, I spent every second looking for you."

She scoffed at that. "That's hard to believe."

"It's true. I mean, I didn't know your name, but I hoped you were out there. And here you are. My own personal miracle."

"You make it sound so easy—like you already know how things will end."

"I've had over four hundred years of watching unions between our people. They're not all easy, but the luceria picked you to be with me for a reason. I know enough to trust that and let the rest work itself out."

She looked away, clearly uncomfortable with the conversation. Neal let it drop, refusing to cause her any more upset tonight. There would be time for her to come around. He could be patient.

"Would you like to try to find the gadget?" he asked.

"I think I can feel it. It's faint, but if I concentrate, I might be able to get a stronger impression of its location."

"You do that. The sooner we find it, the sooner I can take you home."

Neal hadn't come on to her. They were alone together in that cozy house, in front of a roaring fire while the wind blew snow all around them, insulating them from the real world. It was the perfect setup for romance and yet Neal hadn't taken advantage of that.

Part of her was disappointed. Her body was humming with a frenetic energy—an achy need to run her hands over him and let him do the same to her. The saner part of her was relieved. Too much had happened tonight and she was having trouble digesting it all.

Neal was a member of an ancient race. So was she. From what he said, they were destined to be partners in a war against evil monsters—ones she didn't even know existed outside of her dusty books.

And yet, as hard as all that was to believe, what she really had trouble believing was the part where he needed her. He was a big, strong, strapping warrior. He didn't appear to need anyone. If she hadn't felt that need through the luceria, she still wouldn't believe it.

He wanted her, and not just for the night. The impressions she got through their swiftly growing connection were ones of permanence. Forever. He wasn't afraid of commitment, like most men she knew. He craved it.

Not that she knew him well enough to agree to that kind of relationship. For now, she was content to stay with him, see how things went. He might not appreciate her caution, but that was too bad. Caution was all he was going to get.

For now.

The thought whispered in her head, summoning images of the two of them together, making love. She could almost feel the power of his big body moving over hers, driving them both higher. He'd be a demanding lover. She could tell that by his personality. But it was his grace that made her toes curl in longing. A man with that smooth kind of power would drive her crazy. Neal would take her to places she'd never been with a man before, and deep down, she wanted that more than she'd ever wanted any ancient trinket.

Neal came back out of the kitchen. He stopped dead in his tracks, staring at her. His jaw was tight and she could see tension straining his body. He pulled in a couple of deep breaths before he managed to speak.

"I heard that," he whispered.

"What?"

"Your thoughts. The things you'd like me to do to you."

She'd been getting brief flashes from his thoughts since putting on the luceria, but had brushed it off as her imagination. The things she'd felt coming from him couldn't be real. No man had ever wanted her like Neal did.

The proof of that want was straining the front of his worn jeans, making her mouth water.

He took a measured step forward. Viviana didn't move. She didn't want to encourage him to do something he wasn't ready for, and yet the thought of him backing away left a deep ache in her chest.

"I'm more than ready," he told her. "You're the one with questions about the two of us. Not me. I already know how I want it to end."

"How?" she asked before she could stop herself.

"I want us to love each other. To be happy together. To stand side by side and fight the Synestryn. Forever."

"Forever is a long time."

"Only when you're alone and unhappy."

Like she had been her whole life. Mother had always loved her, but Viviana had never truly fit in elsewhere. She wasn't an outcast, but she often thought that was due to her wealth. People would do a lot to overlook the flaws in others when there was money involved.

She didn't want to be included for her money or her status. She wanted to be wanted for herself.

Neal was offering that to her, and doing so as if he had no idea how precious the gift was.

He held out his hand. The iridescent ring shimmered as it grew closer to her, swirling with the colors of parchment and ancient bronze. "I understand that this is all fast for you, but for me, it's something I've been thinking about for centuries. We can be good together. All you have to do is trust me."

Viviana swallowed. So much had happened tonight. Too much. And yet there wasn't a place on earth she'd rather be than right here. With him.

He called to her on some deep level she'd never even known existed. It was as if she were recognizing a long-lost part of herself.

Whatever this thing was between them, it had a magic all its own, and that alone was too alluring for Viviana to resist.

She put her hand in his and a slow, hot smile curved his mouth a second before he kissed her.

Heat bloomed inside her at his touch, swelling until she was consumed by it. His hands slid over her back, pulling her close enough to feel the hard length of his erection. That empty ache inside her clamored to be filled, and Viviana was no longer willing to ignore it.

"I want you," she told him.

A rough groan vibrated his chest. "I want you, too, but we can't. I have to be careful. If we get too close . . ." He didn't finish what he was saying, but his body shook with tension.

Viviana couldn't resist trying to comfort him. She stroked his arms and petted his chest, feeling his muscles tighten beneath her palms.

He closed his eyes as if seeking self-control and his fingers clenched against her hips. She laid her head on his shoulder, and she swore she could hear the creak of swaying branches beneath his shirt. The scent of his skin was intoxicating, and despite his hesitance, she couldn't find the strength to back away.

Heated images flittered through her mind, and the rougher edges told her they were coming from Neal. She was naked, laid out for his visual enjoyment. Her hair was loose, shimmering around her head. Her nipples were tight, and her skin seemed to glow. His dark hand was splayed against her chest, and the matching parts of the luceria throbbed in time with each other.

The image shifted. A red wash covered them, and Neal's body was gleaming with sweat as he moved over her, his muscles bunching powerfully with each gliding move. It wasn't real. It was only a vision in her head, but the effect it had on her was much more than mere imagination.

She was hot, aching. Her clothes were suddenly too tight and itchy. She needed to peel them away and rub herself against Neal, feeling his firm, smooth skin against her own. Maybe if she got him naked, he'd give in and make love to her.

She desperately needed that, needed the release only he could give.

Neal let out the groan of a man who knew he'd been bested. "I can't deny you anything, sweetheart. I'll make you come, but we're going to do it my way."

Chapter Seven

Neal was playing a dangerous game here. Already they were bonding faster than he thought possible. Once the swirling colors in the luceria settled, his life was in her hands. For now, once her promise to him was fulfilled, they could go their separate ways, but if the colors solidified and their connection was complete, then if she left him, he'd die.

He had to be careful, slow down the bonding process as much as possible. As much as he loved the idea of the two of them together, he didn't want to tie her to him with guilt. He refused to allow her to stay with him because he was dead without her. That wasn't fair to either of them.

So he'd find the strength to resist taking her and thereby speeding up the process. He'd give her what she so clearly needed—he refused to let her suffer—but he'd do it with his jeans firmly in place.

She kissed her way up his throat and over his jaw. Her strong grip on his head forced him to bend down so she could kiss him properly. Her soft mouth opened over his, and her hot tongue slid inside, claiming the space for her own.

Neal stifled a groan and went to work like a man on a

mission. The sooner he got her off, the better. He didn't know how long he could resist taking what she so clearly wanted to give.

He wasted no time undoing all the fussy little buttons down the front of her blouse. White lace cupped her breasts, but did nothing to hide her stiff nipples. He bent his head and suckled her through the delicate fabric while he made quick work of the hooks on her bra.

Her soft sound of pleasure filled the air, and her fingers speared through his hair, holding him in place.

Her skirt took only seconds to undo and it slithered down her thighs. Her soft lace panties followed in her skirt's wake, leaving her wearing only her stockings. Those were definitely staying on.

He pulled the bra from her arms and fought her grip long enough to pull back and get a good look.

Viviana was breathtaking. Sweet, slender curves. Gentle shadows cast by the firelight. Delicate bones, womanly hollows. Every inch of her was perfect.

He'd never wanted anything in his life as much as he wanted her right now.

His blood was pounding through his body, demanding that he stake a claim. He could smell her arousal, see the flush of lust darkening her skin. She wanted it as much as he did.

He stared for so long, he began to feel her pull away, her heat evaporating into an awkward kind of shyness.

She covered her breasts with one arm, her mound with her hand. Hiding herself from him.

A primal anger rose up in him so strong and fast he couldn't control it. He took an aggressive step forward, pushing her back against the couch. She stumbled, flailing her arms to catch her balance.

Neal grabbed her arms, easing her down. He held

them away from her body, letting the satisfaction of seeing her again quiet that primal beast. "Don't hide from me," he managed to grate out. "Not ever."

He stripped off his shirt, and then pressed her back against the seat, feeling the velvet rub of her sweet little nipples on his skin.

Viviana let out a soft gasp and dug her nails into his back.

Heat and need flared inside him, blinding him for a moment. But he was touching her skin, and that was enough for now. He'd look at her again when he had her spread out so he could feast on her and make her come with his mouth. He'd take his time looking, enjoying the way perspiration beaded on her skin, and the way she writhed as he held her hips in place.

His lifemark swayed, reveling in the contact of flesh on flesh. His ring hummed happily, urging him to finish what he'd started.

Neal reached between them, parting her damp curls. She was slick and hot, and just the slightest brush of his fingertip over her clit made her lurch beneath him and let out a sharp cry.

He pressed a finger inside her slick body. The tight clench of her muscles around him made him grit his teeth for control. She quivered, pivoting her hips to give him a better angle. She was small, but he could handle that. He'd stretch her gently so when he took her she'd feel only pleasure.

Except that he wasn't going to take her. He was just here to get her off. That was the deal he'd made with himself.

Even as he cursed his decision, he manned up and stood by it, turning his force of will on her body and on how to make it sing.

Viviana wasn't a shy lover. She told him with sounds and small, quivering movements what kinds of touches she liked, and which ones drove her wild. His prim, proper scholar was spread out before him, panting and shaking while he sucked on her clit and pressed two thick fingers inside her. He toyed with her nipples, pinching gently and not so gently in time with his penetrating fingers.

Her breathing caught. Her abdomen quivered. Neal added a third finger and used his teeth to send her over the edge.

She let out a sweet moan and bucked beneath him as her orgasm overcame her.

Neal had never witnessed anything so beautiful in his long, long life.

As her tremors subsided, she pulled him up her body with weak arms and kissed him. She was still shaking, or maybe that was him. He couldn't tell anymore. All he knew was that he was teetering on the edge of driving his cock into her slick, relaxed body deeper than his fingers had a chance of going.

Her hands fumbled at his belt, working it free faster than his blood-starved brain had time to figure out what she was doing. Her slender fingers worked inside his jeans, wrapping around his cock.

Even that was nearly enough to make him come. Only the worry that she'd feel used kept him from letting go and spurting his seed all over her fingers.

He tried to pull away, but he couldn't go far without fear of breaking her arm. "Stop."

She nibbled at his neck, right where the luceria used to lie. His skin was sensitive there, having been starved of touch since his birth. The erotic scrape of her teeth sent zings of sensation down his spine, straight into his balls.

He gasped and gulped for air, trying to gain some thread of control.

By the time he realized what she'd done, his pants were already open and she was pulling his cock toward her core. Her legs were spread wide in welcome, and her wet heat slid against the head of his cock, mixing with his own fluids.

A rough groan shook him. He couldn't pull away. The best he could do was hold still and pray for control.

Viviana grabbed his ass and pulled him forward while she lifted her hips, taking just the tip of his erection within her body.

Glorious tight heat surrounded him, driving away all thoughts but one. He was going to finish what she'd started. And then some.

He drove forward in one smooth stroke, forcing her to take all of him. She pulled in a startled breath and her fingernails bit deep. It only made him want more.

He knew he wouldn't last long. He could feel her trying to reassure him through their link that it was okay, but he ignored it. He didn't want the shallow fulfillment of shooting his load without her. When he came, she was going to be screaming his name in climax while he filled her. That was the only thing that would satisfy this primal need.

Neal took advantage of their connection, opening himself up for her to feel everything he did. He knew what he did was dangerous—that he could be speeding his own demise—but he couldn't help it. He craved that connection, needed it like he needed to breathe.

He let her see herself as he did: beautiful and sexy as hell. He let her feel his consuming need to make her come. He forced her to feel the lust clawing inside him, demanding that he stake a claim on her in every way possible.

Her eyes grew wide and her pupils expanded as she looked at him. Her lips were parted, sucking in great gasps of air as he worked them both toward a fast, hard climax.

It swept over Neal, surprising him in its intensity. In the vague recesses of his mind, he realized he was feeling her come as well, the two orgasms mingling together into one. Sensation sizzled through their connection as his balls drew up close and his seed pumped deep within her trembling body.

She shook beneath him, her slender frame so delicate and fragile under his weight. He didn't want to crush her, but he felt her need for him to stay connected to her.

He was still hard. He could stay inside her as long as she wanted. Whatever she needed, he'd find a way to make it hers. For as long as he lived.

Their connection had definitely deepened because of his lack of control. Not that he could bring himself to regret it. He could never regret being with her like this.

He rolled so she was lying atop him, straddling his hips. She nestled her head against his chest while their breathing slowed and the air cooled their bodies. Her fingers traced the branches of his lifemark.

"The leaves are growing back," she said. "There are little buds now."

Bittersweet happiness filled him. She'd saved him, but for how long?

She pushed up, frowning down at him. "Something's wrong. What is it?"

Her hair was a wreck, her bun askew, and fuzzy strands were sticking out at random angles. It was so cute it made his chest ache when he thought that he wouldn't get to see her look like this again—that this thing they had might be temporary.

Neal forced himself to smile as he felt for the pins holding up her bun. "It's nothing serious. We can worry about it after you find the gadget."

Her hair fell loose over her shoulders, shining and beautiful. His cock pulsed inside her, making her eyes flutter shut.

She gave a soft, sexy moan. "I'm not sure if I can go another round."

"I'm more than happy to find out," he said.

"Don't we need to get moving?"

Neal nodded, hating the truth. "Yeah. We do."

"I can feel it now," she said, grinning with pride. "The artifact. My ability seems to be stronger somehow."

"We're more tightly linked now." Thanks to his lack of control. "You have greater access to my power."

"Does that mean that if we don't find it, we can do that again?"

If they didn't find the gadget, she'd remain linked to him, which would almost certainly result in more fabulous sex. "It does."

"And if I do find it?"

She'd be free of the luceria, free of him, able to do as she chose. Whether or not she slept with him again would depend heavily on whether or not he lived to see it happen. "Guess we'll have to play that one by ear."

Chapter Eight

"There," said Viviana, pointing at a truck-size entrance in the limestone rock face. "The disk is in there."

They were outside an industrial complex built inside a system of caves at the edge of Kansas City.

"Are you sure?" asked Neal as he drove into the main entrance.

Inside, truck-size, man-made tunnels looped around a series of businesses—everything from a granite counter-top manufacturer to a wholesale craft-supply company. The rock walls had been painted white, but were dingy from dust and car exhaust.

"I'm sure," she said. "A few yards that way." She pointed to the right. The new leather of the jacket he'd found for her at the Gerai house gleamed in the dim light. Like his own jacket, the one she wore had been imbued with protective magic. Even so, it still wasn't enough protection to make him feel good about her walking into danger.

Neal turned right and pulled into a parking spot indicated by chipped paint. He killed the engine and shifted to face her.

Dim light poured across her cheek, accenting her regal beauty. She was too delicate for what he was asking of her. Too inexperienced. "Maybe you should stay here. You don't need to come with me."

"How will you find the artifact if I don't?"

"I'll manage." Or he'd fail to find it and she'd be tied to him much longer. He didn't really want her to stay with him because of a technicality, but he didn't want to lose her, either. They hadn't been together long enough for him to prove to her that he was a good man, that he'd always take care of her. That he'd always love her.

And he did love her. He loved everything about her. He'd seen pieces of her mind, felt the warmth of her heart. She was brave and selfless and willing to walk into the jaws of danger for him. How could he not love her?

The amazing part was knowing that if they survived, that love would only grow over time. Such a thought was humbling.

Neal cupped her cheek, loving the smooth warmth of her skin. "You'll be safer here."

"I know what I'm supposed to become—that I'm to use your power to slay the monsters. I never thought you'd be the kind of man to hold me back."

"I'm not. I trust that you'll learn to wield my power; I'm just nervous about your doing so outside of a training environment."

She covered his hand, leaning into his touch. "If I go, we'll find it faster and you can get out faster. If I don't go, I'll be sitting here making myself sick with worry over you and fear that something nasty will slink out of a shadow. I need to do this."

Neal nodded, his respect for her growing. "I understand. I've always felt the calling, too. You're one of us, sweetheart."

He leaned forward and kissed her, savoring the softness of her lips and the sweet taste of her mouth. He could live forever and never get enough of her.

He prayed she'd give him the chance.

Neal pulled back. "We need to go."

"Lead on."

They got out of the truck and headed for an opening that had been cut from the limestone and braced by steel beams. The overhead door had been removed, and based on the way the track was bent beyond use, Neal guessed the door had been ripped away violently. The entrance was blocked by a chain that was draped with a For Lease sign.

Cool air moved over his skin, thanks to the mechanical ventilation system down here.

Behind him were businesses and shops built into the stone. They were all closed at this hour, their parking lots empty and interiors dark. He doubted any of the employees knew they were nestled in among demons.

If he had anything to say about it, he'd take care of their infestation and leave them none the wiser.

He glanced at Viviana. "Stay close. On my left."

"Got it. I do not want to be anywhere near that sword when you start swinging it."

"If things get hairy, you run. Keys are in the truck."

He could see her trembling, but she gave a brave nod. "It won't come to that."

Not while he drew breath, it wouldn't. He didn't think she'd be comforted by that fact, so he kept his mouth shut.

"I heard that thought. You're not going to die. I won't allow it."

He couldn't help but smile. She was cute when she gave orders. "Yes, ma'am."

They passed through the entrance, and the smell of

wet animal assaulted his nose. It was dark, so he chan-
neled a few sparks of energy to his eyes, using their link
to show Viviana how to do the same.

She pulled in a startled breath. "Amazing."

The floor had once been smooth, but was now
cracked and pitted. Abandoned metal racks meant to
hold pallet loads of goods leaned precariously against
one wall. Crooked light fixtures sagged from electrical
conduits along the ceiling. A rusted forklift covered in
dust and cobwebs sat to their left, tossed on its side, and
the remains of a small office stood behind a cracked
glass window.

Whatever had happened here had been unexpected
and brutal.

There were two tall doorways leading deeper into the
network of caves. "Which one do we take?" asked Neal.

"Right."

Neal headed toward it, listening for sounds of movement. His sword was in one hand, ready to strike at anything that got near her.

"It's close," she said.

A second later, she opened herself up to their connection, and Neal felt what she did. A resonant hum
came from beyond the doorway, almost tangible in its
intensity. He could practically see the sound waves emanating out from the disk, reverberating with the magic
the object housed.

He opened his mouth to tell her how amazing that
was when he heard a scuffling noise to their right, inside
the room where the gadget was.

Viviana gasped in fear. Neal gripped his sword in
both hands and stepped between the noise and her.
"Easy," he whispered. "I've got you covered."

Some of the terror streaking through their link

abated and he heard her let out a controlled breath. Power flowed out of him, and though he had no idea what she was doing with it, the feeling gave him a sense of pride. Of rightness.

"That's it, sweetheart. Just like that."

A second later, a flurry of motion exploded from the room as four sgath charged.

Power filled Viviana. It flowed through her veins and seeped between her cells until she was vibrating with it. She sucked it into herself, reveling in the ease with which it poured from Neal into her.

Pressure built within her until she felt like her ribs would burst under the strain. She had to let it out—get rid of the energy before it killed her.

Neal had told her she could wield magic, but he had no idea where her abilities might lie, other than her obvious talent for finding Sentinel artifacts. Unfortunately, neither did she, and it was swiftly becoming too late for thought.

A few feet away, Neal fought the monsters that had charged them. She could sense his need to keep them all occupied and away from her, but there were four of them and only one of him.

In a blur of smooth motion, he lopped the forepaw from one of the beasts as it attacked. Its blood spattered across Neal's arm, singeing his leather jacket. The thing howled in pain and fell back, lapping at its wound.

Two more surged forward to take its place, but one ignored Neal and looked right at her. Its Mr. Yuck green eyes flared with a hungry light and it sprang forward, jaws open.

A vibrant pulse pounded against the inside of her

skull, nearly blinding her. Viviana gathered a ball of power and flung it out at the sgath.

Its body spun in midair, and it let out a pained snarl. It landed hard, skidding over the cracked floor before its sharp claws slowed it to a stop.

It turned, hackles raised, hissing as it slunk toward her.

She hadn't hurt it. All she'd done was knock it around.

Viviana realized then that she was no match for these things. She wasn't a fighter. She was a bookworm. An intellectual. She had no business wading into battle where brawn and blades were the only things that mattered.

Neal roared and spun in a deadly arc. The head of one of the sgath flew up into the air while its body continued to claw at him for another few seconds.

"Pull it together!" he shouted. "You can do this."

She wasn't convinced, but if she didn't do something, they were both dead.

That was the thought that brought a sense of calm down over her. She would not let Neal die, not when she had the power to stop it at her fingertips.

What she needed was a way to cage the beasts long enough for Neal to kill them—a way to protect him from their attack.

Viviana looked around for something she could use. Steel bars would have been nice, but all she saw was a broken pallet stacked with rotted-out sandbags. If she used her power to shove the pallet against one of the things and pin it to a wall, that might work.

The sgath stalking her circled to her left. Neal was too busy fighting off the others to stop it.

She formed a picture in her mind of what she wanted to do and convinced herself she could make it happen.

One by one, the busted sandbags flew off the pallet, freeing it. Elation filled her as she pulled on more of Neal's power, working faster as the sgath closed the distance.

The last bag split open, spilling sand between the wooden slats. She lifted the pallet into the air, seeing a faint wavering of energy connecting her to it as it moved. She shoved on it hard, sucking in as much energy as her straining body would allow, and hurled it at the beast.

It hit the sgath, slamming it back against the rock wall. The thing snarled and clawed at the wood. Its jaws snapped, sending wooden splinters into the air.

The pallet was swiftly crumbling to uselessness.

Panic sliced at her; then she felt a warm touch brush over her mind. Neal. Even during his own life-threatening battle, he was worried about her.

She could grow to love a man like that if they survived.

Viviana held the disintegrating pallet in place while she looked around for another option. The only thing she saw was dirt, sand, and flimsy metal shelving.

What she wouldn't give to have these sgath dead, stuffed, and behind glass in some museum.

Glass. That was it. She needed to put them behind thick, heavy glass.

As soon as the thought entered her mind, the power flowing through her leaped to obey. Heat shimmered from her, making the air waver. The plastic bags left in the pile of sand melted away, creating a chemical stench.

The sgath bashed through the remains of the pallet and lunged toward her, only to stop short as it neared the searing heat that was now making the sandpile glow a fiery orange.

Energy funneled through her so fast she could feel it

chafing her insides. Heat built inside her skin until each breath came out as a puff of steam.

"Too much!" she heard Neal shout somewhere outside her world of heat and pressure. She didn't respond. She couldn't stand to let her focus slip for even a second.

The sand softened, allowing her to shape it into a thick, viscous blob. She kept the heat coming while she sent thick tendrils of molten sand toward the two remaining sgath.

Neal jumped away from the searing heat. She hadn't realized where he'd gone until she felt his cool touch at her nape.

Something changed in that instant. She felt a click, as if a magnet had stuck against her necklace. A heartbeat later, the conduit she'd been using to pull Neal's power into herself opened wide, letting a roar of energy sweep into her.

It was too much. She didn't know how to control it.

She gritted her teeth and concentrated on finishing the job. If she was still alive when that was done, she'd find a way to stop the torrent of power from destroying her.

The molten sand flattened into a plane and shaped itself to cage each sgath inside. The smell of burning hair and the sound of feral screams bounced off the cave walls.

She couldn't breathe. Neither could Neal. Now that she'd taken care of the threat, she realized she'd created another. She'd burned off the oxygen in here.

Black spots flickered in her vision. Behind her, Neal gasped for air.

Viviana cut off the flow of heat, and used the energy seething inside her to push the hot air from the room.

A cold wind swept over them. She sucked it into her lungs as she collapsed to the ground.

Neal eased her down, going right along with her as they crumpled in a heap. His sword clattered against the pitted floor. His arms surrounded her, holding her close. He was saying something against her hair, but she couldn't get her mind to work enough to understand his words.

Across the room, the smoking skeletons of two sgath sat trapped behind grainy, tarry sheets of warped glass.

"Hell of a trick," said Neal. "How about we get the gadget and get you someplace safe?"

"Works for me." She reached out with only a faint wisp of power and saw the artifact glowing in her mind's eye on the floor across the room. It was still inside the carved box, unharmed.

She was too tired to get up, so she pulled it to her. It floated through the air toward them.

"I see you're not having any adjustment issues," said Neal. "You're using my power as if you'd been doing it all your life."

The box landed in her hand, warm to the touch. An instant later, her world went cold, as if all the joy had been sucked from it. Something smooth and warm slid down into her shirt. A high, pained noise of mourning erupted from her. A second later, thick, suffocating darkness fell over her.

Chapter Nine

Neal caught Viviana before her head could hit the floor.

Panic clawed at him, but he kept his cool because he knew it was the only thing that could help her now.

He had no idea what was wrong with her, but it had something to do with his luceria. They'd found the gadget, her promise was fulfilled, and the luceria came off. Just like it was supposed to.

Viviana, however, was not supposed to pass out.

Neal had no idea how many other nasties might be running around in here. He needed to get her out to safety. Or, even better, get her to one of the Sanguinar—their healers—so they could figure out what had gone wrong.

He fished the luceria out from her clothing and fastened it back around his neck for safekeeping. He hated wearing it again, hated thinking that his life would go back to being what it had been—filled with pain and impending death. A life without Viviana.

He had to convince her to give them more of a chance together. A few hours weren't enough for her to know what he did: that they belonged together. She hadn't been raised seeing the proof the way he had. There was no way for her to know except through faith.

He needed her to give him that faith, for just a while longer.

Neal carried her to the truck, lifting her inside. Her eyes fluttered open and her pupils were tiny dots of terrified black. "Give it back," she croaked out, her voice rough, as if she'd been screaming for hours.

He smoothed her mussed hair away from her face, hoping to comfort her. "What, sweetheart?"

Her eyes fixed on his throat and her chin began to quiver. "You can't take it away from me. It's mine. I need it." Her gaze moved up to his. "I need you."

Neal was too shocked to speak. He never imagined she'd want to stay with him, only hoped to hear those words.

Her voice was strained. "Please. I've been alone too long. I know where I belong now."

"Where's that?"

"With you. With your people. *My* people."

She reached up, her slim fingers curling around the luceria. It fell away from his throat and coiled around her hand as if trying to get closer.

Neal took it from her and fastened it around her throat. He didn't want to take the chance that she'd change her mind, so he sliced through his shirt, scoring a line over his heart. "My life for yours, Viviana," he vowed.

And then he held his breath. She had so much power over him. She didn't know all the details of their union, or how his life was in her hands. He didn't want guilt to factor into her promise, so he kept his mouth shut. He'd take what she wanted to give him and count himself lucky for whatever time with her he had.

"I'm staying with you, Neal. You're the only person in

the world whom I can be with and not feel alone. I'm not letting that go. I'm not letting you go. I think I love you."

Neal's heart nearly burst with joy. He never thought he'd get lucky enough to have someone like Viviana in his life, tied to him by both love and duty. She may not have known her own history, but they were going to make their future together.

As he watched, the luceria shrank to fit her slender neck, deepening to a rich bronze color that suited her skin perfectly. The Bronze Lady.

"I know I love you," he told her, and then he kissed her. It was sweet and full of hope and promise, just like the rest of their lives together would be.

CRYSTAL SKULL

JESSICA ANDERSEN

Chapter One

Deep in a rain forest south of the Mexican border

"For an archaeologist who's made the discovery of her career, you don't seem all that happy," Javier said from the far side of the underground cavern, where he was systematically photographing a panel of carved hieroglyphics. Wearing jeans, scarred boots, and a UFC T-shirt, the ex-wrestler handled the high-tech camera as expertly as he wielded their portable excavator and the double-barreled shotgun that was his constant companion out in the field.

Natalie grimaced. *Should've known he wasn't down here just to take pictures.* Her grizzled dig coordinator—and good friend—wasn't big on being belowground. The others must've deputized him.

Settling her headlamp more firmly over her dark ponytail, which was damp at the ends from the cool condensation that slicked everything inside the ancient temple, she focused on the painted clay pots she was supposed to be examining. "I'm just tired."

Which was true. The members of her six-person team had been pulling double shifts ever since she had discovered the cave two days earlier. They were racing to catalog the artifacts before things hit meltdown territory with the locals. Which was imminent.

She had all the necessary permits, but the residents of the nearby village had stopped caring about the paperwork the moment she had peeled back the overgrown vegetation to reveal a cave entrance carved with images of winged, humanoid creatures that matched the local legends of the bloodthirsty bat-demons known as *camazotz*.

Add to that the approaching equinox—which was supposedly when the creatures came up from the underworld and terrorized the villagers—and the fact that a local jaguar had recently developed a taste for livestock, and she had herself a village on edge. There was real potential for a pitchfork-wielding mob to descend on the dig at any moment. They probably would've been there already, if it hadn't been for her connection to American ex-pat and local hero JT Craig.

And how much did that reminder suck?

Javier snorted. "Girl, you showed up everyone who said you were crazy for turning down a season at Tikal and bushwhacking out into the middle of nowhere instead. But you did it. You found a new freaking ruin. Tired or not, stressed or not, you should be happy-dancing from here to base camp and back again. So what gives?"

She shrugged, the motion pulling where her lightweight camp shirt stuck to her skin. "There's no such thing as a 'new ruin.' It's an oxymoron."

"You're the moron if you think I'm letting you change the subject. So give. What's wrong?"

"I'm—" *Fine*, she started to say, then cut herself off because she knew that wouldn't fly with Javier, especially when she wasn't fine. She was restless and stirred up, itchy and twitchy. "I just keep thinking that I'm missing something, that I'm not where I'm supposed to be."

And wasn't that the story of her life?

"We've gotten this far following your instincts. I'm not stopping now."

Which was true. Others might think she was too brave for her own good, going off into a particularly volatile section of rain forest based on her gut feelings and the devil that kept pushing her to do more, *be* more, but Javier and their teammates followed her without complaint.

Still, though, his tone had her glancing over to where he was fiddling with the tripod-mounted camera and attached laptop. "Why do I get the feeling there's a 'but' coming?"

"But if you're feeling off, are you sure that it's about the dig and not about—"

"Don't say it," she interrupted, scowling back at her pots.

"Somebody has to."

"Or not. I've never let my personal life interfere with the work before, and I'm not going to start with JT. Weren't you the one who told me that I've got the dig-site-boyfriend thing down to an art?"

He hadn't meant it as a compliment, either. Ever since he'd married Nikki, the team's bubbly computer guru, he'd been busting on Natalie's long string of short-term, no-harm-no-foul relationships. He had seen her ten-week relationship with the gray-eyed ex–Army Ranger as a step in the right direction.

Or not.

"This time was different. You and JT were—" He broke off when someone shouted his name from topside, the word echoing along the stone tunnel that led down to the sacred chamber. "What?" he bellowed back, setting up a reverb that made Natalie wince.

"We could use you up here," Aaron called.

Natalie breathed a sigh of relief at the interruption. There was no point in talking about her and JT. What was done was done ... and they were way done.

Javier scowled. "Dang it. I just finished setting up this shot. Couldn't the crisis du jour have waited a few minutes?"

They both knew he could've shot five frames in the time it had taken him to set up this one. He'd been stalling so he could push her some more on why she'd ended things with JT. What he didn't know was that it had been the other way around.

Waving him off, she said, "Go ahead. I'll take care of the pictures."

"Come topside when you're done. You should eat something." The *and we're not done with this conversation* was implied.

Once he was gone, she tried to clear her mind and focus on the work at hand. She took the picture he had set up, then started to focus on the next set of glyphs while the attached laptop added the image to the composite they were assembling of the entire carved panel. But instead of framing the next shot, she found herself shifting aside the camera so she could get up close and personal with the hieroglyphs that made up the huge, intricate text.

For a moment, she let herself imagine the artisan who had chiseled the words into the cave wall. He would have known who he was, where he belonged within the hierarchy of the ancients: The scribes had been more than peasants but less than royalty, falling roughly equal with ballplayers and engineers. On some level she envied that—not the stratification, but the identity.

He had probably been a priest, given the religious overtones of the cave. He would have worked in there, hour after hour, painstakingly carving each symbol of a language that had allowed its users to embellish at will, turning words into art.

So beautiful, she thought, trailing her fingers along the carved panel.

It was also an enigma. Everything else in the room belonged to the good guys: The altar on the opposite wall was a carved *chac-mool* that honored the rain god; the winged serpent motifs on the walls represented the creator god, Kulkulkan; the carved and painted rainbows up near the ceiling were a reference to the goddess Ixchel; and the ball-game scenes painted on the clay pots she had been examining paid homage to the sun god, Kinich Ahau. All sky gods, positive influences.

The glyph panel, though, was different.

The nine rows of text—for the nine layers of the underworld, Xibalba—looked like normal Mayan hieroglyphs ... except that in every pictograph that should have contained a human or animal figure, there was a bat-demon instead, a *camazotz*, with sharply pointed ears, tricornered mouth, pushed-in nose, long fangs and talons, and strangely tattered wings.

The locals believed the ancients had built the temple to appease the *camazotz*, and that she risked awakening more of the creatures by excavating the sacred site. But although Cooter, her crazy-brilliant Mayanist mentor, had harped on the value of trusting the natives to know more about their homes than any visitor—however well educated—could, logic said that the legends of the *camazotz* had come from the temple itself, and maybe costumes worn by the members of the bat cult that had probably worshiped there. Not the other way around.

"Chicken and egg," she murmured, trailing her fingers along the writing.

The wonky glyphs meant that she couldn't read the text. Instead, she would have to farm it out to an expert, which was why the photographs, tracings, and other records were a top priority.

So get back to work. But the same gut instinct that had prompted her to turn down the safe-bet Tikal project and disappear into the jungle, and that had eventually led her to the cave, now rooted her in place.

A chill prickled across her skin, an almost electric crackle that was how her gut feelings sometimes hit her. She was missing something. But what?

Frowning, she stared at the panel, touched the carved surface. The silence in the echoing chamber amplified the small sounds of her breathing, making the air seem to throb with the quiet. Her fingertips scraped along the carved stone, from ridge to dip, from one bat-faced demon to the next, the next, and—to something else.

She froze, her pulse going zero-to-sixty as the shape jumped out at her.

There was a bird among the bats.

And it wasn't just any bird. It was *the* bird.

The parrot's head sat atop three stacked circles and wore a flaring headdress of curling feathers in a glyph that was achingly, acutely familiar. Yet the parrot's head didn't correspond to any pictograph in the historical record. She knew that for a fact . . . because she had been searching for it ever since her thirteenth birthday.

"Holy. Shit." She touched the small silver pendant she wore around her neck. She had found the glyph!

All the restless, edgy energy that had plagued her since she'd first set foot inside the cave—hell, in the forest itself—suddenly concentrated itself in her chest. A hot, hard buzz seared through her system, saying: *Do it*.

But do what?

Swallowing hard, she touched the parrot's-head pictogram, stroking a finger along the feathered headdress and down the curved beak. It was really there, really real. It was—

"Ow!" She yanked back her hand and stared at her fingertip, where a thin slice oozed blood. "What the hell?"

Getting in close to the wall, she squinted at a gleam of . . . Was that glass? Impossible. The ancient Maya might have built pyramids and carved intricate writing and art, but they had done it without using most metals or the wheel, never mind glass. They had been knappers and carvers, mostly, which left her with . . .

"Jade," she breathed, seeing the faint blue-green sheen to the material of the thin blade that had been inset into the carving, almost as if its maker had wanted to punish the person who dared to touch the strange glyph.

Or . . . take a blood sacrifice from them. Blood had been the basis for many of the rituals of the ancient Maya. And even, some said, their magic.

When she was around other academics, she snorted at the idea of true magic. The Mayan shaman-priests had been experts at misdirection, using hidden doorways and polished stone mirrors to make the kings and masses believe that they could teleport themselves, move objects with their minds, and summon fire with a thought. Privately, though, she had hung on Cooter's stories about ancient magicians, wishing they were true.

And right then, there was nobody in the room but her.

Do it, her instincts said, coming suddenly so much louder, so much clearer than they ever had before. *What have you got to lose?*

There was magic in blood, at least according to the stories the crazy old Mayanist had regaled his students with, year after year ... until he disappeared into the rain forest. Logic said he'd had an accident or been killed by bandits. Inwardly, though, she had preferred to think he'd found the magic-wielding warriors he had sought. She and Cooter had been very alike—both out of place, both searching for something. She wanted to believe that he had found his place in the end.

Do it.

Senses spinning, heart pounding, she pressed her bloodstained fingertip to the parrot glyph. The moment she made contact, the restless, edgy energy inside her went supernova, and a strange, soundless detonation thudded through her.

She reeled back. "What the *hell*?"

Her hand vibrated, prickles streaked up and down her arm, and a sudden heavy weight on her chest forced her to struggle for breath. Then she simply *stopped* breathing, freezing dead as the carved stone making up the parrot glyph shimmered, rippling and pulsing as though it had suddenly come alive.

Moments later, the glyph and the surrounding stone disappeared, revealing a shallow niche that contained a small, lumpy something.

Holy shit, was all she could think. *Holy shit, holy shit, holy shit.*

That hadn't just happened. It was impossible. Unbelievable.

Only it *had* happened. There was a hole in the wall where the parrot had been. What was more, the humming restlessness inside her had become a warm, satisfied glow, one that had stopped saying, *Do it*, and now urged, *Take it*.

"I can't," she whispered. She had to document the object from every angle before she touched it, had to investigate the trick door. Because it had to be a trick door. The alternative was . . . impossible.

Take it, those deep-down instincts whispered. *This is for you alone. You found the parrot glyph. Your blood opened the door.*

Hand moving almost without her conscious volition, she reached in and touched the solid, lumpy object. It shifted, suddenly gleaming luminous amber as the overhead lights caught the stone.

It was a clear yellow crystal, maybe an inch in diameter, that had been carved with perfect detail into the shape of a human skull.

Take it. Hard, hot possessiveness washed through her. She wasn't aware of making the decision, but suddenly she was picking it up. Cupping it in her palm, she raised it to eye level. The sockets were dark with shadows, save for two pinprick gleams reflecting back from her headlamp, making the skull seem to stare back at her as it warmed against her skin.

Holy. Shit.

"This is a joke, right?" she said, trying to interject logic into a situation suddenly turned incredible. Javier and the others were trying to cheer her up with a gag, riffing off the legendary crystal skulls that were supposed to help save mankind from the so-called 2012 Mayan doomsday.

But how had they managed it? *If they found a trick door, they would've said something*, she thought, glancing back at the wall. *It's a huge—*

Her mind blanked at the sight of a solid stone in front of her once more. There was no sign of the niche; the carvings were back in place ... but the parrot's-head glyph was gone.

In its place was a screaming skull.

Oh, holy shit times a million. The screaming-skull glyph wasn't supposed to exist, either. It represented—according to the doomsday nuts, anyway—a group of warrior-magi who were supposed to save mankind from the rise of ancient horrors at the end of 2012: the Nightkeepers.

"Impossible," she whispered, staring at the screaming skull and feeling the warm weight of the crystal in her palm, the fading sting from her sliced finger.

"Natalie?" Javier called.

She jolted, flushing. "I'll be up in a minute." Her heart hammered in her ears and the rush of blood through her veins had taken on a strange humming sensation.

"I don't think we've got a minute. We need you up here." His voice was too tight, she realized suddenly.

Something had happened topside. *Oh, crap.*

She hesitated. What now? Stay and investigate the skull glyph? Go up and tell the others what she had found? Go up and keep her mouth shut? Something told her that the skull was hers alone. A secret.

"Natalie, *now!*"

"Coming!" Her hands shook as she tucked the skull into an inner zippered pocket of her tough bush pants. Then she bolted up the tunnel. An odd, almost tribal rhythm pounded through her veins, making her feel tough and capable, strong enough to take on the prophesied doomsday. Not that she believed in the end-time. That had just been another of Cooter's stories.

Then she stepped out into the late-afternoon sun, and a cold dose of reality slapped her right across the face.

Suddenly, crystal skull or not, she was nothing more than a five-three, hundred and fifteen pounds' worth of brunette better described as scrappy than scary . . . and she was facing a dozen armed villagers who were holding her teammates at gunpoint.

Chapter Two

When a dark, man-shaped shadow materialized on the jungle pathway up ahead, JT went for his guns.

The shadow spread its arms wide. "Chill, dude. It's Rez."

Scowling, JT rammed the double-barrel back into its scabbard. He was so strung out from three days of 'zotz hunting that he almost couldn't tell friend from foe anymore. Hell, the jungle itself had even become an enemy, crowding too close and putting shadows where there shouldn't be any, like the plants themselves were being energized by the coming equinox.

Just one more day. If he and the villagers could make it through tomorrow night, they would be okay for another few months. He hoped.

"Don't sneak up on me like that. I'd hate to accidentally put a hole in you." *Hello, understatement.* Rez was his closest ally among the locals, one of the few who really knew what was going on.

The village elder was in his late fifties, which was old for the region, but he wore his jade-loaded pistols easily as he stalked toward JT, his expression thunderous. "Where the *hell* have you been?"

Knowing the autopistols, jade-laced ammo, and pump-actions scabbarded crosswise over his back would've clued the other man that he'd been out hunting, JT tensed. "Why? What happened?"

"Your girlfriend found a bat temple two days ago. Which you would've known if you'd been watching her like you said you would."

"She's not—" JT began, then broke off as his blood iced. "She *what*?"

No. Impossible. She couldn't have. In the months she'd been charting the surrounding forest, she had found only three clusters of carved pillars and a small scattering of tumbled stone foundations. There was no way—the gods weren't cruel enough—that she had found a damned temple in the three days he'd been gone.

But Rez wasn't big on jokes, and his dark eyes were deadly serious.

JT's gut headed for his toes on a down elevator to hell. *Natalie.* "Why didn't you fucking *call* me?"

"The satellite signals are all screwed up. Something to do with sunspots."

Or the equinox. The barrier was getting more and more whacked as the end-time approached. And Natalie was in the thick of it, stirring things up with the take-no-prisoners, all-or-nothing enthusiasm that lit her like a beacon.

JT cursed himself. Rez was right—he should have been there. He was the one who had convinced the village council to let her team stay. But there was no point in looking back. They needed to deal with the problem in front of them, do some damage control. "Even if she found something, we should be okay for this cycle. I took out another pair of the tatter-winged bastards late this morning."

Rez shook his head. "We lost a dozen goats an hour ago."

"You—" *Fuck.* That meant there was another pair of demon bats out there.

Which didn't compute—they'd never had two pairs come through together. Then again, they'd never had more than six per quarter, and his tally was already up to eight. He didn't know if the increase was because of Natalie's discovery, or because they were getting closer to the end date. But the whys and hows didn't matter. What mattered was killing the ones that got through.

He set his jaw and ignored the throbbing aches that came from seventy-two hours of freeze-dried rations and minimal sleep. "Okay. I'm going to need ammo, and—"

"There's more. The council decided to boot the archaeologists and seal the temple. They're over there right—"

"Son of a *bitch*." JT took off for the dig site at a dead run, not waiting to hear the rest.

As he pounded through the rain forest, pulse hammering in his ears, he could only hope to hell he wouldn't be too late, because he knew two things for sure: One, there was no way Natalie would give up her discovery without a fight. And two, the villagers wouldn't hesitate to sacrifice the ancient ruins—and possibly the archaeologists—if they thought it would keep the *camazotz* away.

"You can go back inside and retrieve your equipment," the white-haired elder decreed in the local dialect, with Aaron translating for Natalie and the others. "Then go and pack up your tents and trucks. You must be gone from this area by nightfall."

"But we . . ." *Have permits*, Natalie started to say, but then broke off because she'd already pointed that out—repeatedly—and the men clearly didn't give a crap.

There were thirteen of them, a sacred number. Wearing a range of denim cutoffs, tees, and woven textiles, they seriously outgunned her team with a mix of shotguns and automatics, along with a strange-looking grenade launcher held by a hatchet-faced man at the back of the group. She had seen most of them around, had shared meals with at least three. But now they met her eyes with grim determination and no hint of apology.

Swallowing hard, she looked at the cave mouth, where the dreaded bat creatures were carved with their tattered wings spread, their catlike mouths split in silent stone screams. "Please. I can report the discovery without giving away your location. I'll do whatever you want; just don't make me leave now. I need more time."

She was borderline begging and she didn't care. She'd get down on her hands and knees and eat dirt if that was what it took. This wasn't just a career-making find; it was personal.

But the elder shook his head. Through Aaron, he said, "We are out of time. Tomorrow is the equinox, and the creatures are already walking among us."

"With all due respect, the legend of the *camazotz* comes from that." She pointed behind her at the tunnel mouth. "A carving. Stone. Maybe some priests in bat costumes. Whatever's killing your livestock, it's not a six-foot-tall demon with glowing red eyes."

Inwardly, though, she remembered the way Cooter used to growl, *The locals know more about their home ground than you book-smart punks ever will.* And she was acutely conscious of the hard lump in her zippered pocket. If solid rock could disappear and then reappear carved as something else, could she really be so certain that magic and the *camazotz* didn't exist?

She couldn't be, but that wasn't the point right now. "I need another month. One month, that's all."

The elder shook his head. "You have an hour."

Three men handed off their weapons and broke away from the group, unshouldering rucksacks she hadn't realized they were wearing. They knelt several paces away from the cave entrance, keeping wary eyes on the carved monsters as they started unloading flat boxes that were stenciled with U.S. military markings and the words CAUTION, EXPLOSIVES.

"You can't *blow it up*!" She lunged toward the men, but was brought up short when Javier grabbed her arm.

"Natalie, no!" As he dragged her back, she realized that the other villagers had brought up their weapons; their eyes were white rimmed, their fingers on the triggers. They were terrified, and terror could make people do awful things.

Like kill archaeologists.

She clutched Javier's forearm, her fingers digging in. "We can't let them destroy it!"

"Is it worth dying for?" His eyes flared with the temper he reserved for when she was doing something *really* stupid.

"Yes! I found—" She broke off, unable to tell him why. "Damn it."

He shook her. "It's just a ruin. Let's get our stuff and get out of here, like the man said."

But she couldn't do that. No way. Her mind raced. How could she— *Oh, hell.* "I need to talk to JT," she blurted.

She would do anything she could to save the sacred chamber where she had found the crystal skull. Even grovel to the one man she had ever come close to falling for . . . and who had dumped her flat when she'd told him so.

Chapter Three

JT's bungalow, which was a cross between a bunker and the jungle version of a bachelor pad, was surrounded by a twenty-foot-high stone wall topped with wickedly pointed chunks of jade and obsidian. The stones sparkled in the fading sunlight that glinted down through the gap that the walled compound made in the rain-forest canopy.

When the gates were closed, there was no getting inside.

They were closed.

Natalie's heart sank as she let the Jeep roll to a stop. She was going to have to get out and use the intercom panel. *Let the groveling begin.*

She hated this. But the villagers had agreed to give her an hour, and the clock was ticking.

A quick look assured her that the fireproof lockbox under the driver's seat was secure. After the run-in with the locals, she had locked the crystal skull away. She was dying to carry it with her, but she'd be devastated if she lost it. What was more, she didn't trust JT not to hand it over to the villagers if he thought that would settle things down. He had made it brutally clear that he had his life exactly the way he wanted it and didn't intend to do—or let her do—anything to upset that balance.

Well, what do you expect from a guy who's got FREE-DOM *inked in big letters on his forearm?* Her exes would probably appreciate the irony of her being on the receiving end of the "it's not you; it's me" letdown.

Embarrassment—it wasn't heartbreak despite what Javier thought—churned in her stomach as she headed for the touchpad next to the gate. Mildly resenting the fact that he'd never given her the code, she leaned on the buzzer, then stared up into the security camera, trying to fake a pleasant "let's just be friends" smile.

There was no response.

She didn't know which was worse, the thought that he wasn't home . . . or that he was.

After buzzing a second time, she hit the intercom. "JT? It's Natalie. This is business, okay? Not personal. Let me in."

Still nothing.

"Shit." Now what? She couldn't call him with the satellite transmissions on the fritz, which left . . . nothing. A chill skimmed through her at the knowledge that she was forty minutes away from losing the biggest find of her career, along with the first tangible link she had managed to uncover in nearly a decade of searching for something—anything—connected to the locket she had been found with as a baby. Frustration slapped through her, making her skin itch, but she reminded herself that she still had the skull. That was something, right? But the itches didn't subside.

She turned and headed back to the Jeep. She had made it halfway there when the background forest noise went silent. And she realized with sudden sickening clarity that the itch wasn't frustration after all. It was a warning!

The instincts she had been ignoring suddenly lashed

at her, through her, bringing images of jaguars and the recent livestock kills in the area. She was a woman walking out alone, unarmed. *Stupid move, Nat.* Her heart leaped into her throat as she lunged for the Jeep, and the weapon within it.

She was a few paces short of the vehicle when a dark blur erupted from the greenery and slammed into her, sending her crashing into the side of the Jeep and then down. High-pitched squeals battered her eardrums, making her head ring, and she screamed as a dark-furred, red-eyed creature leaned over her, its batlike face splitting into a three-cornered leer of moist, inhuman hunger that she had seen before, carved in stone.

Camazotz!

Instead of arms, it had elongated wings with tattered sails and wickedly barbed claws at the ends of the bony struts. Its dark brown, almost black skin was covered with patches of mismatching fur, and it smelled terrible, like a rotting animal carcass. The miasma brought tears, though not before she saw up close and personal that it was male, its long penis tipped with a leaflike flattening.

Panicked, she tried to worm her way under the Jeep, screaming, "Help me!"

A pair of claws hooked her arm, dragged her out. Pain slashed through her. Terror. Sobbing, she kicked at the creature, but caught only air as it hauled her upright, screeching almost above the level of her hearing.

Its mouth split wide, revealing a black cavern of a throat framed by long, curved teeth.

"*Help!*" Natalie thrashed against the creature's hold. She was all alone, in the middle of nowhere, JT wasn't home, and—

Automatic gunfire slammed out of the nearby forest and into the bat creature.

The bullets ripped into the thing's upper body, blowing back a spray of blackish blood and chunks. The creature reeled and dropped her. But incredibly, horribly, it spun toward the new threat as black ichor rained down from its wounds.

Seeing the flash of a weapon and the curve of a man's shoulder in the forest, Natalie scrambled up and screamed, "Kill it!"

"Get down!"

She flung herself flat as a heavy *thump* split the air and a fist-size missile caught the creature in the midsection and then detonated. Hot, oily black sprayed and the thing flew backward and went down in a limp mass.

"Oh, God. Oh, God, oh, God, oh, God." Natalie lurched to her feet as her rescuer emerged from the rain forest, cradling a big double-barrel across his body.

On one level she recognized JT; she knew his voice, knew the way he moved. On another level, though, the man who stepped out of the shadows and into the fading sunlight was a stranger.

The JT she knew was clean shaven, well dressed, a strangely urbane oasis in the middle of the tropical wilderness. The JT who faced her now shared the same powerful five-ten frame, skull trim, and cool gray eyes. But he wore several days' worth of scruff and hard-used bush clothes, and his body was strung bandolier-style with an arsenal of weapons and ammo. He carried himself with the tough purpose of a soldier, moving on the soundless feet of a hunter. And he had just saved her ass.

He once told her the guns in his foyer were for hunting the occasional man-eater among the big cats in the area. Now she knew different.

"*Chan camazotz,*" she whispered, the nickname the

villagers used for him. Death-bat killer. She had thought it was a metaphor.

Apparently not.

His eyes were hard and hot, almost feral. "Did he get you?"

A harsh, ugly sob ripped itself from her chest. "That was ... It was ... Oh, *JT*!" She flung herself at him.

He caught her, his arms banding around her with crushing force. Relief poured through her as she burrowed into him, feeling the solid strength of his muscles and the way her body fit against his. His warmth surrounded her, and his voice was raspy when he said her name, over and over again, into her hair. At first she thought she was shaking with fear and shock. Then she realized she wasn't the one shaking.

"JT?" She pulled away a little so she could look up at him. "What—"

He interrupted her with a kiss.

There was nothing soft or urbane about his lips on hers this time, nothing civilized about the way he crushed her mouth with his, the way he gripped her. But she was suddenly hanging on to him just as hard.

Heat flared through her, sweeping away the silent agony of the past three days, the heartache, anger, and loss of thinking it was over between them. Because there was nothing "over" about this kiss. It was blatantly carnal and possessive, and everything inside her screamed to be possessed by him.

"What happened to 'I'm not that into you'?" she whispered against his lips.

He slid his hands from her shoulders to her waist, then down to cup her buttocks and lift her up against his prominent erection. "I lied."

She knew she should be demanding explanations, but

she couldn't focus on anything but his taste on her lips and tongue, his hardness against her. She was on fire for him, feverish for his touch. Her fingers trembled as she worked her hands under his shirt, fighting the constraints of his weapons.

"Off," she ordered. "Take it all off." The world spun around her, flaring hot and cold. He said her name, tried to ease her away, but she clung, needing his heat and strength. She had no filter left, no inhibitions. She whispered what she wanted to do to him in vivid and graphic detail, the words tumbling from her as she cupped him through the tough fabric of his bush pants.

He sucked in a rattling breath. "Natalie." He caught her wrist. "We can't—"

Pain slashed through her and she cried out, nearly went to her knees.

He cursed and shifted his grip on her arm. "*Fuck*. He got you."

She stared at the ugly slice that ran the length of her right forearm. It was red and meaty, and the edges of the cut were stained black. The raw heat within her flashed from lust to fever in an instant, and she swayed, disoriented.

"Is it . . ." She didn't finish the question, her words scattering.

"Just a tranquilizer," JT said, his voice rough. "It's on their claws. But don't worry; I've got you. Everything's going to be okay. I'll take care of you, make sure nothing bad happens to you."

But as the world grayed out, her gut said he was lying again.

She just didn't know which part was the lie.

JT eased Natalie to the ground. Her too-pale skin was a stark contrast to her straight, dark hair, and her long dark lashes failed to hide the bruised circles beneath her eyes. Her tipped-up nose and subtly pointed chin, which added to her air of boundless energy when she was up and moving, now made her look delicate. Breakable.

If he hadn't gotten there in time—

"No looking back," he reminded himself. He *had* gotten there in time. Barely.

And now he had to finish the job.

Standing, not letting himself think about anything but the task at hand—because a distracted soldier was a dead one—he pulled his knife from the scabbard he wore on his thigh. Machete-size, but with its blade edged in a double layer of sacred stones—obsidian and jade—it was the only thing he'd found that could do the job.

When he crouched down beside the *'zotz*, he saw that it was most of the way healed, probably just getting ready to start twitching. Although the jade-tipped ammo and jade-filled grenades knocked them down better than ordinary bullets, the fuckers didn't *stay* down if they were intact.

Which was where he came in.

With one clean motion, he slit the thing's throat. As air gurgled and blackish blood leaked into the dirt, he steeled himself, grabbed the *'zotz*'s thick, sinewy penis, and did a Bobbitt on it. That part never got easy—it was a guy thing. But the second he had the creature's limp, creepily warm dick in his hand, the *'zotz* puffed to oily brown smoke and all of it—blood, dick, corpse, the works—disappeared.

"Go to hell," JT muttered. He was no magic user, but the phrase had become his own personal incantation.

With the *'zotz* gone, he returned to Natalie, picked her up, and carried her through the gate into the compound, not letting himself think of what he would've come home to if he'd gotten there a few minutes later.

He carried her over the threshold and into the house, through the main room, and into his bedroom.

Logic said she would have been fine on the couch, but the toxin would keep her asleep through the night, so she might as well be comfortable.

Gritting his teeth, he got her out of her torn, fight-stained clothes and into a tee and sweats that swallowed her small, delicate frame. To his surprise, the wound on her arm was neatly scabbed, with none of the swelling or redness he'd seen the few times he'd been able to get a victim away from a *'zotz*. Still, he cleaned the cut and scrubbed the worst of the sticky ichor off her skin.

By the time he got a bandage on her arm, he was strung tight from a mental slide show of what could've happened if he hadn't gotten back when he did. He shouldn't have taken off into the forest in the first place, shouldn't have—

"Fuck." He lurched away from the bed and headed for the main room, slamming a lid on the what-ifs and making himself deal with the shit he *could* do something about.

First he armed the security system. Then, while he changed out of his hunting clothes and knocked off the worst of the grime, he pulled his phone out and hit up Rez. The call went through, but the connection was shit, with lots of static surrounding a garbled, ". . . never seen anything like it. The damned thing hit us out in the open, right in front of the cave."

JT's blood chilled. Son of a bitch. That was why there had been only one after Natalie. The other one had attacked the temple. "Any casualties?"

"Only the *'zotz*. Did you find your girlfriend?"

Knowing that Rez was harping on the "girlfriend" thing to get him back for disappearing, JT ignored it. "She's sleeping off a claw scratch. Did any of her people see the '*zotz*?"

"No—" Static interrupted. When Rez's voice cut back in, all JT got was, ". . . back at their tents. They didn't see anything."

That was something good, at any rate. Limited the need for damage control. "Get them out of here."

"They won't go without her."

"Make them." JT would've handed her over to her teammates, but he didn't want to have to explain the half-day coma. More, he would need to talk her down when she woke up, find some way to convince her that she had wrecked the Jeep, banged her head, and hallucinated the rest of it. *Note to self: Roll the Jeep into a ditch down the road.*

"About the temple," Rez began, his words barely audible through the static. ". . . council wants to know what you think."

"Blow it," JT said without hesitation. Over the past few years, the villagers had sealed five other caves that showed evidence of '*zotz* activity. Each time, the demon attacks had skipped a couple of cycles. "Then get Natalie's team out. Tell them she's with me, and she'll meet them at the embassy in a couple of days."

"Will do."

JT cut the call, rubbing his chest, where regret ached. Shit, he hated the idea of blasting an actual temple, rather than just an ichor-encrusted cave—ancestor worship was hardwired into his DNA, he supposed. But he'd been searching for the bat-demons' sacred sites, had even talked the council into letting Natalie's team stay in the hopes that their fancy equipment would lead them to pay dirt. And it apparently had, only he hadn't been there to manage the fallout.

Some fucking protector he'd turned out to be.

That failure, too, was probably hardwired. Despite two tours in the Middle East, he knew too damn well that—in this war, at least—his people weren't supposed to be the frontliners. His job was defense and mop-up.

"Shit." He scrubbed his hands over his face, suddenly feeling his age. He wasn't near village-elder territory yet, but his body sure felt that way all of a sudden. "Get some shut-eye," he told himself. "The perimeter's secure."

As secure as he could make it, anyway, given that the *'zotz* suddenly weren't playing by the old rules, the ones that said they came through the barrier only two at a time, and stuck together once they were out of the underworld. Which meant ... Hell, he didn't know what it meant. But it wasn't good.

Knowing he should hit the couch, he headed for the bedroom instead. He stood in the doorway for a long moment, watching the gentle rise and fall of Natalie's chest and seeing the stark white of the gauze four-by-fours he'd taped to her arm.

He shouldn't have admitted that he'd lied about the breakup. As miserable as he'd been for the past seventy-two hours, the situation hadn't changed. He couldn't leave the dark, dangerous slice of forest that had become his responsibility ... and he couldn't let her stay. She was too perceptive, too foolishly brave. Too much of a fighter.

"What am I going to do with you?" he said softly. It was rhetorical, of course. There was only one thing he could do: make her leave. But first he would watch over her, and make sure she slept safely.

Cursing himself for not being strong enough to walk away now, just as he hadn't been man enough to stick around after he'd cut her loose, he lay down beside her. She'd be asleep until midmorning at the earliest, and didn't ever need to know they had spent one last night together.

Her body heat seeped into him, filling some of the empty places and easing the aches. He knew it made him a selfish bastard to take the comfort that he wouldn't have taken—or given—if she were awake. But right then he couldn't make himself care. He needed this. He needed *her*.

Rolling onto his side, he propped himself up on an elbow and let himself look at her, let himself believe that she was there again, one last time. Tomorrow, he would convince her that the *'zotz* had been a nightmare. Then he would drive her back to civilization, where she would get the news that he'd pulled strings to get her permits revoked ... and that he'd started the process a month ago. She would hate him for that. And she would leave.

Tonight, though ... tonight he could reach over and brush at a smudge on her cheek. He could feel the softness of her skin, the warmth of her breath, and—

She turned her face into his hand and gave a soft sigh. JT froze, a bolt of sensation ripping through him when she shifted and rolled over to curl into him, murmuring something soft and sweet.

There was no way she could be waking up this soon.

Except that she was.

Her eyes fluttered open, their depths blurry and vulnerable as they sought his. The air took on a strange humming note, one that resonated deep within his chest and kindled a sizzle of desire he had no business feeling.

"Natalie," he said in a rasp that broke partway. "There

was an—" *Accident*, he should have said, but couldn't stick to the lie. "Ah, hell," he whispered.

He would have taken the kiss, but she reached up as he leaned down, so they met halfway. As their lips touched, the strange vibration in the air changed pitch, lowering until it seemed to hum deep in his diaphragm, emptying his chest and knotting his gut.

When her lips parted, he tasted a freshness that chased away old betrayals. And when their tongues touched, a roaring, possessive heat seared through him.

He wanted to take her, wanted to protect her. Wanted to mark her as his own for tonight, even knowing he would have to drive her away tomorrow.

He rose over her, pinned her without breaking the kiss. He growled when she twined her arms around his neck to hold him close, and sizzling energy raced through him, coming from the relief of having her safe, the adrenaline from fighting the *'zotz*, and three miserable fucking days spent in the forest trying to forget about her.

He tasted her, touched her, crushed her against him, and nearly came when she pulled the bedclothes away and looped a leg around his hips.

Gods, he thought. He didn't say the word, though, couldn't let her suspect the deeply buried part of himself that didn't follow the rules and religions of normal humans. So instead he kissed her hard and pressed against her, trying to surround and protect her from everything but himself.

She got a double handful of his shirt—which was only fair, as he had both of his hands up hers—and twined her foot around the back of his calf, then used the leverage to roll them. Once on top, she rose over him for a long, lingering kiss that made his heart bump.

But then she pulled away, breathing hard, her eyes dark with arousal and confusion. "JT . . ." She trailed off, eyes widening as memory returned. Her body stiffened against his. "What the hell *was* that thing?"

Damn it.

"It's okay," he said quickly. "You're safe here. They can't get over the wall." They couldn't fly until their wings regenerated, and he and the villagers never let them live that long.

And, shit, he was supposed to be telling her it was all a bad dream.

She nodded. "Okay." But she clearly wasn't. Her body trembled. Her mouth worked, but nothing came out as a tear broke free.

The sight twisted something tight inside him, which was a surprise.

On two continents' worth of war, he'd watched lovers grieve, family weep for family, friend for friend. He had sympathized, supported, done his best to avenge the deaths or prevent more killing. But he'd never before felt another person's tears as his own. Not this way.

"Don't cry. Please." He reached for her, but she scooted up on the bed and wrapped her arms around her knees.

Her face was pale, her eyes dark and wide, and her voice broke when she said, "Those things. Jesus, they're *real*. They . . ." She dragged in a ragged, shallow breath. "The hair. And the *smell*. And . . . Holy shit. Holy, holy shit." She stared at the bandage on her arm.

"Breathe," he said, pulling himself up so he was sitting next to her, both of them leaning back against the wall. His arm just grazed hers as she rocked. "Just keep breathing."

Sometimes that was the only thing to do. Keep going. Keep breathing. He'd figured that out the hard way.

Eventually, she started breathing more deeply, matching her rhythm to his, leaning on him a little, her skin warming against his. Finally, she let out a long, shuddering sigh, and said, "So . . . tell me about the bat-demons, *chan camazotz*."

Chan camazotz. An honorable title in the old trading language of the ancient Maya, bestowed by modern-day descendants who didn't—couldn't—understand the irony.

"How do you feel?" he asked, stalling.

She nodded, accepting the evasion. "Woozy. Scared. Freaked-out."

"Don't blame you." He levered himself off the bed. "Let me get you some water."

"Wait. My team. The temple . . ."

"Javier and the others are fine." He paused. "But the temple is gone. I'm sorry." *War demands sacrifice*, he thought, hating that the quote was so accurate, and that he couldn't get the damned writs out of his head no matter how many years he lived in the human world.

She lifted her hand to the locket she wore at her throat, in a habitual comfort-seeking gesture he wasn't even sure she was aware of. "Gone," she repeated tonelessly.

When she said nothing more, he headed for the kitchen. By the time he returned with a couple of water-filled tumblers, her color was better, her expression less haunted. He handed her one of the glasses and sat back down on the mattress, this time facing her. "Drink. You'll want to flush the rest of the drug out of your system."

That was a guess. He'd never seen anyone come around so quickly. Maybe the large number of 'zotz coming through the barrier had somehow diluted their individual potencies. Or perhaps the 'zotz that attacked her had already used up its venom out hunting.

Granted, there was a different, more complicated explanation, one that involved accelerated healing and strength, but that would've been the answer in another time and place. Not here and now. And not Natalie. No way.

She lifted the glass with a hand that still trembled faintly. But her voice was steady when she said, "Okay, JT. No bullshit. What are they? What's going on? And why are you really here? Is it because of them?"

He had told her the sanitized life story he'd told most of the locals and all of the outsiders who had passed through over the years: that he had finished his second tour of duty, made some money during the dot-com boom, and wandered until he found someplace he wanted to stay. Which was all true. What he hadn't told her was why he'd been forced to put down roots in this particular chunk of forest.

He couldn't tell her all of it now, either. "I didn't come here because of the '*zotz*, but yeah, they're why I stayed. They were . . ." He didn't like to remember it, even now. "Rez's people didn't have the weapons or training to handle them. They were trying to fight the '*zotz* on their own, and losing." He paused. "I'm a soldier. That's all I know how to be."

Which was the truth, thanks to an educational system that had been "perfected" over thousands of years but didn't do dick to prepare a kid like him for life in the outside world. He'd thought escaping from the training compound would be the hardest part, but he'd been wrong. Acclimating had been an equal bitch, and he'd never really managed to integrate all the way.

"So I stayed here," he continued. "And I became *chan camazotz.*"

Her eyes were glued to his face. It was pitch-black

outside, and the bedside lamp cast a warm yellow glow that bronzed her pale skin. Her dark hair had fallen from its ponytail. With it hanging down, her bangs cut straight across, and her thick lashes outlining her eyes like kohl, she could have come straight from a tomb painting, an Egyptian princess. A priestess.

Don't go there.

"Demons . . ." she said softly, almost to herself, still touching the locket.

"They're not demons," he said firmly, doing damage control by trotting out the second layer of his prepared story, which he'd never used before because nobody had ever gotten close enough for him to need it. "There's no such thing. The *camazotz* are an evolutionary relic, an archaic species that should have died out a long time ago, but somehow managed to keep going in this one little section of rain forest."

"Okay." She nodded. "All right. That makes more sense than demons arising from the underworld." But something changed in her expression, almost as if she knew he was lying . . . or she was lying to him in return. "What I don't get is why you're hunting them by yourself."

"What's the alternative? Call in the scientific community to 'study' them?" He emphasized the word with finger quotes. "No, thanks. Next thing I know, the fuckers are a protected species with a growing population, and the village is being moved again." He'd seen too many forced relocations to allow that to happen unless Rez and his people wanted to go, which they adamantly didn't. And he sure as hell wasn't leaving; nor was he letting a bunch of eggheads get in there and start experimenting on the *'zotz*. Especially not this close to the zero date.

The secrecy, too, was programmed into his genetic code.

"They need to be exterminated," he said, "not studied."

She nodded slowly, her eyes going shadowed. "So what happens now?"

The question hung in the air, taking on meaning beyond the words.

JT slugged back his water, stalling while his desire to get her the hell out of harm's way jammed up against other, far more selfish needs. He'd partway blown his cover by admitting that he'd lied about not being into her. But he couldn't blow the rest of it, not even for her.

That wasn't just because of the secrecy bred into his bones, either. It was a kindness. It wouldn't be fair to warn humanity that demons were real, and that they were massing for the 2012 doomsday war, only to follow that with the info that the magi who were supposed to protect the earth plane were gone, killed twenty-some years ago by their despot leader.

He couldn't—*wouldn't*—do that.

Go home and live your life not knowing what's coming, he wanted to tell her. *It's better this way*. But he couldn't tell her that without telling her the rest, so instead he said, "Your team will be waiting for you at the embassy. From there, you can either head up to the States, or back out into the field."

"I take it we're not welcome here anymore." It wasn't a question. More, she didn't mention their breakup. Instead, she sat there with her pointed chin tilted slightly, as if to say that if he wasn't going to say anything about their relationship, she sure as hell wasn't.

That should have been a relief.

He grated, "I'll want your word that you won't come back, and that you won't tell anybody about the *'zotz*."

Logic said he shouldn't let her go, but what was his

other option? He didn't have the power to wipe her mind, and he sure as hell wasn't keeping her here, no matter how tempting the option. There was no way he could deal with the '*zotz* with her around, distracting him.

Something unreadable moved in her eyes, but she nodded. "Okay. If that's the way you want it."

A hard pressure shifted in his chest. "It's not—shit." He couldn't say what he wanted to, didn't want to say what he ought to. So he said nothing.

She set her glass aside and slipped off the bed. "I need a shower."

He closed his eyes. "Yeah." *There's no point in wasting effort on could-have-beens*, he reminded himself, but that didn't take away the hollow ache.

"So do you."

It took a second for her words to register, another for him to turn and find her standing there, holding out a hand to him.

His mouth went dry even as his gut fisted on a bolt of lust. "Natalie." His voice caught on the word. "We can't."

"We can. We already have." She dropped her hand, but didn't back down. "I get the rules—just tonight, no harm, no foul, walk away tomorrow and don't look back. I can do that. Hell, I'm an expert at it. Just ask Javier."

"But you said—" He broke off, not wanting to repeat words that had haunted him, taunted him.

"That I was falling for you," she filled in. "Trust me, your reaction took care of that. This is just-a-good-time sex." Something wistful moved in her eyes as she closed the distance between them, leaned in, and brushed her lips across his. "It's thanks-for-saving-my-ass sex." Another soft kiss. "It's I-missed-you sex." A deeper, longer kiss that heated him, hardened him. "What do you say?"

But his mind had seized on three small words that meant far too much: *I missed you*. She said it as easily as she had said, *I think I'm falling for you*. They were facts, and she shared them with an honesty that he could never return.

The past three days had royally sucked, and the next two years without her—or however long he lasted before the *'zotz* got him—would undoubtedly be far worse than he'd imagined, now that he knew what he was missing, what kind of light was being snuffed when the end-time came. But he couldn't tell her that any more than he could admit he wanted her to stay.

So instead, he cupped her face in his palms and kissed her long and deep, until the throb of lust blotted out everything else. Then, still kissing her, he started backing her toward the bathroom, where his solar-heated shower was glassed in on three sides, the panels steamy with the tropical night.

Even as he did so, a warning chimed deep inside him, one that said he should watch his step, that he was in danger of acting like the selfish bastards he'd escaped from. But in that moment, he didn't care.

It was the equinox. And he wanted to make love to her.

Chapter Four

Natalie's entire body hummed with strange, fluid warmth as she gave herself over to the night and the moment. Whether he wanted to admit it or not, JT was right for her; they were right for each other.

But as they paused in the bathroom doorway and eased out of their clothes, piece by piece in the short pauses between long kisses, she knew, deep down inside, that he was wrong about the *camazotz*.

They didn't come from any species that was meant to walk the earth. More, she was somehow connected to them through the parrot glyph, the crystal skull, and the bone-deep instincts that had pulled her to this forest. Was she supposed to fight the creatures, like one of the warrior-priests in Cooter's stories? She didn't know, but the idea both scared and excited her. So did the humming warmth that sparkled somehow gold at the edges of her vision and dulled the throb of fear.

Magic, she thought, the idea not seeming nearly as impossible as it had before. There was magic in the air, and in the way JT groaned when she raked her nails along his biceps, then down along his tattoo.

He turned on the shower, spun her beneath it, and pinned her to the wall with his hard, heavy body, his kisses going rough and needy. He ran his hands up her sides, into her hair, then down her arms to link fingers as they swayed together. In his touch she felt the heady urgency that pounded in her veins, a combination of relief at being back together and the painful awareness that it was only for tonight.

She wanted him, wanted to hold him, have him. They were protected inside the compound; the skull was locked in the Jeep, safe because nobody knew about it except her. If one night was all he would give her, then she'd take it. And she would deal with tomorrow when the sun came up.

The solar-heated water was at once both warm and cool on her skin, adding an edge to her pleasure as they twined together beneath the spray.

Outside the glass-walled shower, the night was seamlessly dark, broken only by a few stars high above, showing through the hole he had punched in the canopy. Before, she hadn't understood why he had pushed back the rain forest rather than living beneath it. Now she got it, and the perimeter made her feel safer. But still, she was acutely aware of how little separated them from the dark rain forest and the creatures that walked within it.

The knowledge added an edge that had her reversing their positions and pushing him back against the wall so she could taste him, biting lightly at his neck, his shoulder, the flat planes of his chest, and then lower down. As she closed her lips over the wide, blunt tip of his cock, he hissed out a breath and leaned back against the warm stone that formed the fourth wall of the shower, one arm braced to hold him upright as the muscles of his powerful thighs moved in time to the slow, grinding rhythm she set.

A harsh groan rattled in his chest, and his free hand

dug lightly into her shoulder, her neck, the back of her head, not holding or directing her, but more proving to himself that she was really there.

Or maybe not. She didn't know, but in that moment all that mattered was that they were there together. She could ride the golden hum inside her, the one that made her feel powerful, reckless, and wicked as she ran her tongue along the thick, distended vein on the underside of his shaft, savoring the places where the texture of his skin changed, and where the touch of her tongue and hands could make him shudder.

"Natalie." He said her name like a prayer, the gritty tone sending new heat sizzling through her as he swept her up in his arms, lifting her and spinning so the warm stone wall pressed against her back and she was the one at the mercy of pleasure. He tongued her breasts, making her arch up against him with the unfamiliar rasp of a three-day beard and the exquisite familiarity of his touch.

She moaned, digging in her fingers, urging him onward, inward, but he kept going with an insistent rhythm that drove her up, far beyond any place they had been before. She cried out—his name, a plea, she wasn't sure—and he answered by kissing her deeply, thoroughly, pressing his body into hers without completing the act she craved.

Instead, he slid his hard length between her legs, along the slick cleft that wept for his entry. Then he anchored her with his hands, spreading her and holding her exactly where and how he wanted her.

"Now," she said, not caring that he'd made her beg. "*Now*, damn you."

His chuckle was low and masculine, with an edge of the effort it cost him to set a torturous pace, pleasuring her without penetrating. She moaned with mounting frustration, then again as the rhythm caught fire within her and she tightened around the empty place where he should have been.

The water was cooler than her body now, cooler than the friction they made together. That contrast, along with the slap of water and skin, the wet slide of his body against hers, combined into a brutally erotic thrill that caught her up, turning her inward. She clung to him, kissed him, tasted his excitement and fraying restraint. And she went over.

She cried out against his lips as the throbbing pleasure took hold, gripping her and leaving her helpless to do anything but dig in, hang on, and ride it out. She said his name, cursed him, begged him, thanked him; she didn't know what she was saying, didn't care as long as he kept sliding against her, hard and full.

Then the storm passed and she went limp. He let her down from the wall; his chest was heaving, his eyes wide and almost wild. His hand shook as he slapped the toggle to kill the water; his steps were slightly unsteady as he led her out of the shower. "Bed," he grated. "Now."

She wasn't arguing.

They toweled each other off and headed for the bedroom, weaving, drunk on lust. The hot, humming power raged through her, making her ache when they lay down together and he kissed her, his hands framing her face, his heavy erection trapped between them, throbbing against her skin.

Then he shifted and slipped inside her. She saw stars and comets, felt the pounding of her blood and his as he shifted to match their palms on one side, and then twine their fingers together.

Her eyes fluttered open and she looked down at their

joined hands. She had lost the bandage in the shower, but the cut must not have been that bad. It was barely a faint, faded line now, matching up with the word tattooed on his left forearm: FREEDOM. The alignment seemed somehow profound, sending a new spear of sensation through her as his eyes met hers, and he began to move within her.

It would have been smarter to look away, to close her eyes and lose herself to the physical pleasure. Instead, she stayed locked on him, looking into him and letting him see too much.

New needs rose up in her, clawed at her until she surged against him, clung to him, urging him on and then racing ahead, her body bowing beneath his as the leading edge of another orgasm caught her unaware. It took her outside herself, to a place of push and pull, action and reaction, until she would have done anything, given anything, to reach the climax that beckoned just out of reach.

Her vision blurred; her eyes drifted shut. He whispered to her: "Natalie." Just her name, yet in a soft, moved voice that touched her more deeply than it should have.

"I missed you." She hadn't meant to say it again, hadn't really meant to say it the first time. But he answered with a body-locking shudder of passion, a surging stroke that put her over and took him with her.

She clung to him as the world shattered around her, pulsed through her, lit her up with warm liquid gold.

Crying his name, she pressed her face into the crook of his neck so he couldn't see into her eyes, where she knew there was no hiding that she had lied when she said she could handle a no-harm-no-foul night with him. Because if she had been in danger of falling before, she edged that much closer now as he came inside her, grating her name and a male litany of, "Oh, yes, oh, there, oh, *gods*, oh, fuck, yeah."

They clung, shuddering, and then easing as their bodies unlocked. Then, though she knew she probably shouldn't, she curled naturally into the too-familiar cuddle they had developed in their six-week stint as lovers.

Her heart hurt from the comfortable warmth of his body against hers, the touch of his breath in her hair, the pressure where he still held her hand, and the way his grip gentled when he slipped into a doze. That in itself was a sign of his exhaustion. Always before, he had fallen asleep after her and woken before she was up. Not so now. His arms went lax and heavy around her; his breathing slowed and deepened.

Cuddling in, she closed her eyes. And didn't come anywhere close to falling asleep.

She was wide-awake, her brain churning. Oddly, though, she wasn't overthinking what had just happened between them; her mind was caught on something else, something that stayed tantalizingly out of reach when she tried to focus on it.

She frowned and opened her eyes, then eased back to look at him, trying to find the tiny detail that had caused her instincts to kick in.

Rather than softening in sleep, his features had become even fiercer, as if he couldn't let go even when unconscious, afraid that something important would slip away.

Tenderness tugged at her. She touched his jaw, tracing the rasp of stubble. He hadn't shaved since they'd broken up, she thought, and wondered whether he'd been out hunting the creatures all that time, keeping moving, not slowing down long enough to think. Restless. Itchy. Twitchy. Like her.

Don't talk yourself into something that isn't there, she told herself. But warmth coursed through her as she let herself mentally replay their lovemaking: his deep rumble of sexual completion, his earthy praise, his—

Her belly knotted when she figured out what had been bothering her.

Just now, in the throes, he had said *gods*. Plural.

Oh. Shit.

There was nothing wrong with polytheism ... but it was an almost unthinkable choice for a man who had grown up, as he had claimed, in a deeply religious family smack in the heart of the Bible Belt. Which meant he hadn't, or at least not entirely.

Was it another lie? Or something that went deeper?

Her heart thudded as the getting-to-know-you stories he had shared about his childhood suddenly seemed too pat, almost rehearsed. *More lies.* Who was he, really? How did he fit into this place, with these creatures? He was one of the good guys, a soldier, just as he'd said— that much she was sure of. But she didn't know who he was beyond that.

Thoroughly chilled even though she was still lying beside his big furnace of a body, she slipped out of bed and pulled on borrowed clothes, adding a sweatshirt against the bone-deep cold that had chased away the golden warmth.

Pausing in the doorway, she looked back at his sleeping bulk. "Who the hell are you?" she whispered. Inwardly, though, she was thinking, *Who the hell am I?*

Was she a piece of whatever was happening in this place, or was this just the ultimate in orphans' fantasies:

that she was the lost child of powerful people, abandoned with a magic necklace that brought her back to where she belonged?

Or not, she thought, still staring at JT. She didn't do lies, didn't do liars.

But what was the truth?

Turning away from him, she padded out into the main room and took a long look around, not sure what she was searching for, but figuring she would know it when she saw it.

A half hour and two cups of coffee later, she found it: the seam of a hidden door disguised to look just like the rustic, exposed-beam interior of the main room. After that, it wasn't hard to identify the pressure pad that triggered it—the disguise was cursory, more to fool casual visitors than to evade a determined search.

She hesitated, nerves sparking even as her instincts said, *Do it*.

Blowing out a breath, she whispered, "Okay. Down the rabbit hole we go." She wanted, needed the truth about what he was hiding, what it had to do with her.

As she opened the door and pushed through, she was braced to find almost anything. What she got was a plain, workmanlike space with a computer, filing cabinet, and other office detritus.

Not letting herself hesitate—she had already crossed the line—she woke the computer, wincing when a solar converter kicked on somewhere else in the house. But the machine was password-protected, and she was no hacker. So instead of messing with that, she searched the rest of the small space, rifling through desk drawers, and then the filing cabinet. There, she found four journals, arranged by date, going back nearly a decade.

She pulled out the oldest one and cracked it open,

but then stalled at the sight of his distinctive, crabbed writing.

Did she really want to do this? He had lied to her, it was true. But reading his personal papers wouldn't make that better; it would just make her guilty of something, too. Maybe finding the office was enough—she could call him on it and see what he said. More lies, probably. But with her body still warm and loose from their love-making, she wanted to give him the chance.

She moved to shut the journal, but then a word jumped out at her, and she froze. *Xibalba*. It whispered in her mind. *Xibalba*. It was the Mayan underworld, the root of evil and the source of the villagers' bat-demons. Which most definitely weren't the cryptic species he had claimed them to be.

Another lie.

Damn it, JT.

Taking a deep breath, knowing she wasn't going to like what she found but unable to walk away now, she opened the journal all the way, and began to read.

When the demons first come through the barrier, from Xibalba to the earthly plane, their flesh is raw and exposed, and they're newborn-weak. They hunt animals in the beginning, the bigger the better, because they need the blood volume to power up. They drain the bodies dry, then take the skins to cover themselves—it knits somehow, so the skin becomes theirs, everywhere except the wings. In order to fill in their wings, they need human skin.

They were sneaky this time, taking only a few animals from each herd. It wasn't until Rez's family went missing that we knew for certain. And even then, they hid the bodies in their damned burrow.

Skinned and drained, and left there for the poor bastard to find.

We go hunting tomorrow, and I hope to hell I don't fuck it up. Some chan camazotz. That first time was a fluke and blind fucking luck, and now they've gone and made a hero of me. Mostly because they need one, and the real heroes are gone.

I don't even know if the jade ammo will work for me. We're still eight years out from the end-time. If things are bad now, what are they going to be like two years from now? Six? Fuck me. I never should've come down here. Because now I'm trapped.

"Son of a bitch," she whispered, her skin chilling to prickles of gooseflesh as things started to line up in a patchwork of fact and fiction—or what she had thought was fiction, even though old Cooter had sworn it was all true.

Her fingers trembled as she closed the journal, then laid her hand flat on the cover. Her scientist self should've been electrified by the grim discovery—it was a huge find, way more important than the temple. But she couldn't get excited, not over this.

JT hadn't just lied about his background and the '*zotz*. He had lied about everything.

"Snooping, Natalie?" he said from the doorway, voice neutral.

She looked over as her heart thudded and her stomach gave a sick churn that was mingled with heat and heartache. He was wearing a tee and jeans and had one hand braced on the doorframe, so the FREEDOM tattoo faced her. He didn't look angry so much as haunted. Caught.

She hated that she had to blink back tears. "How much of our relationship was you keeping track of me and my team, and using us to find tunnels the *camazotz* might be living in?"

It wasn't the most important question in the grand scheme, but it was the one she wanted answered first, damn him.

He looked away. "Some of it."

"How much?" The burn of tears went to a wistful ache. *Give me something. Tell me the sex was about us, at least.* She couldn't have been that far off. Could she?

He didn't answer for a long moment, just stood there staring at her. Then, finally, he muttered an oath and jerked his head toward the kitchen. "Come on. If we're going to do this, I need some damned coffee."

She sat for a long moment, holding the journal in front of her like a shield. Then she got up and followed him into the other room. "Got anything stronger than coffee? I think I'm going to need it."

Five minutes later, armed with drinks and sandwiches, JT faced Natalie across the narrow butcher-block bar that separated his kitchen from the rest of the main room. He was strangely calm.

She had seen a *'zotz*, heard him call on the gods, and read enough in his journals to figure out that he'd been using her. There was no point in denying any of it. And he was so godsdamned tired of being alone.

She was his lover. More, she might be impulsive, but she wasn't irrational. Once she understood what was going on—as well as he did, at any rate—she wouldn't blab when she got back to civilization.

Hell, he was almost glad she had found the hidden room. Their lovemaking just now had changed something inside him, or maybe it had been changing for a while now. He didn't know. All he knew was that he wanted her to understand who he really was. No more lies, no more secrets.

"How much did you get from the journals?" he began.

Something shifted in her eyes, but she said only, "Enough to know that the *camazotz* aren't anybody's cryptic species."

He took a deep breath, orienting himself. "Okay. Twenty-six thousand years ago, there was a..." He trailed off as he heard the words echo in other voices, other times, handed down from father to son, generation after generation. "Scratch that. Screw the history. What matters is that there's a barrier of energy that separates the earth from the underworld. It's been destabilizing over time, making it easier for things like the *camazotz* to get through weak spots and come to earth. It's my job—if you want to call it that—to make sure they don't get far."

"'Over time,'" she repeated. "You mean as we get closer to the winter solstice of 2012."

His gut tightened at the reminder that the end date was way too fucking close for comfort. But he nodded. "Yeah. On the zero date, there's a good chance that the barrier will collapse entirely, releasing all of the nasties that've been banished to the underworld over the past twenty-six millennia." He waited for her disbelief. Didn't get it. Cool fingers walked down his spine. "Why aren't you making noises about meds and rubber rooms?"

"Beyond having been attacked by a demon?" She paused, blew out a breath, and said, "I used to work for this professor who was obsessed with the 2012 dooms-day. He was always telling us stories about the end-time war."

"A nut job, you mean." But something dark and nasty moved through him. Stories. He had known storytellers, once. An entire culture of them, gone in a night, killed by a king who had dreamed of a great victory and had led his people into a massacre instead.

She tipped her hand. "In some ways. In other ways, Cooter was one of the smartest people I've ever met. And it was hard not to see how his stories lined up exactly with the historical record."

"What stories?" He forced the question through gritted teeth.

Her expression went wary, making him wonder what she saw in his face, but she answered, "He told us about a race of magic users who have lived in secret among humankind, century after century, guarding the barrier against the occasional demonic breakout and training for the zero date, when they would become our saviors."

"Son. Of. A. Bitch." He lurched to his feet, heard the chair crash to the floor behind him. He wanted to pace, wanted to run. Instead he stood there, vibrating with an anger that had gone cold and sour with age.

She rose to face him, eyes wide with excitement and dawning wonder. "I'm right, aren't I? That's why you're out here fighting the *camazotz*. You're one of them. You're a Nightkeeper!"

She might as well have said, "You're my hero," because that was the way she was looking at him.

Bile rose. "Not in a million years."

Anger flashed in her eyes. "Stop it," she snapped, advancing on him and drilling a finger into his chest. "No more lies. It fits with Cooter's stories. *You* fit. You're exactly how he described them: You're a trained fighter, charismatic as hell, and"—she paused, her cheeks pinkening—"the most sensual, sexual man I've ever met." She met his eyes. "That's part of your religion, isn't it? Sex magic."

Something twisted inside him. "I'm no magic user."

"But you're a Nightkeeper."

The moment he had decided to tell her the truth, on some level he had known it might come to this. He'd built his life on living in the moment, dealing with the crisis in front of him, and didn't want to look back at a past he had finally managed to forget. But for Natalie, whose enthusiasm and impulsivity had both charmed him and gotten her in a shitload of trouble, he would do it.

"The Nightkeepers are gone," he said bluntly. "Back in the eighties, their king got it in his head that they could prevent the apocalypse by attacking the barrier at a sacred site in Mexico. He ordered every able-bodied man and woman into the battle, nonoptional." He paused, forcing back the memories that tried to come. Apparently, he hadn't forgotten any of it. He'd just blocked out the nastiness. "They all died, not just the fighters, but the children, too. Every fucking one. The demons slaughtered the warriors and then went after their home base, wiping it off the earth and turning it to godsdamned dust."

That was the only explanation for why, when he'd gone back, he'd found only an empty box canyon where the training compound had been. And it was why he'd never been able to find anyone else like himself in years of sending out the signals his parents had taught him, until he'd finally given up.

Her lips parted, but no sound emerged. He couldn't tell what she was thinking—hell, he barely knew what *he* was thinking, except that he'd gotten only halfway through smashing her illusions.

He made himself keep going. "But the thing is, the stories tell only part of what it used to be like, the part that makes them seem like heroes." He paused. "I don't know if the world is better off without them. Maybe not, given that the barrier is getting thinner by the year. But the thing is, I know for damn sure that *I'm* better off without them. Because I wasn't lying when I said I wasn't a Nightkeeper. . . . I was one of their slaves."

Chapter Five

"A slave," Natalie whispered, reeling not just from that revelation, but from all of it. Her gut told her that this was the key to understanding JT, that this was the truth. And oh, holy crap, what a truth. It was unbelievable, impossible, yet instinct also said this was what she had been looking for. This was the reality.

The doomsday war was real, and it was coming. *Oh, God.*

She leaned on the breakfast bar, mind spinning as she tried to take it all in. But even as she grappled with the realization that this was far, far larger than just the two of them, she was acutely aware of the rigid set of his shoulders, the wariness in his face as he waited to see how she would react.

He had called himself a slave. Cooter had never said anything about slaves. But he *had* mentioned another race that had lived with the Nightkeepers. "You're talking about the *winikin*."

He flinched. "I don't like the word. *Aj winikin* means, 'I live to serve my master,' and I fucking don't. Nobody should have to." But something changed in his expression and he said cautiously, "We didn't usually make it into the stories."

The *we* sent a shiver through her. This was really real. It was really happening. She was talking to a *winikin*. One of the hereditary protectors of mankind's salvation. One of the people they were going to need if the war was really coming.

Holy. Shit.

Trying to keep her voice from shaking, to stay cool when on some level it felt like JT had suddenly changed in front of her, becoming even more than he'd been before, she said, "The way Cooter told it, the *winikin* were a vital part of the society. They raised the Nightkeepers, taught them, protected them. It was their job to make sure that if anything happened to the warriors, the children would survive to start over."

"Nobody ever asked if we wanted the job," he said flatly. "Not back when the first *winikin* were magically bound to the Nightkeeper bloodlines, and not later. It wasn't voluntary. None of it was. If the magic tagged a kid for *winikin* training, he got trained, period. Once he grew up, if the magic chose him to be blood-bound to a mage, he went through the ritual, no discussion. A bound *winikin* couldn't have a family of his own, couldn't have a life of his own. His mage had to be his first and only priority. If—" He broke off, a muscle pulsing at his jaw. "It doesn't matter anymore. They're all dead. It's over."

"They ..." She trailed off, her stomach tightening. Cooter's stories had all been about duty, destiny, and heroes fighting to save the world. Not this. Nothing like this. He hadn't talked about the magic being used to press children into service—he had made it sound like the two races had worked together, relied on each other. But even as she scrambled to catch up with that change in paradigm and the dull horror of doing the math and realizing they were less than two years to the end date, she couldn't get past the excitement of finally getting down to the truth . . . and starting to grasp what it might mean for her.

A *winikin*. JT was a *winikin*. *Holy crap*.

Even now, as he leaned back against the counter and crossed his arms over his chest so his biceps bulged beneath his tee, she felt the punch of his presence, the animal magnetism that put a thrum of warmth in her veins. She could just see the edge of his tattoo, which had gained new meaning. *Freedom*. But although he might think the Nightkeepers' world was gone, it remained ingrained within him. He had lied to her, yes. But he'd done it to protect her, the same way he had tried to break things off between them before she got in too deep.

It was too late for that, though—she was right in the middle of things. And the more she heard, the more she suspected she'd been involved for a long time. Like her whole life.

"They're not all dead," she said softly. "You're here."

"There was a resistance, a faction of magi and *winikin* who thought the king was challenging the gods by planning to attack the barrier. There were fifty, maybe sixty rebels, including my parents and me. We were all planning to disappear the night of the battle. But the royal council found out and came after us." He paused, his eyes gone dark. "When they started pounding on the door, my father gave me the keys to the Jeep he had hidden in the hills beyond the canyon, and sent me out the window. He told me to leave and never look back. I was ten."

"Oh, God. I'm sorry."

"It was a long time ago."

Drawing a deep breath to settle the sudden churn in

her stomach, she said, "Was it the summer solstice of 'eighty-four?"

His face blanked and his skin went chalky. He took a step toward her, but then jerked to a halt. "How did you know that?" His voice was a pained rasp; his eyes searched hers.

"Because that was the day I was abandoned in the bathroom of a maternity ward in Albuquerque. I was about nine months old. There was no note, no identifying information. Only this." She removed her locket, thumbed the clasp, and held it out to him by the chain. The pendant spun, letting the light glint off the two ovals of polished obsidian contained within it. The one on the left was carved with the parrot's-head glyph. The other one was so scratched as to be indecipherable.

He reached out and took the locket with a hand that shook ever so slightly. "Dear gods."

Her heart stuttered; her whole world contracted to this moment. "I've been searching for the parrot's-head glyph ever since my thirteenth birthday, when my parents told me I was adopted and gave me the locket." When he didn't say anything, just stood staring at the locket, she pressed, "What does it mean?"

He touched the carving, his blunt fingertip making it seem small and delicate. "This is the symbol of the parrot bloodline. The magi of each bloodline wore the symbols on their inner forearms, along with glyphs for their magical talents and such. The bound *winikin* wore smaller bloodline glyphs, one for each member of the bloodline, and a larger one for their charge, along with the servants' mark." His fingertip moved to the other, scratched side of the locket. He rubbed where the original lines were barely visible. "This was the servants' glyph. The *aj winikin*."

"The—" She broke off as her blood hummed in her veins. "I'm like you? I'm a *winikin*?" Sudden warmth flared through her, lighting her up and making her feel powerful. Invincible. *Magical.*

He snapped his head up to glare at her. "Your parents were *winikin*. You're free." His voice was rough, his eyes dark. "You've lived your whole life in the human world. You should consider yourself lucky, and get the hell out of here while you still can."

"No way." She lifted her chin. "I've been looking for answers more than half my life, staying on the move because I never felt like I knew who I was or where I belonged. Until now."

"Natalie . . ." He held out her locket, grim faced. When she stepped closer to take it, he brushed his knuckles along her cheek. "Don't. Please. This doesn't change anything."

He was wrong. It changed *everything*, at least when it came to her plans. As for the two of them . . . she didn't know. He wanted her, but he also wanted his freedom. And she didn't know if she could work with that.

"I'm not leaving," she said after a moment. "Not if I can do something to defend the barrier." Beneath the thrill of the discovery was a thick underlayer of fear that bubbled up at the thought of what they were really talking about here. The end of days. The end of *everything*. This wasn't just about the two of them. It couldn't be. Swallowing to wet a throat gone suddenly dry, she said, "Let me help you."

"Help." He said the word like a prayer, but shook his head. "You don't get it. There's nothing you can do to help, and I can't risk being distracted."

"I can take care of myself," she said, stung. "And what

do you mean, there's nothing I can do? What about the magic?"

His mouth thinned to a line. "There's no magic without the Nightkeepers."

She lifted the locket, only then realizing that she had clenched her hand around it in a tight fist. "But I'm a parrot. This proves it."

"That *suggests*," he emphasized the distinction, "that you're descended from the *winikin* of the parrot bloodline. The *winikin* weren't magic users. They were just support staff."

Her pulse hummed in her ears. "What if I'm not a *winikin*?"

Cold anger flared in his expression. "You're sure as hell not one of *them*."

Careful, her gut warned. As far as he was concerned, the Nightkeepers had been another sort of enemy. But she had to know. "Are you sure?"

"Positive. For one, you're too small. They were . . ." He trailed off, eyes darkening. "Bigger and stronger than normal humans. They were the ultimate warriors—they fought harder and longer, healed faster. You couldn't take your eyes off them." He shrugged. "They were gods on earth." Something must have shown on her face, because his expression sharpened suddenly. "Why?"

Heart pounding, she pushed up her right sleeve to show the thin white scar. When his eyes went wide and white rimmed, she nodded. "Yeah. It healed. And you said I came out of the drug sooner than you expected."

"That's—" He broke off. "There's another explanation. There has to be."

"That's not all. You said I shouldn't be able to do magic? Well, I'm pretty sure I already have." She described how the parrot glyph had disappeared at the temple. She tried not to let it hurt when he stalked away from her to brace his hands on the back of the couch, head hanging as if he didn't want to look at her. She finished, "There was a little space behind where the glyph had been. In it was a yellow crystal skull."

His head jerked up and his face went gray, practically matching his eyes. *"What?"*

She had to fight not to back up as he crossed to her and gripped her arms, hard. Instead, she clutched him in return, refusing to back down. "And that's not all. I think it was magic that pulled me to this region, magic that helped me find the temple. And when we were making love—"

"Where's the skull?" he interrupted.

"What? It's safe; don't worry. It's in the Jeep lockbox. But why—"

"You left it *outside*? Gods help us!" He tore away from her and bolted for the mudroom, snapping over his shoulder, "Stay here!"

He slapped off the security panel on the run, grabbed a gun and a long, sheathed knife, and slammed through the door. Seconds later, the motion-activated lights blazed to life as he pelted barefoot across the courtyard.

Shit, shit, shit, shit, shit. The curse hammered with the pounding of JT's pulse and the thud of his footsteps on the packed dirt as he hurtled through the gate, shotgun first.

He skidded to a halt the second he got a good look at Natalie's Jeep. *"Fuck!"*

The vehicle was off-kilter on a shredded tire, the driver's door hung open on a single hinge, and the interior was ripped to shit, dripped with ichor, and smelled like week-dead cow. The lockbox hung askew, open and empty.

Too late. He was too fucking late. "Son of a bitch!" At the sound of a noise behind him, he spun, but kept his finger off the trigger, knowing damn well who it was. "I told you to stay inside!"

Natalie stood there, staring at the Jeep, stricken.

He was already on the move, taking her arm and hustling her back through the gate. "Come on. We can't stay out here."

He was headed for the house, but just inside the walled enclosure, she dug in her heels and yanked away. "Wait. Just wait a damned minute!"

Rounding on her, he snapped, "Why? So you can cast a spell on me? What's it going to be—temporary amnesia? A sleep spell? Why not teleport us straight to wherever they took the damned skull?" He knew he wasn't being fair, but he'd just started to comprehend the idea of her being a *winikin*—there was no faking the locket—when things had hung a quick left straight to hell.

She couldn't be a magic user—she had all the physical hallmarks of *winikin* ancestry in her dark coloring and eyes, and the Nightkeepers always bred true. No way they would mix their precious blood.

But the evidence was there. He couldn't deny the scar. And the skull . . . What the hell were they going to do about the skull? More, what was he going to do about *her*? Whatever her bloodlines, whatever her powers, she didn't have the right training to stay here and fight. Not to mention that she was reckless, too willing to throw herself headlong into danger.

But he couldn't just chase her off, not now that she knew that she, too, had a connection to this chunk of godsforsaken forest. And not now that he knew there

were more *'zotz* on the loose. The tatter-winged fuckers had somehow trashed the Jeep without tripping the
alarms. What else could they do now?

He was all too aware that it was almost dawn. The
day of the equinox.

Gods help them.

"Tell me about the skull," she said, pressing. "What
can it do?"

Nothing without a Nightkeeper, he thought. But he
didn't say it, because suddenly that didn't seem as clear-
cut as it had minutes earlier.

"When the Nightkeepers' long-ago ancestors used
the barrier to trap the demons in the underworld, they
created thirteen life-size crystal skulls that together balanced the energy flow across the planes. They hid four
of them on earth, sent four to the underworld, and sac-
rificed four to the sky gods. They kept the last one, and
used magic to divide it into thirteen smaller replicas. One
was given to a female seer in each of the major bloodlines. They became the *itza'at* seers. The visionaries."

She exhaled softly. "The skull can tell the future?"

"When wielded by a fully trained *itza'at* mage. It's no
use in a fight."

"If that's true, then why did you haul ass out there?
And why did the *camazotz* take it?"

Knowing they had moved past the point of conve-
nient lies, he said, "When a skull is separated from its
wielder, it broadcasts powerful magic. Once you brought
it up out of the temple, any creature with a link to the
barrier would have been able to zero in on it." His gut
tightened. "The *'zotz* that attacked you was probably
coming after the skull, but once it saw you, it decided
to have a snack first, add some skin to its wings." He
deliberately paused, letting the gory details sink in. "As

for why they took it, power is power. Destroying it in an equinox ritual could fuel some serious magic."

Her eyes flared. "*Destroying* it? No. No way. We can't let that happen. We have to get it back."

"Natalie—"

"Don't 'Natalie' me, JT. If I'm a *winikin*, then I'm a protector by nature, right? And if we're free, then that means we get to pick what we want to protect. You chose your village. I'm choosing the skull that belongs to my bloodline."

"It doesn't belong to your bloodline," he gritted between clenched teeth.

"It does if all of the magi are dead," she countered neatly. "Why else would I have been the one to pick up its signal?"

"I—" He broke off. "Damn it." She was right. And it was a plausible explanation for why she looked like a *winikin* but seemed to have some connection with the magic. In the absence of a better option, the power was reaching out to the D-list.

Only in this case, D stood for *danger*.

"The *camazotz* would have brought it to their hell-mouth for any sort of ritual," he said finally, wishing she didn't have a point. "That's the hole in the barrier where they're coming through, one that takes a hell of a sacrifice to get open. Theoretically, it should be inside a big-ass temple, but I'll be damned if I can find it. And if I haven't managed to track it down in seven years of searching, there's no way you're going to find it in less than a day."

She just looked at him, unblinking. "I told you. I can sense the skull. I can lead us to where it's gone." In that instant, her certainty reminded him all too strongly of how the old king had looked as he stood at the front of the meeting hall, talking about his plans to attack the barrier.

JT's blood chilled. "Natalie, for gods' sake."

"Tell me about the hellmouth. Can we use it to get into Xibalba?"

"That's not funny."

"It wasn't a joke."

Frustration sparked through him. "Do you seriously think we can take out the underworld itself, just the two of us?" When the argument edged way too close to those old, blood-soaked memories, he veered off. *Don't dwell. Move forward.* "No way. We're not doing this. I'll tell you what we *are* doing: You're going to go inside and lock up where it's safe, and I'm going after the '*zotz* that busted up your Jeep. I'll track them, find them, and kill them."

She closed the distance between them and wrapped a hand around his arm, gripping right over his ink. "My instincts are good, always have been. And right now they're telling me that if we don't get the skull back, everything you've seen up to now is going to look like a warm-up act."

Memories churned, souring the back of his throat. But he said only, "Go inside and stay there. Let me do my job."

"It's— *Behind you!*"

Whatever else she might have said was drowned out by a whip crack of leathery wings and the high screech of a '*zotz* in attack mode.

"Get inside!" JT bellowed, and was relieved to see her bolt for the house. He spun and ducked, then brought up the shotgun and fired at the incoming blur as it soared over the damned wall, its wings fully extended. And intact.

Not for long. Blasting away, JT shredded the bat-faced bastard's wing membranes, rage flaring at the sight of the pale, smooth skin. Human skin. *Shit, Rez. What the hell happened?*

The thing flapped hard and then slammed to the ground short of him, keening in pain and fury. Eyes gleaming coal red, it scrambled to its feet and lunged for him, mouth splitting in a tricornered screech.

He unloaded the second barrel into the creature's face. Chunks and ichor sprayed, and he moved in fast, whipping out his blade and making the necessary cuts—throat and dick—before it could recover.

It puffed to greasy-ass mist, leaving him crouched there, breathing hard. "Son of a—" Another blur hurtled over the wall; another screech raised the hair on the back of his neck. *"Shit!"* He slapped for his ammo belt but wasn't wearing it. The shotgun was empty, the—

"JT, *down*!" Natalie shouted from the house, punctuated by a door slam as she bolted back out with one of his shotguns.

He pancaked it into the dirt and she fired over him, nailing the *'zotz* center-mass. The thing went down hard, and he got himself up and running. Knife. Dick. Gone. He stared at the place where it had been, trying not to see the pink skin of its wings.

"Come on." She was beside him, pulling on his arm, trying to drag him into the house. "There might be more."

"There will be," he said hollowly, not sure how he knew. "They're coming through too fast. They must have used the skull to stabilize the hellmouth somehow. . . ."

"Exactly. And we're going to need more than a couple of empty shotguns if we're going to be any good out there."

That snapped him out of his daze. "Natalie . . ." He trailed off at the sight of her.

Barefoot and wearing his sweats, with her long dark hair swinging into her face, a stone-edged knife stuck in her waistband, and a double-barrel held one-handed, she looked nothing like the fiery, driven researcher whose boundless energy had lured him from the role of observer to that of lover. Her eyes were fierce and determined, her expression set, and she held her body with a hunter's stillness.

Before, she had made him think of joy and laughter, reminding him that there was a larger world out there, one worth saving. Now she reminded him of the warrior women he had once lived among. The change terrified him. Yet at the same time, it gave him something strange and unfamiliar.

It gave him hope.

"Okay," he said with a short, soldier-to-soldier nod. "Let's arm up. I'm sure Rez could use the extra help."

But as they headed inside, she said, "Just defending the village isn't going to be enough. We need to get that skull back."

Frustration beat at him—that she wouldn't listen to reason; that because he had been making love to her instead of hunting, the *'zotz* had taken human victims and patched their wings; that he and Natalie were the only ones at ground zero when there should've been hundreds of magic users holding the barrier.

"I know you want the skull back," he said carefully as he reset the security system—futile, maybe, but at least they might get some warning of an incoming attack. "Believe me, I do, too." Though not for the same reason. She saw it as her identity. At the moment, he considered it an enemy asset. "But while we're trying to find the hellmouth, the *'zotz* will be going after the villagers." The certainty curdled thick and cold in his veins. "More people are going to die."

"Yes, they are." Her eyes were shadowed with grief, her voice steady with purpose as she swapped his sweats for her beat-up clothes from the day before. "But how many will die if the *camazotz* use the skull for an equinox ritual?" When he didn't have an answer for that one, she nodded. "Thought so. Which means we need to get the skull back and destroy the hellmouth."

He scowled, hating the hell out of the situation. "I should've run you and your team out of the area when I had the chance."

"I would've come back." Fully dressed now, she moved to face him, so they stood toe-to-toe in the center of the main room. She looked up at him, reached up to cup his face in her palms. "It's time to stop defending your perimeter and go on the offensive."

"*Winikin* don't do offense," he grated, trying not to notice how her warmth seeped into him, trying not to remember the things her soft scent made him want to dwell on.

"I do," she countered. "So what does that make me?"

"Mine," he rasped. And he leaned down and kissed her long and deep, trying to let his touch tell her what he couldn't say aloud.

Damn it. He was way out of his depth and sinking fast. He didn't know what she was or what the gods intended for them—if, indeed, the gods were still in charge. All he knew was that his life had been changing since she had come into it; *he* had been changing. And he didn't want to be alone anymore.

As he molded her body against his, rampant desire raced through him, a mix of sexual need and hard, hot protective urges. He wanted to lock her in the house and keep her safe, wanted to surround her with a protective force field, wanted to—hell, he wanted to put her in a bubble where nothing could touch her except him.

But as he gentled his kiss and slid his hands down her arms, so their fingers linked and held, he knew that would make him no better than the masters he had once served. Because it wasn't what she wanted. She wanted to be out there, in the thick of the action. She wanted to find herself, wanted to find answers.

"You scare the hell out of me," he said against her mouth.

Drawing back, she looked up at him, her eyes smoky with passion, her lips moist and full. "We have to go after the skull, JT. I just know it, deep down inside." She flattened her palm over his heart. "I know it in here."

He closed his eyes, for the first time in his life wishing that he were a magic user. Because then he could've hit her with a sleep spell and kept her safely snoring until the equinox was over. Except that she was right. They couldn't ride this one out. Something had to give.

And that something, apparently, was him.

"Okay. We'll do it your way." He pressed his forehead to hers, holding her a moment longer. Then he let her go and stepped away. "Come on," he said, heading for the trick door that led to his office . . . and the weapons cache beyond. "If we're going after the bastards on their own turf, we're going to need some serious firepower."

Chapter Six

As they headed into the forest, Natalie didn't know whether it was the approaching equinox or the knowledge that the two of them were doing what they had been born to do, but the magic was working. She could see a golden sparkle in the air; it flowed in a thin, translucent ribbon, leading her onward as the blue-black of dawn became the gray of morning.

Behind her, JT was heavily armed and carrying enough explosives to collapse a dozen nesting tunnels. And if part of her worried that he would want to simply collapse the hellmouth, sacrificing the skull to avoid a direct fight, she had decided that she would deal with that if and when it happened. Because one thing was certain: She had to get the skull back. It was a tangible link to the magic. More, it was *hers*.

"This can't be right." He kept his voice low, but the concern in his tone was evident. "We've circled around. The village can't be more than five, ten minutes west of here, max. There's nothing in this area but a couple of carved pillars. No temple, no hellmouth."

"We're practically on top of it," Natalie said, looking back over her shoulder at him as she stepped between two wide tree trunks and through a waist-high layer of thick, leafy ferns. "Trust me."

"It's not about trust. It's—" He broke off. "Gods help us," he whispered, the words coming from both shock and prayer as he looked beyond her.

Natalie spun. And gaped.

The clearing that opened in front of them held the broken pillars he had mentioned. But that wasn't all. Where before there had been only a few scattered stones, now there were dozens of intact pillars as well, their carvings crisp and new, the bat glyphs prominent.

The pillars formed a circular perimeter around a huge opening where the earth had fallen through to reveal the path of an ancient underground river. The dry riverbed came up to almost the surface on one side, then sloped down and split into three dark-mouthed tunnels, where tributaries had once flowed. The cave walls were incised with hieroglyphs; the central tunnel had life-size *camazotz* carved on either side.

There was no sign of the creatures themselves, but the air smelled of rotting flesh. This was their home. Their origin.

Gods, Natalie thought, the plural seeming suddenly right.

She had walked right across the clearing a few days earlier and it had felt like solid earth. Either the equinox had opened the hellmouth, or the skull was somehow involved.

A shadow moved within the central tunnel.

"Get down!" JT hissed, yanking her below the level of the leafy ferns, where they would be hidden. Once they were both down, he parted several fronds and looked through. *"Shit."*

A line of skeletal, patchy-skinned *camazotz* were

emerging from the center tunnel, their steps slow and uneven.

He whispered, "They must've just come through the barrier, which means they'll be hungry and looking for hides." He glanced at her. "Can you still sense the skull?"

Her stomach shimmied. "It's down that same tunnel."

"Probably leads straight to the hellmouth."

"So what's the plan?" Her blood pounded with the need to reclaim the crystal skull.

"There isn't any plan." His expression went hard and closed, becoming that of the man who had dumped her. "We can't go down there."

Her heart clutched. "I thought we had an agreement."

Regret flickered in his eyes. "Natalie, be reasonable."

"And let those bastards have the skull?" Panic kicked at the thought, coming from the instincts that hadn't ever failed her. Except, maybe, when it came to him.

"Going down there would be suicide."

"So is doing nothing. This isn't just about one equinox. It's about the next two years, and you damn well know it."

In the clearing, the gaunt *camazotz* started disappearing into the forest in pairs, all headed toward the village.

JT's eyes darkened. "We need to help them fight off those things," he said urgently. "You're right that this isn't about one grand gesture; it's about a long-term war. And you don't know for certain that getting the skull back will do a damned thing to change the outcome." He paused. "Or do you?"

She hesitated. The lie would change his mind, and he'd lied to her plenty. But she couldn't do it. "It's an educated guess." A wish. A hope. "The skull brought me here. Hell, for all I know, it brought you here, too. We can't just let the bastards have it. This is our ..." She trailed off, knowing he didn't want to hear about duty or destiny. Not after what he'd lived through.

His eyes softened. "Natalie—"

A crash in the brush behind him, away from the tunnel mouth, had them both going for their weapons.

"Stay here," he hissed, his expression shifting to that of the hard-eyed hunter in a split second. "I'll be right back." He disappeared noiselessly, with only a faint swirl of foliage to show where he had been.

She hesitated for a moment, but knew she didn't have a choice. She had to get the skull back, no matter what it took. And she couldn't afford to give him the chance to stop her.

So, chest hollow with fear and heartache, she slipped out of the ferns and headed for the clearing, following the ribbon of yellow light.

Counting himself damned lucky that the commotion had come from a sleek jaguar that had been in no mood to rumble, JT slipped back into the fern patch. And stopped dead.

She was gone.

He had known on some level it was going to come down to this. But he hadn't known that it would make him feel like a thousand toxic claws had just dug into his soul. Pain lashed through him, and he lunged across the ferns to scan the clearing.

The *'zotz* were gone and there was no sign of a commotion. But there was no sign of Natalie, either.

"Godsdamn it," he grated under his breath. She hadn't waited for him, hadn't trusted that he was trying to do the right thing, too. And now she was down there alone.

Every instinct he possessed screamed for him to follow her. She was his. He loved her, damn it. He loved her sloe-eyed dark beauty, loved her damnable bravery. Hell, he even loved the fact that she wanted to find her past, her place.

He had to go after her, protect her. But how? He was only one guy with some guns. He didn't have an army backing him, didn't have—

He froze as the terrible idea came to him full-blown, as though it had been sent by the gods themselves. Or their dark counterparts. *Oh, holy fuck*, he thought, his gut clenching on the, *No way. No fucking way.*

It was an unbearable answer. And it might be the only chance any of them had.

He bolted for the village, yanking his cell as he ran.

"Come on, come *on*!" But the call didn't go through. The barrier was in full flux. *"Shit."*

He ran hard, sacrificing stealth for speed.

A blur came at him from the side. He nailed the '*zotz* with both barrels of his shotgun, but didn't stop to finish it off, just kept going.

At the gunshot, shadows oriented on him, closed on him. He fired as he ran, blasting a hole in the demons' net and dodging a claw slash on the way through. Then— *Thank fuck!*—he burst through the trees into the clearing that surrounded the village.

His gut clutched at the sight of the villagers dressed in the ceremonial garb of their Mayan ancestors, ready for the equinox rituals they hoped would push back the demons for another few months. The shotguns and grenade launchers they carried were a stark contrast to the brightly colored woven textiles, feather-and-jade headdresses, and bold, geometric face paint they wore.

When he saw JT, Rez shouted the equivalent of, "Make a hole!" in his native language. The villagers opened fire, knocking back the pursuing *'zotz* as JT lunged through the defensive perimeter, his heart hammering for him to *hurry, hurry, hurry!*

He gripped Rez's forearm. "I need your help."

"Anything, *chan camazotz.*"

He had known that would be the answer, but it only added to the weight of responsibility that suddenly descended on him, nearly crushed him. "Natalie found the main temple. I want to attack it and shut them down for good. But I can't do it alone."

Beneath his feathered headdress and black zigzag paint, Rez's expression firmed. "I'm with you. How many others do you need?"

Time telescoped, and JT felt the terrible weight of his decision. "Everyone." And even that might not be enough. But the village's fate would be decided one way or the other today. By the end of this equinox, they would all be free . . . or they would all be dead.

"Hurry," he urged as Rez started snapping out orders, sending the older children to collect the younger ones in a sturdy central building, which would be guarded by the few warriors they would leave behind. The rest would follow JT as soon as they had loaded up on ammo.

Hang on, Natalie, he whispered deep in his soul. *We're coming.*

He just hoped to hell they weren't already too late.

Natalie's heart hammered as she crouched behind a broken pillar as a pair of new *camazotz* passed way too close for comfort, headed into the forest. When they were gone, she exhaled shallowly and thanked the gods that the newborns' perceptions were as weak as their bodies. She had gotten lucky so far. She only prayed her luck would hold.

Slipping from concealment, she headed for the central tunnel, shivering as she entered and the temperature plummeted. Stalactites dripped down from the tunnel's ceiling, and a snail trail of water ran along one side, glistening in the pools of sunlight that were let in by a series of natural skylights created by fallen-in sections.

The ribbon of golden energy connecting her to the skull beckoned her onward, but she hesitated, looking back over her shoulder at the bright blue sky of a jarringly beautiful spring day.

"Damn it, JT," she whispered. She would've given anything to have his solid, centered presence by her side. But he hadn't come after her. She was on her own.

The tunnel went from dark to light and back again as she passed beneath the ragged openings, then mostly dark as it angled downward. She didn't dare use her flashlight, but there was light once more up ahead. She fixed on it, kept moving toward it, feeling her way along the slippery stone track, which grew treacherous as the incline increased.

Breathing through her mouth to avoid as much of the stench as possible, she paused when she reached a sharp bend in the tunnel. Moving carefully and staying low, she peered around the corner. And caught her breath, stomach knotting. *Oh, sweet Christ.*

Beyond the corner, the tunnel dead-ended in a roughly rectangular cavern, which was open to the sky, with stalactites spearing down from the ceiling, dripping into pools of stagnant, slimy water. The opening was crisscrossed with vines and branches, turning the sunlight green and dank. In one corner, several reddish, glistening things hung in the shadows. *Bodies,* she thought, her stomach knotting with horror. But she fixed her attention on the chamber's sole occupant: a huge black-furred *camazotz*.

It faced the far wall, where a tall panel of carved hieroglyphs rippled fluidly with strange energy. The creature's fully intact wings were tucked tightly around its back, and it wore two heavy stone yokes, one around its throat and another that hung low on its hips, protecting its genitals.

Oily brown energy hung around it, moving from the *camazotz* to the pulsing wall and back. As she watched, a shadow moved on the other side of the swirling panel, and then the ripples parted and a stringy, skinny *camazotz* fell through. It landed wetly and struggled up with red hatred burning in its eyes as it glared around the cave.

Holy shit. Natalie swallowed a surge of fear that threatened to lock her in place. This was it. This was the source, the hellmouth. More, as the big *camazotz* turned to shove the newborn aside, she caught a flash of yellow hanging on a cord around its neck.

The crystal skull!

She was moving before she was aware of having made the decision, lunging across the chamber and unloading the pump-action into the newborn as she came. Black ichor splashed and the creature flew backward. She didn't waste time finishing it off, but kept going, firing the rest of her jade-loaded shells into the bigger demon's abdomen, knocking it away from the wall.

With surprise on her side, she got inside the huge *camazotz*'s guard. As it roared and swung at her, she dodged, grabbed the skull, and used her knife to cut it free from beneath the stone collar that protected the creature's neck.

The *camazotz* shrieked and raked at her with teeth

and claws, but the moment she had the skull clutched tightly in her hand, strange heat detonated inside her and the shimmering gold energy was suddenly *inside* her. It poured into her, filled her up, made her feel faster and stronger, like a trained fighter rather than her usual small, scrappy self.

Pivoting beneath the creature's next attack, she ducked, got the knife up, and carved a long furrow in its wing membrane. When the *camazotz* jerked back, screaming in pain, she spun and bolted for the tunnel.

Thud. Two more of the creatures dropped straight into her path, their intact wings spread wide. Their eyes burned like coals and their mouths split in three-pronged shrieks. Fear slashed through the golden glow of magic as she spun, skidded on ichor, and went down. She rolled and scrambled up, but more wings boomed, more demons hurtled down from up above, darkening the chamber as they blocked out the light.

Heart hammering, she ducked a claw swipe and rammed the butt end of the shotgun into a gaping three-cornered mouth. Then, breath sobbing in her lungs, she chucked the empty gun, pulled her autopistol—her last real weapon—and started blasting away, trying to drive the creatures back.

But the pistol lacked the knockdown power of the shotgun. The creatures kept coming, then fell back, parting to let their giant leader through. His burning-coal eyes were locked on her, on the skull. The stench enfolded her, bringing panic.

Heart hammering, she backed up, slammed into the wall, and couldn't go any farther.

Oh, shit. Oh, shit-shit-shit. Terror poured through her. She was done. She was dead. She was—

"Natalie, *down!*" The shout paralyzed her for a second, but then her body took over and she threw herself on the slimy floor as a hail of gunfire cut through the space where she had been. Black liquid sprayed and the big *camazotz* reeled back, mouth splitting in a shriek of pain that soared above her hearing, then was drowned out as dozens of other weapons opened fire in a deafening salvo.

She scrambled partway up, watching in gape-jawed shock as the past came alive and Mayan men and women wearing bright ceremonial tunics and headdresses, their faces daubed with war paint, poured into the chamber. But rather than stone clubs and wooden spears, they were armed with grenade launchers, shotguns, and knives. Moving with almost military precision, they formed two lines. The warriors in the front line mowed down the *camazotz* and advanced, while the second line went to work with their knives, cutting the bat-demons and banishing them to oily smoke.

And in the center of it all was JT. Wearing his hunting clothes, bandoliers, and a snarl of feral rage, he fought the huge *camazotz* knife against claw, trying to get past the stone yokes that protected its throat and genitals.

Her heart surged. He had come back for her. He was fighting for her, going to war for her. But he had lost his guns, and none of the other warriors had a clean shot.

And as she watched in horror, she saw his footing start to slip.

JT! Jamming the skull into her pocket, she bolted for the combatants. She wouldn't let him down.

"Natalie, no!" he shouted. "Stay back!"

She ignored him and went in high with her knife, aiming for the tied sinew that held the collar in place. She slashed through it and then, as the creature shrieked and spun, she went for the ties on the hip yoke. And missed.

"*Natalie!*" His voice was anguished, the demon's rage palpable as it lunged for her.

A blur caught it from the side as JT rammed into the much larger creature, somehow managing to drive it aside and take it down. Roaring, he plunged his knife into its exposed throat, ripping through skin, tendon, and vessels with one convulsive slash.

The *camazotz* leader arched and writhed, flailing with its now-ragged wings as JT cut through the hip ties and hacked the thing's dick off with a grisly sawing motion.

For a second nothing happened. Then the *camazotz* disappeared.

The belch of foul, oily smoke dissipated quickly, leaving JT and Natalie together in a small oasis of calm, while around them the villagers mopped up the last of the creatures.

His eyes fixed on her, dark with emotion. His mouth silently shaped her name.

Relief hammered through her, alongside a hard, hot flush of victory. "*JT!*" She flung herself at him, wrapped herself around him, and burrowed in tightly when his arms came up to band around her. "You came back for me," she said against his neck, then pulled away to look into his eyes. "I guess you *are* into me, after all."

"I love you." He said it without pretense or preamble. It was stark. It was the truth.

She hadn't been braced for it, hadn't been expecting it, and the shock left her gaping.

His expression clouded. "I know I'm a bad bet. I'm barely civilized on a good day, and I'm more used to keeping secrets than telling the truth. But I'll work on it, I swear. You said once that you were falling for me. If you'll give me another chance, I'll—"

She cut him off with a kiss. It started soft, as a way

to shut him up, but quickly gained heat and depth, becoming a grinding grapple of relief and the mad, powerful joy that thrilled through her like liquid gold as she pulled away. "I'm not falling for you anymore. I already fell." She met his eyes, saw the truth there, the solidity that anchored her restlessness. "I love you, too."

His face blanked and then flushed; his eyes glowed with love. "Natalie, I—"

"*Chan camazotz!*" Rez shouted.

They jolted apart and spun, dropping into defensive crouches, knives at the ready.

But there was no way to defend against what they saw. Not with knives. Maybe not even with jade-tips.

A huge shadow darkened the glittering swirl of the hellmouth. A harsh rattle gathered, stringing the air tight as the swirls thickened and took on form and substance, going from shadow to a deep, fiery orange that froze Natalie to her marrow.

Her stomach dropped. She didn't know what was about to come through, but every instinct she had ever possessed, ever relied on, said that if it got through, they were all dead. "*Christ.*"

"We can leave," JT said tightly. "We can blow the tunnel from topside. That might keep it trapped." But he didn't move, except to load his shotguns, eyes fixed on the hellmouth. Because they both knew that whatever was trying to come through, it wasn't a *camazotz*. And it wasn't going to stay trapped for long.

"I think—" She broke off on a low gasp when a sharp pain stung her upper thigh. She slapped for the spot, afraid she'd been tagged by a claw swipe. But her fingertips encountered a hard lump instead of blood. The skull.

She dug in her pocket, hissing when the stone burned

her fingertips, then whispering, "Holy shit," when she pulled it out.

The crystal skull was glowing gold, its hollow eye sockets gleaming red, not the fire of the *camazotz*, but a deep bloodred crimson that made her heart sing.

JT let out a low, reverent oath. "Magic," he said softly. "You're a magic user. A skull wielder."

But she shook her head. "I don't think so. I think ... I think I'm just its transportation." She couldn't feel the warm golden glow anymore. All the power was once again collected within the skull itself.

"*Chan camazotz*," Rez said again, his voice low and urgent.

"I know." JT lifted his shotgun as the fiery orange swirl bowed inward, the barrier stretching membrane-thin and showing hints of a smoky creature with six-clawed hands and a wide slash of a tooth-filled mouth.

Sacrifice hurts. The words whispered deep inside Natalie, though she wasn't sure if they were a memory or something else.

She opened her hand and looked down at the crystal skull, the gleaming stone that was now streaked with blood and ichor.

It was gorgeous. It was powerful. It had belonged to the bloodline her family had served. More, it had called to her, perhaps from the very beginning. And the stories said the magi would wield the skulls in the end-time war.

Yet the magi were gone. And JT had said a terrible sacrifice was needed to open a hellmouth. Her gut said another would seal it for good.

"Stay or go?" he asked, voice tight.

He was offering to let her make the final call. More, he had led the others into battle, sacrificing what he believed in to save her.

Could she do anything less?

Raising the skull, she balanced it on her palm and stared into its bloodred sockets. For a moment, she felt a stir of warmth, saw a spark of gold. Felt a farewell. Almost a benediction.

Then, as the bulging barrier shuddered and started to give way, she flung the skull into the split.

Red-gold light flashed supernova-bright as the skull disappeared into the hellmouth. And then the world went crazy.

Chapter Seven

The hellmouth solidified in an instant and then *shattered*, sending oily brown shrapnel spewing through the chamber. JT grabbed Natalie and spun them, putting himself between her and the needle-sharp spray, which peppered his back and arms, burning him.

There was a roar and a flash. Then nothing. Even the pain faded; the shrapnel spray had left no mark, no blood.

And they were alone. Safe. The place where the hellmouth had been was nothing more than a plain section of cave wall, a powerless blank.

JT shifted his grip on Natalie as the chamber echoed with a sudden, unexpected silence. Her arms came around him, and for a moment they just held each other.

Then Rez let out a whoop. The cry was picked up by the others, their cheers echoing off the surrounding stone and heading up to the sky. It was less a victory cry than a battle shout, a clamor of defiance against the demons.

But one held longer than the others, rising up in a wordless howl of grief. Still holding on to Natalie, JT turned to see a young man, little more than a teen, kneeling by the hanging corpses. He had lost his headdress, and his war paint was streaked, turning the slashing stripes to black tears.

"Oh." Natalie breathed the word, tipping her head against his to lean on him, taking comfort. Giving it.

"Hell," JT rasped.

The others fell silent, and then several closed on the grief-stricken boy, while the rest dispersed to check on the too-still bodies scattered around the chamber. Rez pulled the teen to his feet and led him away, keeping an arm wrapped around the young man's shoulders, talking to him in a low voice. A villager crouched down beside one of the bodies, shook his head, and rose, hands coming away painted red with blood.

"Damn it," JT grated. He did a head count, didn't like the number he came up with. But the air was clear, the '*zotz* gone, the hellmouth sealed.

"I'm sorry," she said softly. "If I hadn't . . ." She trailed off, shaking her head. "No. This was what had to happen. I just wish they didn't need to be involved. I wish . . ." She glanced over at him, her eyes going wary. "I wish we had real backup, real knowledge, and a plan for the next couple of years."

He understood what she was asking. A week ago, even a day ago, he would have pretended he didn't, doing his best to avoid the fight. *Defense, not offense.*

Now he turned to face her squarely, meeting her eyes when he said, "The old training compound was located in New Mexico, in a box canyon near the Chacoan ruins. They had—*we* had a saying: 'What has happened before will happen again.' If any of the Nightkeepers and *winikin* survived, they will have rebuilt on the old site."

She went very still. "Are you sure you're ready to go back?"

He leaned in, touched his lips to hers. "I'm not going back. I'm finally moving forward." He didn't know what the future held, knew only that they would face it together . . . and that he couldn't hide anymore.

Her lips curved beneath his; the kiss deepened. And as the sunlight splashed through the opening far overhead, warmth hummed through him, and golden light sparked at the edges of his vision.

"Magic," she whispered.

"Not magic," he corrected. "Love." But maybe in the end they were two sides of the same power. And maybe—hopefully—that power would be enough to see them through the next two years . . . and beyond.

RED ANGEL

DEIDRE KNIGHT

Chapter One

It was a special kind of tacky that greeted you on the postholiday shelves of the Sandfly, Georgia, Piggly Wiggly. Not exactly primo wrapping paper selection, particularly not for a hostess gift for one of the richest and oldest families in Savannah. Somehow, Sunny figured, their swanky bottle of Dom Pérignon wouldn't look quite right presented in a tinfoil poinsettia *sack*.

She cast a wary glance at her best friend, Kate Rabineau. "You should've bought a gift bag downtown, Katydid. The selection would've been much better than here at the Pig."

"Let's just grab something that the bottle will fit in." Kate glanced impatiently at her watch. "We're late as it is."

"Oh, and whose fault would that be?" Sunny reached for a bag covered in lime green elves and frowned.

"Sunny Renfroe, don't you get started on me," Kate said. "You know I had to look just right today."

They were having brunch with the Angel family—Mason, Jamie, and Shay were fifth-generation demon hunters, and although lately two of those siblings had become friends to both Sunny and Kate, Jamie Angel was a bit of a holdout. He didn't much respect Kate's kind; something to do with her being a vampire and his being a hunter and all that. In other words: Jamie was among the *uninformed*, the kind who naturally sought Kate's blood and life. It had taken a good deal of persuasion by his siblings for him to call off the hunt on the Rabineau family.

But in the end, the fact that Kate was now engaged to Mason Angel's best buddy, Dillon Fox, had won that battle. Since then, Dillon had permanently joined Jamie's paramilitary group of demon hunters, and Jamie had respected the vampiric cease-fire. But it didn't mean Jamie liked Kate any better, and for some reason, his sister, Shay, was determined to change that fact.

Hence, they'd arrived here, at the Piggly Wiggly down the street from the Angels' plantation, surveying nearly week-old wrapping paper and cards.

Sunny planted her hands on both hips. "All that's left are marked-down Christmas leftovers." She retrieved a poinsettia-adorned bag, the kind made specifically for champagne and wine gifts. "This thing's tackier than my mama's light-up lawn reindeer."

Kate snorted impatiently. "I'm not the one who wants to impress Jamie Angel."

"Which is why you took an extra thirty minutes fixin' your hair?"

"This is your cockeyed plan, not mine," Kate disagreed.

"And Shay's. Don't forget, this get-together was her idea, too."

Kate retrieved the bag covered in neon lime elves. "Let's make her laugh . . . and snub Jamie at the same time. We can tell him this was closest thing we could find to the Grinch."

Sunny wasn't so sure; maybe it was her Southern

manners, but she wanted something pretty. "Give me another second," she told her friend. "I'm gonna look down in the wine section."

Kate glanced at her watch again. "Dillon's waiting for us out in the car. I don't like leaving him so long."

Sunny smiled at her friend. "Honey, Dillon's fine! He hunts demons and you never fret for a minute. Why should you worry if he's sitting out in the parking lot?"

Kate glanced away, saying nothing, but Sunny understood. Dillon had been blinded by a mortar round while serving with his unit in Iraq, and although his guide dog, Lulu, was with him nearly everywhere, and he was fully independent and part of the Shades, Kate's love for him ran deep. So every now and then she became a bit too protective—usually when Dillon wasn't around to catch her doing so.

Kate released a tight breath. "Okay, sure, and I'll keep looking in this aisle."

Sunny strolled toward the shelves filled with wine and beer. Bingo—at the very end of the row, she saw an absolutely lovely bag with sequins and tassels. She was about to grab it when a horrific stench reached her nostrils. The hair on her nape prickled, her body tensed, and her otherworldly senses kicked into high gear.

With one sideways glance, she saw the demon over near the checkout lines. His blazing red eyes were laser-locked on Kate, who stood obliviously looking at gift cards. Even if Kate had turned, she never would've seen the rapacious creature. She wasn't a hunter, didn't have the sight—and she wasn't what Sunny was, either.

Kate Rabineau was, however, a magnet for creatures of darkness who craved her blood because of the supernatural strength it would give them. Demons like this one regularly stalked Kate—and Sunny, because of her unique destiny, routinely destroyed them. Day in, day out, Sunny safeguarded her dear friend, all without Kate's knowledge that Sunny wasn't human, not even close.

Summoning her power, Sunny created a shield illusion. Everyone in the store would see an image of Sunny, just another African-American woman shopping in the aisle of the Piggly Wiggly, when in fact she was already moving faster than any human eye could track. She had surging handfuls of power in both palms, and threw that destructive energy toward the vicious demon.

He glanced up, red eyes growing wide in surprise.

"Eat this!" she cried in a voice that only the demon or other angels might hear.

Long fangs were exposed as the demon roared in terror, but the sound and his paltry life were instantly snuffed out by her assault. The blazing glory engulfed him instantaneously, and he dissolved before her eyes. Only the echo of his hoarse cries remained, and even that extinguished a moment later.

Sunny stood there, gasping for breath, and couldn't help smiling when she realized she was standing by the express checkout lane. That was exactly what she'd served that sinful creature: an immediate departure from the world. No more torturing of humans, no more stalking of vampires for their rare blood. She had the urge to don a cashier's apron. "Next!" she'd love to cry, and get some more vile beings dispatched. As it was, though, she had a brunch to attend. Which pretty much summed up her life here on earth; it was like being a supernatural double agent, where you pretended to be normal while kicking ass on the sly.

Summoning her power, she bounded back to the place where she'd stood in the aisle, released the mirage that she'd kept in place, and grabbed the gift bag.

One enemy down, all in a day's work for a vampire's guardian. Now to make sure that Kate didn't suspect a thing, which was always the trickiest part of the job.

"So let me get this straight. You want a *vampire* to spend New Year's at our house." Jamie Angel looked at his younger brother, Mason, who, just like Jamie, was committed to hunting and destroying all creatures of darkness. Vampires included. At least until very recently.

"That's the idea," Mason agreed, his expression pure innocence as he raised the newspaper just high enough to avoid Jamie's sharp gaze.

In a city the size of Savannah, the paper was still relevant, especially in their line of work. Checking out the obits, reading about unsolved local crimes, even scanning the business section—all were important in pursuing leads regarding paranormal activity.

At the moment, however, Mace was using the newspaper as a shield, which pissed Jamie off, seeing as how he had every right to be worked up. The Angel family had spent generations battling demons and vampires, and now Mason's marine buddy, Dillon Fox, had gone and *gotten engaged* to one. A vampire. That was bad enough, especially since Dillon was part of the Shades, their elite paramilitary group of hunters. But no, apparently it *wasn't* bad enough: Now Mason had invited Dillon and his bloodsucking fiancée over to watch bowl games on New Year's Day.

Jamie took a long sip of sweet tea. "You know where I stand on Dillon's upcoming marriage to that . . . that . . . Oh, good God, I can't even say it, much less imagine her on our property. Daddy's probably rolling over in his grave as it is."

Mason lowered the paper just enough to give him a pointed look. "Don't be a vampist, Jamie."

"Political correctness doesn't extend to vampires, brother. Nor do social invitations, at least not from me. Isn't it enough that I've called off the hunt for the Rabineaus?"

Mason sighed. "It's a party. Everyone's coming."

"Everyone," Jamie repeated, and then cursed under his breath.

"Everyone who matters, at least to me. I'll have Nik. Shay'll have Ajax. The rest of the Spartan brothers are coming. And you can invite whichever skanky chick you're seeing right now. Who is it this week again? Tori? Tawny? Titty?"

Jamie flipped him off. "Her name is Terri Lynn Sweeney, and she's a nice girl."

"Just like all the women you date. Natch. Met her at a strip club, did you?" Mason snickered, his green eyes filled with mischief.

"I've only been out with her a few times," Jamie said. "And it was a bar, thank you very much."

"Okay, well, shit yeah, you bring your girl, I bring my guy, Shay brings her husband ... and Dillon Fox brings his fiancée. No biggie at all." Mason resumed reading the paper as if they were discussing the latest shift in stock prices.

Jamie stepped forward and yanked the newspaper out of his brother's hands with an irritated gesture. "I'm not gonna sit back and let this house get desecrated by a vampire, not even a supposedly 'friendly' one. Not on my watch, bro."

Mason scowled at him. "This isn't a church, Jamie."

"No, but it's something just as sacred to me. My home. Our *family's* home for six generations." Jamie stalked over to the credenza, where Shay had laid out Sunday brunch, and began loading a plate with biscuits and cheese-grits casserole and scrambled eggs. "Color me impolite, but I just don't like the idea of your pals eating hoppin' John and lounging around on Mama's favorite settee."

"Jesus, you're the one who recruited Dillon for the Shades. Hasn't he done good work since joining the team?"

"Of course," Jamie acknowledged softly. Blind or not, Dillon Fox had turned out to be one hell of a hunter, with an almost uncanny sixth sense for tracking demons. "But he loses points for his choice of spouse. He was supposed to *investigate* her, remember? Not fall in love and get engaged to her."

Mace sat back in his chair. "Kate Rabineau's a good woman. If you spent any time with her . . ."

"I've known her since I was eight years old!" Jamie bellowed. "And I've known she was a vampire and to be avoided at all costs since then, too. Your battle buddy's got some piss-poor judgment with his choice of a mate."

Mace leaned back in his seat and stared at Jamie for a long moment. "Do you even realize how many times Dillon had my back while we were in combat? He saved my life more than once, just so you know, and that means I give him the benefit of the fucking doubt. In all regards. If he's in love with Kate, if he says she's to be trusted, then that's good enough for me."

Their sister, Shay, whistled as she walked in the dining room. "Plus, he's hotter than Sunday pancakes."

Mason got a gleam in his eyes at that observation. "Yeah, well, there's a reason I nicknamed him Foxy."

Since Mace had come out to them two months earlier, he'd become more forward and vocal about his sexual orientation—including how hard he'd fallen for one of the Spartan immortals, Nikos Dounias. Lately Nik spent almost as much time at the plantation as he did over at the warriors' compound, and just as many nights in Mace's room.

No wonder Mason had so much sympathy for Dillon's falling in love with someone unexpected, someone otherworldly to the extreme. His own lover was a good twenty-five hundred years old, hardly the girl—or even boy—next-door type.

Jamie sank down into the chair again, spreading a starched napkin on his lap. Since their mother's death nine months earlier, Shay had worked hard to fill the void she'd left behind, and that included upholding their family traditions: Sunday brunch, fine linens, pimento-cheese sandwiches, antique china, the whole nine yards. This while she was emerging as one of the best demon fighters Jamie had ever seen. Which meant that Shay, in a very real sense, had become the lady of their family home, and if she wanted to entertain vampires, her vote carried more weight than his own.

Which irritated the ever-living tar out of him. He was their big brother, damn it. He led the Shades, and he was supposed to call the shots around here . . . but he was also supposed to be a gentleman. That was how his mama had raised him, and it was obvious that putting the kibosh on Dillon and Kate's invitation didn't fall under the "mannerly" category.

But it was more than that, and deep down he knew it. He was the eldest, but both of his younger siblings had settled down, while he kept burning through girlfriends like a book of matches. Hell, who was he fooling? It had been years since he'd had a legitimate "girlfriend." He dated. He hooked up. He prowled. But he rarely had the same girl in his life for more than a few weeks, and until recently, he'd liked it that way. His line of work wasn't exactly conducive to healthy, intimate relationships, not when he spent nearly every night patrolling the streets of the city and taking down vile, evil creatures.

Shay walked over to where he sat, and wrapped her arms about his neck. "Come on, Jamie. It'll be good for you to open your mind a little. Besides, Kate is bringing a *friend*," she trilled, giving him a quick kiss on the cheek, and releasing him from the embrace.

"Sissy cat, I'm not interested in dating anyone seriously. Least of all a vampire." He wasn't about to admit that over the holidays, starting at Thanksgiving and culminating on Christmas Day, he'd realized how very alone he was.

Mace leaned back in his seat, sipping his iced tea. "She's not a vampire. She's what Kate calls a 'Normal.'"

Shay pulled out a chair and sat down beside him at the table. "Just chill and it'll be fine, Jamie. And I really think you might like her friend Sunny. She's nothing like your usual type. . . ."

"Booby and blond and none too bright," Mason volunteered helpfully.

"Nope, none of that describes Sunny, but she's . . ." Shay stared into space for a moment, smiling. "She's kind of weirdly magical. I don't know how else to put it."

Jamie took a bite of scrambled eggs and said, "In other words, she's got a great personality. Code words for 'not very attractive.'"

"Oh, not at all." Shay laughed. "She's absolutely gorgeous."

"And single," Mason clarified. "I might be gay, bro, but I can still appreciate a nice-looking woman. Trust us—Sunny's hot."

"Why else do you think I made sure Kate was bringing her along?" Shay laughed, giving Jamie a conspiratorial wink that he pretended not to see.

Great, his siblings were tag-teaming like crazy. Were they reading him like one of the lore volumes their family kept down in the cellar, deciphering his emotional codes like some complex and ancient text? Or maybe he'd been more obvious than he realized. On Christmas Eve, Jax had given Shay a gorgeous ruby ring... and then he'd walked in on Nik kissing Mason under the mistletoe. It had been like a one-two punch, proof that he was painfully single while everyone else he cared about had found true love.

After that, he'd poured himself a double Scotch and gone to bed. Alone. And wished that, just once, he had someone special of his own to hold close on the unseasonably cold holiday night.

He stabbed a fork into his cheese grits with an irritable gesture. "So what y'all are saying is it doesn't matter what I want. Kate and company are coming, and that's it."

"No." Shay reached for the frosty iced tea pitcher and began pouring herself a glass. "But I *am* saying you'd better deal, because they're gonna be here in five minutes—ten, tops."

"What?" Jamie roared. "It's not New Year's for another three days!"

Shay slid into the seat beside him. "Well, it's like this. Apparently someone—not saying *who* ..." Very slowly Shay swung her gaze in Mason's direction. He got a sheepish look, and stared down at his plate. "But someone slipped the word to Dill that you're not too keen on this whole thing."

Jamie flung his napkin onto the table and shoved out of his seat. "Bastard."

"Vampist," Mace shot back. "They're my friends. And as I recall, you're the one who told me you'd always ac-

cept me and the people I care about. . . . Remember that
tap dance? Nothing I'd ever do that you'd judge, yada,
yada?"

Mace had him there. It had been his big-brother pep
talk the night Mason told him he was gay.

Jamie sighed and stared at the ceiling. "I think I'll go
sit on the veranda and smoke a cigar until they leave."

Shay frowned at him, her light blue eyes narrowing
like lasers acquiring a target. "Oh, no, you don't, James
Dixon. They're coming over for brunch so we can plan
the menu for the party."

"Be sure to pick lots of garlic recipes. And I do mean
lots of 'em." With that retort, Jamie grabbed his plate
and stormed off toward the kitchen. Maybe he could
hide in the pantry until the invasion was over.

Sunny sat up in the backseat of Kate's BMW. "Holy
cats! This place is crazy big." She peered out the window
at the mile-long sandy drive and the long row of live oak
trees that lined both sides of it. "I can practically smell
the money."

Kate grunted, glancing at Sunny in the rearview mirror. "Don't be too impressed. . . . Trust me, I grew up
with these people."

"You grew up with *me*, too." Sunny rolled down the
window, the smell of the nearby river and marsh filling
her nostrils. She smiled, closing her eyes, savoring the
familiar low-country scents. The river and marshes and
creeks ran in her veins at this point, and she offered a
quick prayer that she could always stay in Savannah, all
the more because of how Kate needed her protection.
The run-in at the Piggly Wiggly had been only one of a
dozen such encounters in the past few weeks alone.

Kate made a sound of disgust. "Yes, but unlike the

Angels, you never wanted to destroy me, my family, and anyone else like me," Kate retorted, speeding up a little as they continued down the seemingly endless driveway.

"No, girl, I love you. Always."

Kate had been Sunny's best friend since the fateful day in fifth grade when trashy Raylene Gibbs had called Sunny the N-word, and Kate stood up for her. Of course, Kate hadn't known that Sunny wasn't your average ten-year-old—just as she remained unaware of Sunny's true nature even now, some sixteen years later. And that Sunny had been planted in Kate's life for a very particular reason. Certain secrets had to be kept, no matter how much you loved and cared for someone, and Sunny's carefully guarded mission fell into that category.

Dillon spoke up from where he rode in the passenger seat, his guide dog, Lulu, curled across his feet. "Y'all are pals with Shay, and Mason's good people," he drawled, his Nashville accent sultry as ever.

"I have no problem with *Mason*. In fact, I'd say we're friends now," Kate said. "It's his stupidly arrogant and prejudiced brother I can't stand."

Sunny gave Kate a look in the rearview mirror. "Jamie doesn't like black people?"

If that was the case, then this brunch shindig wasn't going to be very enjoyable—at least not for Sunny.

Kate shook her head. "Far as I know, he only has issues with my kind. Thinks he's some big-deal hunter. Smells of too much cologne. Reeks of sexist ladies' man. And as we all know"—Kate glanced sideways at Dillon, who appeared slightly amused—"he despises vampires."

Dillon reached for her hand, staring ahead, eyes unfocused. "Aww, Jamie's not that bad. He's just a little misinformed, especially about the woman I love. I'm gonna straighten him out today, baby.

"But tell me, really," he said, rapping the window with his knuckles. "What *does* it look like here? Mace was always so embarrassed about his family's money. Really played it down when we were in the corps. I never even realized he was loaded for the first few years I served with him."

Sunny gazed up at the expansive live oaks, their branches gnarled like an old woman's hands, Spanish moss dripping downward like heavy lace. "Beautiful," she murmured appreciatively. "A little eerie. Magical. The whole place feels like something from a fairy tale."

And she'd seen plenty of magical, beautiful, amazing places over the centuries. But this particular property felt as if it were under a heavenly spell.

"You haven't even seen the house yet!" Kate laughed. "Sunny Renfroe, you better be strong when we face off with Jamie Angel. If you're this starstruck by his family home, you might drool all over him when I introduce you."

Although she'd lived in Savannah for most of her human life, Sunny never had met Jamie. Her own circle didn't intersect with his high-society one, and even though Kate was old money, their friendship was unique. Beyond that, the Rabineaus were old guard, but kept their distance from most of Savannah society because of their vampire heritage.

Then a thought occurred to her. Although she'd not met Jamie, his brother, Mason, was certainly easy on the eyes, not to mention smart and thoughtful. Maybe Jamie had at least some of Mason's tough-yet-sensitive appeal.

Sunny perked up. "So, tell me, Katie, girl. Is Jamie handsome?"

"Yes, he's hotness," Kate muttered. "And it sucks. It's why he's so full of himself. He's got these big green eyes, dimples . . . He's like six foot three, I think? Six-four maybe? Broad shoulders, rock-hard physique. He looks sorta like Mace, but taller and . . . prettier. Know what I mean? Mace has that rough edge to him, whereas Jamie's smoother. A little preppy."

Dillon laughed. "I don't think I'd ever call Jamie Angel pretty. Then again, I've never seen him. But I've *heard* him with a semiautomatic taking on a legion of demons, and smelled their blood all over him. And all the while he's using that smooth Southern charm on the bastards. If I were a girl, I'd say that's smokin' hot . . . not pretty."

For some reason, Sunny flushed at the thought of meeting Jamie. Dating and boyfriends did not fall under her job description. The implications of forming a romantic relationship for someone like Sunny were, well, just too complicated. So she avoided those kinds of entanglements, but lately she'd been feeling restless. Maybe it was because Kate had fallen in love, and her friend's happiness highlighted the differences in her own life and those of the people she cared about. She was so alone, and even though her bosses forbade love relationships with humans . . . the longer she lived as one, the harder that mandate became. And the truth was, it hadn't been easy to begin with. Just as Kate had done for all those years before meeting Dillon, Sunny longed to feel *normal*.

The fact was, Sunny ached to have a man's strong arms about her, yearned to feel more human than she did on most days. And she desired something that could never happen, not for her. She dreamed . . . of falling in love.

Chapter Two

"James Dixon, get your butt on down here!" Shay called up the stairs, then offered Sunny and Kate an extremely apologetic look. "I am so sorry. He knows better than this."

"Coward," Mason muttered. He bent down and gave Sunny and Kate each a brief kiss on the cheek, welcoming them warmly, then clapped a hand on Dillon's shoulder. "Come on, Foxy. Got a new Glock I wanna show off." The two of them, led by Dillon's guide dog, headed down the hall.

"Jamie!" Shay called out again. "You're not getting out of this one."

Sunny's face flushed hot with shame. She hated feeling like some odious obligation, a pariah for Jamie Angel to avoid. And even though rationally she realized his issues were with Kate, not her, it didn't take the sting out of being so blatantly dissed.

She pasted a smile on her face and tugged on Shay's sweater sleeve. "Forget it, girl. Let's go eat some of your famous grits casserole."

One look at Kate, and Sunny could see her friend wasn't feeling even that generous. She was glancing all about the entry hall as if looking for an escape route.

"I'm telling you . . . this is a mistake," Kate said. "You're rock awesome, Shay, but Jamie's always been a jerk to me. Let's just, I don't know, let's forget the plan. Heck, we can have New Year's out at my family's beach house on Tybee!" she said brightly. "I mean, why not?"

"Because, Katie, you're not going to let this guy intimidate you or snub you." Sunny sniffed at the air, feeling her dander rise. As an African-American woman who'd spent her whole earthly life in the Deep South, she had some experience with prejudice and being socially overlooked; she wasn't about to stand by and let that happen to Kate. Besides that, even when it came to fairly harmless insults, Sunny remained highly protective of Kate.

Shay clearly shared that emotion, and began trotting up the stairs in a huff. "I'm gonna find my brother's sorry ass. Don't you two worry. *James Dixon!*" she bellowed at the top of the steps. She kept calling for him upstairs, sounding completely put out with her brother.

Sunny shook her head in disbelief. "Talk about rude. Where's that boy hiding?"

"I'm not hiding anywhere," a deep, highly masculine voice drawled from behind her. "Ready or not, here I come."

Slowly Sunny pivoted on her booted feet, and found herself face-to-face with the closest thing to a human angel that she'd ever seen. Maybe his name was downright prophetic. With his bright, luminous green eyes, beautiful face, and broad shoulders, she'd have sworn he was hiding a pair of wings on him somewhere.

With a half-cocked, sexy grin, he extended his hand. "Jamie Angel," he said, his voice pure gravel and seduction. "You must be the *friend*."

Sunny blinked up at him, confused, overwhelmed by how outrageously handsome he truly was. "Friend?"

"Yeah, the one my sis is gunning to fix me up with." He raked a slow gaze down her body, lingering for too many seconds on her full breasts. "Now I can see why."

Kate bounded forward and swatted him on the arm. "James Angel, you shut up now. This is my best friend, and I'll not have you . . . pawing at her."

He held up both hands innocently. "I didn't lay a finger on her."

"No, you just clapped your hound-dog gaze on her like she was fine china at a yard sale. Sunny Renfroe isn't cheap and she sure isn't your type."

"Who says she's not?" Jamie asked huskily, never moving his sultry-eyed gaze from Sunny. "You, Kate? We already know I don't trust you or your kind, so why should I put any faith in your evaluation of my 'type'?"

"I'm standing right here!" Sunny cried. "Would you both chill the heck out and stop talking about me like I'm not even in the room?" She stomped a foot, flushing at the way Jamie's light green gaze slid back to her. She returned the stare, tilting her chin defiantly. "Good Lord almighty, Jamie Angel, you're as bad as they all say. Worse, maybe."

One elegant eyebrow lifted. "Who all?"

"Just about every woman in this town . . . your own sister, even."

Jamie rolled his eyes. "So Shay wants to fix us up, and yet she's warned you that I'm a scoundrel?"

Sunny couldn't help laughing. "Bull's-eye. Her exact word for you."

"Think that's the first time I've heard her call me that?" He stepped much closer, smiling down at her so broadly that his dimples deepened. "What do you say I show you around the place? Take you for a walk down to the creek marsh?"

Those were the words he used, but the message in his eyes suggested something much, much more dangerous. It was as if he were playing a game with her, seeing how far he could push her boundaries while he toyed with her.

Sunny squared her shoulders and drew in a cleansing breath. She had a mission here, and it didn't include getting ogled by—or ogling—the subject of said mission. "Look, let's have a nice, pleasant round of introductions, and then we can all—*all* of us—go sip a little tea, whatever."

"It's brunch, Shay style. In the formal dining room." Jamie gave a gallant half bow, and the elegance of the gesture was at total odds with his worn cowboy boots and faded jeans. Preppy? Not so much. Or maybe he was just tricked out in his Sunday casual.

He extended his hand again, and smiled his fallen-angel's smile once more. "Nice to meet you, Sunny Renfroe. And just for the record? You can be my type anytime."

The devil. Sunny flushed even hotter, and glared at him. He knew she found him beautiful; he *knew* that every woman, throughout his short mortal life, had found him sexy, at least to some degree. His gaze drifted down her body, and he actually cocked his head sideways for a better look at her long legs, which were highly visible because of her miniskirt. She flushed, hoping she hadn't missed cleaning off some obvious speck of demon's blood.

"Nice," he said in a slow, simmering tone. "Very, very nice."

She'd been around men with money before; they had a tendency to believe they could buy or own anyone or anything that suited their fancy. Well, she sure as heck wasn't a show horse or an antique vase or any other object of beauty he could purchase when the whim struck him.

Sunny planted a hand on her hip and repaid his assessing study. She started on his face, taking in the strong jaw covered in light beard growth, then lingered on his full, luscious lips. But she really kicked into gear by dragging her gaze down to his hips and mimicking his earlier gesture as she angled for a better look at his rear.

Then, with a nonchalant shrug, she said, "Nice."

Jamie looked pleased with himself, puffing out his chest. That was probably why Sunny couldn't resist adding, "I mean, if you like white dudes with wimpy physiques. That kind of nice . . . I guess."

"Wimpy?" Jamie repeated in disbelief. He was built, and at six foot four, no one had implied he wasn't strong and muscular since he'd grown seven inches in the ninth grade.

Who was this chick? Shay had said she was human, yet something was different about her. She sure didn't *smell* like a vampire, didn't have that tangy scent that was coming off Kate. In fact, she actually emanated a kind of gardenia aroma, one of heavenly sweetness. Among Jamie's many spiritual gifts, he was what he termed "a smeller," for lack of a better word. It was more than having the sight, which he'd had since he was not quite ten years old. Being able to spot demons was just one part of his unusual abilities. He could also identify supernatural entities based on the way they smelled. He'd even, occasionally during Easter, smelled the Holy Spirit while in church. A perfect aroma unlike anything found on earth.

Sunny, with her high-heeled boots and short skirt, smelled pure and sweet. Could she somehow be a demon, masking her true nature by an act of subterfuge? No, that wouldn't work, because their entire property was warded against demons and dark spirits. Besides that, there wasn't a demon within a half-mile radius that he wouldn't sniff out.

"What *are* you?" he blurted, catching another whiff of her downright gorgeous scent.

She laughed, a light, tinkling-chimes sound, smiling so hugely that her big brown eyes crinkled at the edges. It was an innocent, totally surprising sort of smile, one that spoke of goodness and true joy.

She looked up into his eyes, her own lovely brown ones sparkling. "Oh, honey, puh-lease! Just because I put you in your place, now I'm suspect?" she teased. "Is it really *that* uncommon for you to get as good as you give, Jamie Angel?"

And he actually blushed. He, the always smooth, ever-unflappable guy, felt heat creep all the way down his neck. It wasn't what she'd said—it was all in how she was smiling up at him, the warmth in her gaze, the gentle mockery in her eyes. She was so unlike the women he always dated, with their rode-hard-put-up-wet expressions, their stale flirtations . . . and yet she *was* flirting. Wasn't she?

"Speechless, are you?" She laughed lightly, and finally broke their long, shared glance by turning to Kate. "He's a pussycat, baby," she told her best friend. "All meow and no bite at all."

He frowned back at her, his earlier flirtation gone. Initially, he'd been playing a role with her, one that was intended to annoy the crap out of Kate Rabineau and possibly even tick off Shay for having set him up like this. But all that was changing by the millisecond because of one simple fact: Sunny was ravishing, with honey-dark skin that had a glow to it, almost as if she'd been touched by the sun. Her eyes were wide set and almond-shaped, with long, dark lashes. They gave her a mysterious look—they were also sexy as living hell. Ordinarily, he'd have been all over her for the duration of her visit, but he was truly unsettled by the unusual, eerie innocence he sensed in her. It was downright otherworldly, and he couldn't be wrong about that fact.

"Jamie?" Sunny prompted, staring up into his face. This time she sounded almost . . . concerned.

He studied her, rubbing his temple. There had to be a way to pin down her true identity and nature. His mind whirled, grasping at any number of possibilities. The radiance of her burnished skin was lovely, but it wasn't normal or human. This chick literally seemed to glow a little.

He squinted down at her, as if somehow his sight might kick into overdrive and cough up the goods on the woman. "I . . . Seriously, Sunny. Where'd you come from?"

"I grew up here, in Savannah."

"From what age?"

"Since I was a kid," Sunny said, eyeing him oddly. "Why?"

He turned to Kate. "Do *you* see it?" he asked, even though he knew she was the last person who'd validate any theory he might form about her best friend.

Kate didn't balk or deny, but she did stare at him as if he weren't quite speaking English. Then she turned sideways and took a good long look at her friend. After a moment she shook her head in confusion, facing him again. "Jamie, what *are* you talking about? I'm the only vampire in this house right now."

He shook his head numbly. "She's not a vamp."

"I'm glad you can see that." Sunny laughed, the sound musical, beautiful. Strangely soothing and hypnotic.

"No, trust me; I realize she's not a bloodsucker."

Sunny scowled at him. "Now, that, Jamie Angel, is just plain rude. And you here, in your big plantation house, I'd think you'd know better how to treat a lady."

"I'll treat you to the full-court press once you admit it." He gave her a slow, devilish smile, his trademark. It never failed to unravel female composure, and get him whatever or wherever he wanted.

Sunny just scrunched her nose up at him, utterly unaffected. "Admit what?"

"That you're not human." He folded both arms across his chest with a self-satisfied gesture. "Not even close."

"Of course Sunny is human." Shay came trotting down the stairs. "And about time you showed up. First, you vanish when we've got guests coming. And now? You harass them. Good work, big brother. Thanks for being completely embarrassing."

Jamie pointed at Sunny, sputtering, "How . . . how can you not see it, too?"

"*Jamie.*" Shay eyeballed him hard, but before he could explain that he really was just calling it like he saw it, his sister linked arms with Sunny and Kate. "Come on, ladies. Let me show you some proper hospitality. Just ignore Neanderthal James."

Jamie skulked behind them, slowly meandering toward the dining room in their wake. Something about Sunny Renfroe wasn't right; he was sure of it. He didn't get an evil vibe off her, but his senses were definitely picking up that she was supernatural in nature. He just didn't know if she was a threat. He knew enough about evil, too, to realize that it often came dressed up and looking pretty . . . and a lot like what you most wanted. Also, it wouldn't be smart to forget that the wards protecting their property had been compromised several times lately.

Yet how could he explain the instant attraction he'd felt awaken inside of him, an almost magnetic pull toward Sunny Renfroe? He prided himself on never reacting this strongly to any female; he had far too many walls in place to do so.

Besides, she wasn't even his type, although he'd always had a thing for big brown eyes like hers. And for curls, and she a head full of light brown corkscrew spirals that tumbled to her shoulders. Watching those curls bounce as she walked into the dining room, he had to fight the urge to rush after her and stroke one, wrap it around his pinkie.

But evil often came looking pretty and full of seduction. He vowed to remember that. He'd assumed a position of détente regarding Kate and the Savannah-area vampires, but whatever Sunny was . . . Well, he'd made no promises not to expose or hunt other paranormal creatures.

After everyone had wrapped up brunch, Mason brought out a margarita machine, and the vampire crew all seemed to think that cocktails in the afternoon was a splendid idea.

Pain in the ass, that was what it was. Jamie had hoped they'd already be heading out the door by now, not settling in for the long haul. He'd participated in enough Cinco de Mayo celebrations to realize that one margarita had the mystical quality of becoming two or three.

Jamie tailed Mason into the kitchen, where he stood, starting to read the machine's directions.

"So tell me you saw it, too," Jamie hissed under his breath.

Mason glanced up at him curiously. "Saw what?"

"That Sunny girl is supernatural in nature. It can't be good, either, considering she's cavorting with known vampires."

Mason laughed, and started reading the directions again. "Having a vampire in the house has your dander all in a knot. Chill and be nice to them."

"I was plenty polite to them both. I even pulled Kate's chair out for her at the dining table."

Mason smirked. "Well, don't you get the good-citizenship award for gentlemanly excellence?"

"Damn it, Mace, take this seriously. I'm telling you—that female ain't right. She's not human, and she's here, in our house. What's to say she's not doing recon work as we speak? Trying to find the way into the cellar to destroy some of our lore?"

"I can hear her laughing in the dining room," Mason told him matter-of-factly. "Sounds really sinister, too, man. Better go arm yourself down in the cellar, get that new Glock of mine."

As if to underscore Mason's sarcasm, at that exact moment he heard Sunny's light, sweet-sounding laughter as she said, "He's not _that_ hot."

Him. They were laughing at him; he knew it.

"She is not human," he ground out.

"What are you saying, then? That she's a demon?" Mace gave him a hard-boiled stare, the kind of glance he'd probably used to intimidate privates and even squeaky-new lieutenants under his command back in his Marine Corps days. " 'Cause we both know she wouldn't have made it past the wards if that were true."

Jamie sighed. "Didn't stop you from suspecting Juliana a few months ago, the fact that she'd gotten past the protections—and it turned out you were right."

"Partially right," Mace corrected. "Juliana had accidentally bound herself *to* a demon. She wasn't one.... That's how she was able to get past the wards."

"So then why are you automatically assuming I'm wrong, not that maybe I could be on to something? Just like you were on the right track with Juliana. But no, I'm half-cocked and seeing things that aren't there!"

"Jamie, come on, now." Mace set the directions on the kitchen counter and turned to face him. "I'm listening to you."

"But you don't believe me."

"I didn't sense a damn thing about her—so to speak." Mason laughed and Jamie gave him a mirthless look in return. "I could sense Juliana's demon from the moment I laid eyes on her," Mason argued. "With Sunny, I get nothing. Shay's obviously got nothing, too."

"Maybe I'm just a better hunter than you both."

Mason rolled his eyes. "Oh, you did not just say that."

"I'm the eldest, which means I've had the sight longer than either of you."

"You're the head honcho, bro, but that don't make you the most talented in our bunch. You *are* wrong sometimes."

"Name a time."

"Uh, how about now? It's not just Shay and me against you on this one. Dillon's developed a really strong gift with his hunting, too. So that's three of us who don't sense anything wrong with Sunny."

Mason's boyfriend, Nikos, came into the kitchen right then, and Mace's eyes lit up when he saw that Nik had arrived. "Hey, you know how to work a margarita machine?" he asked as Nikos gave him a quick kiss.

They shared a flirtatious glance as Mace handed over the directions, and it was clear that Mason had already halfway forgotten his conversation with Jamie. It was annoying to be around people who had recently fallen in love, and Jamie rolled his eyes, thinking about how passion blinded people to plain good sense.

Wait. That was it. . . . He could use that very thing against Sunny. Get her guard down, then learn the truth. She'd responded to him physically, even though she'd tried to knock him down a few pegs. He'd seen the lust and arousal flare in her eyes, and he'd smelled the desire radiating off her skin, too.

Come New Year's night, he'd find a way to get much, much closer to the woman and, in the process, discover her secret. Then again, why wait at all? What was wrong with enacting his seduction plan today with the power of a few margaritas?

Chapter Three

"Think you can hide from me out here?" Jamie Angel stepped onto the upstairs balcony, where Sunny had been sitting for a few minutes. She loved the bubbling sounds of the creek and marsh. For the end of December, it was an unusually mild evening, and the light breeze from the water was soothing.

And, yes, she had been completely avoiding Jamie for hours, the balcony only her latest effort in that battle. He was too hot, too sexy, and way, way too dangerous. That, and he'd made an obvious point of trying to pursue her ever since brunch. The long afternoon had stretched into early evening, with the holidays clearly making everyone relaxed. Around three p.m., Mason had broken out the margarita machine he'd received as a Christmas present from Shay, and now pretty much everyone was feeling a little bit toasty.

Jamie sprawled into a wicker chair beside her, draining the last of his margarita. "You didn't answer me, Sunny." He propped his booted feet up on the balcony railing, tilting his chair back onto two legs in a relaxed, sexy posture. "You've been avoiding me," he observed. "Why?"

"Because you're a bad boy and I know your kind."

She shifted in her own chair, knowing she should leave, yet finding that she lacked the will to do so.

"What happened to me being a *pussy*cat?" He said the last word with a wicked grin.

She rolled her eyes. "You just proved my point most elegantly."

He smiled at her, and for once it didn't seem manufactured or intended to accomplish anything. And it absolutely melted her heart. To see a glimpse of the real Jamie, for just a moment, affected her more strongly than any of his flirtation or innuendo ever could. There was genuine sweetness there. She sensed that he hid it from almost everyone in his life—and that he guarded his heart just as vigilantly.

After a long moment during which it seemed their gazes were locked, neither able to look away or stop smiling at the other, he faced forward again. Reaching in the pocket of his denim jacket, he retrieved a cigar and slowly began trimming it.

"You mind?" he asked as an obvious afterthought, gesturing with the cigar.

She shook her head and rose to her feet. "I was just about to go inside anyway."

As she started to walk past him, Jamie blocked her exit with his left leg, trapping her close against him. "Not so fast, Sunny Renfroe."

There was danger in his tone, but as she looked down into his light green eyes, there was a heap more flirtation.

"I have plans for us," he said, and before she could blink, he reached out and ran one hand along her upper thigh. Slowly he stroked her there, his touch so lingering and sensual that her eyes watered. "Yep, you're as good as I thought you'd be," he whispered throatily. "Better."

She should've shoved him out of the way; she

should've hightailed it to the other side of the veranda. Instead, she stood mesmerized, feeling her skin practically burn as he caressed her leg again, a little higher.

"Why you been avoiding me, huh?" He gazed up at her through slightly lowered lashes. "I'm beginning to think you don't like me very much."

His fingertips rode up beneath the hem of her short skirt. Her breathing increased and her heart thundered so hard that blood rushed in her ears.

"But you *do* like that. I can tell." His beautiful eyes became filled with desire. "So do I."

When his fingertips snaked their way much higher, nearing the edge of her panties, Sunny came back to her senses. Taking hold of his hand, she forced it from underneath her skirt. "Jamie ... you need to stop ... now."

"Why?"

For Jamie, it undoubtedly was that simple: If you liked someone or were attracted to them, you hooked up. No attachments, no entanglements, just pure, uncomplicated pleasure.

Not in her world.

He continued staring into her eyes, waiting for some kind of answer, and only then did she realize that their fingers had become entwined, neither of them letting go. "Because I don't even know you."

"But you could. . . ." He gave her a suggestive glance. "In fact, it's downright biblical. To 'know' me. Very Old Testament, since that was the euphemism they chose."

She flushed. "That's disrespectful."

"God invented sex," he said matter-of-factly. "I happen to believe in God *and* in great lovemaking. I don't see a conflict of interest."

Oh, for me there's one, she thought, trying to still the crazy tempo of her heartbeat and breathing.

"Well," she said on an unsteady exhale, "I don't believe in having sex with someone I just met."

He gave her a ravishing smile, his deep dimples popping into view. "Now, that, Sunny Renfroe, is a full-on crying shame."

He released her hand and turned to light his cigar. Instantly she missed the warmth of his touch, the heat that he'd been stoking inside of her. Stupidly, she had the urge to cry out, *Never mind. Let's start over!* But the moment had been lost.

Jamie puffed on the cigar, blowing the smoke away from her. It curled into the dim light coming from inside the house. He leaned back in his chair again, and it threw him into the shadows. Sunny hated not being able to see him clearly. He had some of the most beautiful human eyes she'd ever seen, so bright, so vivid, especially the way they contrasted with his naturally golden skin.

"So how long does it take, then?" he asked casually.

"For what?"

"Until we've known each other long enough to have sex. For me to seduce you properly. A few hours? A couple of days? A week? Because I'm a very determined man. You should know that."

Sunny leaped to her feet. "I've gotta go."

"Oh, come on, sugar bug. Don't be like that. I'm not trying to scare you off. Sit down and hang out with me for a while. Tell me why it is you've been here most of your life, but I've never met you."

Sunny stood, frozen, trying to decide whether she dared risk staying, because Jamie did scare her—tremendously so, but not because she thought he'd ever harm her. Not that he could overpower her if he tried, not with her otherworldly abilities. It had all been in that one look he'd given her, the hidden sweetness that all his bravado and flirtation masked. Her heart had flipped over inside her chest, her breathing had grown shallow— and she'd known she could fall in love with him. Quickly, swiftly, tumbling all the way down as she fell.

And caring for any human in *that* way was strictly forbidden.

"Jamie, I really need to go back inside right now," she said, starting toward the porch door.

"Oh, come on and take a load off." Jamie wrapped one strong arm about her waist and brought her right down onto his lap before she could even react.

She found herself leaning into a chest that was hard and muscular, her own soft breasts pressing far too close against his strength. His breath was warm on her cheek, and although she expected him to try to kiss her, he did something far more surprising. He reached out and caught one of her curls between his fingers, his breath hitching momentarily.

"God, you know what's amazing about you?" he murmured. "I love your hair. It's beautiful. Well, I mean ... if I had to isolate just one thing, it would be your eyes. I could lose myself in your eyes, Sunny. But I do love these curls."

Very gently, almost tenderly, he began stroking her hair, as if he meant to soothe away her fears of him, her anxiousness about what he was asking for.

He looked deep into her eyes, and although it was dark, she could see intensity in the depths of his gaze, almost as if he were searching for something. Only then did she realize she'd begun trembling slightly. He frowned. "Hey, now. I won't hurt you, sweetheart. I'm all meow, remember?"

She splayed an unsteady hand against his chest. "I forgot about the possibility of teeth and claws."

"Nah, I don't bite and I don't scratch. Well ..." He laughed low in his throat. "That is, I'll stick to the parts you *want* nibbled and toyed with."

Her eyes slid shut. "Jamie, I ... I'm not used to this."

"Being held by a man who wants to give you pleasure? A gorgeous thing like you? I find that impossible to believe."

"Trust me."

"Now, see, *you* don't seem to trust *me*. Am I coming on too strong? Or is it an issue with me in particular? Because from where I'm sitting, you on my lap and my arms around you, I wouldn't be anywhere else right now. And what is that perfume? You have the most unusual scent all over your skin. It makes me want to taste you."

"Jamie!" She pushed at his chest in frustration. "You *are* coming on too strong. Way too strong."

"And yet you're still sitting squarely in my lap. I don't see you rushing to escape." He held his hands up in surrender. "And I'd hate for you to go, but maybe that's best. So long as you promise I can see you again."

She shook her head, turning away from him, and still didn't move from atop his lap. "I'm not ... not experienced. I don't ... I *can't* do this. Okay? Please just let me go."

He cupped her cheek, slowly urging her to face him. For a long moment, he looked into her eyes. "Sunny, baby, how is that possible?"

"You're the one who didn't think I was even human," she said, distress mounting. His myriad signals were confusing, the way he vacillated between seduction and teasing and now gentleness. She found it harder and harder to sort out his intentions.

"Well, are you?"

"You've had your hands all over me. Don't I feel human?"

He caressed her cheek. "You feel soft and beautiful and warm." He sighed, his eyes drifting shut. "Good Lord, you feel ... like everything I need." Slowly he encircled her in his arms, holding her close, like a treasure.

He made her whole body burn with those words and his touch, but he didn't confirm that he'd let go of his suspicions. She had to break contact before he used his famed hunting skills to deduce what she really was.

"You should let me go," she insisted.

He took one long puff on his cigar, studying her, but not releasing his hold on her body. "You're sure?"

"Please."

Releasing her gently, he helped her back to her feet with polite grace. Straightening her clothes, she took a step toward the French doors that led to the home's interior. But before she could open them, Jamie was behind her, pressed close to her body.

His warm breath brushed against the nape of her neck. "I'll give you an hour to reconsider," he whispered seductively. "I'm not in the habit of begging, but I want you something fierce, Sunny Renfroe. I promise I won't hurt you, and I won't dishonor you ... but I will make you feel things you've never known before. If you're willing to risk all of that, meet me down by the creek in exactly an hour. Look for the glass gazebo to the right of the dock. I'll be there waiting for you. Don't disappoint me ... please."

She turned to look at him, but he was already moving back into the shadows.

He'd basically begged her to come to him. What was he thinking? It was like he'd temporarily lost his mind around the woman, become enchanted.

Jamie stared through the glass porch doors and

watched Sunny hurry toward the sofa where Shay and Kate sat. She kept neatening her hair, her clothes, and he smiled at how shy she really was. She hadn't been lying about her lack of experience; he was sure of it. But as she sat down stiffly between his sister and Kate, he panicked slightly. Was she going to tell them what he'd just done? If she did, there was no way she'd ever show at the gazebo, and that disappointed him fiercely—and not just because he wanted to ferret out her true identity.

He hadn't expected her innocence to seduce him. Now he wanted to give her everything he'd just promised . . . and much, much more. If he learned her true nature in the process, that would be an extra bonus, but it was no longer his main desire or concern.

Shay turned to Sunny, saying something, and he held his breath, wondering if Sunny would confess all. Well, it wasn't like Shay or Kate should be surprised. He *was* Jamie Angel, after all, and if they expected him to avoid Sunny Renfroe, then his little sis shouldn't have suggested he might find the woman appealing.

He turned, not wanting to see whether Sunny blabbed about his proposition . . . or his failed seduction attempt. With a heavy groan, he leaned against the side of the porch and closed his eyes. His entire body was on fire, absolutely burning for Sunny. Tonight was supposed to be about subterfuge, about unlocking all her clever mysteries. Instead? He was fully fucking smitten with the female. Not good.

Beyond that, he was harder than stone inside his jeans, which meant the next hour would be painfully slow—if she even showed at the gazebo. Reaching between his legs, he rubbed scraping denim against his erection, aching for Sunny with downright frenzied intensity. No woman in years had affected him so strongly and instantly.

Wait! That was it. He opened his eyes with a start, hand still poised against his groin. No other woman had ever brought such heat into his body. Ever. She'd clearly placed some kind of erotic spell over him, proving her supernatural nature; otherwise he wouldn't be wound so tight.

He would go to the gazebo, wait for her, and seduce her. Then, when he had her beneath him, he would pry the truth out of her.

Sunny hadn't dared ask Shay or Kate what a glass gazebo was, and sneaking away from the party had taken some clever maneuvering. In the end, she'd said she wanted to walk down to the creek to get away from all the noise, and from the way Shay's eyes had gleamed, her friend had clearly guessed what was *really* going on.

Shay had smiled broadly and warned her to be careful, which Sunny took to be more than a passing caution about her brother and his scoundrel's ways.

Sunny had to be losing her mind to court the kind of danger that Jamie Angel was offering, and yet? She hadn't found the strength inside herself to stay away. Despite the fact that she was violating every rule of her job description, even knowing that she might be seriously reprimanded, or even possibly lose her position, she couldn't stop herself from following the gorgeous, seductive man.

He wasn't wicked; there was no guile in him. Yet he attracted her with his frighteningly powerful magnetism. All her years and she'd kept herself pure. What would her supervisors say? They answered to God, and none of her kind was supposed to mingle sexually with humans. Ever.

So here she stood at the end of the dark, tree-lined path, staring at the distant shape of what had to be the glass gazebo. She'd used her own radiance to find the way in the dark, but that wouldn't do now that Jamie might see, so she lifted her cell phone and used it to illuminate her path. The moon was overhead, too, but it was only a sliver, so while it definitely set the atmosphere, it didn't provide much brightness.

Stepping carefully, she neared the structure; it appeared almost Japanese in design, which seemed at odds with the antebellum style of the home. She'd seen something like it before, but couldn't think where. She was about to search for a door, when Jamie opened one for her, peering out at her. In shadowy relief, he seemed much larger, like a massive, solid sculpture, and she hesitated.

He answered by seizing hold of her wrist and tugging her inside the gazebo with him, closing the door tight behind them both. They fell against the glass panes, instantly in each other's arms.

"You came to me," he breathed in the darkness.

"Well, you asked so nicely." She laughed, and he pulled her much closer. She could hear his heart's fast, aroused tempo beneath her ear.

"You make me want to be nice."

"Which is so much better than naughty."

"Now, that, my darling, depends entirely on what kind of naughty you're talking about." He traced the length of her nose with his fingertip, studying it intently. "Anyone ever tell you that you've got an adorable nose?"

She burst out laughing. "Okay, I'm thinking you aren't nearly so smooth as you think you are! Talking about my nose, Jamie Angel." She giggled some more, especially when he looked genuinely offended for a moment.

"Cutting down my moves now, are you?"

"I have a *silly* nose, so you were really reaching." She'd always thought it turned up just a little bit too much.

He bent down and very sweetly kissed her there. "It's got an attitude. It says, 'I've got pluck and determination.'"

"My nose tells you that?"

"Uh-huh. And it tells me to do this, too." Without asking permission, without a word or a sound beyond a low groan, he covered her mouth with his own. It was an unapologetic kiss, a commanding one, and he pressed her tighter against his chest.

Before she could stop herself, before she could consider the potential reprimands—or trouble with heaven itself—she opened her mouth eagerly to him. He slipped his tongue between her lips, creating a circular, slow pressure, until she dared to reciprocate the motion. Something changed right then, a next level of heat and fire passing between their bodies.

This kiss . . . was more than a kiss—it had to be. It was a kind of claiming, with Jamie moving his hands into her hair, twining his fingers all in it, even as he pressed her up against the glass door. He used his hips to pin her there, and she gasped when she felt his very hard erection push into her belly.

He broke the kiss, moving his mouth to her neck. "What's wrong?" he murmured, lowering his head until his lips were against her throat. He began suckling and nibbling there, then, with a laugh, released a husky *meow*.

She dragged at the air, trying to find her balance. *I felt your manhood, and it scared me . . . made me want you even more.*

"I'm afraid," she admitted quietly, aware that she'd begun shaking slightly.

He kissed the column of her throat, trailing wildfire across her skin. He stilled, his mouth poised against her collarbone. "Won't hurt you," he rumbled. "Trust me."

"I don't know what to do."

"Baby. Baby. You are doing everything I want or need," he said, then flicked his tongue against her throat, licking her there.

With a trembling hand, she reached up and stroked his hair, leaning against the door to steady herself. He moaned slightly at her gentle gesture, nuzzling her, then turned his cheek until it rested in her palm. In that moment she realized he really wasn't a threat, or anywhere near as tough as he wanted the rest of the world to believe. It was just as she'd sensed on the veranda earlier: He possessed a very tender, gentle streak that he did his best to hide from everyone around him.

She'd done her research on him before today, and knew that he'd seen the darkest side of the universe as a result of being a hunter. Maybe that had caused him to put those walls up, or maybe he spent all his bravery in the field, and protected himself in love. That thought filled her chest with painful loneliness, a palpable sadness for the emptiness he lived with. She ran her fingers through his hair even more tenderly, wanting to soothe away all his monsters.

"You feel so right, Sunny Renfroe," he whispered in reaction. "And nobody ever feels right in my arms."

She stilled, instinctively knowing that he'd just made a very deep, intimate admission, maybe without even fully realizing it. Her eyes teared up suddenly at the idea that this strapping, gorgeous man—this battler of demons and the forces of darkness—clearly felt alone.

She caressed his cheek slowly, the heat between them simmering, briefly changing to something far more tender.

Just as quickly, the moment passed—or he forced it to. He stood upright, bracing both arms about her so that she was framed against the door. With a long, searching gaze into her eyes, he whispered, "I wish you'd become my lover tonight."

Jamie stretched out on the wicker chaise longue that occupied the center of the glass house. He'd brought the chair out here after his mother's death, when he'd needed a place away from his family, away from the Shades and the Spartans. Somewhere quiet where he could think. It faced the flowing creek and marsh grass, and late in the day he liked to amble out here and drink a glass of wine.

But he'd never, not once, invited a female to this place of sanctuary. That alone should've tipped him off that Sunny was bounding past any of his own protective wards, yet he kept trying to tell himself that it was all about identifying her supernatural nature. She didn't feel evil and sure as heck didn't taste it. She was the diametric opposite of all the nasty creatures he fought. But after years with the sight, a decade of hunting, he had to know exactly *what* she was. If she wouldn't admit it, then he'd use his sensual skills to pry the facts out of her.

The only problem with that little plan? He could feel himself falling fast and hard, which meant she wasn't the only one who was scared.

He sprawled out on the chair and gazed up at her.

She stood uncertainly beside him, arms folded tight across her breasts. He needed to make her laugh, get her to loosen up a little.

"You are sixteen going on . . ." he sang, laughing.

She swung her gaze to him, dark eyebrows quirking together in confusion. So he explained. "*Sound of Music.*" He gestured about them. "They had one of these glass houses in that movie. It's why my mama wanted one. Daddy had it built for her before I was born."

She smiled, a gorgeous beam of sunlight brightening up the night. Unexpected. Thrilling. He wanted to keep her smiling forever.

"I knew this place looked familiar. I love that movie."

"Perhaps I should chase you around on the benches and twirl you in my arms, then." He lifted an eyebrow. "Naked."

Her smile faded and she wrapped both arms about herself again.

Everything in her demeanor screamed *virgin*, and it made him feel guilty . . . but not for long. He wasn't just after her identity. He'd meant what he'd said on the veranda—he wanted to give her more pleasure than she'd ever known. Wanted to see her react to his touch, glimpse the fire in her almond-shaped eyes as she lay beneath him and he stroked her deepest places.

She glanced away, toward the creek, looking uncomfortable, and that wouldn't do at all. He reached for her hand, pulling her closer to where he lay. "Sunny."

She kept her gaze averted, even as their fingers threaded together. He could feel a light sweat on her palm, and he frowned. "Why are you so afraid of me?" he asked softly.

Finally, she met his gaze. Her own eyes filled with desire and heat and, yes, fear.

"Tell me," he urged, sitting upright and taking her other hand.

"I'm not afraid of you."

"Then what?"

"I'm afraid of me!" she cried impatiently. "I don't know what to do. . . . You're experienced and suave, and I . . . I still want you, even though I shouldn't."

He broke out into a huge grin, his heart beating much faster. "That's my girl."

"No," she insisted, disengaging her hand from his grasp. She looked up, as if searching for some answer from heaven itself. "I'm . . . not supposed to . . ."

He rose to his feet. "Is it a spiritual thing? You don't think a good girl should have sex or something? I already told you where I stand on that one. God invented the act of making love."

She shook her head again. "Not for me, He didn't."

He thought on that statement for a moment, trying to place it within any context that would explain what or who she truly was. He decided to go straight for broke, as he'd always been a gambling man.

"Sunshine, be honest with me, okay? Are you really human?"

She pressed both hands to her face. "Please don't ask me that again. Don't push me anymore."

At that precise moment, a flash of lightning rent the sky, throwing them both into staccato relief. He caught a glimpse of her extreme dismay, a rivulet of dampness on her cheek.

Then all was dark again. It had to be a sudden storm, because the night sky had been clear only a few minutes earlier. Only, no storm, not even in the low country, came up this fast in December.

Again, bright light flashed, a peal of thunder vibrating the glass all around them. Sunny turned from him, head bowed.

Every emotion inside of him was at war—he yearned to comfort her, to make love to her, to interrogate her. Instead, he found himself stepping behind her and very gently wrapping his arms about her waist. Drawing her back against his chest, he simply held her.

"You don't have to tell me," he whispered in her ear. "It's okay. We can take our time, too. There's more than tonight."

He'd not promised a woman more than one night . . . ever.

Sunny stilled in his arms, then shocked him by starting to laugh. "You can actually go a little slow, scoundrel?"

He stroked her hair, smiling, and then kissed the top of her head. "Not normally. But you're not a normal girl."

She sighed. He shouldn't have pushed her again, not even subtly. Turning in his arms, she leaned her cheek against his chest. "I wish I were," she said wistfully.

He angled his mouth to kiss her again, but lightning speared the darkness, seeming to suspend between them endlessly. That was the moment when he saw the massive, winged figure on the other side of the glass . . . staring at Sunny with eyes as bright as moonbeams.

"Uh, Sunny . . ." He cradled her head against his chest protectively, wanting to shield her. "There's something I should tell you."

She nestled closer, seeming more comfortable in his arms. Now, of all the damned times.

"Mmm-hmm?" she inquired sweetly, eyes closed.

The creature shifted its headlight gaze and fixed it hard on Jamie. It was impossible not to see the intense disapproval, even as blinding as that glance was. Jamie pressed his eyes shut instinctively. That was no demon, and it certainly wasn't a winged Spartan.

It was, however, a kind of being that Jamie had seen on rare occasions while fighting in the fiercest spiritual battles.

"Sunny, I really need to know. . . . It's important." He paused, stealing a breath. "Your secret . . . You wouldn't happen to be an angel, would you?"

Chapter Four

Kiel. Her heavenly supervisor. Of course he'd come, and hadn't wasted any time about it. Sunny blocked Jamie from her superior's furious gaze, stepping in front of him to act as a shield. Although she had no hope of hiding Jamie—not physically, since he dwarfed her—and not from Kiel's knowing, piercing stare.

"Jamie, you have to go. Fast," she warned him, stepping closer to the glass wall that separated her from Kiel. Just a thin pane of glass, a tiny sliver of a veil between holy wrath and Jamie Angel.

"I'm not leaving you right now. That creature looks pissed."

"He's very angry, yes."

"Because I kissed you."

"Because *I* disobeyed." She tried to keep her voice calm, but it was difficult with Kiel's gaze and size growing more intimidating by the second.

"Is he going to hurt you? Are you an angel, too?"

She glanced back at Jamie in exasperation. "*Yes*, I'm an angel. *Yes*, you were right: I'm not human. Now let me do damage control before you get hurt or blinded just by being near him." She pointed at Kiel, jabbing her finger. "He's a whole other level, okay? He's serious stuff, and you can't be in his presence. And whatever you do, don't look into his eyes!"

"*You're* trying to protect *me*?" He sounded shocked, bewildered, and all the while he kept gaping at Kiel. Kiel, who, at any moment, would undoubtedly shatter the glass all around them with his fury and power.

"Jamie!" She yanked open the door to the gazebo and started shoving him out onto the path. "Get on back to the house. And please, please don't tell Kate . . . or Shay. Anyone. Please keep my secret for me."

He stared at her for one last second, squeezing her hand. "I don't want you to get hurt because of what I did," he whispered.

"Then leave me."

At last, he spun on his heel and walked into the darkness, and slowly she breathed again.

From behind her, Kiel spoke, now inside the structure. "You've been rebellious." His vibrato filled the gazebo, making the glass itself sing with his voice and power.

She kept her back to the massive angel. "It wasn't my intention."

"But it happened, Sunera."

She pressed her hands against the glass, trying to steady herself. "James Angel is overpowering."

"To a *true* angel?" Kiel's laughter rumbled and she watched as the glass panel beneath her palms cracked. "He bears the name as a prophetic sign of his power, but he is only a mortal. You've grown weak during your human years."

"You're the one who put me here, in a human body, as a ten-year-old. You made me human."

"It was your task to serve as Kate Rabineau's guardian, to protect her from the forces of darkness in the world. To stand between her and the evil that would seek to use her power for gain. To guard her against any harm, whether by human or demonic hand."

"And I've done that!"

Kiel's voice grew much quieter. "It was also your task, Sunera, to develop understanding and compassion by living as a human."

She planted a hand over her heart. "I may be an angel, but I still feel, still care.... I still experience human passions because I've been living in human form for almost seventeen years."

Kiel's power sang through the air. "You forget yourself," he rumbled. "As you did with James Angel just now."

She turned and faced the mighty one who had intimidated her for centuries, the one she held in high esteem ... yet always feared. Kiel blazed like the sun, mere feet away from her. She looked up at him, shaking all over.

"Will you send me home, then? Is that it?"

"You have work to do here on Earth. Important work protecting Kate. Although the Angel clan no longer seeks the lives of vampires, Kate remains vulnerable to other hunters, ones who don't understand that she is not evil, only rare. And I don't need to remind you of the demons who seek her blood."

Sunny hung her head, feeling ashamed, fearful for Kate's safety. She couldn't believe that she'd nearly compromised her position as her best friend's guardian angel—the thought of anyone else being assigned to Kate made her blood run cold. Kate was *her* duty, *her* charge. She couldn't falter again, no matter how badly she wanted Jamie.

"Don't punish Kate because of my indiscretion."

"This is but a warning, young one." Kiel's glowing, humming wings spread wide, until his shadow covered her. "However, indulge these human passions again and there will be a price."

A price. She would be sent back to heaven, taken out of the field until she'd earned the right to serve as an earthly guardian again.

Who would watch over her best friend, who would protect her—as a pure-blooded vampire, Kate would always be at risk from hunters and dark forces that sought to harm her. Even though a vampire, she was still an Earth dweller, and the heavenly angels watched over every person on Earth—human and vampire.

"But Kate?" she asked, her heart clenching.

"Kate would be granted another guardian."

As a whole, vampirekind was misunderstood by their human counterparts. There were so many false myths and legends, and Hollywood hadn't helped any of that misinformation, leaving vampires open for hunting. So they needed protection at least as much as humans did, and God made no distinction, protecting both groups on Earth. The problem, though, was that their special abilities meant that they could spot the usual heavenly guardians, with their wings and otherworldly nature. That was why Sunny had been sent to safeguard Kate in human form, without her glory and angelic appearance. Her natural radiance, too, she kept concealed unless she absolutely needed it.

Throughout the eternal age before that, Sunny had served in heaven, and occasionally as a guardian angel for humans on Earth. But being paired with Kate, and assuming human form, was a first-time experience. Now it seemed that she'd failed miserably.

"Don't leave Kate in danger because I've made a

mistake," she pleaded, bowing her head respectfully to Kiel.

He smiled gently. "Our approach next time would be different. But don't force our hand. Perhaps with another mortal your disobedience might have been more easily overlooked."

Was that why Kiel had come so quickly? It had something to do with Jamie's calling and his abilities as a hunter? Her mind raced.

"I'd barely finished the kiss and you were here," she ventured, hoping he would give more details. "That's fast, even for you."

Kiel smiled, adding the wattage of another sun to his already blazing beauty. "I was alerted."

Her mind whirled. "I've seen no guardians around Jamie ... unless there's someone like me, an angel in human form? But if that were true, I'd have sensed them. I don't understand why Jamie, who fights such dark forces, is left without his own guardian."

Kiel's expression grew somber. "He is *not* alone."

"But I haven't seen—"

"James Angel and his siblings have special guardians, but they are instructed to keep their distance lest they interfere."

"Interfere? Interfere with what, sir?" She couldn't mask her anger. It was their job, as angels, to protect and watch over humanity. She'd never once heard of guardians who "kept their distance." The thought that Jamie—or Mason and Shay—might be less than well protected galled her.

Kiel regarded her calmly. "Sunera, Jamie and his siblings fight demons, darkness. They are in the battlefield nearly every day. If their own guardians were visible or intrusive, then the demons would spot them. The Angels' ability to fight would be nullified, because the demons would cower and not come near. We both know that they are drawn and compelled to battle human hunters like the Angel siblings."

"While we are forced to stand aside and watch the bloodshed and pain."

"We cannot interfere with free will. You know the parameters."

Sunny thought of how oddly gentle Jamie had been with her, the way he'd ignited her, even while seeming vulnerable. He was beautiful, and demons sought his blood every day . . . while his guardians were held at bay by heaven itself. "You're using them, and that's not right."

Kiel rumbled his displeasure at the comment, and she heard another glass pane crack. "They are endowed with spiritual gifts that few humans ever even know about. The Lord has called them. . . . They embrace their gifts."

"And you put them at risk with inadequate coverage. No wonder I never saw any angels around them . . . and I couldn't understand, not from the first time I met Shay. It's like you're dangling them as bait, without sufficient protection. If their guardian angels keep that kind of distance, they're practically on their own."

"*Enough!*" Kiel roared, a blast of warm wind filling the space. His wings expanded; his countenance blinded her.

She fell to her knees, trembling. Impertinence never was tolerated by her commanders, and she hastened to make amends. "Forgive me."

Instantly Kiel's strong hand touched the crown of her head, his fury vanished, replaced by kindness and compassion.

"You care deeply for all humans, and these Angels are your friends. Trust me when I say we do not leave them at risk. Jamie is guarded by angels, the Shades by many more. They watch from afar unless needed. Even Jamie has seen his guardians on occasion, in the midst of heated battle. That's how he recognized what I am the moment he saw me. Jamie alone has three guardians."

She looked up in shock, still kneeling. "Three?" She'd never heard of a mortal with three guardian angels. Even two was exceedingly rare.

Kiel smiled again, gentleness in his bright, glowing eyes. "You see now that he is special."

Yes, Jamie was special; she'd figured that out the moment they'd kissed. Before. There was something so powerful and beautiful in him, he almost seemed like he *was* an angel, and not just by name.

Kiel continued, "You understand why you must not allow him to touch you again?"

She nodded, tears filling her eyes. "Yes, Kiel. I understand."

"Then why the tears, young one?" He patted her cheek.

The tears came harder and she shook her head, avoiding Kiel's strong gaze. "I should not say."

He forced her to look up at him. "You should not hold silent."

There weren't words. How could you tell another angel that your deepest wish, the gravest, most important desire in your heart, was to be human? To know what it was to love another human, to experience the power of that love in mortal life? All these years, watching from afar, Sunny had felt an outsider, forever looking through the glass at what she never could have herself. That feeling had intensified tenfold once she'd been sent to Earth as Kate's personal guardian, after being placed in human form.

And now recently, having watched Kate find such beautiful love with Dillon, all that longing had multiplied even more. When Kate had been a little girl, and Sunny was watching over her already, Kate's favorite movie had been *The Little Mermaid*. Even then Sunny had identified with Ariel, longing to be human, to find her place on Earth. Now she felt as if she'd found her very own song in Jamie's arms, only to be denied her voice.

She could explain none of this to Kiel, nor would she try.

But his eyes revealed a deep understanding of those unspoken words. "This is why touching them intimately is forbidden. It unlocks emotions that should never belong to us." For a moment, Kiel's gaze grew long, almost sad, and she wondered if he'd walked this same path of temptation himself at one time. But then he looked back at her. "Do not kiss James Angel again, continue in your role as Kate's guardian, and all shall be well."

She nodded, wiping at her tears. "Yes, sir, understood."

All shall be well. But how could it be, now that she knew what it was to be in Jamie Angel's arms?

Jamie stared numbly at the flat screen. All around him, his family and friends were laughing and talking, cheering on the bowl game, but he could barely hear a word. Sunny Renfroe was an angel. He, a man who'd spent his entire adulthood trying to serve God with his demon fighting, had kissed someone sacred. Someone pure.

Surely he'd be damned to hell. Certainly a giant heavenly hand would materialize any moment and for one specific purpose: to yank him off the sofa and send him straight to the fiery pit.

You just didn't go and seduce an angel. Never mind that she'd shown up at his house disguised as a human.

Who are you kidding? You knew she wasn't a mortal from the moment you met her.

He'd known, and yet he'd contrived a plan to seduce her, and look what had happened. He'd quite possibly caused her a great deal of harm, while he continued to live his everyday human life.

"Jamie? Did you hear me?" Shay dropped down onto the sofa right beside him. "You're zoned. What's wrong?" She studied him, seeming genuinely concerned. "And you look like you just saw a dark legion or something. You're actually pale. And your eyes are bloodshot."

He rubbed his temples; his head had been hurting ever since he'd looked at the glowing angel—he'd done that before Sunny had issued the warning. Now his head throbbed and his eyes burned.

"Jamie," Shay whispered again, glancing around at the others who talked and laughed, oblivious to his torment. Shay knew him far too well. Without waiting for him to reply, she took him by the hand. "Come with me."

He shook his head. "Can't talk about it," he mumbled, closing his eyes.

Shay leaned right up against him. "You're scaring me, so I'm not giving you a choice. You either come with me down to the cellar, or I turn off the television and alert Mason, Dillon, and everyone else to the fact that you've obviously been spooked."

"And Sunny," he suggested miserably. "Don't you want to alert her, too?"

Shay glanced around the room. "She didn't come back with you?" his sister asked in surprise. "I just assumed . . ."

He didn't say a word, just kept rubbing his burning eyes.

"Talk to me, Jamie," Shay insisted. "Let's get out of here so you can tell me what's going on."

He rose from the sofa with a weary sigh. "This life of ours . . . it really does suck sometimes."

*   *   *

Jamie pulled volume after volume off the shelves of the cellar library. This small downstairs room, adjacent to their wine cellar, housed all their family's lore on demon fighting, the occult, God, angels ... you name it, and they had texts about it.

Shay sat at his desk in the antique swivel chair, watching his frantic movements. "What are you doing, James Dixon?"

"I'm not ready to talk about what happened."

"I didn't ask you to."

"You did earlier," he argued, retrieving a particularly weathered volume about angelic beings. "It's why you followed me down here."

"Nooooo," Shay said. "I followed you down here because I'm worried."

"About Sunny." He carted another three volumes to the table and deposited them, then returned to searching the shelves.

Shay rocked back in the chair, watching him. "I have a distinct feeling Sunny is perfectly fine. Whereas you're the one who's got that deer-in-the-headlights expression permanently frozen on your face."

He couldn't tell Shay about what he'd seen, what he knew. Sunny had begged him not to, and hadn't he caused her enough trouble already? How could he violate her last request of him?

Last request. The words caused a chill to chase down his spine. What if she never came back to the house? What if that huge angel had ... What would the guy do? Whisk her back to heaven? Destroy her? He couldn't even contemplate what would happen when an angel received a scolding.

Well, that wasn't entirely true. When Lucifer and his

crew had rebelled, they were cast out of heaven . . . and they became demons.

The chill he'd experienced became full-on tremors as he prayed and begged God to give Sunny a break. This had been his doing entirely. She shouldn't have to suffer for his folly and sin.

Shay walked toward the table where he was massing the various volumes—books he hoped might explain why or how an angel would live as a human. He'd never even heard of such a thing, much less encountered it. Sure, he'd seen angelic entities on the battlefield from time to time; he knew Mason had as well, even while fighting over in Iraq. But angels in human form? Not charted territory for any of them.

Shay began thumbing through the stack, reading off titles. "*Angelic Host: Configuring the Armies of Heaven*? *Understanding Heavenly Powers*?" She laughed. "So, you took Sunny on a walk and accused her of being an angel or something? Jamie, she really, truly *is* human. You gotta get over this obsession."

He swallowed hard; he hated keeping secrets from Shay or Mason. It had never worked in the past, not for any of them. Like that corrosive pain Mace had lived with until he'd admitted to his family that he was gay.

Surely Sunny wouldn't have begged him to keep her secret from Shay if she'd understood how intuitive his sister was, the way she'd needle and prod him until he admitted why he was so upset.

He paced the small, dusty room in agitation; upstairs several of their friends began shouting as the football game took some intense turn.

At last he faced his little sister. Pressing his back against the tallest shelf, he bolstered his courage with a quick prayer. "Sissy cat, she *is* an angel," he blurted.

She laughed. "Oh, shut up."

He, on the other hand, didn't laugh at all. "I am deadly, completely serious. But you can't tell Kate or Mason or anyone else. She begged me to keep the truth about her a secret."

"She is not an angel." Shay gave him an incredulous smile. "Geez, you're really wound up tighter than I thought. What happened?"

He sagged against the bookshelf. "Shay. She. Is. An. Angel. It's true...." And then he admitted the worst part of all. "And I totally made out with her. And got her in trouble," he added in a rush. "This scary, huge angel showed up to ... chastise her, I guess. I dunno. But I kissed her, and now she's maybe going to be punished ... and I'm probably going to burn in hell. And the worst part? I don't care. I just want ... I want to hold her again. Kiss her again. And she's a flippin' angel! What's happening to me, Shay? Huh? Am I losing it or what?"

Shay stared at him, light blue eyes wide and incredulous, but said nothing.

"Are you tracking with this shit, Sissy cat? I think I'm falling for an angel. Maybe I really will burn in hell now."

He stared at his sister, waiting for some kind of reply, but she wasn't the one who answered.

"I asked you not to tell."

Jamie whipped his gaze to the open doorway; Sunny stood there, her own eyes bright with unshed tears.

"I thought you'd keep my secret ... after everything we shared," she murmured, and Jamie watched his sister's eyes grow even wider.

Chapter Five

"Shay, I need to be alone with Sunny." Jamie met Sunny's gaze with smoldering determination. His eyes were bloodshot, undoubtedly from the few moments he'd looked at Kiel. Sunny hoped his vision wasn't damaged, and had to fight the urge to rush to his side, to ensure that he was all right.

Not one of them spoke. Shay sat in the chair, stunned and unmoving. Meanwhile, Jamie kept on looking right at Sunny, almost as if he could see into her, inside her rapidly beating heart. Shame filled her throat with bile. Embarrassment caused her to stare at the floor.

Shay moved wordlessly toward the doorway, and before Sunny could stop her, she drew Sunny into a tight, reassuring embrace. "It's okay," she murmured against Sunny's cheek. "We won't tell anyone else. I promise. We both do. You are safe with us; I promise you that, too."

Sunny nodded as Shay released her, hurrying up the worn wooden stairs that led to the first floor. She watched Shay vanish, desperate to look at anything except Jamie Angel. She couldn't blame him for telling Shay, not really—and yet, it still stung, after all she'd risked just to kiss him.

Wrapping her arms about herself, she shivered, avoiding Jamie physically. But she should've known he'd have none of that, and his large, strong hand touched her shoulder.

"Are you all right? Safe now?" he inquired softly.

She bobbed her head, staring at the floor. "It will be okay."

"Then look at me, Sunny," he murmured, stroking her upper arm. He was doing it again, getting physical with her when he should keep his distance.

She swerved away from his caress. "It's all right for now, but only if we don't touch again. Kiss again. None of that can happen. Ever."

"I hate that. I can't tell you how much I hate it." His voice was husky and filled with emotion. "But I don't want you to suffer anything 'cause of me."

She put her back to him, fighting tears. "And you don't want to burn in hell. Like you said to Shay," she remarked with a trace of bitterness.

"I'm not worried about me! You know that." He placed strong hands on both her shoulders, forcing her to turn and face him. She didn't want him to see her tear-filled eyes. The pain in her heart was about him—and yet it so exceeded the bounds of this moment. It stretched over centuries of loneliness, the aching for someone to have as her own, not just to watch over, nor to protect objectively.

He slid two fingertips underneath her chin, tilting her face until their gazes locked. "I've hurt you. I'm so sorry."

She pressed her eyes shut. "You don't understand. How can you?"

"Make me understand. Tell me what's going on inside you right now."

His hand was still brushing beneath her chin, and she shoved it away in frustration. "Didn't you hear what I said? No more touching. I could be punished if we do."

He smiled at her. "That wasn't sexual. Just to be clear. I'm sure your team would know that."

She walked to the far side of the room and began idly thumbing through a stack of leather-bound volumes, unstacking and stacking them. "I wish I were human. And for an angel, that is a sin," she said after a moment. "Falls under 'thou shalt not covet.' "

"But you look completely human. I've seen a few angels in my day, and you're not like any of 'em."

She gazed down at one of the books on the table. *Angels Among Us.* Only then did she realize that every volume in the pile was about her kind. "You pulled all these out? To find out more about me? Us?"

He leaned against a tall bookshelf. "Force of habit in my line of work. Encounter something you don't know, research the hell out of it." He barked a laugh. "Pardon the choice of words."

She walked across the room and sat down at the rolltop desk. "I'll make it easier on you. I'll explain exactly what I'm doing here on Earth. But then, Jamie? We can't *ever* be together again, not even as friends."

A long time ago, Jamie had taken to making short-term bargains he didn't exactly intend to keep. This was one of those times. Somehow, some way, he was determined that he'd be able to see more of Sunny. He couldn't imagine *not* seeing her now. Friendship, perhaps, but he wanted far more. On the other hand, he'd meant what he said: He didn't want to cause her to be hurt or punished, and he really didn't want to tick off God in the process.

He'd learned another habit in his years as a hunter, too: Sometimes you really could get your way even if it meant bending supposed spiritual "rules." This was also one of those times. Or so he darn well hoped and prayed.

Sunny brushed a hand through her curls, her agitation obvious. "I'm Kate's guardian angel," she said after a moment. "What we term an earthly guardian, sent in human form."

Jamie processed that revelation. He'd never read or heard of such a thing, but that wasn't surprising, since she and her fellow human guardians looked and seemed . . . human.

"I'm sorry, but vampires need guardian angels? That's what you're telling me? Are there many of you?"

She shrugged. "I don't know. I'm not on the priority list when it comes to information. I'm what you'd call . . ." She laughed unexpectedly, but sadness lurked in her gaze. "I'm lower-rung, Jamie."

"Lower-rung among the most powerful beings God ever created. That's top tier of everything else," he said, momentarily trying to forget that he'd kissed her. So long as he compartmentalized his lust for her from her angelic nature, he could keep it together.

"I'm what they call a 'young one.'"

"What's that mean? You haven't been around since the beginning? Since creation?"

She smiled and his heart skipped a beat. She was so beautiful, even in the midst of a difficult conversation. The way her eyes sparkled, lit with an inner fire of goodness and light. The way she looked at him, as if he were the most important person in her universe at the moment.

She didn't explain her laugh or answer his question,

just kept smiling faintly. Some of the tension eased between them, and he relaxed, leaning against the shelf.

"You can tell me," he encouraged. "Whatever it is, I can handle it."

"I have no doubt about that, James Angel. No, I'm not one of the originals. More of an afterthought, a later model, so to speak."

"That makes me feel so much less creepy." He snorted. "I mean, nothing like knowing you're lusting after one of God's heavenly host to make you feel like you should be on some offender list, somewhere."

"You probably are," she said, her smile fading. "Unfortunately, we both are."

"Yeah, there is that," he agreed. "So how old *are* you, then, exactly?"

"I don't know. My human self is twenty-seven, though, for whatever that's worth."

He glanced sideways at her, his brow furrowed. "How can you not know?"

"We're not made to remember. It creates too many complications. I remember this life, here on Earth as Kate's guardian . . . and some memories from before I was sent down here. Maybe a few hundred years' worth? But that's about it."

"Wow. That's . . . Don't you ever wonder what you *don't* remember?"

She shook her head. "I'm invested in this life." She patted her chest. "Being Sunny Renfroe. It's who I am right now. If anything, being an angel teaches you about the importance of every second of life, how precious every moment really is."

It was exactly how he felt about being a hunter. So much time spent serving and witnessing demonic death

had taken a toll, but it had also caused him to understand the precarious balance between life and death,
good and evil. Still, despite all that he'd seen, he hadn't
ever encountered anyone, male or female, remotely like
Sunny Renfroe.

"You're an anomaly for me. I mean, don't take that
the wrong way," he rushed to clarify. "But I've never
seen a damned thing about human guardians, not in the
lore, not out in the field. Actual guardian angels? Yeah, I
think I've seen my own a few times while in the heat of
battle. They're big and scary like your boss guy. But you?
Nothing like you, not ever, Sunny."

She smiled her wide, enchanting smile once again.
"Well, Jamie Angel, not that you *know* of."

"But I knew you weren't human within moments of
meeting you." He couldn't help beaming with pride. He
wanted her to admire his skills and abilities, wanted to
prove that he could be worthy of her interest, her care.
He wanted her to love him.

He realized it right then, a quicksilver thought, right
through his heart. He wanted this woman to love him,
body and soul. Eternally or not. Even though he had
only known her for a day, he already realized that he
was falling for her. Hard. He could almost taste how
badly he ached for Sunny to turn those wide-set brown
eyes on him and whisper words of affection.

And it was utterly forbidden.

He stared at the floor, trying to still his racing
thoughts. She'd said something, but he couldn't seem to
focus or hear.

"Hmm?" he tried, gazing at his booted feet.

"I was explaining about Kate. Why I'm her guardian."

He forced himself to glance upward, trying his level

best to appear composed. "I'm sorry; I was just ... processing. Taking it all in," he said, not wanting her to read his thoughts or his heart. "So Kate ..."

"Because she's a vampire, her guardian must be in human form. Otherwise her special sight would reveal the angel's identity."

"And that's the part I don't get. You're saying angels watch over vampires?" He gaped at her, unable to keep the revulsion out of his voice. "Why would God protect a band of bloodthirsty creatures like them?"

Sunny's eyes flashed with mild anger. "Jamie, did you not just hear me? I'm Kate's guardian angel. Please don't speak about her so disrespectfully ... or her kind. They're God's creatures, too, and they aren't evil. They're also very vulnerable, and as you well know, God protects his own."

It was going to take a while for him to think of vampires as vulnerable or as "God's own," but he also recognized that Sunny would know far better than he would. Made him more than thankful that he'd recently called off any plans to hunt vampires. At least there was one thing he'd done right in this whole fiasco, and maybe that would chalk up a few heavenly points in his favor.

"Okay, vampires aren't evil. Noted. I'll be sure to update the company files. So tell me, then—how did Kate luck out and get you?"

"It's the way with all vampires. Their watchers are sent like I was ... into their lives. Friends, relatives, neighbors ... we take a number of roles in the vampire's life, but the purpose is always the same: to guard them from demons—" She stopped short for a moment, anxiously fiddling with the hem of her sweater, obviously hesitating for some reason. "And we protect them from misguided hunters, ones who believe the falsehoods and myths about vampirekind. People like . . . you."

"That might just be the worst I've felt all night, Sunny Renfroe," he said, kicking himself for all the years he'd tormented Kate, needled her about one thing or another.

She shook her head vehemently. "You're a good hunter, Jamie. Excellent. You didn't know. . . . It was part of why I came today. I thought, well, maybe I could help you understand in some way. Influence you."

"You certainly affected me," he said in a voice that sounded seductive, even to him.

Sunny didn't miss his tone or implication, rising suddenly to her feet. "And now I've answered your questions," she said with false brightness. "I should go find Kate. . . ."

He caught her arm, spinning her toward him. She pushed back against his chest, but not very hard—and not very convincingly. He slid one hand around her lower back, not holding her too close, but near enough. "I have to see you again, Sunny. Friends. We can be at least that, right?"

Her palms still rested against his chest, and he swore he felt the heat of her skin through his long-sleeved T-shirt. "Friends?" She searched his face, brown eyes flicking back and forth across his features. Perhaps she was trying to read his true intentions.

"Just friends. I want more, but . . ." He pressed his nose against the top of her head, inhaling the lavender scent of shampoo. "I'm realistic."

"Yes, of course. You want to be friends with a guardian angel. Both your feet are planted firmly on the ground."

"We already are friends," he countered. "Wouldn't

you say? So I'm really just arguing for a continuation of the status quo."

She sighed into him slightly, then stepped backward. "You are a highly persuasive individual."

"I try my best." He gave her a flirtatious yet simultaneously sweet smile, a contradiction, just like the man himself.

Sunny walked to the other side of the room without answering, and at first he thought she never would. But then she paused at the bottom of the steps, turning toward him. "Okay. Friends for now . . . unless I hear an objection from Kiel. And if I do? You might never see me again anyway."

Chapter Six

"Shay, honey, it's me." Sunny cradled the phone against her ear. She was still lying in bed, barely having slept at all last night. "I got a favor to ask."

This favor was the closest thing to a plan of action that Sunny's many sleepless hours had yielded. Drawing a breath, she laid that plan on her friend. "You know those books that Jamie had in the cellar last night? Any chance I could borrow a few of 'em?"

"I wish." Shay sighed into the phone. "Jamie holed himself up down there last night after you left, and he's not budged ever since. No way would he let me take anything out of the library. Frankly, Sunny, he's not been in his right mind since you left."

Sunny closed her eyes. "He's gotta leave the cellar sometime, right?"

"But not long enough that I could let you borrow any of those books. He'd ask too many questions, all of them about you."

And he'd want to know why Shay was removing those volumes, which would elicit a firestorm of problems, as well as potential amorous attention once Jamie realized Sunny was the one after the texts. Which was so not what Sunny needed right now. She'd been hoping to come up with a subtle way of investigating their "problem" without Jamie knowing. Like she'd told him, she was a lower-rung angel, and it wasn't as if she had many answers, but during the night she'd come to hope that maybe—just maybe—some of his family's many volumes about angels might help them. Might even point out a way they *could* be together, a way she might fall to earth without turning dark or sinning.

"Sunny, I have to tell you . . . Jamie can be incredibly stubborn. He won't let this thing with you go easily."

"But, Shay, he doesn't understand. If he did, he wouldn't be doing all that research."

"Then why did *you* want to read all those same books?" Shay asked innocently. "Just a sudden random interest in learning more about your own kind?"

"I kept praying, all last night . . . hoping there might be some way."

"You can't blame my brother for hoping and praying for the same thing." Shay laughed into the phone, lowering her voice. "That kiss you two shared, it must've been out of this world."

Sunny's face flushed and she covered her eyes even though Shay wasn't there to see her shyness. "I think I could love him." Sunny reached for a pillow, pressing it against her cheek, wanting to hide in shame.

Shay made a happy little squealing sound into the phone. "That means we've just got to solve this problem."

"It's more than a problem!"

"A compatibility issue, that's all. God *is* love. You of all people know that, more than any of us. So if He is love, and you think you could love my brother, then maybe it's not as forbidden and impossible as you seem to think."

Sunny opened her mouth, about to argue and explain Kiel's warnings, but Shay was too excited to hear.

"Sunny, doll, I have an idea. Just keep an open mind and I'll be over in an hour."

Shay sat down across from Sunny on the sofa. She clasped her hands together, excitement glinting in her eyes. "I don't know how much you know, as an angel. About me or us, I mean."

Sunny couldn't help smiling. "I'm limited in my scope. So don't worry; I don't know the secret stuff you wrote in your diary at fourteen."

Shay reached for the big purse she'd plopped on the floor. "What about my gifts? Jamie's and Mason's? Know anything about that?"

"Just that you're all very gifted hunters. That's all."

Sunny peered into Shay's purse, wondering what she was pulling out of it. Suddenly her friend produced a big sketch pad and charcoal pencils. Shay placed them both on her knees and then faced Sunny. "I'm a prophetic artist. That's one of my gifts, and that means I can sketch the future or visions or sometimes get heavenly insight. I'm a prophetess."

Sunny grinned. "Oh, yeah, that—that I'd actually sensed. Sorry, forgot to mention it. It's in the way your aura glows. It's pearl colored."

"Really?" Shay's eyes went wide. "I don't see auras. None of us Angels do. That's freaking cool."

"Just like humans, heavenly guardians have different gifts. That's one of mine."

"Like how I draw and see things, learn things." Shay nodded in understanding, opening her sketch pad. "Oh, and I should warn you, Sunny—I kind of zone out while I do this."

Shay slowly began moving her pencil across the blank page. Her dark eyebrows knitted together; her pale blue eyes became glazed as she stared down at the page. After several silent moments, she began a rocking motion as she drew, humming a strangely monotone tune that sounded a bit like a hymn.

Sunny rose quietly, moving to the sofa where Shay sat, intensely curious as to what her prophetic drawing might reveal. Shay kept working, oblivious as Sunny settled beside her on the couch.

Very quietly, Sunny stole a look at the sketch, and her breath caught in her throat at the vicious scene on the page. Jamie lay prone on the ground, a heavy metal chain wrapped about his throat—held firmly in the hands of a hideous-looking demon. And if anything might have frightened her away from Jamie, if any image could have convinced her that she didn't belong in his life, the rest of Shay's sketch did just that.

Because standing over Jamie's prone body, radiating with heavenly power . . . stood Sunny herself.

Sunny pressed a hand to her lips. "That's terrifying."

"What?" Shay turned to her, blinking in surprise—almost as if she were coming out of a deep trance.

Sunny pointed to the drawing. "Look at it. He's in danger . . . because of me."

Shay studied her own drawing for a moment, then shook her head in disagreement. "That's only one possible interpretation."

"You got another?" Sunny's heart leaped, no longer lodged quite so firmly in her chest.

Shay pointed to the image. "Yeah. Maybe you're meant to fight *with* him. Maybe you're supposed to be a team. . . . You're together in this image."

"And he's in trouble because of that."

Shay shook her head. "You're watching over him here, helping," she said, then gave Sunny a long, significant look. "Looks to me like you're about to save his butt. And that's exactly what fighting partners do: watch each other's backs."

Sunny buried her face in both hands. "Oh, honey, but that's not what I'm called to do. I'm Kate's guardian, not Jamie's."

"Sometimes mission priorities change. That's true on Earth, so I'm guessing that might be true for heaven, too."

Sunny's hands fell to her lap. "If I only had information, some way to know that you're right."

Shay smiled, a conspiratorial gleam in her eyes. "Uh, Sunny? I didn't just bring my sketch pad." She reached inside her big purse and retrieved three dusty volumes, leather-bound, with ancient writing on them. "I brought these, too—smuggled them out of the cellar without Jamie knowing. I say it's time we go to the source and look for real information."

"About what, though?" Sunny's thoughts were whirling, confused. So much was happening, and so quickly.

Shay's voice became much quieter. "Whether angels can ever choose to become fully human."

Night finally came to Savannah after what felt an almost interminably long day. Jamie had spent many hours researching angel lore down in the cellar, including what would happen if one fell to Earth, and he'd only come up empty-handed. There appeared to be no way that he could hope to pursue a relationship with Sunny, yet it didn't stop his heart from hoping. Stupidly hoping.

And one tiny verse in a rare ancient Greek text had given that sparking hope a bit of kindling. It was from the book they called *The Hunter's Lexicon*, a set of instructions to demon hunters from the oldest times. In

it, Jamie had discovered a passing reference to human
atonement. That should a hunter engage inappropri-
ately with a heavenly guardian, he should atone by spilling demon's blood.

He would've been out on River Street tonight anyway. Knowing that hunting his demonic quarries might
absolve him, possibly even Sunny, of his sin of wanting
her was an extra benefit. Perhaps if he could just fight
hard enough, kill enough demons, then perhaps he
might be worthy of Sunny. Perhaps God might *deem*
him worthy, his sin forgiven.

The cobblestoned walkways of bustling River Street
were always the perfect hunting ground, and so he'd
enlisted Mason, the two of them rolling into downtown
after ten p.m. This time of night was usually when some
of their worst nemeses began preying on unsuspecting
tourists, taking advantage of the inebriated state of the
humans to do some soul sucking or body possession.
Jamie and he dressed in all black, fading into the riv-
erfront, unnoticeable to most of the partygoers out at
the bars and restaurants. The cops were on their side,
and always turned a blind eye to their subtly concealed
weapons and paramilitary gear.

Walking beside him, Mason sighed heavily. "Dude,
would you stop glowering like that?"

Jamie turned to his brother. "I'm not doing anything
but my job," he said defensively. "Just scanning the perimeter, looking for the usual perps, like always. I tell
ya, if Thrastikas shows up down here tonight, I'm in no
mood to issue any pardons."

In fact, that higher-ranking demon would make a perfect atonement. He'd performed a litany of vile deeds
in the past month—including motivating a stabbing that
Jamie had witnessed firsthand. The victim had spent

weeks in ICU. That demon needed to go down, and Jamie was ready to off the beast. Besides, Thrastikas had been after Jamie's blood for a while, and tonight was the perfect time to end their feud.

Mason grinned, his own eyes searching the dark side alleys. "I thought Thrastikas was your best friend. That you wanted to turn gay together."

"Okay, that's beyond disgusting, so I won't even go there."

Thrastikas had thick leather wings that were prone to making earsplitting noises when they beat together. He also wore manacled chains about both legs that clanged and dragged loudly, which only emphasized his permanently hunched shoulders and crooked back.

"In fact, that's about like me saying you wanna go straight with—"

Mace hit him on the arm, silencing him. With two fingers he indicated the side alley, and sure enough, who should be lurking in the shadows along with a lower minion but Thrastikas himself.

Jamie reached to his hip, where he had a dagger sheathed, and slid the powerful blade into his palm. Beside him, he felt the whisper-quiet motion of his brother doing the same; one of Mason's best fighting skills, in fact, was how lethally quiet he could be. Stealthily, he and Mace crossed the street, concealing themselves against the bar that stood adjacent to the alley where the demons were waiting. And Jamie had no doubt that that was precisely what the pair were doing—waiting for unsuspecting humans to molest and violate.

Jamie paused in the shadows, Mace right behind him. If they didn't enter the alley directly, the demonic duo might vanish into the dark. But if they waited, they might have a better chance of ambushing the pair, espe-

cially if the demons left the alley and ventured out onto
River Street. Jamie's heart hammered in his chest. No
matter how many times he'd gone on the hunt, he never
ceased to get an adrenaline rush that made his entire
body grow taut. He also never failed to remember that
one false move, and his current demon battle could be
his last.

Mace touched his arm, pointing to the alley, signaling
that he wanted to advance first. Jamie shook his head;
Mace might be the marine, but Jamie was the leader of
the Shades. No way would he let his brother take point
in such a potentially dangerous situation. Jamie adjusted
the dagger in his palm, securing his hold on it. He'd go
right for Thrastikas's throat; Mace could take down the
demon's little sidekick. Turning, he met Mace's stare
and showed him the middle finger—it was their long-
standing joke, their way of indicating the leader was going after the biggest, baddest demon dude in the mix.

Mace gave a curt nod, and Jamie swept into the
alley—and crashed right into the thick barrel chest of
Thrastikas himself. Neither of them expected the impact,
and it sent Jamie sprawling onto the alley's pavement.
Thrastikas staggered, his feet momentarily tangled in
the heavy metal chains about his legs.

But his minion, despite being small and clearly of the
dumber, lower variety of demon, moved fast. Perhaps
because he was so little, Jamie didn't have time to process, but the critter flung itself at Jamie's head, beating
him with its scaly wings.

Jamie swatted at it, lashing out with his dagger, and
the acrid-smelling demon slumped lifelessly on Jamie's
chest. He flung the wicked thing across the alley, rolling
to his feet. Mace had Thrastikas by the leg chains, the
demon prone on the ground.

Thrastikas lashed at Jamie with a clawed foot, drawing blood from Jamie's calf. He kicked back in return, raising his dagger. It was time to finish this foul demon once and for all. The atonement might help, too. Might provide Jamie an opening with Sunny . . . or at the very least, earn him points for good behavior.

"I'm going to finish this. Now," Jamie said.

Mason tightened the chains in his grasp. "I've got him, bro."

Jamie lunged forward, prepared to slice the blade across the demon's throat, but as he moved in for the kill, Thrastikas used his chain-bound legs to knock Mace across the alley with a painful cry. That one moment of distraction was all it took; right as Jamie lunged, the demon's massive wings unfurled and he soared heavenward, clanking chains swinging in the air.

Mace groaned, rolling onto his side protectively. "Oh, man, he nailed me in the balls. Hurts like a mother."

Jamie knelt beside him, still searching all around the alley and the street for any sign of their enemy. But both Thrastikas and his minion were gone. He'd missed the real action he'd come here for, and now Mace was going to need a little recuperation time. Maybe that was a sign he should study the lore for more ideas. After all, he would be seeing Sunny again in just a few more days, and he had a lot of work to do between now and then if he hoped for any chance of a relationship with her.

Chapter Seven

"I don't understand why you don't want to come." Kate stood in Sunny's kitchen, dressed up for the New Year's Day party at the Angels' plantation—an event that Sunny had decided she couldn't possibly attend. Not after seeing Shay's prophetic drawing, and the danger she possibly represented for Jamie. Even after spending the past days tirelessly studying the ancient volumes on angels, she'd found no plausible way that she could choose to fall, not without being destroyed or turning evil. Shay had promised to retrieve more volumes, but Sunny just couldn't put her heart into the quest. Kiel's warnings still sang in her ears. Which meant that, despite Jamie's desire for friendship, it was impossible. Sunny was too attracted to him, out of her right mind when around him. She was lucky that Kiel hadn't appeared to her a second time to further warn and chastise her.

"Sunny, I just don't get it. You had a good time out at the Angel place the other day." Kate glanced at her watch. Dillon was waiting in the car, and they were a little late as it was.

"I sure did. Shay and Mason are fabulous—"

"And you thought Jamie was *hot*. I saw the way you looked at him," Kate teased. "And, by the way . . . where was it you disappeared to the other night, exactly? I noticed you both vanished for a good long while."

Sunny turned back to the counter, focusing all her attention on the dough she was rolling out for a chocolate-filled pastry. Whenever she felt restless, like she did right now, cooking helped settle her nerves and restore her serenity.

"I can't go anyway," she argued. "I'm covered in flour and my hair's a hot mess."

Kate sashayed to her side and began playing with Sunny's hair. "I could make it beautiful in five minutes flat. You can change clothes, and you don't even need mice or a pumpkin—just go to the ball."

Sunny waved her off with a forced laugh. "It's a football party. No glass slippers allowed."

"But there is one definite prince who will be there."

Sunny planted a hand on her hip. "Now he's a *prince*? You despised Jamie until three days ago."

Kate shrugged. "It was a shocker, but he was pretty nice to me. And to you . . . and you like him, so he's off my shit list. At least until he makes a wrong move with you."

Sunny averted her eyes, rolling the dough some more. Kate didn't miss her avoidance tactic, and took hold of her arm.

"Sweetie, did Jamie do something to hurt or upset you? Is *that* why you won't go?" her friend asked in concern. "If he did—"

"No!" Sunny blurted. She didn't want Kate blaming Jamie for anything, or trying to press him for details, either. "No, no, he's fine." She sighed, burying her face in both hands. "And beautiful! And he was really sweet to me. Oh, Kate, what am I gonna do?"

"So you *do* like him?" Kate pried at her hands, trying

to get Sunny to look at her. "Then why not go? I mean, I know he's a hound, but I didn't just see the way *you* looked at *him*. . . . He couldn't take his eyes off you the whole day. And that kind of attention from the perennially single Jamie Angel? It's a downright miracle. So you have to come tonight, Sun!"

Sunny pulled out of Kate's grasp and paced the small kitchen, wringing her hands in agitation. "If I go, he'll start everything up again, and . . . and . . ." *I'll fall in love with him. And I might just fall from heaven if I do. And there could be dangerous repercussions for Jamie as well.*

"And?" Kate prompted, rolling her hand impatiently.

"*And* he's got too bad a rep for me. I just can't trust him," she lied, offering a quick prayer for forgiveness.

Kate sighed, studying her from across the room. "All right, then," she agreed reluctantly. "I guess if you're sure. Just seems like, I dunno, there could be something between you two. Something worth taking a chance on."

Sunny pasted a smile on her face. "Now that you're engaged, you're in love with love. You want everyone to be as happy as you."

"Of course I do! I wish there were a whole pack of Dillon Foxes for all my girlfriends. But he's one of a kind, so I have to work with what's available. And Jamie Angel is very available."

Sunny stared past Kate's shoulder. "He deserves genuine love with a good woman," she said, her chest tightening. "Someone kind and real, someone he loves deeply. Yes. I pray that Jamie finds that." Sunny glanced away, blinking at sudden tears. She'd never wanted anything so much as to be that very woman for Jamie. To be the one to kiss away his pain, to chase away that dogged loneliness she'd sensed inside him.

"Oh, my God," Kate whispered wondrously. "You don't just *like* him. . . . You fell for him hard."

Sunny wiped her eyes, forcing a bright smile onto her face. "How in heaven's name could that have happened?" she sang. "We only spent a few hours together."

Kate gave her a knowing smile. "A lot can happen in a few hours. Look at me and Dillon."

She had to hustle Kate out of the apartment, or her best friend was going to slowly wheedle and cajole far too much out of her. Slipping an arm through Kate's, Sunny walked her slowly toward the door. "You go to the party with your own prince. Have a great time and text me later, okay?"

Kate stopped by the front door, looking at her uncertainly. "I can't believe you're being such a coward about this. It's not like you at all."

Sunny's face flamed hot. "I'm not being a coward!"

Kate wrapped both arms about Sunny, holding her tight. "I'm praying that you find the love of your life, too. Just be sure you don't tuck tail and run when you do."

Kate and Dillon entered the foyer, and Jamie just kept staring past them through the still-open front door. Waiting. Expecting Sunny to come strolling in behind them, her big dark eyes dancing with light. He leaned a little sideways, trying to see down the steps.

"Uh, Jamie," Kate volunteered hesitantly. "Sunny's not coming."

He blinked back at her. There had to be some mistake. Friends. They'd agreed to be friends. She wouldn't have stayed away from him, not if she felt like he did. She couldn't have managed to keep her distance—it had taken every bit of his self-discipline not to show up at her apartment in the past few days.

"So, dude, just us," Dillon added, following Lulu's lead into the house. He carefully passed a gourmet shopping bag into Jamie's hands, hesitating until he was sure Jamie had hold of the parcel. "Sorry; no Dom Pérignon this time. We did bring some good wine, though."

But you didn't bring my Sunshine. All he could do was blink back at Kate, trying to understand why Sunny would've stood him up. Even if it wasn't a date, they'd had plans for the party.

"Why didn't she want to come?" he asked, trying to keep his tone bland.

"I honestly don't know, Jamie." Kate shook her head slowly, a meaningful expression in her eyes. Had Sunny told her something about him?

He'd spent the past days aching to see Sunny again, fighting the compulsion to go after her, to beg for a way they could be together. Only his absolute respect for her and her wishes had held that plan at bay. Then he'd woken exhilarated this morning, his first thought that he'd be with her again today. The whole morning had been a study in finding ways to expend his nervous energy. First, a six-mile run that had done almost nothing to calm his libido. Next, several hours spent reading one of the volumes about the Grigori, the fallen angels mentioned in the Apocrypha. He'd read page after page, searching for any hint that Sunny might find a way to become mortal, some loophole where they could be together without it being a grave sin.

His reading had yielded no hope whatsoever. Just like all the other lore he'd studied for the past few days.

So at last, he'd pinned all his anticipation on the simple act of getting to spend time with her. It was a gorgeous, unseasonably warm New Year's Day and he'd planned to walk her down to the dock. He already had one of their most expensive vintages from the wine cellar chilling in a cooler down there—along with a pair of his grandmama's silver wine goblets. He'd even brought out a hand-crocheted lace tablecloth for them to sit on. It was truly what Sunny Renfroe deserved—the full-court press.

Full-court press. He'd thrown the words out to her the other day in jest, and here he stood in khakis and a button-down and polished loafers and . . . she simply wasn't coming.

Kate stared up at him, searching his face; he had no doubt that his extreme disappointment showed in his eyes. "I'm sorry," she said with surprising sympathy. "I tried."

He nodded, scuffing one of his shoes against the hardwood floor of the entry. "I guess she didn't . . ." He couldn't even finish the statement.

I guess she didn't care about me, didn't want to be near me. I guess I was wrong about what happened between us. . . .

Even though he knew better—Sunny had been more than obviously attracted to him. The stakes between them were just too high, and he got that.

Kate stepped close and rose onto the balls of her feet, whispering in his ear, "Go after her, Jamie. She's well worth pursuing."

She stepped back, giving him a conspiratorial smile, then followed in Dillon's footsteps.

Sunny lay on her sofa, Kleenex box in hand, watching *When Harry Met Sally.* Perfect. A movie about friends. . . . Well, at least they'd started out that way. Why didn't *she* possess the strength of will to take Jamie up on his offer of friendship?

Because, just like Harry and Sally, she knew that she and Jamie would wind up falling in love. She couldn't really see someone as strong-willed and eager as Jamie Angel wasting much time without going for what he wanted, either.

"Kiel," she whispered, fresh tears starting, "am I being tested? Is that it? Why else would I have to hurt like this?"

No answer. Kiel came to her only at the most important of times, and apparently one lowly guardian's tears didn't qualify as urgent. She dabbed at her eyes and tried to focus on the movie, but was interrupted by the front doorbell. Who would be dropping by on New Year's Day? Her mama might be out walking around downtown—and if it was her mother, she'd instantly notice Sunny's mood and teary eyes and want to know every detail of what was troubling her daughter. After "adopting" Sunny when she was sent to Earth—her parents had no clue about her true nature or age—her mama had always been overprotective, loving Sunny all the more because she felt so blessed to have her.

Tiptoeing to the door so that whoever was on the other side wouldn't hear her, Sunny looked out the peephole of her apartment door.

"God, help me," she whispered, and, wiping her eyes one more time, began unlatching the door.

Jamie waltzed right into her apartment as if his arrival on her doorstep were an everyday thing. As always, he dwarfed her, but somehow in the cramped space of her apartment, he seemed even taller and more broad shouldered. And she'd have sworn that the man was even handsomer than the last time she'd seen him.

As they walked together into her living room, she assessed him as inconspicuously as possible. Whereas the other day he'd been in grungy jeans and a T-shirt, today he wore a dark purple Polo button-down, one that made his green eyes more vivid than usual. He also had on neatly pressed khaki pants that emphasized his very fine physique. Oh, how she'd fibbed when she'd claimed he looked wimpy. Everything about Jamie Angel's physique spoke of power and strength, and she'd spent several long nights imagining what it would feel like to have that body atop her own. To have him deep inside her, loving her.

And she'd spent the *days* repenting for such wicked desires.

When they reached her living room, he turned and faced her. His expression was like granite, full of determination. "I've decided there has to be a way."

In the background, Meg Ryan was faking her orgasm, and Jamie lifted one eyebrow. "Perhaps you should take that as a sign about you and me. About what could happen, the pleasure—"

"Stop!" She held up both hands, desperate to silence him. "Just stop right now, James Dixon."

He reached out and caught one of her curls between his fingertips, stroking it languidly. "You caught my full name when my sis used it, huh?"

"It apparently works when one needs to be forceful. Or get your attention." She swatted his hand away from her hair.

He smiled his fallen-angel, sinfully gorgeous smile. "Oh, you've got my full attention, baby. But you already know that." Once again, his hand found its way to her hair, his eyes narrowing in pleasure as he stroked first one soft curl, then another.

She gaped at him. "I thought you were worried about burning in hell!"

"I thought *you* responded to my kiss in a very human way." He drew one long curl to his lips, kissing the end of one tendril. "It's just your hair, Sunshine."

She ducked out of his reach and retrieved a hair band from around her wrist, gathering the curls into a ponytail so he wouldn't play with them again. He looked disappointed, but slid both hands into his pockets obediently.

Wordlessly, she stalked toward the kitchen, where the pastry was baking, and Jamie began to wander around her apartment. It was the second floor of a brownstone, a completely open floor plan. Without continuing his bantering innuendo, Jamie gazed about the place, taking in her myriad plants and flowers, the primitive art on the walls. "You have a real talent for growing things. But then again, you're full of life, Sunny Renfroe. I'm not surprised."

She opened the oven and checked on the pastry, and Jamie grinned. "And a talent for cooking," he added. "That smells delicious . . . just like you do." He said the last in a bedroom voice, low and full of temptation.

She closed the oven, shaking her head in disbelief. He was behaving exactly as she'd imagined, pressing her with unstoppable energy and sensuality.

"Why did you come? Just to torment me some more?" she demanded, hoping he couldn't tell how hard she'd been crying. Unfortunately, he spotted the wad of used tissues on the floor at that precise moment. Bending down, he picked them up, frowning sharply. He balled them in his fist, seeming almost angry.

He strode to where she stood in the kitchen, moving in extremely close. "I couldn't stay away," he admitted in a husky voice. "I couldn't even try to keep my distance. I meant what I said. . . . What if there is a way we could be together?"

Two more steps and his arms were about her waist, even though he knew the risk to both of them—especially to her. She pushed at his chest. "Do you want me to be punished? Sent back to heaven . . . or worse?"

His eyes slid closed and he dropped both hands to his sides. "No," he said in a hushed voice. "I just want to have you in my life."

"Jamie." She studied the floor. "You barely know me. You're just caught up in . . . what I am. The way that makes you feel."

He moved right back to her, planting strong hands squarely on her shoulders. "Sunny, it's not what you are. It's the way *you* make me feel. Don't you get it? I've been dead inside . . . the things I see, the creatures I kill. It's all I know. To actually care for a woman? To believe in the possibility of love? I buried that a long time ago."

"But you *can* love." She reached a trembling hand to his cheek. "I see your heart and it's beautiful."

His eyes grew bright. "My heart's been cold for a long time. But then you came along, and you're . . . so good. So pure and beautiful and, God forgive me, incredibly sexy. It's like . . . I could change. I could care. I could . . . I could love you, Sunny."

"That would be a mistake."

He shook his head adamantly. "Perfect love casts out fear. That's what the Bible says."

"I'm not afraid, Jamie. I'm here for a reason. And intimate relationships with humans don't fall under the job description."

"They made you human. You said so yourself the other night," he argued. "How can they put you here, expect you to live a mostly human life and not have someone of your own?"

She turned away sharply; his words tore at her heart.

Suddenly his arms came around her again, and he was kissing her nape. A sweet kiss, an almost chaste one, just a brush of his lips against her skin, a back-and-forth pressure. "Go to dinner with me tomorrow night," he begged. "As friends. Only friends, I swear it."

She had to steady her breathing before she could even answer. "You're not capable of interacting with me that way," she finally groaned. "Look at you right now."

He kissed her nape once more, slowly trailing his tongue across her skin. "I'm gonna find that loophole, Sunny Renfroe," he whispered, pressing his mouth to her ear. "And when I do, I'm going to make love to you, make you feel things you've never been allowed to experience." He pulled back, looking deep into her eyes. "And I'm going to make you mine. Until then, yes, we'll only be friends ... but you still get the full-court press. Starting tomorrow night."

Chapter Eight

As Jamie and Sunny reached the upstairs of the Mansion's restaurant, the maître d' led them toward their table. As she followed him, Jamie placed a guiding hand against the small of her back. It was a gentlemanly gesture, an almost protective one, but it still set her skin on fire. Tonight was a dangerous gamble, one that defied the intent of Kiel's express orders, even as it followed the rule of his law.

That was when she realized exactly *where* they would be seated. "Sir, the table you reserved," the maître d' announced, revealing a private, candlelit table for two in the tower turret. "Just as you requested."

"Jamie," Sunny warned. More than a gamble, this was a terrible, terrible risk, one with a potentially treacherous outcome.

He waited for her to slide into the round banquette, and as she did so, she noticed that the restaurant's most romantic table also had a set of silver velvet curtains. Would the two of them be closed in alone after their meal was served? Before? Her pulse skittered in a crazy tempo and Jamie seated himself right beside her.

She gasped softly once they were left alone, the luxurious curtains halfway drawn around them. The rounded bench seat pressed their bodies closer together than she'd have liked, but she couldn't seem to force herself to scoot farther away from Jamie. Everything in the turret twinkled and glowed, from the artfully arranged candles along the windowsills to the silver and gold sequins on the tablecloth. It was more romantic and dreamier than any place she'd ever been for dinner. An obvious and deliberate tactic on Jamie's part, too.

"You called ahead," she murmured, daring to glance up into his bright green eyes, even more beautiful than usual because of the candlelight.

He brushed light fingertips along her cheek. "I wanted you all to myself," he said quietly. "I'm already very greedy when it comes to my time with you, baby."

"This is only friendship," she reminded him unsteadily, trying to calm her erratic breathing. "You agreed to the terms."

He stopped touching her and began staring pointedly at her lips, sensual heat in his gaze. "I love your mouth. I keep dreaming of feeling it against my bare skin, all *over* my body."

She stared down at her menu, avoiding his gaze. "You agreed. . . ."

"I haven't done anything untoward, have I?" he asked, studying the wine list. "Haven't disgraced either of us, or fondled you? Surely your bosses won't complain just yet."

No, but your three guardians are watching from somewhere, even if I can't see them. And Kiel sees everything I do. . . .

"I think champagne would be lovely." His selection made, he slid the leather-bound wine list onto the table, turning his full attention on her. "Now, tell me what it was like when you became human. What you remember about your childhood . . . I want to know about your family, the one that raised you. I have questions, lots of questions."

"Why do you want to know all that?"

"Because a strong second to how much I want you, my sweet Sunshine? Is how badly I want to know everything *about* you." He faced her completely, resting a forearm along the back of the banquette. "I booked the table for the whole evening. So start talking and don't leave anything out."

Jamie's attention never wavered, not for one moment of their time together. Even after their meal was served, he would take a bite or two, then turn back to her, asking about some detail or another. Why had the angels chosen the Renfroes as her mortal family? Was it their faith, their position in society? How had she concealed her identity from them, starting at ten years old when they'd adopted her, never realizing that she'd arrived on Earth only a month before?

His fascination with her was endless, and to his credit, he didn't touch her again throughout the evening. He slowly sipped champagne, his green eyes always on her while she talked. A few times, she saw him reach out for her hand, then catch himself, retrieving his champagne glass instead.

After almost two hours, Sunny was worn-out with talking. "It's not fair. You've had all the questions. Maybe I had a thing or two to ask you." She tried laughing, feeling suddenly shy.

He waved her off. "I'm boring. Why do you think I can't keep a girlfriend?"

"Because you don't let anyone close, Jamie," she said seriously. "I see your game." He glanced away quickly, whispering something unintelligible under his breath.

She leaned closer, wanting to hear. "What did you say?"

He turned back to her. "I'll let you in. I mean I would . . . if . . ." He gave her a wistful look. "I know, I know. . . . Never mind."

She saw genuine pain flash in his eyes, and tried to lighten things up. "We never would've worked anyway. I mean, a black chick and a white dude? In *this* Southern city? Good grief, the tongues would wag and wag, especially given your family name. The Junior League would have group-wide heart failure."

"Sunny, it's not 1950 anymore," he disagreed. "Nobody cares who I see. Besides, I don't move in high society very much anyway."

"James Angel, be truthful now." She gave him a wide-eyed, chastising look.

"Okay, okay," he admitted, laughing. "I can't bullshit one of the heavenly host."

"Jamie!" She clamped a hand over her own mouth at his irreverence.

He shrugged. "So I hit a few of the society parties now and then. I don't belong in that world. We have money, but we're freaks in this town. The main thing . . ." He leaned closer, sliding his arm along the back of her seat without actually touching her. "The most *important* thing is, I'd have been proud to have you on my arm, Sunny Renfroe. So proud."

Her vision instantly blurred and she stared at her plate wordlessly. Jamie's warm hand encircled her nape and he rubbed the cordons of her neck, very tenderly massaging her. "I didn't mean to upset you."

She blinked at the tears, knowing she should force his

hand away. He couldn't touch her, couldn't transgress the rules of interaction.

And she couldn't find the strength to stop him. "I'd have been proud, too," she whispered, wiping at her eyes. "To be on your arm, to know you were mine. But I can't afford to even *dream* about that."

He scooted closer, the hard muscles of his upper thigh pressing into hers. He slid his hand down around her shoulder, cradling her close. "Dreaming isn't a crime, sweetheart," he whispered in her ear, letting his lips graze the lobe with an almost-touch. "God puts dreams inside of us for a reason."

She shook her head, searching for the strength to scoot away, but he just leaned a little closer, holding her against his side. "I never much dreamed I could fall in love," he admitted huskily. "Not ever. Not till you walked in my house the other day."

She looked up into his eyes plaintively. "Please. Don't make this harder, Jamie. You saw what happened in the gazebo."

"Your boss? Yeah, don't think I'm not scared. I may be a tough guy, but I realize this is serious business."

She lifted fingertips to his cheek, caressing it briefly. "Then stop touching me."

He smiled gently. "You're touching me, too."

She dropped her hand as if scalded. "I won't. Not again."

"How can you be so sure?" he asked, obediently sliding a few feet away along the banquette, putting safe distance between their two bodies.

Her throat tightened painfully, but she forced herself to meet his gaze. "Because I won't see you again, not after tonight. It was a mistake. There's too much desire, too much we both want . . . and can't have."

Jamie planted his fist on the table angrily. The silver-
ware and china clattered; his champagne glass sloshed
some of its contents onto the cloth, but then he slammed
his hand down even harder. "I've spent my whole adult
life serving the righteous by hunting demons. So tell me
why, Sunny?" He turned to her, desperation darkening his usually bright eyes. "Why have I been given this
dream of you, only to have it denied me?" With a brutal gesture, he reached for his champagne, draining the
glass's remaining contents. "How can falling for you like
this be wrong or evil? Maybe I should burn in hell, but I
can't stop how I feel. . . ." He glanced away sharply, wiping his own eyes with the back of his hand.

She'd never wanted to touch a human more than she
did Jamie Angel in that moment. Not to arouse him, not
to pleasure herself. She simply wanted to draw him into
her arms and hold him, comfort him.

There were no rules against compassion. The curtains were closed; they were completely alone and un-
observed. Without questioning or second-guessing for
another moment, she opened her arms wide and pulled
Jamie close, wrapping him tightly in an embrace. He bent
his head against her shoulder, sliding his hands about
her waist. She felt the fast rhythm of his heart beating
against her own chest, smelled the masculine scent of
his skin, the fresh, clean aroma of shampoo in his hair.

She reached, threading her fingers through that
straight, soft hair. Just one stroke, maybe two. Surely
that would be overlooked.

Except . . . he moaned. Right in her ear, an eager,
hungry sound that said one or two more caresses would
only ignite the fire between them all over again. Make
them burn harder and hotter, take them beyond the veil
to the place of punishment and retribution.

She drew in a ragged breath, pressing her mouth against his bristling cheek, feeling his own lips against her jaw, her throat. He pulled at her waist, drawing her closer, closer, until she was halfway on his lap, feeling his thick erection beneath her thigh.

Had to stop, had to put an end to it . . . but she didn't possess the strength of will to do so.

"Belong to me, Sunny," he begged, his mouth finding hers. "Please find a way."

There was no rule that could be bent. They'd been doomed before they'd ever so much as kissed the first time.

With both hands, she pushed at his chest, sliding away from him and back onto the banquette. Jamie kept reaching for her, his gaze imploring as it swept over her face, her body. She was about to explain the facts again, when his BlackBerry rang, vibrating on the table beside him.

He stared at it for one long moment, and she saw Mason's name on the caller ID. "Damn it." He whipped the phone to his ear. "What's going on, Mace?" he demanded irritably. She couldn't hear what his brother said on the other end, but Jamie lowered his voice, turning away. "I told you not to disturb me. That tonight was important," he whispered.

She couldn't help smiling, even as her heart broke . . . for Jamie and for herself.

"Where?" He suddenly sat up tall in the seat. "Midnight? All right."

He replaced the BlackBerry on the table with a sigh. "Work," he muttered, staring down at the phone, seemingly lost in thought.

"What's happening at midnight?" Maybe if she could pull his attention back to the real world, he'd forget their own anguished interactions.

Jamie raked a hand through his hair. "Usual crap. There's this demon Thrastikas that's been gunning for my ass lately. Apparently . . ." He waved it off. "Doesn't matter."

She sat forward, her own senses on full alert. What if this was the same demon that Shay had drawn the other day? The dangerous one, with that death grip on Jamie? Even if it wasn't, something about this midnight meeting felt dead wrong. As a guardian, she was wired with a full load of senses that ordinary humans didn't possess, and right now they were warning her about Jamie's safety.

"Jamie, please tell me what is happening at midnight," she repeated intently.

"Mason wanted to let me know he set a trap for Thrastikas down in Bonaventure Cemetery. That demon soul-sucked a couple of tourists today and Mace is pissed. So he's decided that we're going to take him down tonight once and for all."

The hair on Sunny's nape bristled. This plan wasn't right; danger awaited Jamie—she was sure of it.

"I don't think that's a good idea."

He cast a dubious look at her. "I don't have to take you home for another hour."

"It's not about me. It's dangerous, Jamie."

"Like I said, the usual stuff," he said in a dull tone. She'd hurt him tonight, and she didn't like the idea of his being in the field in his current emotional state. The pain he was suffering would put him in jeopardy, make him more vulnerable than usual.

She shook her head adamantly. "I'm serious, Jamie. Don't go tonight. Please."

Maybe she should tell him about Shay's drawing, but the image could be interpreted in any number of ways. For all she knew, Jamie would try to use it to argue that she belonged in his life; otherwise a demon might kill him. So she opted to keep the drawing's existence to herself.

He leaned back against the banquette and gave her a long look. In the candlelight, his eyes gleamed bright, filled with unmasked heartache. "You're telling me we have no future, Sunny. You've made that point indelibly clear. That means all I've got is my calling as a hunter," he said bitterly. "I might as well focus on my job . . . since I won't have you."

She reached for his hand, but he averted the gesture. "Jamie, listen to me," she begged. "Don't start taking crazy chances. Not because of me or because we can't . . ."

She wasn't able to finish, because the phone rang again, although she couldn't see who was on caller ID this time. After a moment, Jamie said. "All right, I'll get moving. Yeah, yeah, I know. Give me thirty."

Before she could object again, or explain about an earthly guardian's keen sense of danger, Jamie began tracking down the server and handling the bill. When she tried to take hold of his hand while they waited for the valet, he got another phone call, and walked away from her to answer it. The drive to her apartment was only a few blocks, and despite several efforts, she wasn't able to convince him that he should stay far away from Bonaventure Cemetery tonight.

Chapter Nine

Jamie didn't like the smell of things. Literally. He wasn't even over the locked gate to Bonaventure Cemetery yet, and the acrid, rank scent of demons already had his stomach roiling, something that almost never happened after so many years as a hunter. As he slung a booted foot over the top of the wrought-iron gate, the stench intensified. This was going to be an ugly battle—all his senses told him that.

Sunny warned you to stay away. An angel from the heavenly host cautioned you that this fight was a dangerous one.

He'd been too hurt and distressed to heed her warning, but more than that, he'd wanted to lose himself in a good fight. Gashes and claw marks would heal, so he welcomed them, wanted to feel that pain, the rawness of it. Yes, his body would heal even as he knew his heart never would recover from this particular emotional hit. He was convinced he'd lost Sunny forever, so why not bring on the battle wounds? God wanted him as a hunter but wouldn't grant him the deepest wish of his heart? Well, fine. Then he was here to fight, to put his life and body on the line. Maybe if he was lucky, some badass demon would get the best of him this time, and put him out of his misery for good.

Only that would mean never seeing Sunny again ... unless he bumped into her at the gates of heaven. And his death would hurt her; he was sure of it. He knew that their current situation wasn't because she didn't care for him. He had total confidence that she'd been feeling every beautiful, conflicted, and tormenting emotion that he had tonight.

She was simply smart enough to have a healthy fear of God in the matter, whereas his heart—his human soul—had wanted to believe there was some way they could be together. Precisely because he did love and fear God, he possessed a ridiculous heap of faith that Sunny was meant to be in his life.

Until the restaurant tonight. Something about her saying that she'd never see him again had stabbed him more deeply than he'd thought possible. Her words had been final, and he'd known it. She would never be convinced to search for any loophole to their situation; he'd glimpsed that resolution in her eyes.

So he really didn't have anything left to lose in this battle, which meant he shouldn't fear the shrieks and caterwauls that started up as soon as he climbed over the gate. With a quiet *thud*, he landed on the loamy ground inside the cemetery, squatting and listening keenly. Mason, Shay, and another one of the Shades, Evan, were already here, and he searched the ten-o'clock position for where they were supposed to be posted.

In the moonlit shadows, he could make out his brother's form, with Evan and Shay crouching beside him. It wouldn't be midnight for another thirty minutes, but they knew from experience that demons had difficulty

understanding the human passage of time. Although
demon stench was in the air, Thrastikas couldn't possibly have arrived yet, or Jamie would hear the demon's
clanking chains. The links were long, permanently manacled to the creature's ankles, and they sounded his arrival like a death knell wherever he went. At least for
Jamie and the other hunters who had the supernatural
ability to hear and see demons.

Even though Thrastikas hadn't shown, there was still
no telling how many of their enemies were massed already in the cemetery, so Jamie moved clandestinely toward Mason and Evan, keeping low to the ground.

Mace caught sight of him and motioned with his
hand, indicating with two fingers that they were tracking a pair of the enemy. Jamie took up position behind a
live oak nearby, poised with his semiautomatic for when
the creatures came within striking distance.

Right then, a shriek like a banshee's rang out in
the treetop just above Jamie—much too close above
him. Swinging his weapon, he prepared to fire, but he
didn't even get a chance. Thrastikas dropped from the
tree, tackling him like a ten-ton deadweight, swinging
several of his mighty chains overhead. His eyes were
beady and red, and the chains made a whistling sound
in the air as they whipped toward him. Dimly, Jamie was
aware of Mason and Evan firing their weapons, but then
heard more shrieks as an explosion of light pierced the
darkness.

With a quick gaze to the left, he saw a demon horde
move in on the other hunters, blocking them from aid-
ing him. Shay cast a desperate glance in his direction,
then turned to fight off the leather-winged creatures advancing upon them all. He was isolated, going head-to-
head with a demon who particularly wanted his blood.

Again Thrastikas swung his chains overhead, growling at Jamie. "Hunter, your blood is mine. And after this fight—I'll have your soul."

His angel had been right: This was a trap, and now they'd been lethally ambushed.

Sunny, sweetheart . . . I'm sorry, he thought. He wished with all his might that he could see her even once more, just as the massive chains made contact with the crown of his head.

The last thing he heard was Thrastikas's wicked cackling. "James Angel, welcome to hell."

Sunny gunned the gas pedal of her Camry, wishing for once that she were in angel form. If she could've engaged her wings, her supernatural ability to move among physical places quickly, she'd already be in Bonaventure.

She'd tried to sit this one out, wrestled to respect Jamie's wishes to engage the enemy tonight, even if it meant risking his life recklessly. But the more she'd paced her apartment, thinking about Shay's sketch and remembering the visible pain she'd seen in Jamie's eyes back at the restaurant, the more she couldn't stay away. Not while he had some kind of crazy death wish because of her decision.

And what if he was right about there being a way for them to be together? There was at least the slim possibility, enough of one that she wanted Jamie to know that he shouldn't put his life on the line recklessly. And that he shouldn't give up on them, not just yet. They could study the lore together, read every volume, try to find a loophole.

She was almost to Bonaventure Road when a humming sound began in the car, the seat beside her instantly filled with light. She nearly swerved right off the road, unable to see anything because of Kiel's luminescence.

Thankfully, he toned his brightness down right away. For once, she saw him as he rarely appeared—more human. His warm eyes were the color of golden wheat, his skin like burnished bronze. His hair was an unearthly mix of red and blond and gold, the combination creating one of the mystical colors that didn't exist anywhere but back home.

"Sunera," he chided quietly. "You are nearing an abyss right now with James Angel. Dinner was not wise."

She shook her head, focusing on the road straight ahead. "Sir, he's in danger. Tonight. He's going to a demon battle, and when he spoke of it, I knew . . . I sensed . . ."

"This is what it would be like every time he went to war. You know, more than any *human* female, the danger he faces."

She glanced sideways in shock. "Are you saying there actually is some way I could be with him?"

Kiel gave her a bare hint of a smile, one that seemed to conceal a thousand secrets. "Even angels have free will, Sunera."

Being a lower-level guardian, Sunny still didn't know many things. There was so little that her superiors had taught her about her angelic nature, including the choices available to her. "Free will to do what? I can't have Jamie—you've already said so."

"Free will to do what is right," her superior said cryptically, but she'd have sworn there was an odd sparkle in his eyes. "I tried to guide you down the easier path. But in your heart, you know what the right thing is. You've always known."

"Sir, sir," she cried, turning down the road that led toward the cemetery. "How can I know the right thing? You've told me he's off-limits, told me there's no possibility, but now . . . has anything changed? I'm confused."

"Faith is the evidence of things unseen," he said, quoting scripture. "Lean on your faith. Perhaps it will open up a new course for you."

She opened her mouth to beg for more information and guidance, but he was already gone. All that remained was a slight warm glow in the empty seat beside her. And two highly significant, meaningful words, a compass in the midst of her confusion: free will.

Jamie's forehead throbbed from a deep gash Thrastikas had inflicted with the chains. Blood dripped into his eyes, and he kept trying to wipe it away so he could see to fight. He and the demon had squared off, but unless Mace or Evan managed to free himself from the fracas and come to his aid soon, Jamie knew he wouldn't last long. The demon had tossed away Jamie's semiautomatic first thing, then managed to get hold of his knife and dispose of it as well.

So he was head-to-head with a particularly malevolent demon with nothing but his bare hands to use as a weapon. He assumed fighting stance, offering a prayer for strength and assistance. For several long seconds, the red-eyed demon glared at him, his ugly leather wings brushing together. The appendages created an earsplitting sound, and the demon grinned in pleasure at Jamie's pained reaction.

"You've been a splinter in my ass for long enough, hunter," Thrastikas growled, and once again began swinging the chains overhead, allowing them to gain momentum as he ran at Jamie.

In a blur, Jamie was dragged to the ground, the thick, rusty links wrapped tight about his throat. He gasped and coughed, trying to draw even a single gulp of air, but the force was too tight on his windpipe.

With both hands, he grasped at the chain, frantically trying to loosen the pressure so he could breathe, but the demon only tightened his hold, laughing viciously. Jamie scrabbled at the ground with his boots, flailing as he tried to fight back.

"A fitting end," Thrastikas taunted. "A torturous death for one who has tortured me for far too long. Now, like so many of my brothers have done by your hand . . . you will die."

Jamie gagged, still clawing at his throat, trying to get a bead on his comrades, but they were much too far away to help him now; he could hear them fighting farther in the distance. He was on his own, at least until the other hunters could dispatch the demon horde.

Everything began to grow darker, dimmer, and Jamie knew he was dying. Instead of struggling, he let his thoughts go to Sunny. Pictured her bright, lovely eyes, the warmth and care he'd seen reflected there. Her purity. Her sweetness.

That was what heaven would be like. Death would be like Sunny Renfroe.

Maybe he was dead already. The darkness suddenly grew golden and bright as a sun, the penumbra overshadowing Thrastikas. Jamie couldn't even see the demon in the blaze of glorious light. Heaven. He was already there, the transition far easier than he'd always imagined.

And Sunny was there with him! She stood in the center of the glowing energy, beaming down at him, pure love in her eyes. He smiled back, trying to reach toward her, but he remained prone and his body wouldn't obey. Of course not, he was only a spirit now, no longer a physical being . . . although it seemed he should be able to walk and move in heaven. Just as it seemed that his throat shouldn't hurt and burn so harshly and the gash on his forehead shouldn't throb still. The afterlife was a lot more painful than he'd expected.

Sunny knelt beside him, gently touching his throat, and the sharp pain dissolved. Then, with a light brushing of her fingertips against his forehead, that pain vanished as well.

"Sunny?" He gasped the word, sounding gritty like sandpaper. Lifting both hands to his throat, he tried to loosen the chain, but it was no longer around his throat.

"Be still and don't try to talk," she soothed, stroking his hair.

He peered up at her, not understanding what he'd just experienced. He'd have sworn he was in heaven when she appeared in that halo of light. "Am I ... dead?"

She pressed a tender kiss to his forehead, caressing his cheek. "No, my love. You're going to be fine. You're safe."

He might be safe, at least for now, but Sunny wasn't! There were demons all around; Thrastikas might hurt her. In alarm, he tried to sit up. "You gotta get out of here," he warned hoarsely, but she pushed him back down easily. He caught sight of Thrastikas's crumpled form only a few yards away; his wings and body had been scorched, the chains melted. His once-beady red eyes stared lifelessly, all the hellfire gone from their depths. Sunny had done that; Sunny had used her angelic power to turn his enemy to an ashen heap.

"Sunshine," he whispered hoarsely. "Thank you. I'm sorry ... so sorry about ..."

"Shh, just rest, Jamie. Rest." She kissed him softly on the lips, and it was warm, strange. Different from any other time they'd shared a kiss. So much so that whatever she did caused him to fall fast asleep immediately.

*   *   *

Sunny watched Mason and Evan hoist Jamie's still form into the backseat of Mace's pickup truck. She'd given him a holy kiss, placing him in a deep, healing trance. Although she'd instantly mended his wounds, the emotional and spiritual trauma of coming so near to death needed to be healed as well, and that took time.

Once Jamie was laid out on the seat, looking peaceful—and so fast asleep that he began snoring loudly—Mace turned to her. "I don't get it." He shook his head. "We were knee-deep in battle with some truly wicked demons, and then . . . they went ghost on us. And where did you come from?" He pointed at Sunny. "*You* were suddenly here and then all the demons were gone. And Thrastikas was toast back there. He was scorched against the ground. What's up with that?"

Sunny gave him an evasive smile. "Well, I was worried about Jamie." She turned and peeked at him one more time, wanting to reassure herself that he truly was all right.

"So you came out into the thick of a demon battle? Really, now," Mace continued, popping her on the arm. "I don't believe you. There's got to be more to it than that."

Shay started pushing Mason toward the driver's side. "Leave Sunny be. Isn't it bad enough that she's got to contend with Jamie? She doesn't need you, too."

He stopped in his tracks. "Contend? From where I'm standing, sissy, there's a lot more than *that* going on between those two."

Shay gave her brother another shove. "Just drive. There's no big conspiracy here."

He was still muttering about vaporized demons and supernatural forces when Shay closed his truck door, giving Sunny a brief and conspiratorial grin. "Thanks, sweetie," Shay said. "I know we all owe you our lives. Or at the very least we owe you Jamie's life. That you cared enough to come out here . . ."

Sunny lifted her finger to her lips dramatically, and whispered, "Shhhh. If he hears, it might go right to his head."

Shay burst out laughing. "Oh, my gosh, you so totally have my brother's number already."

I so totally love *your brother already*, Sunny nearly blurted in reply, but turned back to her car instead. Her work tonight had only just begun.

Chapter Ten

How long am I supposed to wait? I need to see you, Sunny. Give a guy a break, why don't you? You're killing me here....

Sunny smiled, reading Jamie's latest message on her iPhone. He'd texted her repeatedly during the past three days, and every time Sunny had indicated that it wasn't time yet, but that she definitely wanted to see him. That she had some big news. Something that would give him hope, but she needed time.

She'd been reading and delving into every book on angelic guardians, messengers, and hosts that Shay could shuttle over to Sunny's apartment. And the more she read, the more convinced she became that because of her love for Jamie, she truly could exercise her own free will. That she wouldn't turn dark as a result, not if guided by her faith—and no matter how hard she prayed, she always received the same answer: that she was meant to be with Jamie. Even though it seemed to fly in the face of everything she'd been called to do—and even though it contradicted Kiel's initial chastisement—she knew it was her destiny.

But she'd needed time enough to prove that to herself before telling Jamie such big news.

And he'd just about gone bonkers with the waiting. Patience, she was learning, wasn't high on James Angel's list of virtues.

Still smiling, she texted back, *I've been working on something for you. . . . Patience, big guy.*

Almost immediately he fired another volley:

Are you saying we can be together? Are you implying you figured out a way? I can't take much more of this. . . .

When she didn't text back right away, her phone began to ring, and she beamed. It was kind of silly, but it felt good to be pursued—and felt more than wonderful for Jamie to be the one doing that pursuing.

She answered the phone and he plunged right in. "I'm all out of patience," he blurted. "Are you home? I'm walking out to my truck right now. . . . I'm coming to see you."

"Really?" she said demurely. "Right now?"

He was silent for a moment, as if he'd expected her to object or dodge. "You . . . It's okay if I do?" He sounded entirely disbelieving, stunned even.

"Do you like lasagna?"

Another pause, then, "Hell, yeah. Wait, you want to cook for me?"

"James Dixon, you sound so shocked. I'd reckon you were used to dinner invitations from single women." She opened her pantry and began retrieving spices and spaghetti sauce and pasta. "I mean, aren't you supposed to be God's gift to every girl in Savannah?"

"Not anymore. There's only one girl I want, and you know it," he answered very quietly, and then she heard him suck in a breath. As if he were bracing for her rejection, for words she would never say again, the dreaded, *We can't be together.*

But she wouldn't give him her news over the phone.

It had to be done in person, when she could kiss him and hold him for hours afterward.

"Well, good, then," she said lightly, "I'll even have fresh bread for you. See you in a little while."

And with that she hung up the phone before he could cajole her for more information. It was thirty minutes from Isle of Hope to her apartment. She had a lot to accomplish in that very short amount of time.

Jamie took the steps to Sunny's apartment two at a time. He'd driven here at breakneck speed, lucky as hell that he'd not been stopped for a ticket, but he couldn't have slowed down if he'd tried.

She had good news; she had to. Something he wanted to hear. And she knew that there was only one thing that he would count as a happy announcement right now: that they had a future together.

He paced around on her stoop and ran a hand over his hair, trying to neaten it up. He'd been so hell-bent on storming her gates that he'd not even bothered to shave or change into nicer clothes. He was wearing faded jeans and a frayed green polo, but he didn't even care. He just wanted to be with Sunny, was desperate to hear her say that she'd found a way for them to be a couple.

Before he could ring the bell, Sunny opened the door. She leaned against the doorjamb smiling up at him with a sexy expression in her eyes. "Well," she drawled, "you must've broken the sound barrier with that drive over here, James Angel."

He was speechless. Unlike him, she'd made herself absolutely gorgeous, wearing a sleek pair of black jeans with a black cashmere turtleneck. Her hair was pulled back with a brightly colored silk scarf patterned in purple and red and black. He wanted to take that fabric between his teeth and untie it so he could run his hands all through her light brown curls.

"I . . ." He blushed, staring down at his scuffed boots, feeling stupidly shy now that he was here. "I couldn't get here fast enough, sweetheart. But you already know that."

"What's with gabbing on my front stoop, then? Come here." She grabbed hold of his arm, pulling him inside the apartment.

The moment the door was closed, Sunny was wrapping her arms about his neck, tugging him down for a kiss. Unlike all their previous kisses, this time she was bold, not hesitating for even a heartbeat as she backed him up against her front door. It turned him flat on, Sunny being so direct and aggressive.

It also caused his heart to slam inside his chest. Sunny wouldn't be so eager if . . .

He broke the kiss they'd begun. "Sunny, baby." He gasped. "Are you telling me . . . Can we . . . Is this allowed?" He didn't quite dare hope, even as he'd spent the past days desperately praying and dreaming of this very moment.

She beamed up at him, her almond-shaped eyes alight with fire and passion and . . . love. Cupping his face between both palms, she blessed him with a radiant smile, one that was lit with just a touch of her supernatural glow. "Yes, Jamie," she whispered, bobbing her head.

"Allowed to be together? To fall in love? To be lovers?" he rushed to ask, clinging to her hips. "Please tell me I'm understanding this right."

She nodded again, her smile widening. "Yes, my love, I believe we can be all those things."

His vision instantly blurred and he sagged against the door behind him, a heavy, crushing weight instantly lifted off his body and soul. "H-how?" he stammered, bunching her sweater in both hands. It was almost as if he feared she might still fly away, that he might lose her, so he had to hold her tight.

She leaned her cheek against his chest, sighing contentedly. "I finally understood what could be done after Kiel came to me again. That night of the demon fight . . . when I was driving out to stop you."

"You shouldn't have put yourself in danger like that," he admonished. "Not for me."

"Of course for you! I love you; why wouldn't I?"

He sucked in a sharp breath, desire and hope spiraling like crazy inside his heart. Had she really just confessed her love for him?

"You love me?" he murmured, cradling her even closer against his chest.

She pulled back and stared up into his eyes. "I've chosen to fall so I can be with you. I think some angels might consider that love."

"Sunny, no, no," he argued, panicking. "You can't do that. Fallen angels turn into demons. They become evil and dark. . . . No way, sweetheart. Not for me."

"You don't know as much as you think you do, hunter," came the answer from behind her, a rumbling noise like the sound of thunderclaps and music combined.

A bright beam of light filled Sunny's living room, and he tried to avert his eyes this time, but thankfully the gigantic angel toned down his glory somehow. Kiel stood in the center of the room, appearing mostly human, although his golden-tan eyes were unlike any Jamie had ever seen in a mortal.

"Young ones, it was a difficult test," the entity sang, a broad smile filling his face. "As Sunera now knows, God ordained and allowed your new love to endure a trial.

For a purpose . . . that you would know the strength of your feelings for each other. Know the importance of being destined to love and fight together."

"Fight together?" Sunny asked in surprise, but Jamie noticed that the rest of the mighty angel's announcement didn't seem to shock her at all.

"James Angel, you have a new battle partner in Sunera. You will pair with her as you fight demons and darkness. And, Sunera? You are now reassigned to James."

"What will that entail? I'm not sure I understand."

Kiel's eyes gleamed like diamonds. "Your role will be different from when you were with Kate—and she will be given a new guardian. You and James Angel will fight as one, true battle partners. Angelic strength matched with his hunter's skills. You're meant to complete and balance his power. Your faith, dear one, had to find this way . . . and it did."

Sunny turned to face Jamie. "I read the lore," she admitted sheepishly, and only then did he notice the small stack of leather-bound books on her coffee table. "Shay kept bringing me books, volume after volume. No matter how much I kept thinking I should give up . . . I couldn't give up on *you*, Jamie. On us."

Kiel beamed. "But you did not learn everything, Sunera. As of this moment, you are now this human's partner, his mate . . . and his wife."

"His *wife*?" they blurted simultaneously. They hadn't gotten married; they'd barely even kissed before tonight.

"It is declared so by heaven itself. No earthly ceremony is necessary." The angel's eyes sparkled. "Unless you want one, that is."

Jamie gaped. He'd spent years terrified of settling down, of making a commitment to any woman—much less marrying one. But as he gazed back at Kiel, the messenger's words seeping into his brain, he felt lighter and more alive than he had in years—and was shocked to realize he wasn't afraid at all.

"So we're already married, and she'll still be an angel of sorts?" Jamie clarified. "My own personal guardian angel?"

"I don't have to fall?" Sunny chimed in, her dark eyebrows furrowing in confusion.

Kiel stepped much closer, seeming larger and taller the nearer he came. "It *is* a kind of fall, to become human in this life and mate with a mortal," he answered Sunny, the words vibrating so strongly that the potted plants rocked where they sat on the windowsill. "Your willingness to fall in order to experience love has set you on an uncharted course. And what happens after that, Sunera? It will be as unknown to you as it is to all humans. . . . Your future in heaven remains a mystery. That is what it means for *you* to fall. That you live out your years as a human . . . although one with certain special angelic abilities. But you will not be given answers about the afterlife or future missions."

Jamie looked into Sunny's eyes, needing to know that she was comfortable with the arrangement, but all he saw reflected in her gaze was joy and genuine love. No doubt glimmered in her warm brown eyes, not even the slightest hesitation.

When he turned back to thank Kiel, the angel had already vanished, leaving a radiant glow in the center of the living room.

"This means," he said, spinning Sunny back into his arms, "that tonight's our honeymoon night, sweetheart."

"This can't be the way you imagined things happening between us," she whispered apologetically.

"Everyone always said I'd have a shotgun wedding one day. I just never imagined an Angel would wind up with an *angel*." He laughed, untying the scarf from her hair. "I like it loose, so I can run my hands all through your curls." He twined a particularly tight ringlet around his pinkie, loving how soft it felt.

Sunny stared up at him through half-lowered lashes. "Jamie Angel, you have a fixation with my hair."

"Because it's sexy as ever-living..." He coughed, seeming to catch himself. "Uh, heaven."

"But be serious for a minute," she argued as he angled for a full-mouthed kiss. "I know this is totally sudden."

He slid both hands low about her, cupping her perfectly rounded ass in both palms. He gave a rolling squeeze, tightening his hold until she gasped in pleasure.

"Sudden?" he murmured against her lips. "This past week's been one long, slow-motion hell for me. Wanting you, needing you ... tasting the bitterness of denial. And before that? Years of loneliness and emptiness right up until the moment I found you. No, this isn't sudden, Sunshine. This is my destiny. *You* are my destiny."

With a graceful motion, he bent down and scooped her up into his arms. "And this is you, my darling, about to be carried over the threshold to the start of our happily-ever-after. Where I'm going to make you fully and truly my wife ... in every way."

Chapter Eleven

Jamie carried her over the threshold of her bedroom with a flourish, pausing to glance around. "More flowers." He stood cradling her against his chest, taking in the African violets and orchids and amaryllis blooms, an awed expression on his handsome face.

"I'll plant some for you, if you'd like," Sunny suggested, flushing as she realized that she'd soon be living with him as his wife. And wasn't that just the sort of thing wives did? Plant flowers, cook food, provide a loving home? "Maybe . . . in the kitchen. I mean, if Shay won't mind."

"Shay? She'll never stop gloating about anything you want to do for me. And thanking *you* for shattering my confirmed bachelorhood." He nuzzled her cheek playfully. "Besides, I have a feeling you and Shay will be making over my family home . . . I mean, your *new* home," he corrected with a huge grin. "Good thing I have a big-ass bedroom so we can share it comfortably."

"For a man who's been notoriously unable to settle down, you're handling our 'shotgun marriage' with shocking ease." She glanced up into his eyes, some small part of her still worried that Kiel's mandate might overwhelm him, scare him away.

He stared down at her, serious in his expression. "Sunny, forget my trail of women, okay? Lord knows I want to. And Lord knows they wanna forget me!" He laughed, but there was a trace of regret in his gaze. "Thing is, I just hadn't found you yet, but once I did, I was ready for . . . well, everything we're gonna share. And I do mean *everything*." He glanced pointedly at the bed, then asked uncertainly, "The question is, though, are you ready? For this?"

She leaned forward, capturing his mouth with an answering, exuberant kiss. She was more than ready. She needed all of James Dixon Angel right now, and she wanted to make that fact abundantly clear. His tongue darted within her mouth, creating a tantalizing motion, teasing at her own tongue.

Still kissing her, he moved toward the bed, then playfully swung her down onto the mattress with a light bounce. He might as well have been tossing a feather, he handled her weight so effortlessly, which caused her to think of those hard muscles she'd felt beneath his clothes. And reminded her that she was about to see him in all his naked, masculine glory. She, who had never seen a nude human male—ever.

"Jamie? You know I don't . . . know . . ." She panted against his cheek as he lowered himself between her legs, nudging them apart with one hard, strong thigh.

"I'm gonna show you everything, Sunbeam," he promised, sliding warm, calloused hands up underneath her turtleneck. Instantly her nipples puckered, reacting as his palms moved up along her slender rib cage. Such warmth, such self-assurance, the way he touched her, coasting those strong hands upward until he cupped one breast in his hand, leaning all his weight on the other elbow. Her nipples tightened even more, beading beneath the silk and lace of her bra. She arched into his touch, wanting to feel his fingers rub back and forth over her sensitive flesh, and as she did, he settled more firmly between her thighs. A hard ridge pressed into the vee of her open legs and she lifted against it, needing him closer—desperately wanting all of him much closer.

In reaction, he began a kind of rocking motion, back and forth between her legs, mimicking what they both craved. The clothes simply had to go, or she'd never have all of him. Fumbling with the buttons of his shirt, she tried to unfasten it, but her hands were trembling too badly. Easing her hands out of the way, he locked his eyes on her with a blazing, heated gaze and made quick work of his own shirt, until it fell open about his hips. She gasped. Literally. He had a chiseled physique that was even more stunning than her ripe imagination had dreamed. She sank back into the down pillows and gazed up at him in awed wonder. He had tight pectorals with dark pink nipples that were as puckered as her own. And that chest was nearly hairless, smooth and sculpted, giving way to cordoned abdominals that made her pulse race. Much lower, she glimpsed a line of curling hair that vanished into the waistband of his jeans, a trail of pleasure that practically begged her to follow.

He began to lower himself atop her again, but she darted a hand to stroke that soft thatch of hair, dipping two fingertips beneath his waistband to trace the scandalous path. She met resistance in the form of cotton boxers and Jamie gave her a sensual smile. In one easy motion, he rolled off of her and onto his side, unsnapping his fly with an easy flick of his fingers. He tugged his jeans zipper to half-mast, then guided her hand there, obviously wanting her to finish the job.

"Have at me, baby," he murmured, leaning into the pillow and closing his eyes. "I want to feel your hand all inside my pants, I admit it."

It was an admission and a gesture of full surrender, and she doubted Jamie Angel was much in the practice of giving himself over to a woman quite so fully. Undoubtedly he'd spent his entire romantic life dominating and avoiding intimacy.

Tentatively she gave his zipper a light tug, being gentle because of how it bowed outward with his erection. Slowly she managed to lower it, and much to her shock, his firm length bounced free and into the palm of her hand. It was warm, the flesh so much softer than she'd have imagined, and she traced her thumb over the tip. Dampness formed beneath her touch, and she jolted. Surely a man didn't come this easily . . . did he?

Jamie opened his eyes with a lazy, aroused look. "Just what I want . . . Keep going, Sunshine."

There was so much she didn't know and should've asked Kate. Or at least read in a book, but she'd always been afraid of being reprimanded if she explored human sexuality. Now here she was feeling stupidly clueless. She touched his tip again and even more dampness beaded beneath her touch. Jamie growled in obvious pleasure, and she paused again.

"You're amazing, sweetheart. Nobody's ever touched me like you. . . ." He urged his hips upward, seeming to beg for more.

"You're not . . . done? But you're wet. . . ."

He barked a laugh and pulled her atop him, pinioning her close against his chest with both arms. "On second thought, let me show you a few things," he promised huskily. "I want to give you a different kind of heaven."

*   *   *

She was tighter than he'd imagined, but then again, he couldn't remember the last time he'd made love to a virgin. Actually . . . that would be never. His women had always been loose and ready and dismissive of foreplay, so taking it slow with Sunny was a revelation. Every time he stroked any part of her, she purred or moaned, and when he slid his fingertips between her legs, caressing the slick folds, her eyes flew open. She stared at him, panting, as he slowly slid first one finger, then a second inside of her. By the erotic look in her eyes, he was pretty sure she'd never fully known what to expect.

"I'm your love tutor," he teased, stroking a little deeper inside her, a back-and-forth friction that had her whole body warming against his own. "And you are an outstanding pupil, my Sunbeam."

She nodded, swallowing hard. "I want to learn everything. Feel everything with you, Jamie."

It was time; she was ready and wet and thrusting her hips against his palm. He drew a deep breath, knowing that she'd have a fleeting moment of pain with what he did next. Lowering himself between her thighs, he paused as their hips pressed close together. For one endless moment they both seemed to hold their breath, eyes unblinking and locked on each other. Everything would change; their entire future was suspended in this breath-stealing instant.

Finally, she gave a resolute nod, wrapping her arms tight about his neck and pulling him close. "Now," she urged on a sigh. "Now, my love."

He surged inside her, feeling slight resistance, then only her grasping warmth, her welcoming fire. "Oh, God above, yes!" he half groaned and half prayed.

She dug fingers into the small of his back, surging upward as he plunged deeper into her. For an innocent, she knew exactly what she wanted—her body's instincts providing more direction than he ever possibly could.

They rocked together, and he lifted her right thigh up about him, wanting to be deeper inside her slickness, hungry to give her even more pleasure. She wrapped her other leg tight about his torso, embracing him with her thighs—and giving him the fullest penetration. As he hit that sweet spot, she cried out, throwing her head back against the pillow and clutching his shoulders. He felt her quiver about his hard length, and couldn't restrain himself any longer, either. Quaking all over, he plunged deep into her, riding out waves and waves of pulsing pleasure. With one hand he gripped the headboard, squeezing as the strong orgasm shot through his whole body; with his other he clutched her hip, urging her upward with every one of his thrusts.

And then a blissful stillness descended upon them both. A serenity that he'd never once known before in his life. They lay entwined, he exhausted atop her, she sprawled beneath with her legs still half hitched around his hips. After a moment, he lifted a sweat-slicked palm to her cheek, wiping away some dampness there. She blinked up at him wordlessly, wondrously, and he'd never seen more love in any woman's eyes than he did in Sunny Renfroe's right then.

"My wife," he said softly, brushing a wayward curl out of her eyes, "I do have one thing to correct you on."

She lifted both eyebrows high. "I did something wrong? While we—"

He silenced her by pressing fingertips to her lips. "You are perfect. That was beyond perfect. No, but what you said about me being God's gift to the women of Savannah?"

She nodded, and he stroked her lips with his thumb,

smiling down at her. "Yeah, well, truth is . . . you're God's gift to *me*. That's the real way of it."

She beamed up at him, then began to giggle, clamping a hand over her mouth.

"What?" he asked.

"It's just . . . you're God's gift to me, too."

"And that's funny why?" he asked, frowning slightly.

"When I was little, I always did want a hound dog."

He rolled with her until she was splayed atop him, her breasts bouncing lightly against his chest, her legs spread wide about him. "For that, Mrs. Angel, I shall be forced to exact a penalty. Besides, I'm not a dog, remember? I'm your great big pussycat."

"And that makes me your catnip," she said as he felt his groin stir to life anew.

He pushed up against her still-damp opening and released a low, seductive meow right in her ear.

Yes, heaven. Sunny Renfroe was his heaven on earth.

Read on for a sneak preview of the next novel in
the Sentinel Wars series by Shannon K. Butcher,

BLOODHUNT

Coming from Signet in August 2011

The color of suffering was a dark and sickly yellow, and Hope Serrien knew she'd see it on a night like tonight.

A cold front had swept down over the city, slaying any hope that spring was coming soon. Power lines glistened with a layer of ice, and icicles dripped from street signs. The sidewalk under her feet was slick, but even that couldn't keep her indoors tonight. A night like this brought death to those who had no place to escape the cold.

And cold wasn't the only enemy on the streets. There were things out here. Dark, evil things. People were going missing, and Hope feared they hadn't simply moved on to warmer climes.

Sister Olive was a middle-aged woman who ran the homeless shelter where Hope volunteered. She'd insisted that Hope stay indoors tonight, but the nun had never truly felt the frigid desperation of having nowhere to go. She'd always had a warm, safe place where she knew she belonged.

Not everyone was so lucky.

Hope shifted the canvas bag on her shoulder and walked faster. She always carried sandwiches and blankets in case she ran into those in need—those who refused to come to the shelter. With any luck, they'd all have better sense than to be stubborn on a night such as this.

She scanned the street, paying close attention to the dark crevices between buildings and inside recessed doorways. That glowing, yellow aura of suffering was hard to miss.

Or maybe Hope had just had a lot of practice at spotting it.

If Sister Olive knew how Hope found people in need—if she knew Hope could see auras—the nun would probably have had her committed. Good thing that wasn't something that came up in normal conversation. Hope wasn't sure she could lie to a nun.

A flicker of unease made Hope pull her coat closed more tightly around her neck. She'd seen things at night—things she knew couldn't be real. Dark, monstrous things that slinked between shadows, hiding from sight. Their auras were black. Silent. She couldn't read them, which made her question whether the monsters even truly existed outside of her imagination.

She probably should have brought one of the men along with her to ward off any problems. But how would she explain to her escort how she knew where to go? It was better to do this alone and keep her secrets. Fitting in among normal people was hard enough when she *didn't* draw attention to her ability.

Hope forced herself to head toward the one place she hadn't yet searched for those missing souls. She hated getting near the run-down Tyler building—it brought up too much pain and confusion, too many bad memories. She'd promised herself that tonight she'd put her ridiculous fears aside and look for her friends there.

The three-story brick structure rose into the night sky. The lighting here hadn't been maintained, leaving deep pools of darkness to hover about the building like an aura of decay.

A heavy *thud* and a screech of wrenching metal rose up from behind the structure.

There was definitely someone back there. Or some-*thing*.

Images of those dark creatures flickered in her mind. Her muscles locked up in fear, and for a moment she stood frozen to the pavement.

The real danger out here tonight was the cold, not monsters, and the longer people were left to suffer in it, the more dangerous it became.

Hope forced her legs to move. Her first steps were slow and shuffling, as if her own body was working against her. Then she picked up speed slowly, shoving all thoughts of monsters from her mind.

As she crept down the alley that led to the back of the building, she heard more noises that she couldn't quite identify. There was a grunt of pain and the rattle of wood tumbling about. Once, she thought she heard a woman's voice, but she couldn't be sure. The only woman she knew who was too stubborn to come inside out of the cold was her friend Rory.

Hope cleared the corner, and the first thing she saw was the gaping hole where the overhead door had been ripped open and partially off its track. The metal looked as if it had been punched in with a giant fist, leaving jagged shards behind.

From within the opening, Hope saw a brief flash of color—the sickly yellow of suffering.

Rory.

Desperate fear washed over her, making her lurch forward through the ragged opening. It was too dark inside to see, so she fished inside her satchel for the flashlight she always carried.

A feral growl of rage rose up from her left. It wasn't a human sound. Not even close.

Primal fear surged through her, and she had to fight

the need to curl into the smallest space possible so she could hide.

Her search for the flashlight became frantic, her gloves hindering her as she fished around in her bag.

She located the hard, heavy cylinder, only to have it slip from her grasp.

Heavy, pounding steps shook the floor. A woman cried out in fear somewhere to Hope's right.

Hope grasped the flashlight and powered it on as she ripped it from the bag. The beam of light bobbed around, catching motes of dust as it passed.

Hope aimed it toward the sound of torment. The light bounced off something huge and shiny. Something pulsing with muscle and moving so fast, she couldn't keep the light trained on it.

Its aura was black nothingness.

Panic gripped her tight. She needed more light to ward off this thing. Something as hideous as that would hate the light. She felt it on an instinctive level, as if she'd been taught how to protect herself from the monster.

Hope swung the light around to the employee entrance next to the pulverized overhead door, hoping there would be a switch nearby. Surely whoever came in through that door would need to have access to lights, right?

The beam of light shook in her grasp, vibrating with the trembling of her hands as she searched. It seemed to take forever, but as she neared the door, she saw a series of switches.

She sprinted over the dusty floor, praying that the power here was still on—that whoever was trying to sell this place had left the electric on for potential buyers.

Hope shoved up all four switches at once. There was a muted *thunk*, then an electric *buzz*. Light poured down over the room, and while many of the bulbs were burned out, it seemed as bright as the surface of the sun compared to a moment ago.

She blinked and turned, forcing herself to look at what her flashlight had touched.

The room was large and open. Lines that had been painted on the floor to outline separate areas were now covered in dust. A stack of wooden pallets had been toppled, and the dust from their fall had not yet settled.

Across the room was a giant, hulking creature poised over someone she couldn't quite see. All she could tell was that they were surrounded by that yellow aura of hunger and suffering she'd come to know so well.

The beast's head swiveled toward her, the movement sinuous and fluid. Its green eyes fixed on her, and she swore they flared brighter for a brief moment.

An unnatural fear rose inside her, screaming for her to run. Hope knew what this thing was. She didn't know its name or where it came from, but she knew that it wanted her blood.

A roar filled her ears as a distant memory tried to surface. Her head spun, and she clutched the wall behind her to stay on her feet.

Please, God. Not now.

As much as Hope wanted to remember her past, she wouldn't survive the distraction. She fought off the memory, mourning its loss even before it passed.

The beast snorted out a heavy breath, sending four curls of steam into the cold air. Its mouth opened, revealing sharp, wicked teeth.

Hope was sure the thing wore a sinister grin.

"Run!" shouted a man.

She couldn't see him, but it was his aura that peeked

out from behind the monster. It pulsed with a flare of bright blue courage, and a second later the monster roared as if it had been struck.

Now that its attention was no longer focused on Hope, her knees unlocked and started working again. She needed to find help. Fast.

She had turned to do just that when she caught a glimpse of an aura peeking out from behind the toppled pile of pallets.

Hope rushed over and found a man lying unconscious on the floor. One side of his face was darkened with a bruise, and in his loose grip was a board covered in the same shiny stuff that coated the monster's skin.

His aura was faint, the colors flickering like the flames of a dying fire.

He wasn't going to make it if she didn't do something.

Across the room, a crash sounded as the fight wore on. Hope didn't waste time figuring out who was winning. It was going to take all her strength to get this man out of harm's way. Just in case it was the monster who won.

She shoved the pallet that was pinning him down off his legs. His jeans were dark with blood.

Hope patted his face, hoping to wake him. His eyes fluttered open, but she doubted his ability to focus. His pupils were huge, and sweat covered his brow. "Logan. I need Logan. Poison. He can fix it."

Hope didn't know how he knew that, but she doubted he'd waste his breath lying.

Her gaze slid across the room to the fight. The man battling that beast must be Logan. She had to help him. She had no idea how to defeat the monster, but she'd seen a length of metal pipe near the door, and she wasn't afraid to use it.

If you like bad boys, hot magic, and high stakes, be sure to check out Jessica Andersen's latest installment in the Nightkeeper series,

STORM KISSED

Available from Signet Eclipse in June 2011

Reese didn't know Cancun that well, but she knew cities. She knew the taste and smell of their dark underbellies, and understood the creatures that ruled them.

She also knew that if Strike and his crew went looking for her, they would start with the airports, bus terminals, and hotels, all the normal places that normal people went to. So, heart thudding sickly in her chest, she headed for what her gut told her was the bad section of town and flung herself into a warren of narrow streets that dwindled rapidly to alleys, losing layers of respectability in the process. And becoming entirely familiar.

Scrawny alley cats and lean, hard-eyed mutts of both the human and animal variety slunk in the shadows.

This was her world.

As she worked her way deeper into the maze, moving fast but not too fast, she was aware of beady eyes watching her from shadows, and the way they shifted, sending a silent message flashing ahead: *Grab her. We'll share.*

A minute and three alleys farther in, a lean-hipped youth with shark-dead eyes and a four-inch blade dangling from one hand moved out from behind a Dumpster and gave her a spittle-flecked, "Hey, baby, you looking for me?" in English rendered almost singsong by his thick accent.

She rattled back in barrio Spanish, "Get these cops off my ass and you can have whatever you want."

"Fuck that." He disappeared himself, and the shadows melted away. They wouldn't stay gone for long, but the threat of the cops had bought her a few minutes, a little space to think.

Not that she wanted to think. It hurt too damn much.

Dez. God. Throat so tight it hurt to breathe, she kept going until her gut told her she had gone far enough, and then picked out a narrow, open-ended alley that smelled pretty much like every other alley on the planet—a mélange of piss, body odor, and rot, with a spicy overtone that said she was far from home.

Putting herself about halfway down the alley, she scoped out her exits, both horizontal and vertical, before she leaned back against a padlocked doorway, causing her .38 to dig into her lower back. Then she braced her hands on her knees, let her head hang for a second, and concentrated on not losing her shit.

Dez was alive. As in not dead. Which meant . . . "Nothing," she told herself, hating that her voice cracked on the word. This didn't change anything.

She couldn't *let* it change anything. He wasn't her cowboy or her white knight, wasn't her best friend, wasn't her partner, wasn't anything to her anymore. She had saved his life by putting his ass in jail long enough for Fallon to get the guys who were gunning for him, and then cutting the deal that had gotten him out again. Word had it he'd even straightened up—to a point— while he'd been inside. She doubted he had found God, but she had hoped he had found some perspective, and maybe even a few shreds of the guy who had saved her ass back in the day.

That had evened them up. A life for a life. Which meant she didn't owe him.

Her stomach rumbled.

This isn't your problem. She didn't need to get involved—hell, she *shouldn't* get involved. She should give the info to Fallon, and let him decide what—if anything—to do about it. And if the thought brought a twist of grief and regret, she made herself ignore them both as she dug into her carryall, going for the false bottom where she kept a second set of IDs and plastic that would get her home and ought to keep her off the radar unless Strike and his people had major clearance or a big-ass back door into the system.

Given that they were looking for Dez, the latter seemed a far stronger possibility, as did their being paramilitary. He hadn't been—wasn't?—an acronym kind of guy.

Dez. God. Her throat closed; a sob rattled in her chest, but she made herself keep going, her fingers shaking as she popped the bottom of the carryall.

Then, unexpectedly, a strange tickle shimmied down the back of her neck and her instincts kicked hard. Oh, shit.

She spun, but didn't see a damned thing. Then a strange crackle laced the air, displaced air *whoomp*ed, and Strike freaking *materialized* right in front of her. He looked around, saw her, and looked profoundly relieved.

Relieved? What the hell? She went for her .38 reflexively, but his expression shifted to one of fucking-get-it-done determination. Moving lightning fast, he grabbed her wrist with one hand, twisted, grabbed the gun with his other hand, and chucked it away.

"Sorry about this," he said, which didn't make any sense, either.

Then the air crackled. The shimmies got worse. And sudden vertigo slammed into her, tunneling her vision.

"What . . . ?" Heart hammering, she reeled, tried to run, and staggered drunkenly instead. She had been drugged!

She felt herself falling, felt strong arms catch her in an impersonal grip. Then there was only a strange, shimmying darkness that took the world away but left the panic behind.

Don't miss the next thrilling installment in
Deidre Knight's Gods of Midnight series,

RED MORTAL

Coming from Signet Eclipse in April 2011

Leonidas swung Daphne down off the horse and into his arms. Cradling her close, he stared into her pale blue eyes until his breath hitched. *Lovely* didn't begin to cover her ethereal beauty. A demigoddess, an immortal creature of Olympus, a Delphic Oracle . . . and, of late, a Goth girl. Any *sane* king would've kept his distance and never taken on the challenge.

But he'd come up the hardest way, in the Agoge training school of Sparta, where he'd clawed for every crumb he'd ever gotten. It had been true survival of the fittest, with Leo struggling to thrive like a desperate weed in the sundried bricks of that place. That was when he'd learned to face any challenge, physical or psychological. He'd brought that iron-willed strength to Thermopylae, to all the battles he'd waged in the old days and ever since, and he wasn't about to start backing down now.

Daphne belonged to him; it was only a matter of fully claiming her before the Highest God himself. In his human life, he'd loved his wife, Gorgo, deeply, but now, all these years later, he could no longer recall her face, much less her touch. But when he kissed Daphne, something unearthly, mystical, ignited inside his heart; it was an eternal love, the kind that could survive the bonds of death and rebirth. And if that bastard brother of hers continued to separate them by intimidation, Leo wasn't above waging war against the cruel god. He'd done so already, besting Ares in two recent battles.

She slid both arms about his neck as he lowered her

slowly to her feet. She was light, so light, in his grasp—
and yet so fully a woman that his breath hitched as her
breasts pressed against his thick chest. For one long moment their gazes locked—Daphne with her thin arms
twined about him, her breath warm against his skin as
she pressed her face into the crook of his neck. His lips
parted slightly, and he nearly pressed his mouth to hers.
But no . . . Not yet.

There was something he wanted much more than a
kiss. To feel her body, that lithe, feminine body, beneath
his own much larger, bulky one, just as he'd promised. Maybe it would be awkward, a bit inelegant, but
he didn't care. He always had been the bull dreaming
of making love to a fairy queen, of holding a butterfly
against his warrior's chest. And he'd had plenty of practice taking Daphne without hurting her—all in his fantasies. He would be gentle with her now; he vowed it.

Rummaging through his saddle bag, he located his
crimson cape. He'd brought it intentionally, with a particular plan in mind. Keeping one arm about her waist,
he unfurled the crimson fabric with a romantic flourish,
making a blanket for them in the crisp field of grass. He
watched the Spartan cloak settle and, swallowing hard
in anticipation, he turned to Daphne. Her blue eyes had
grown wide, and a rosy flush infused her cheeks as she
stared at the makeshift bed. She chewed her lower lip,
seeming troubled. Wasn't this what she wanted?

But then she turned back to him, her pale blue eyes
flashing with heat and desire, all hesitation completely
gone. He seized the moment, pulling her into his arms,
and into a fervent kiss. Pain spiked through his right
knee as they sank to the ground, tumbling together—
the ancient war wound had been hurting more with each
passing day. But for once, he ignored the torturous in-

jury, losing himself in Daphne's arms. Her hands were in his hair, tangling in his short, thick curls, grasping as if she couldn't possibly have enough of him.

Shifting his hips, he used his thigh to part her legs, and settled heavily there. He was an imposingly large man, and she was so delicate and small by comparison. He tried to go slowly, but after all these months it was hard to rein himself in, especially when she drew her knees up about his legs. The shifting movement positioned his groin squarely against her intimate place, and he ached to feel her, damp and wet with desire, and to stroke her there.

She seemed to crave that very thing because she squeezed her thighs, lifting and urging him onward with a muffled, enthusiastic cry against his neck. In response, he began a subtle rocking motion, each thrust tightening his groin even more, every motion causing her to respond in kind, the two of them mimicking the act he so desperately longed to complete.

"Oh, gods, Daphne." He released a low, hot groan against her neck. He could smell the sweet aroma of arousal on her skin, feel the way her pulse fluttered beneath his lips. "Daphne mine, you're blessed torture."

She smiled up at him, a gleam in her eyes. "I want to make you hot and bothered and unable to hold back. I want you begging me. . . ."

He released a groan of frustration and desire. "So . . . that's your evil plan. I hope you will see it through to the very end."

She tangled her thin arms about his neck, pulling him closer. Pressing her lips against his temple, she whispered, "I intend to rule the universe, with you my only subject."

He pulled back, gazing into her eyes. "Are you saying

you would consent to be my queen?" he asked, searching her face. He'd spent the past year so intent on simply capturing her that he'd never even contemplated formalizing their relationship.

She answered by holding him closer, drawing his mouth to hers for a kiss. He grew so aroused that he ached with it, his cock pushing painfully against the metal zipper of his pants, and his balls tightening like bowstrings.

But she didn't shy away; in fact, she kissed him harder. She stroked her tongue against his in slow, tantalizing sweeps, each time seeming to taste him more deeply. Her hands roamed his back, his hair, his shoulders. In response, he cradled one palm beneath her buttocks, drawing her upward on a twin surging motion of their bodies.

After a moment, when he felt drunk with that kiss, she finally pulled away. Sinking back against the ground, her breathing came in ragged, uneven pants. "Leo, I want you ... more than I've ever wanted you."

He stared down into her eyes, the clear blue of them like gazing into the Aegean ... but with a tempest coming. He kept his body atop hers, suspended there, wanting her with more desperation than he'd ever felt before. And yet an invisible force held him in check: the knowledge that she would likely leave him again after this. Every separation from her became more unbearable. . . . What would such a parting be like once they became lovers? Unendurable, he was certain.

"Daphne." He leaned up on both elbows, staring at her solemnly. "Promise me you won't vanish on me, not after this. Not if we become ... if I take you, uh ... make ..." His face flushed, and finally he clamped his mouth closed, giving up on the effort. Why did his asinine shy streak always surface with Daphne, and when he most needed composure?

"Go on, Leo," she prompted, smiling up at him with gentle patience. She placed a cool palm against his heated face. "You know you can speak your mind with me."

He drew in a sharp breath and started again. "If we are lovers," he managed to force out, "then you will stay."

She stroked his cheek, studying his face with an intensity he didn't quite understand. As if memorizing his features, trying to ensure she knew every line, every scar. "I won't go again, Leonidas. Not this time," she vowed, threading her fingers through his hair.

Suddenly her eyes grew wider, and panic filled her gaze. Her hand froze, still twined in one of his short, wiry curls.

He frowned at her. "What's wrong?"

She shook her head mutely, her gaze flicking over his countenance with silent intensity. What had she just seen in him? What was causing her to be so fearful that she began trembling beneath his big body?

"Daphne, tell me," he urged, but she responded by tugging his head downward decisively. She covered his mouth with hers and sank her tongue deep inside his mouth, as if she meant to consume him, take him into her very core and hold him captive. It was the most fervent, aggressive kiss she'd ever given him. She began pulling at the hem of his linen shirt, working it upward. He complied hungrily, breaking the kiss only long enough to strip out of the rough fabric.

Her small, warm hands swept over his back. She didn't seem to notice the hideous scars that marred his shoulders and middle back, kneading her fists against his muscles, moaning into his mouth as they kissed.

He cupped a hand firmly along her nape. "Daphne," he murmured against her lips, "I love you. I love you with all that is in me, and—"

He wasn't able to finish; a hard male laugh rang out, piercing the field's mellow, late-day quiet like a pistol shot.

Shannon K. Butcher

BURNING ALIVE
The Sentinel Wars

Three races descended from ancient guardians of mankind, each possessing unique abilities in their battle to protect humanity against their eternal foes—the Synestryn. Now, one warrior must fight his own desire if he is to discover the power that lies within his one true love…

Helen Day is haunted by visions of herself surrounded by flames, as a dark-haired man watches her burn. So when she sees the man of her nightmares staring at her from across a diner, she attempts to flee—but instead ends up in the man's arms. There, she awakens a force more powerful and enticing than she could ever imagine. For the man is actually Theronai warrior Drake, whose own pain is driven away by Helen's presence.

Together, they may become more than lovers—they may become a weapon of light that could tip the balance of the war and save Drake's people…

And don't miss
Finding the Lost
Running Scared
Living Nightmare

Available wherever books are sold or at
penguin.com

JESSICA ANDERSEN

NIGHTKEEPERS
A Novel of
the Final Prophecy

*First in the acclaimed series that combines Mayan lore
with modern, sexy characters.*

In the first century A.D., Mayan astronomers predicted the
world would end on December 21, 2012. In these final years
before the End Times, demons from the Mayan underworld
have come to earth to trigger the apocalypse. But the modern
descendants of the Mayan warrior-priests have
decided to fight back.

**"Raw passion, dark romance, and
seat-of-your-pants suspense, all set in
an astounding paranormal world."**
—#1 *New York Times* bestselling author J. R. Ward

Also Available
Dawnkeepers
Skykeepers
Demonkeepers
Blood Spells

A THRILLING SERIES FEATURING SEVEN IMMORTAL
SPARTAN WARRIORS PROTECTING MANKIND—
AND CONFRONTING PASSION ALONG THE WAY...

DEIDRE KNIGHT

Red Fire

A Gods of Midnight Novel

Eternity has become a prison for Ajax Petrakos. Centuries after
he and his Spartan brothers made their bargain for immortality,
Ajax struggles to maintain his warrior's discipline. His only
source of strength is his hope that he will soon meet the woman
once foretold to him—the other half of his soul, Shay Angel.

Ajax searches for his destined mate on the haunted streets of
modern-day Savannah, but he isn't the first to find her. Shay,
the youngest of a powerful demon-hunting clan, can see the
monsters that stalk the steamy Southern nights—an ability that
draws the deadly attention of Ajax's worst enemy. As Shay and
Ajax race to solve a chilling prophecy—one that could spell
Ajax's death if they don't succeed—a fated passion arises,
threatening to sweep away everything in its path.

<u>Also in the series</u>
Red Kiss
Red Demon

Available wherever books are sold or at
penguin.com

S0015-111510